SECOND CHANCES

The Kate Corbin Story

SECOND CHANCES

The Kate Corbin Story

By

SUSIE RIGSBY

*To Susan
Best regards
and Happy reading
Susie Rigsby*

Black Oak
MEDIA

Second Chances: The Kate Corbin Story

Copyright © 2012 by Susie Rigsby
Front cover illustration Copyright © 2012 Kitty Tuma Hitt
Interior Design by Michael Kleen

First Edition published by Black Oak Media, Inc. in 2012

All rights reserved. No part of this book may be reproduced or transmitted in any form or by any means including photocopying, recording, or by any information storage and retrieval system, without written permission from the copyright owner, except for the inclusion of brief quotations in an article or review.

All characters appearing in this work are fictitious. Any resemblance to real persons, living or dead, is purely coincidental.

First Printing Summer 2012

ISBN-13: 978-1-61876-007-4

Published by Black Oak Media, Inc.

To order copies of this book contact:

Black Oak Media, Inc.
Rockford, Illinois
www.blackoakmedia.org
orders@blackoakmedia.org

Printed in the United States of America.

This book is dedicated to my daughter,

Susan Lori Prather

for pushing me to *get it done*.
I could not have done it without you
...and I love you.

ACKNOWLEDGEMENTS

With the writing of this book, my first, I realize I couldn't have done it without the assistance of a special few who offered their time, talent and suggestions. Luckily, I had some of the best ever to help me with getting Second Chances: The Kate Corbin Story published. I must thank Tim Robinson, a Canadian who knows how to edit, and even provided me with a few tips about Canada. Thanks to Kitty Tuma Hitt for the beautiful cover art. Special thanks to the manuscript readers: Jan Berry, Josie Brooks, Kate Dunmire, Jeannie Harbour, Mary Jo Harrison, Ginnie Kuhn, and Brenda Tasky. To Judy Spagnola of Book Trends, thank you for believing in Kate's Story. Last, but certainly not least, thank you to my publisher, Michael Kleen of Black Oak Media, a super guy to work with.

"It isn't fair. Holy Mother of God, it just isn't fair," Dixie said, shaking her head as she was digging around in her purse for a Kleenex and pack of cigarettes. "It's too much for one woman to have to endure. Makes you wonder what kind of a God would do this to someone like Kate, especially after what she's already been through."

PROLOGUE

When Tom Miller, the Human Resources administrator for the Black Gold Coal Company, engaged the turn signal on the company's Ford Taurus sedan, he noticed there wasn't another vehicle in sight on this oil and chip country road. Not that it mattered because Tom was a creature of habit, engaging the turn signal every time he changed directions.

    Today, traffic was the least of Tom's concerns in this small community of Oakville, Illinois. At the moment, his mind was elsewhere, thinking about the numerous other times he'd driven over Corbin Lane. Those were the good times, when a select few of the company employees would gather at Mack and Kate Corbin's home on Friday evening after work. Kate had jokingly dubbed those events her "$5 after work parties", claiming it was a great way to unwind after a stressful week. Not to mention those parties worked as cheap relaxation therapy for Mack. Being a best friend of the Corbin's, Tom had attended just about every one of those $5 parties.

    There was always an abundance and wide variety of alcoholic beverages readily available for consumption at those BYOB (bring your own booze) parties where, if anyone did happen to over-indulge, Mack would insist they remain as house guests until the next morning. Kate would throw out a pillow and blanket, offering the family room sofa as a safe haven. The next morning, those over-night guests who had accepted the Corbin hospitality would awaken with a well-deserved hangover, get a whiff of hot coffee wafting through the air, and then somehow manage to get up and stumble into the kitchen. Tom had been forced to accept that hospitality a few times himself.

Those after-work parties had abruptly come to an end after the Corbin's only child, Caleb, was killed in a freak one-vehicle accident. The boy's funeral was still quite prominent in Tom's mind. He wondered too, as he glanced over at his passenger and the company's Occupational Health Nurse, Dixie Collins, if she was going to hold up under the pressure. Theirs was a rotten job that was never easy under any circumstances, but when personal feelings are involved, then the job can become utterly unbearable. It would be a miracle if Dixie's composure didn't slip, especially since she and Kate had been so close.

Sitting in the car with her hands clasped together, Dixie didn't have much to say after leaving the hospital's emergency room. She wasn't accompanying Tom on this trip simply because it was her job; she wanted to be there for Kate. Shortly after being introduced to Mack's wife, she was invited to join Kate's small investment club. The two women had become best friends and spent a great deal of time together.

Looking over at Dixie again, Tom realized that she was close to the breaking point. He had to give her credit though, because the nurse had managed to maintain her composure... until now. Even in the hospital's emergency room, hoping that by some small miracle Mack could survive, she'd held up and handled herself as a true professional. She'd adhered to the procedures she had been trained to follow during an emergency situation. It hadn't been easy.

The company's standard operating procedure regarding underground accidents had been implemented before the mining of coal ever started. When an employee was injured underground, the emergency medical technicians were trained to administer first aid until the injured person could be transported to the surface. From that point on, the company's nurse was to be responsible for the injured party's care and treatment until they could be transported to the nearest hospital.

When it was first announced over the underground mine's page-phone that a miner was down, Dixie had listened intently to the medical technician yelling for someone to get a stretcher. Shortly afterward, the information concerning possible injuries was being relayed directly to the nurse. She was then required to contact the hospital's ER physician, advising as to the extent of visible injuries and what should be expected.

It was a written rule that an injured person's name was never to be broadcast over a page phone. Dixie had no idea that it was Mack Corbin being transported from underground and hoisted to the top of the shaft. Had she known, Tom wondered how well Dixie would have performed.

"Stop the car, Tom," Dixie said with an unsteady voice, tears welling up in her eyes. "I don't think I can do this."

Dixie's slim body shook as if suddenly chilled. Tom stopped the car, allowing the nurse a few moments to regain control of her emotions. He couldn't let Kate see the nurse in Dixie's present state of mind.

"Damn it, Dix, I don't like this shitty job any better than you do. I'd rather cut off one of my arms right now than have to tell Kate about Mack. Unfortunately, we don't have any choice. She has to be told and it's our job to see that it gets done."

"It isn't fair. Holy Mother of God, it just isn't fair," Dixie said, shaking her head and digging around in her purse for a Kleenex and pack of cigarettes. "This is too much for one woman to have to endure. Makes you wonder what kind of a God would do this to someone like Kate, especially after what she's already been through."

Tom had been thinking the very same thing. "If Kate's able to think anything at all after what we tell her about Mack, I'd think it would be that God has forsaken her. That's why we have to make sure she hears this from us before it hits the five o'clock news. And if I know Kate, that small TV in the kitchen will be on while she's preparing Mack's dinner." Hoping he'd allowed Dixie enough time to regain control of her emotions, he asked, "Are you ready now?"

Dixie inhaled another deep drag from the cigarette before rolling down the car window, tossed it out, and then looked over at Tom. "No. But you're right that it's our job, so let's get this over with. I can't bear the thought of watching Kate fall apart right before my very eyes. This will destroy her, Tom. My God, Caleb hasn't been dead three months yet, has he?"

"About that," Tom replied as he shifted the car into gear and headed up the lane again. Like Dixie, he knew finding the right words to tell Kate about Mack would be extremely difficult, but watching her fall apart would be unbearable. There just wasn't any easy way to do his rotten job.

They rode in silence the rest of the way.

When the company car pulled into the driveway, Caleb's huge Saint Bernard lumbered out to greet the visitors. The dog followed as Tom and Dixie walked toward the porch. When they reached the front door, Tom pushed the doorbell and heard the inside chimes alerting Kate that she had company. A few moments later the door opened and Kate greeted them with a warm smile.

"My goodness, what brings the two... of..." Kate's words began to fade away with a look of apprehension. Familiar with both Tom's and Dixie's job descriptions, their somber expressions alerted Kate that something was wrong... terribly wrong. "Oh, my God! Mack's hurt, isn't he?"

Tom was fidgeting with his hat. "There was an accident, Kate."

"Accident! What kind of accident? Where is Mack? Is he at the hospital? Take me to him now." Kate was already starting to panic before she saw the tears welling up in Dixie's eyes. Then she looked at Tom again. "*NO!* Oh God, no! Please don't do this to me! Please... don't... don't you dare do this to me. He can't be... please... please don't tell me Mack's not... coming home."

"We don't know exactly how it happened, Kate. The Safety Department hasn't given out a full written report yet. We just know a large rock fell out of the roof in a cross-cut. It landed on top of Mack," Tom said in a pathetic attempt to explain.

"Oh God, this isn't for real. It can't be happening." Mack couldn't be gone. He just couldn't. It had to be some kind of mistake.

Every hour of Dixie's professional training escaped her as she watched Kate slowly backing away from them, into the living room entranceway. Because of the huge lump in his throat, Tom was unable to say anything more.

"It was instant, Kate. Mack didn't suffer. He never regained consciousness," Dixie said, watching Kate collapse. Tom quickly grabbed Kate up into his arms. With tears welling again, Dixie looked up at him. "I don't think she'll ever be able to survive this."

Kate had finally reached the point of resenting the constant push of pills at her and needles into her, realizing it was no longer a matter of having to go along in order to get along.

1 | CHAPTER ONE

... One year later

Severe emotional trauma. That was Kate Corbin's diagnosis written in her medical chart. Well, it had to be called something, didn't it, since the term *nervous breakdown* is not a medical term. In Kate's particular case, the psychiatrists had noted the cause of her condition as extreme and repetitive trauma. By accident, Kate once had the opportunity to read her own chart, after which she often wondered if this was a term that referred to patients who had literally fallen apart at the seams; poor souls who'd lost all recognition of anyone or anything around them, ceasing the ability to perform normal every-day functions. Whatever the diagnosis meant, there was never a doubt as to Kate's emotional condition when she was first admitted to the mental hospital. The trauma she'd endured had definitely been extreme.

But, as the psychiatrist's prognosis had indicated, it was felt that Kate could, and would, get better with the passing of time. It had been a slow come-back for Kate, but she appeared to be much better after only a year of treatment. Since she was obviously on the mend, the doctors felt that Kate was ready to start the process of rebuilding her life. She had seemingly learned to cope with her losses, could even talk about Mack and Caleb without breaking down, or so the staff psychiatrist had determined.

And since she was now able to discuss every event that had led to her breakdown, wasn't it a given that facing the outside world again would follow? After all, and as Kate had often

11

thought, wasn't that what those mind-fixing shrinks expected of her? Discussing the untimely death of Mack and Caleb was now a matter of choice for Kate, an achievement that had to be mastered if she expected to obtain a release from this place.

The day she'd been admitted and for several months afterward, Kate had been totally unaware of where she was, much less why she was there. Gradually, the hospital's staff had forced Kate to understand what had happened. Accepting it was the hard part. In the beginning, her psychiatrists feared Kate would become suicidal, intent on joining her deceased husband and son, because living without them could not possibly be any kind of life.

They were right.

For months, Kate lay motionless in the hospital bed with her eyes fixed on the ceiling, completely out of emotional reach. When she woke up screaming, a nurse would come running into Kate's room and mercifully inject her with their mind-numbing sedatives. No longer having a reason to live, Kate had simply lost her will to do so.

Eventually, the shock and trauma of Mack's and Caleb's death subsided and she began to respond to the voices, independently managing to do whatever she was told. The nurses had gently and slowly forced the will to keep going back into their patient, just as they'd gradually talked her into eating the food.

Kate had finally reached the point of resenting the constant push of pills at her and needles into her, realizing it was no longer a matter of having to go along in order to get along. There were other options and things would have to change if she ever expected to be released. The psychiatrists would never consent to her discharge until they were confident their patient was lucid.

A scheduled meeting with Kate's psychiatrist had been arranged for this morning. A breakfast tray was brought to her room at the usual time, but the thought of food was repulsive to Kate. Instead, she'd picked up the cup of black coffee, taking a sip as she glanced into the mirror. She stared at the reflection of her anorexic-looking body. Once a full-figured woman, Kate was now consciously aware of her appearance, noting the pallid skin stretched over her emaciated frame.

If that wasn't bad enough, and to make matters even worse, her dark eyes were deep-set in their sockets, the look of a woman whose life was about ready to end from a dreaded disease. The dark, puffy bags under both eyes left an impression of a highly addicted drug-user in need of serious rehabilitation, or else a good fix.

As if it would make a difference and hoping for as much, Kate picked up a hairbrush and began pulling it vigorously through her long auburn hair. There wasn't a trace of shine in the thick soft mane that Mack had insisted she never cut. Now dull, limp and lifeless, Kate's hair was a reminder of the way she felt.

But if she was going to meet with the staff psychiatrist this morning, then an effort had to be made toward improving her physical appearance. Getting the good doctor to believe she now thought like a normal person with good sense became part of Kate's plan. Doing this would not be a problem for Kate. She willed herself to easily present that very impression.

She'd showered early, dressed, and applied a small amount of eye makeup. She'd even borrowed a tube of lipstick from one of the nurses, adding a little color to her lips. She'd brushed her hair until it held a noticeable hint of sheen, or so she thought. There wasn't much to be done about the puffy, dark circles under her eyes, tell-tale evidence of sleepless nights.

Those annoying dark circles had seemed to deepen since Kate had asked to not be given any more sedatives. It was a pleasant surprise when the psychiatrists agreed to her request, even though she was certain it was more of a medical move on their part, wanting to observe their patient's reactions after the medication was stopped. She'd put forth great effort toward getting back to a normal state of mind, but for some reason, sleep refused to become a part of that effort and simply wouldn't happen. Even so, Kate had remained adamant about not taking the nightly sedatives.

The slacks and blouse she'd chosen to wear for her appointment with the psychiatrist had once fit beautifully. But this morning, the clothes hung over her frail frame, noticeably too loose. However, the rose colored silk blouse did tend to complement Kate's complexion, which helped a little. And for that, she was thankful.

Kate was grinning as she walked out of her room, thinking a small amount of humor could be found in getting discharged from this mental hospital. She would be in possession of a legitimate document to affirm that Kate Corbin was a normal person. Now wouldn't that be something to brag about? After all, how many in the world today had documented proof of their normalcy.

After all the pain, heartache and loneliness Kate Corbin had suffered during the past months, a trained psychiatrist carefully observing Kate's features might easily perceive she had once been a very beautiful woman. Dr. DuPuis, the newly employed staff psychiatrist could easily arrive at the same conclusion. He was still reading Kate's medical records when the intercom on his desk began to buzz. The psychiatrist glanced up at the time on the wall clock before answering.

"Yes, Peggy?"

"Kate Corbin is here for her appointment, Doctor."

"Thank you. Please, send her in."

There was a look of surprise on Kate's face when she walked into the office and was met by a young and unfamiliar psychiatrist sitting behind Dr. Hill's desk. She wasn't at all prepared for the personnel change. "Oh! I'm sorry. I must be in the wrong office. I'm sure my appointment was with Dr. Hill this morning."

"You're in the right office, Kate. Dr. Hill decided to take a vacation this week. He graciously offered me the use of his office while he's away and asked me to meet with you during his absence. Please, come in and sit down," Dr. DuPuis said, pointing to a chair. "By the way, you look very nice this morning."

Kate smiled. "You should be careful about offering a compliment such as that, Doctor. Your nose might suddenly begin to grow."

Dr. DuPuis chuckled as he looked into the open file on his desk. "Do you think?"

"I do."

Getting on with the job he'd been asked to do, he told Kate, "I've just been going over your chart, Kate. Dr. Hill's notes indicate you want to go home."

Kate didn't much care for the idea of dealing with a different shrink, especially one with such a young appearance. "Yes, that's correct."

Looking directly into a patient's eyes was a thing with Dr. DuPuis, convinced that the eyes could reveal a great deal about a person. Thinking Kate's eyes looked very tired, he asked, "Do you really feel you're ready for that, Kate?"

"I wouldn't ask if I didn't, Dr...?"

Dr. DuPuis stood up and extended his hand across the desk to Kate. "I'm sorry, how rude of me not to have introduced myself. I'm Dr. Brockton DuPuis, a new member to the hospital's staff. I don't think Dr. Hill has officially announced it yet, but I understand he plans to retire soon and I'll be taking his place."

Sizing up the young psychiatrist as they shook hands, Kate bit nervously at her lower lip with a look of reservation. She was, however, still prepared to play mind games. After all, if you've met one shrink, then haven't you met them all?

"Congratulations. Dr. Hill will be a difficult act to follow, but I'm sure you'll do just fine," Kate said.

"Thank you." Smiling, Dr. DuPuis sat down and turned his attention to the open file again. "I've read through your entire file this morning, Kate. You were dealt a tremendous amount of tragedy and great loss in a very short period of time. When you were first admitted, Dr. Hill had his doubts as to whether you would ever be the same again. However, his latest notes indicate you've made great progress toward a full recovery."

Knowing whatever she said would have to make sense, especially with a young shrink she'd only just met, Kate chose her words carefully. "To be quite honest with you, Dr. DuPuis, I rather doubt that I'll ever be the same again. But I do have to try and start over, don't I?"

"That's certainly what we're hoping you can do." He finished making a few notations in the file, after which he looked at Kate over his small, wire-rimmed glasses, quick to notice her thin appearance when she took a deep breath. "Tell me, Kate, what are your plans for the future? Have you decided yet about what you're going to do after you leave here?"

"Oh yes, I have. There's a bit of unfinished business in Oakville that I'll have to deal with, like selling my property. The house and grounds would be too much for me to maintain. Then I'm going to visit my sister in Toronto. I was invited to stay with her for a while," Kate told him.

Dr. DuPuis smiled again. And even though Kate was unable to read any thoughts this young psychiatrist might have about her case, his smile was warm and he looked sincere. Kate wondered if a psychiatrist's ability to conceal their thoughts was something that made them good at their profession. She tried to relax.

"Dr. Hill thinks very highly of you, Kate. His notes indicate you're a college graduate."

"I have a BS in Education.

"Do you expect to pursue employment in that field?"

"Perhaps, but I'm not thinking that far ahead right now. I expect it's going to take some time for me to get everything settled in Oakville before I leave for Toronto. Financially, I understand I'm quite sound, so I don't have to seek employment in order to support myself. Eventually, I do hope to find some type of work that will help to fill the... void." Kate felt the familiar lump in her throat. She hated the word *void*. It was so empty.

Dr. Dupuis studied his patient for a few moments, said nothing as his eyes looked deeply into Kate's once again, then finally, "I'll take care of your release, Kate. I agree with Dr. Hill that it's time for you to go. The fresh air and warm sunshine should do wonders for you."

"Thank you."

"I'll write you a prescription for *Ativan*. I don't have to tell you the drug helps if you have trouble sleeping. It will be up to you as to whether or not you need it."

"I'll have the prescription filled just in case I do, but let's hope not," Kate said.

He was making additional notes to Kate's file and wasn't looking at her when he asked the next question. "Will your parents be coming for you when you're released?"

"No, my parents live in California. Mack's parents will be coming to get me," she replied.

Second Chances

A mental picture of her parents flashed through Kate's mind, causing her to smile, wondering what kind of an impression her father's pierced ears and long gray ponytail would make on Dr. DuPuis, or the many trinkets, beads and exotic clothing her mother usually wore. Would the young psychiatrist be quick to judge Sam and Laura Lingle as two aging hippies who had refused to change with the times, never wanting to live any other way or be any different?

The very idea had almost caused Kate to chuckle out loud.

Kate and her sister, Emily, had grown up with and been accustomed to living with the hippie lifestyle of their parents, even considered it as just a way of life. Kate loved her parents, yet couldn't remember the last time she'd seen or heard from Sam or Laura. For whatever reason, it really didn't seem to matter anymore. And she hadn't planned to visit her parents any time in the near future. She wasn't that fully recovered. Not yet.

Mack's parents had insisted on Kate staying with them until she was ready to leave for Toronto. Peter and Maureen Corbin were more like devoted parents than in-laws to Kate. They had been wonderful to her during the past year, never failing to make the long trip every weekend to see how their son's widow was doing. Kate knew Mack's parents loved her dearly, assuring her that their home was hers for as long as she wanted. Kate was truly grateful for their kindness. The thought of staying in the house she'd helped Mack build was way too painful for her. It simply wasn't going to happen. She would empty the structure of its furnishings, sell it, and find another place to live.

Dr. DuPuis closed Kate's medical file, stood up and extended his hand to her once again. He felt positive that Kate had a plan for putting everything back into perspective concerning her life. He sincerely hoped that plan would work for the pretty lady.

Susie Rigsby

"Here, Kate, let me carry your bags," Peter offered and picked up the two suitcases, noting the light weight of each. "There's not much in your luggage, is there?"

"No, but then again I suppose it's more than I came with," Kate replied.

2| CHAPTER TWO

Maureen Corbin had been in a frenzy all week about bringing Kate home from the hospital. Anyone would have thought she was going to pick up a newly adopted baby daughter. Peter had been aware of his wife's anxiety as they waited for the day to arrive when they would make the trip to get Kate. Needless to say, it troubled him somewhat.

"I can't wait to get Kate home with us, Peter. I'll put some meat back on that boney frame of hers," Maureen bragged, her plans already in place for improving Kate's physique.

"Now, Honey, I've told you not to get yourself all worked up about Kate staying with us. Kate knows we'll always be here if she needs us, but we have to remember that she's still a young woman. She might be thinking it's time to make a new life for herself and we shouldn't stand in Kate's way," Peter told his wife, hoping to prepare Maureen for Kate's inevitable departure, his mind never clear as to whether he and Maureen needed Kate more than she needed them. And that too had often troubled Peter.

Peter Corbin had always been a down-to-earth and sensible man. When Caleb was killed, he'd been the sole pillar for the whole family to lean on. He'd stood like the Rock of Gibraltar when Mack was killed, even though his own heart was breaking. He fully understood that if he hadn't been there during Maureen's grief over Mack, then simply to survive would have been impossible for his wife. Like Kate, she'd lost her only child, but she still had her husband.

Kate was standing by the window and looking impatiently at her watch when she spotted Peter's car pulling into the hospital's spacious parking lot. She'd been waiting for her in-laws to arrive for what seemed like forever. What few belongings she'd kept at the hospital had been packed for well over an hour. Dr. DuPuis had personally delivered Kate's official release papers earlier that morning, so she was more than ready to leave the depressing environment once and for all.

The scent of expensive perfume preceded Maureen as she opened the door and entered Kate's hospital room. With her arms extended to Kate for a hug, she said, "My goodness, Katie, don't you look just beautiful this morning. Do you have all your belongings packed and ready to go home?"

Home, Kate thought, literally detesting the sound of the word.

"I'm more than ready to leave this place, Maureen, if that's what you mean," Kate said, smiling as she looked directly at Peter while embracing Maureen. "I can't thank the both of you enough for coming to get me. Gosh, Maureen, what is that fragrance you're wearing? It becomes you so," Kate said, knowing the compliment would please her mother-in-law.

"It's called *Happy,* darling, which certainly fits the occasion with you getting out of this dreadful place," Maureen replied, delighted that Kate had noticed the perfume's fragrance.

"Here, Kate, let me carry your bags," Peter offered, picking up the two suitcases that were sitting on the hospital bed, noting the lightness of each. "There's not much in your luggage, is there?"

"No, but then again I suppose it's more than I came with," Kate replied as she took one last look around the small room, making sure she hadn't forgotten anything. "Let's get out of here. This place is starting to depress me and that's the last thing I need right now."

With Maureen on one side of Kate and Peter on the other, the threesome walked together down the corridor toward the building's exit. It appeared as though Kate's in-laws were guarding her to ensure no one grabbed Kate away from them.

A male nurse had spotted Kate and called out to her in a teasing manner, "Hey, Kate, don't tell me you're breaking out of here today?"

"That's right, I'm outta here, Jonathan," Kate affirmed with a small chuckle. Kate's small amount of laughter quickly touched Peter's heart. How long had it been since he'd heard Kate laughing for any reason? Too long, and that was for sure.

"Hey... all right!" Jonathan shot back, sticking his two thumbs up into the air to give Kate an affirmation. "You gotta promise to look me up if you ever decide to get married again, Beautiful."

"You're already married," Kate said and laughed again.

"Yeah, but I'd kick that woman out just for you, Sweetheart," he said, just before blowing Kate a goodbye kiss. "You take care of yourself, Kate. And don't ever let me see you in this place again."

"God, I hope not," Kate whispered quietly.

After exiting the hospital, the walk through the parking lot to Peter's car felt refreshing. Kate's lips curved into a faint smile when Peter hurried ahead to open the car doors. *Always the gentleman*, she thought, and suddenly realized how noticeably kind the years had been to Peter. He really hadn't changed much at all, maintaining his tall and slim, but broad-shouldered and straight physique. His blue eyes twinkled and softly crinkled when he smiled. She'd always thought of Peter as a handsome man and with his thick, snow-white hair, he reminded Kate of the movie star, Peter Graves. Peter was such a soft-spoken man that a person might have expected him to start apologizing before he ever said hello.

With a charming disposition that was smooth as silk, Mack had often remarked that his father would have made a great politician. But Peter's interest in politics ended with whatever column he had written in reference to a certain law that had just been passed or a pending piece of legislation, or editorials on upcoming elections and political candidates. He was a journalist and a highly successful newspaper publisher.

Even though it had never been Mack's intention to follow in his father's journalistic footsteps, Peter had expected Mack to take over the newspaper and do just that. Needless to say, Mack's parents were quite disappointed when he announced that instead of taking over the family newspaper business, he wanted to study mining engineering. Peter never quite understood where, when or how Mack's ambition to be a mining engineer had come about. He spent countless hours trying to change his son's mind, but eventually realized that it wasn't going to happen. Mack's heart was set on the vocation he'd chosen to make a living.

Mack graduated Magna Cum Laude with a Masters Degree in Mining Engineering from the University of Rolla, and as any father would have, Peter beamed with pride over his son's accomplishments. Even before his graduation, Mack had received several employment opportunities from various major coal companies.

Therefore, it came as no surprise when Mack accepted a position with the Black Gold Mining Company, the third largest energy provider in the nation. The employment offer had been a dream coming true for Mack and Kate. The company had just finished building a new state-of-the-art underground mine in the same county where Mack was born and raised. Mack had held on to the hope of residing close to his parents while raising a family of his own. And his wife couldn't have been happier. Their marriage had finally given Kate the roots and family she'd forever dreamed of having.

Within no time at all, Mack was getting promotions and climbing the ladder of success in upper management with the coal company. Watching his son's quick advancements had convinced Peter to sell the newspaper business and retire. That sale had provided Peter with a sizeable amount of money to invest, but with the untimely deaths of their son and grandson, Peter and Maureen Corbin were left without an heir. Kate was the only other person left to inherit their investments and other assets.

"Kate, would you like to stop and get a bite to eat?" Maureen asked, thinking there was no time like the present to start adding a few pounds to Kate's frail frame.

Peter glanced up to look at Kate in the rear-view mirror. She looked so frail in the back seat of his spacious Lincoln Town car. From the moment they'd left the hospital parking lot, Kate had done nothing but stare out the window.

"That's fine with me if you both would like to stop," Kate replied.

"Would you like a full meal or just a sandwich, Honey?" Maureen was hoping for a full meal reply.

Poor Maureen, Kate thought, knowing her mother-in-law meant well, but didn't understand that food was the last thing on Kate's mind at the moment. "Oh, it doesn't really matter. A sandwich would do just fine for me, but stop wherever you both would like to eat."

The corners of Kate's mouth lifted slightly as she was suddenly remembering the way Mack would always laugh, just before telling her to go for Peter's wallet when his father offered to buy a meal. *"Order the biggest damn steak you can find on the menu,"* Mack would say, and it was as if she could hear him saying those words to her right then.

Maureen shot her husband a disgusted look when Peter pulled into the parking lot of a fast food restaurant. "Oh, for God's sake, Peter! You surely don't expect Kate to eat this crap, do you?"

Peter frowned, but the tone of his voice remained unchanged. "Pray tell me what's wrong with this place, Maureen? I happen to like the hamburgers here."

Kate immediately came to his rescue. "This is fine with me, Maureen. Really it is."

Maureen shot Peter another disapproving look. "Peter, you know darn well how those little hamburgers this place sells can tear up a person's digestive system. They're nothing more than small rectal rockets and the last thing Kate needs is a raging dose of diarrhea. I really had a restaurant in mind where we could have a nice selection of healthy vegetables and fruits, along with a nice cut of meat. I certainly wasn't planning on cholesterol city here."

Peter ignored his wife and parked the car.

It was only after they were seated inside and had their food that Maureen finally gave up and quit complaining. Dabbing their French fries into the ketchup, the air had seemingly cleared over the disagreement of where to eat, even though it was very apparent that Kate was picking at her food.

Maureen reached over and patted Kate's hand. "Honey, you need to eat up. You're going to waste away to nothing if you don't."

"I'm really not very hungry, Maureen. I guess the anticipation of getting to go home has my stomach a little upset." *Home,* Kate thought. The word didn't sound right. Besides, she wasn't going home. She didn't have what she thought of as a home any more. She was going to stay with her in-laws. The emptiness Kate felt of not belonging anywhere had never left her, nor did she expect that it ever would. No matter where she went, it would never be a home to Kate... not without Mack and Caleb.

"Well, I bet I can fatten you up when we get you home again. In fact, I've already baked a batch of your favorite oatmeal cookies. I have some other goodies just waiting for you too. We'll get that body of yours back into shape in no time," Maureen said, most assuredly.

Peter looked apologetically over at Kate before turning to his wife. "Maureen, did it ever occur to you that maybe Kate doesn't want you to fatten her up?" Then he looked at Kate with concern in his voice and on his face. "There's no telling what kind of diet you'll have to endure when we get home, Kate, but probably a lot of liver."

"You keep out of this, Peter. I know what's good for Katie and I'll handle it," Maureen scolded, using that tone of voice again.

Peter reached for his hat and winked at Kate. "That's what I'm afraid of. Come on, let's get out of here and get back to God's country."

When they were back on the road again, Kate wondered why Peter had referred to Oakville as God's country, since it wasn't at all the way she now thought of the small town. Oakville was where her whole world had fallen apart in a matter of a few short months. It was a place she dreaded to even think about, much less return to again. And if it was God's country where they were headed; Kate felt even more certain that she didn't belong there anymore. She closed her eyes and pressed the side of her forehead against the car window, not saying another word during the return trip to Oakville.

Kate took a deep breath, inhaling the scent of Peter's pipe tobacco. "I love the aroma of your tobacco. It reminds me of..." she stopped, unable to finish the sentence. It was the first time she had even come close to mentioning Mack's name to Peter.

3 | CHAPTER THREE

Just as she would have expected, the overall appearance of the home where Kate's in-laws resided had remained unchanged. The historical two-story colonial brick dwelling was covered with ivy vines across the front. Black wrought iron railings were mounted on each side of the wide and winding brick steps that led up to the front porch. Healthy-looking, violet and pink petunias were hanging down from over the top of four wrought iron window boxes. Yard lights were evenly spaced on both sides of the brick walkway that was lined with colorful begonias. Mack had often remarked that the house was an extension of his mother, but actually reminded Kate more of Peter in a masculine sort of way.

Kate was quite envious of Mack's family life when she was first introduced to his parents. The Corbin clan could have easily passed for the perfect "Ward and June Cleaver" family of the "*Leave It To Beaver*" television series. Peter with his quiet and serious ways and Maureen looking as if she was a model for Vogue magazine at any hour of the day.

Kate's admiration for his family actually amused Mack, because in reality they weren't any different than most other families. The Corbin clan had their share of disagreements, but it only took place behind closed doors. They did appear to be the "perfect family" in front of others. Kate had revealed so very little to Mack about her own family, but after meeting Sam and Laura Lingle in person, he could well appreciate Kate's opinion of his parents. Even so, he'd readily admitted, "My parents are human too, Kate. They aren't perfect."

"Your parents adore you, Mack. I'll bet neither one has ever gotten very angry with you," she'd teased. "And I'll just bet neither one has ever raised a hand to you."

"Now that's where you're wrong. I can remember Dad whipping me once when I was a little kid," he'd confessed.

"Just once! Is that all?"

"What do you mean *'is that all'*? Are you kidding? Do I look stupid? Once was enough to convince me never to give my dad another reason to whip me again," he said, barely managing to look serious.

"How so?"

"I was always a good boy after that," Mack replied and burst out laughing. But Kate wasn't laughing and he knew why. "What about you, Katie? Has your old man ever tanned your hide?"

"Never. My parents were convinced that inflicting physical pain on a child was not a necessary form of punishment. They thought love and peace resolved everything, either before or right after smoking a joint."

Realizing that Kate's parents were hippies and their mode of living or example of parenthood wasn't exactly a normal way of life, Mack refrained from any further serious conversations with Kate about her family. It wasn't until after they were married and Caleb was born that he'd taken a stand about the Lingles... though ever so subtle.

Kate's first and only thought as Peter pulled the car into the garage was to rid herself of that hospital-like odor she felt certain had saturated her skin and clothes. She headed straight for the bathroom in need of a long hot shower. Adjusting the water's temperature to as hot as a body could stand, she lathered up with a scented soap and scrubbed her skin with a loofa.

After stepping out of the shower and wrapping herself in one of Maureen's soft, fluffy towels, Kate stood in front of the full-length mirror and observed the unfamiliar image. *That can't be me,* she thought, moving closer to the mirror for a better look. But she backed away when the mirror's image began to speak, cutting away at Kate. This couldn't be for real.

"I don't get it, Dearie. Why are you even here?" the image asked. "I thought you'd just gone off somewhere and died."

Second Chances

Kate stared at the reflection for several moments before she replied. Then finally, "God knows I tried."

"Yeah. Right. Well apparently you didn't try very damned hard or else you'd have gotten the job done. Furthermore, don't think for one second that you're fooling God, me or anyone else," the image shot back.

Kate took a deep breath. "So, okay then, I didn't go off and die. So... what now?"

"What now? Just who are you trying to kid here, Dearie? Not me, I hope. You are on the run. You can't wait to get out of here. And just look at Mack's poor parents. Well, what the hell do you care?" The image scoffed at her.

Why is this happening to me? And why now? "Don't say that! I do care. I love Mack's parents. I've always loved them. Peter and Maureen understand why I can't stay here."

"Yeah, yeah, sure they do. Okay. So go ahead, run away and try to forget all about the life you once had here in Oakville. Who gives a damn anyway?" The image was fading away before Kate had a chance to reply. Desperate now to talk to Peter, she hurried to get dressed. If anyone could understand the way she felt, Peter could.

She found Peter on the front porch sitting in the swing, asking as she sat down beside him, "Mind if I join you?"

"I'd be delighted. It's a little cool out here this evening, Kate. Should I go inside and grab one of Maureen's sweaters for you?"

"No, I'm fine, but thank you." Kate said before taking a deep breath, inhaling the scent of Peter's pipe tobacco. "I love your tobacco's aroma. It reminds me of..." stopping short in mid-sentence, unable to finish because she hadn't yet mentioned Mack's name to Peter.

"You were about to say the aroma of my tobacco reminds you of Mack, weren't you? It does me too, Kate." Peter's eyes shifted upward toward the starlit sky, as if he might see Mack somewhere up there in the heavens. "I swear to God, I still think of him every time I light up my pipe."

"I'm sorry, Peter. I shouldn't have brought it up."

"Nonsense, Kate, don't say that. I live with his memory too. Not a day passes that I don't think about Mack and Caleb. I

27

know it's been hard for you, sweetheart, but life does go on. And so will you." He reached over to pat Kate's hand. "Besides, haven't you heard it said that no one is ever really gone as long as they're remembered by those who loved them?" Peter pulled another puff of his pipe. "Mack will never be gone to me."

Kate took another deep breath, grabbing one more whiff of the tobacco's scent. Then, thinking it best to change the subject, she said, "I'd like to drive over to the house tomorrow and look around, Peter. I want to dispose of its contents as quickly as I can."

"I figured as much."

"Yeah, well, the thing is, I don't know if I can do it alone or not. Would you mind going over there with me?" she asked, sounding a bit distraught.

"You don't have to do anything alone, Katie. Of course, I'll go with you."

Kate smiled. "Thank you. I'll need your support."

"You'll always have my support. Maureen's too. You should know that by now. You're all the family we have left. We've loved you like a daughter from the moment Mack brought you here. No matter what you decide to do, all we want is for you to be happy," he said before puffing on his pipe again. Giving Kate a concerned look, he removed the pipe from his lips. "Kate, I realize you're still a young woman with a full life ahead of you. I don't want you to get so caught up in feeling sorry for Maureen and me that it alters your thinking about what you want to do in the future. Don't ever think that we expect more than you can give. I'm behind you all the way, no matter what you decide. Is that clear?" He reached over to put his arm around Kate's shoulder, giving her a hug.

"Yes, Peter, it is. Thank you. I know the past fifteen months have been hard for you, too. And I really do understand what you're trying to tell me. I'll take care, I promise. But we both know if I stay too long that it's only going to make it worse for Maureen when I do leave. And I do have to go. I can't stay here with all these memories. I'll drown in them if I do."

"You don't have to plead your case with me, Honey. So don't even try. I must say, however, that I'm glad to see you have

Maureen all figured out. She's been worse than an expectant mother ever since you agreed to stay with us."

"I know. Perhaps I should have given more thought to coming back and staying here for a while. Maybe it wasn't such a good idea after all. But there's no way I could have gone back home." Then Kate laughed, rather softly. "Would you just listen to me? I don't know why I'm still calling that place home. It's not my home any more. Home is where the heart is and there's nothing left in that house for me. Mack and Caleb will remain in my heart until the day I die, but I can't surround myself with their things. I'd wind up right back in the nuthouse if I did. I've got to do this my way, Peter, regardless of whether it's right or wrong."

"I know that, Kate. And I understand where you're coming from. But Maureen, well bless her heart, she's different, kind of like an old mother hen. The sad thing for Maureen is that she's running out of little chicks."

Susie Rigsby

"Baron! Oh, my God! What's happened to that dog? He looks so woebegone and skinny," Kate said, taking in the dog's thin and pitiful-looking body; a reminder of her own pronounced appearance.

4 | CHAPTER *FOUR*

Returning to the home she and Mack had built together affected Kate exactly as she'd thought it would. Nothing had been moved and memories of Mack vividly returned to Kate as she looked at the smoking stand next to his favorite chair. Mack's pipe was still in the smoke stand where he'd left it, as if it were only yesterday. Kate picked up the pipe and gently rubbed her fingers over the stem, just before slipping it into her pocket.

Then she walked over to the gun cabinet and immediately noticed that it was empty. She glanced back at Peter. "Where are Mack's guns?"

"I took them over to my place, Kate. I didn't think it would be a good idea to leave them here. I'll gladly give them back when you get settled again. I took his rabbit hounds too. I went ahead and moved the pen and doghouses to my place as well. You can't let good rabbit hounds run loose and it was easier for me to take care of them at home. I hope you don't mind," Peter said, feeling guilty he hadn't told her sooner.

"Don't be silly. Why would I mind? What would I do with Mack's dogs anyway? You keep the guns and the hounds. Mack would want you to have them. I think you should have his gun cabinet too. You do still hunt, don't you?" she asked, running her fingers over the cabinet's smooth wood.

"A little. I guess I'm not as alert or agile as I used to be," Peter told her, hating that truthful admission.

Kate walked away from the gun cabinet, toward the dining room. "I think it would probably be best to hold an

31

auction, Peter. What do you think? I have no idea what this stuff is worth or what it might bring. I just know I don't want to keep any of it. Please feel free to take whatever you want. The same goes for Maureen."

"What about his clothing?" Peter asked.

"His clothing? Are Mack's clothes still hanging in the bedroom closet?" She couldn't believe it, but then where else would Mack's clothing be? Everything in the house was the same as it had been on the last day of Mack's life.

"Maureen felt we shouldn't do anything with his clothing without your permission. She didn't have the heart to ask while you were still in the hospital, afraid it would set you back." Peter nervously pushed at the carpet with the toe of his shoe, as though he didn't know what else to say, then added, "If you'd like, Maureen could donate his clothing to the church for their annual rummage sale."

"*NO!*" Kate shot back before thinking. Then she saw the shocked expression on Peter's face. "I mean... why don't you just give his clothing to the Salvation Army? They can always use good clothes and they'll give you a receipt to use as a charitable donation on your income taxes. I think that's what Mack would have wanted." And it was true. Mack gloried in all the itemized deductions a taxpayer was allowed on a tax return.

"Whatever you say, Kate. I know a good auctioneer. I'll get in contact with him for you," Peter said.

"Good. I'll call a realtor and get the house listed. I don't plan to wait around for the house to sell, Peter. I can do the paper work by mail or give you Power of Attorney to close the deal for me. If you'll be responsible for the property's upkeep until the house sells, I'll put money in an escrow account for your time and expenses," Kate told him. She wanted to move on without delays of any kind from anyone.

"You don't have to worry about any of that, Kate. It's not a problem. I'll see that everything gets taken care of the way you want," Peter said, following Kate into the dining room.

When Kate unlocked the French doors and walked out onto the deck, she heard Caleb's dog barking as it came around the corner of the house. A look of disbelief was on Kate's face when she spotted the Saint Bernard. Baron looked nothing like the same dog she remembered.

"Baron! Oh, my God! What's happened to that dog? He looks so woebegone and skinny," Kate said, taking in the dog's thin and pitiful-looking body; a reminder of her own pronounced appearance. When the dog reached the deck to greet Kate, she knelt down on her knees and hugged Baron. The dog was licking Kate's face, slobbers going everywhere. She gave Peter a look, as if to say she couldn't believe he'd let Caleb's dog get into such a shape.

"Don't look at me that way, Kate. We took Baron to the vet because he wouldn't eat. The vet said there wasn't anything physically wrong with the dog. He was just grieving for his family. Caleb left him first, then Mack, and then you. I guess the poor dog didn't know what to think. We thought sure he'd die because he wouldn't eat. I loaded him up in the truck several times and took him home with me, but he wouldn't stay. He sleeps in the same spot at the front door every night. I suppose he's still the guard dog around here. It's for sure no one would bother anything with a big dog like Baron lying around. I think he's just been waiting for you to come back."

Kate stood up. "Well, I'm here now and I won't leave this dog again."

When they were ready to go, Kate lowered the tailgate on Peter's truck and called to Baron. The dog jumped into the truck bed without hesitation. That night, and for the first time since the large Saint Bernard had become a part of Mack Corbin's family, he slept across Peter Corbin's front door.

Kate was inside.

Susie Rigsby

"I take it by the extra large canine out front that my favorite sister-in-law has arrived," Gordon said, giving Kate a hug.

"What do you mean by your favorite, Gordon? I'm the only one you have," Kate teased. "And just how did you manage to get past that big dog?"

5 | CHAPTER *FIVE*

Getting away from the small Illinois town of Oakville where she'd once spent the happiest years of her life was foremost on Kate's mind. It had only been two weeks since her release from the hospital, but Kate had completed her business affairs in record time and was ready to depart for Toronto. Getting away had not happened soon enough as far as Kate was concerned. Her *Jeep Cherokee* was packed with everything she intended to keep.

Peter had contacted a realtor to sell Kate's house and agreed to handle the details of the sale. From that point on, anything that would need Kate's attention in the future could be handled through the mail. As expected, the property had appraised well because it was fairly new and situated in a beautiful country location. Kate was prepared to accept an offer of any kind, even one less than the market value if need be. Remembering Mack's words that it wasn't good for a house to sit empty for very long, all she really wanted was for the home to sell and be occupied again.

It seemed as if the day for departure was never going to happen, but it had finally arrived and Kate was more than ready to go. She logged on to the Internet the night before, pulled up *Mapquest* for driving directions from Oakville to Toronto, then printed the detailed information in order to memorize the routes.

She'd finished off a third cup of coffee with Mack's parents and thought it best to take advantage of Maureen's clean bathroom before leaving. As Kate checked out her appearance in

35

the mirror to make sure everything was in place, she noticed the dark circles had finally disappeared that were once so prominent under her eyes, and color had returned to her cheeks again. She removed one of the combs from her hair, running it through the heavy mane for a better grip.

Satisfied with her appearance, Kate sighed as she took another hard look at her reflection in the mirror. She wasn't surprised when the mirror's image frowned at her, then tauntingly asked, "Well, Miss Priss, don't you look just like a woman about to bust out of here?"

This isn't going to get to me. I won't let it. And yes, she was ready to go. "It's time."

"Sure it is. You're just going to drive off and leave those two people behind that love you so much. Go on and make a new life for yourself. Who cares? Right?" The voice was condemning and the image stared disapprovingly at Kate.

Looking sternly into the eyes of the mirrored image, Kate whispered, "If you're trying to make me feel guilty, then give it up because that won't happen. Mack's parents understand why I can't stay. I'll come back to visit and they can visit me. But I'm leaving. So you might as well shut up and leave me alone."

The image smiled smugly. "Okay, Okay! Have it your way. Go on and get out of here. Just don't think you're getting rid of me, Lady, because I'll still be with you."

"You know, I sort of thought so," Kate said, smiling as she turned to open the door, leaving before the image had time to fade from her sight.

She had tried to convince herself that she wouldn't feel guilty about leaving Peter and Maureen, but that didn't keep a lump from forming in Kate's throat as she was saying goodbye. And damn it, she didn't want or need to harbor such an emotion, but it hit her anyway. She'd been doing just fine and holding her own until Maureen broke down and began to cry when they said goodbye. That's when the guilty feelings began to overtake Kate.

Then she turned to look at Peter. The poor man looked as if he had just lost his last and best friend in the world. After giving Kate a big hug, Peter ushered her toward the Jeep, insisting she get an early start, saying he'd made the long trip to Toronto before and knew it was tiring. As she hugged Peter for the last time, Kate

Second Chances

inhaled the lingering scent of pipe tobacco on his clothing. It was Mack's scent.

Kate hadn't realized after solidly packing the back of the Jeep from front to rear that there wouldn't be much room left for her dog, which meant Baron would have to ride in the front passenger seat next to Kate. With that in mind, there was only one way for a dog like Baron to travel... and that was *in style*. During an earlier Wal-Mart shopping trip, she'd spotted a boy's small straw hat on sale, something her traveling companion would definitely need for the trip. She made sure the hat fit, then cut holes in the top for Baron's ears. Before starting the Jeep's engine, Kate placed the hat securely on top of the dog's head and laughed.

They were now ready to roll, she thought as she opened the compact disc case sitting on the console. She selected a Rod Stewart cd, pushed it into the player and looked over at the dog. As the sound of Rod's raspy voice began singing *"If We Fall In Love Tonight"*, Baron turned his head toward Kate with a pitiful look, one that a Saint Bernard can easily give.

Kate rubbed her hand over the dog's back and grinned. "What? You don't like the music? Or is it your new hat that you don't like? Well, it really doesn't matter, Big Dog. I don't want to hear any complaints from you about the music or the hat."

The dog knew she was speaking to him, but ignored Kate since it wasn't a direct command that he was trained to understand. With his tongue hanging out and slobbers dangling down both sides of his mouth, Baron was perfectly content just to be with Kate.

"Once we get to Toronto, I guess you know our first order of business will be cleaning up this Jeep. No telling what it's going to look like by the time we get there," she told the dog. Oh well, Baron was worth it. The dog was all she had left of her life with Mack and Caleb.

* * *

Emily Juenger was on pins and needles while waiting for her sister's arrival. But then she knew Kate pretty darn well and Kate would get there in due time, which was, of course... Kate's time. The Juengers lived on the North side of Toronto and even though

Gordon had sent Kate excellent driving directions to their home, she wasn't familiar with the huge city. Emily knew it was silly to be so worried because Kate had a cell phone and would call if she got into trouble.

Even so, there was still good cause for Emily to worry. A woman traveling that distance alone was enough to make anyone worry. But Kate had said she planned on taking her time, wanting to do a little sightseeing along the way. In fact, Kate's exact words were, "Don't get your drawers in an uproar, Em. I'll be there when I get there."

Yeah. Right, Kate.

Emily looked at her watch again. Kate should have been there by now. Maybe it was Kate's remark that she had reservations about staying with them that had Emily so nervous. Maybe Kate had changed her mind because of Gordon, a spotlessly clean dentist with an obsessive-compulsive behavior about dirt and germs. Kate had said she wondered just how much Gordon could take of a dog like Baron hanging around his home. It made her feel a bit uncomfortable about staying with Emily.

Kate hadn't been discharged from the hospital when she'd accepted Emily's invitation to visit. At the time, she hadn't given Baron that first thought. Later, she told Emily on the phone, "I really don't want to stay with you for very long because of Baron. We both know how Gordon feels about dogs."

Emily had just laughed at her. "Don't be silly. Baron will be fine. Gordon will just have to get used to your dog, that's all."

"Is that right? Well, you'll need to keep two things in mind about my dog, Em. First, when Baron shakes his head, he can throw a slobbering goober a good five to ten feet. And second, he shits like an elephant. Either action could send your clean-freak husband right into orbit," Kate warned.

Just to imagine Kate's dog taking a crap in front of Gordon was hilarious to Emily. "That's not your problem, Kate. It's Gordon's. He'll have to deal with it."

"Oh, yeah? Well, about the first time Gordon gets hit with one of Baron's big goobers, or he accidentally steps in a pile of dog shit with his spit-shined shoes, that's when I have a feeling the welcome mat will get ripped from the Juenger doorstep for Baron... and me," Kate joked, sounding more like her old self.

"You just get that big dog loaded up and head your hind end up here to Canada. I can't wait to see you," Emily said.

The two sisters hadn't seen each other since Mack's funeral. Emily had flown in to be with Kate during that terrible time, but didn't stay for long. She knew Kate was in such a state of mind as to barely realize that Emily was even there, or that there was anything Emily could have done for her sister.

Emily wasn't real sure that Kate was aware of anything at that particular time. All her sister's heartache and sadness had simply been too much for Emily. After the funeral, it was much easier returning to Canada than to stay and endure the misery. Besides, she knew Kate would never know the difference.

Gordon had been a real problem back then as well. His lucrative dental practice had been put on hold and patients were waiting for his return. Not to mention that Gordon's tolerance for Emily's parents was only good for a few days at a time. He had never accepted the Lingle's hippie way of life, quickly concluding their lifestyle had been the main reason for the extreme closeness between his wife and her sister. Laura and Sam had been too wrapped up in each other to be overly concerned about their daughters. There was either a protest march they had to attend against the political system they thoroughly hated, or else they were at a meeting somewhere in the area with their groupies. If nothing else, they just sat around smoking marijuana together and in a world of their own.

That's not to say the Lingles didn't love their darling little daughters, but more that their lifestyle simply didn't include their children. It very well could have, if Kate and Emily had only adapted to their Hippie ways. Fortunately, both girls had minds of their own and being a Hippie wasn't for them.

Gordon had never tried to hide his resentment toward Emily's parents. Of course, there were several other reasons he disapproved of Sam and Laura Lingle, and should anyone ask, Gordon could have named every one of those reasons in a New York minute.

Luckily, Kate and Emily weren't bitter about or scarred by their childhood. The girls had always felt loved by their parents even though they knew at a very early age that Sam and Laura were different. Their parents wanted the girls to assume the responsibility of caring for each other, which was exactly what the sisters had done. Never once did they ask Sam or Laura to attend a school function or activity that most other parents attended. Instead, the girls attended those school functions for each other.

After attending high school classes all day, the sisters had taken part-time jobs and worked late into the evenings, saving their money together. As they grew older, they learned how to shop for each other, shared everything, and never asked their parents for a dime.

It was during Kate's senior year that she'd met and fallen in love with Mack. After watching Kate's fairy tale courtship and beautiful wedding, Emily had been greatly influenced by Mack's undying adoration of Kate. He simply couldn't get enough of the woman. It had been Emily's dream to someday marry a guy that was just like Kate's husband.

With his tall, husky physique, Mack's perfect stature gave the appearance of an imposing person, or better yet, a man to be noticed by all. He had this gorgeous mass of blonde curly hair to go with those intensive sky-blue eyes. Mack was so ruggedly handsome that whenever he smiled, it instantly melted a woman's heart. He was definitely the kind of man to admire.

Emily used to tease Mack about women blatantly staring at his backside when he walked through a shopping mall. Mack would burst into laughter and accuse her of smoking Sam's wildwood weed for saying such a thing. She could still hear him laughing at her. She missed that man.

Impatiently, Emily looked at her watch again. What could be taking Kate so long to get there? Standing at the window and still watching for Kate's Jeep, Emily's thoughts drifted back to when she'd first met Gordon. He was nothing like Mack, but that hadn't stopped Emily from falling madly in love with him. Mack, an avid sportsman, had enjoyed all sports but particularly of hunting. Gordon didn't care much for the idea of killing any animal, but definitely enjoyed the more quiet sport of fishing. Mack wasn't afraid of getting dirty. Gordon detested any kind of dirt.

Unless it had something to do with mining coal or making love to Kate, there wasn't anything that Mack took very seriously. Gordon was nothing but serious. Both men, however, had the same quality of love and devotion for their wives. Emily was satisfied her marriage was good, like Kate's had been. The only thing lacking in the Juenger marriage was a child. And Gordon wasn't ready for children.

It was getting close to five o'clock in the evening when Kate's Jeep pulled up into the Juenger driveway and Emily ran outside to greet her sister. Baron barked excitedly as the women whirled around in the driveway, hugging each other.

"Oh, Kate, let me look at you. My goodness, you look so thin and I'm so envious," Emily said, trying not to show her concern.

"It's probably a good thing I got out of Oakville when I did, Em. I think Maureen was hell-bent on fattening me up. She poked so much food at me that I could have ended up looking like the Goodyear Blimp if I had eaten it all, which I couldn't. Baron did all right though. He got the leftovers," Kate joked, looking back at Baron in the Jeep. "Is Gordon home yet?"

"No, he works late on Thursdays. It's just us. Come on in. We'll have a glass of wine while we wait on him for dinner."

"Okay, but let me get Baron first," Kate said and opened the Jeep's passenger door. Baron jumped out and shook, throwing goobers everywhere just as Kate had previously described, then lumbered over to one of Gordon's prized shrubs and hiked his leg. Kate glanced at Emily, who had not taken her eyes off the big dog. "Why are you looking at Baron like that, Em? I told you about him. Remember?"

Emily smiled. "Yes, I do. And I was just remembering what you told me."

"What?"

"That he probably does shit like an elephant. Christ! He really is huge! I guess I didn't remember Caleb's dog being so large." Emily's arm was entwined with Kate's as they headed for the house. When they reached the front door, she stopped and turned to Kate, not quite sure what was expected in the line of hospitality for the dog. "You aren't... I mean... he isn't going to come inside... is he?"

Kate laughed. "No, he'll stay out here by the door. Don't worry, he won't run off."

"I don't think I was really worried about it, Honey. I was probably hoping for it," Emily teased.

After getting settled in the family room with their wine, Emily tried to remember the last time she had actually sat down with Kate and had a long talk. Even though they had always remained in close touch with each other, their lives had been totally different.

Try as she did, Kate couldn't remember the last time she'd been with Emily either, although she was sure Emily had been by her side during Mack's funeral. Emily had been faithful about writing to Kate during her stay in the hospital too.

"So, how are you?" Emily started, raising her glass to Kate.

"I'm beat from the long trip, but I don't think I'm crazy any more if that's what you're asking," Kate said, chuckling.

"Smart ass. That's not what I meant and you know it."

Kate smiled. "I know. I'm doing better, Em. Naturally, I still have a hard time dealing with the fact that Mack and Caleb are gone. There are times when I still can't believe it, even though I know it's true. I don't think I could have stood much more of Oakville. People made a point of telling me over and over how sorry they were. I'm sure they meant well, but they kept looking at me like I was some kind of freak, like they couldn't understand what had happened to me," she said and took a sip of wine. "Honestly, Em, I didn't realize that I was in a mental hospital those first few months. I guess my mind just snapped. God, I was so consumed with grief over Caleb that I could never imagine anything happening to Mack. If I'd just been paying closer attention, I would have known."

Emily looked puzzled. "Known what? I don't understand."

"I'd have known that Mack didn't have the heart to go on living after we lost Caleb. His grief kept growing, gnawing away at him all the time, even while he was trying his best to console me. I didn't even have enough sense to see what was happening to him. Mack was never one to take chances underground. He always knew when a roof was working, about ready to fall, and he drove right into that crosscut anyway." Trying not to cry, Kate wiped a tear away from each eye with the tip of her finger. "I'm sorry. I thought I was all cried out of these stupid tears, but I guess not."

"Don't do this to yourself, Kate. Mack loved you more than life itself. He would never have left you, not intentionally." Emily turned her glass up and took a drink.

"But he did leave me, didn't he?"

"Kate, it was an accident, for God's sake," Emily argued. "Mack would not have gone into an unsafe area if he'd known. And you know it."

"That's what I keep trying to tell myself, Em. Then I think about what all those good and God-fearing folks in Oakville tried to tell me? I can just hear them saying it to me now. 'Honey, we know these are real hard times for you to accept, but you have to trust that what happened was God's will.' I had reached the point where I just wanted to scream every time I heard those words," Kate said, exuding the bitterness.

It worried Emily that there was so much resentment in Kate's voice. It wasn't healthy to carry those feelings. "That shit will eat you up alive if you let it, Kate. Don't go there."

"Sorry, Em, but I already have," Kate said before taking another sip of wine.

Then they heard the front door open, alerting them to Gordon's presence. Still wearing his white dentist jacket when he walked into the family room, Kate thought her brother-in-law looked as dapper as ever.

"I take it by the extra large canine out front that my favorite sister-in-law has arrived," Gordon said, giving Kate a hug.

"What do you mean by your favorite, Gordon? I'm the only one you have" Kate teased. "And just how did you manage to get past that big dog?"

Gordon chuckled. "That was easy enough. I offered him a bite of my candy bar. Wouldn't you know that damn greedy dog devoured the whole thing," Gordon replied before kissing Kate on the forehead, then glanced over at his wife and winked. "Does your gorgeous sister have dinner prepared for us? I'm starved."

Emily got up and headed for the kitchen. "What else is new? It's in the oven, Gordon. All I have to do is dish it up. I'll go put dinner on the table while you visit with Kate."

"Sounds like a great idea." Gordon agreed, heading straight for the built-in bar to fix a much-needed scotch and water on the rocks. Then he sat down on the sofa beside Kate, reaching over to pat her leg. "It's good to have you with us again, kid. Are you going to be okay now?"

She smiled at Gordon, who always said exactly what he thought. "I guess no one ever died from a broken heart, Gordon. I have to be living proof of that."

"No, I guess not, but I know it's been rough for you, Katie. You just need to stay here with us for a while, relax, and get your bearings. You may not think it now, Sweetie, but life does go on. And so will you," he said.

As if you would know, Kate mused after listening to Gordon's words of wisdom. "You sound like my shrink, Gordon. He kept saying that very same thing to me. It's what I'm going to do with the rest of my life that has me a bit puzzled, though I'm sure something will eventually turn up for me. Hey, thanks for giving me a place to land for a while. I'll do my best to try and stay out of your hair."

"I don't have enough hair left for you to worry about, Sweetheart," he joked. Then he got serious. "I'm glad you're here, Kate. I hope you know that our home is your home for as long as you like."

Peter had often said those same words and to hear them again, Kate suddenly felt a bit melancholy. "I know. And I really do appreciate your hospitality. I probably should rest up for a while. After which, I think maybe I'll look around for a place of my own in the country. I love it up here in Canada, but Toronto is too large with too much concrete for me. Besides, this is no place for Baron." She knew that last remark would strike a nerve with Mr. Impeccable. Gordon had never liked dogs or cats and he'd often told Mack he didn't.

"The best you could hope for with a dog that size, Kate, would be that he'd go out and play in the traffic," Gordon joked. Kate gave him a look and Gordon immediately realized his dog joke wasn't funny.

"Gordon, that dog is all I have left of my life with Mack and Caleb. Where I go, the dog goes."

Knowing he had offended Kate about her dog, Gordon attempted to clear the air. "Hey, Kid, cool down! I was only joking. Haven't I already bonded with your dog? He ate my whole candy bar, didn't he?" Gordon patted her leg again. "Tell you what I'm going to do. I'll help you unload your stuff after dinner," he offered, wanting to change the subject. "Looks to me like you're traveling light."

"You wish. Wait until you start unloading that *stuff*. You'll be sorry you ever offered to help," she said and smiled at him.

Shortly after dinner, and as he said he would, Gordon helped Kate unload the Jeep. It didn't take long for a tiredness that resembled jet lag to claim what little energy Kate had left. Saying she thought it was time to call it a day, she convinced her sister that a hot shower and a good night's sleep would do wonders. Kate was alone in her room by 9:00 P.M. and mighty glad to be there.

*   *   *

In the privacy of their bedroom, Gordon thought about Kate's physical appearance as he began to undress. She'd felt so thin when he'd embraced her. Kate had always been a beautiful woman, but today she didn't look so good. "Jeez, Em, she looks like hell, don't you think?"

Emily flashed him a furious look. "You kill me, Gordon. She lost her only child fifteen months ago. And three months after that she lost Mack, a man she loved more than life itself. After that, she's spent a year as a patient in a mental ward. So do you honestly think Kate's supposed to look like a picture of health? Losing Caleb about had her done in, losing Mack just finished her off. To be honest, after seeing Kate this way, it makes me wonder if I ever want to have children." Emily had been thinking a great deal about Caleb. She couldn't have grieved more for her nephew if he'd been her son.

"I'm sorry, Honey. I know she's been through a lot. I didn't mean that the way it sounded. Honest, Em, I swear. You know I love Kate as much as you do. I'm just concerned about her, that's all," he apologized.

She knew Gordon meant well. "I know. I'm sorry for the way I snapped at you. I just feel so sorry for her and it's like I don't know what to do or say. I feel so helpless myself at times."

"Kate's going to be okay. We just have to give her plenty of time to get back into the groove again. She's plenty strong-willed enough. Once she regains her physical strength and gets her body back into shape, then I think everything else should fall into place."

"Do you think?"

"Well, I sure do hope so."

Looking up at the star-lit sky and not-quite full moon, Kate's mind was saturated with memories of Mack and Caleb. She was in her own little world when she heard Mack's voice. "What's the matter, Sweet Pea? Can't you sleep?"

6| CHAPTER *SIX*

The bedroom Emily had fixed up for Kate's visit contained all the comforts of home, including a television and private bath. The king size bed looked inviting enough and, as tired as she was, Kate thought surely the sleep she so desperately needed would happen for her tonight, but for some reason the hot shower she'd taken earlier had done nothing to relax her aching muscles.

Lying in an unfamiliar bed with her eyes wide open, Kate realized that sleep wasn't going to come as easily as she'd thought, or at least hoped it would. For one thing, the bed was much too large for one small-framed and thin woman. She still wasn't acclimated to sleeping without Mack, often wondering if that would ever happen.

After tossing and turning for what seemed like hours, Kate finally gave it up as a lost cause. Looking at the clock, Kate couldn't believe it was only 1:00 A.M. when she reached to turn on the bedside lamp. Leaving the bed of misery she'd been lying in, she walked over to the window and opened the curtains. Looking up at the star-lit sky and not-quite full moon, her mind was saturated with memories of Mack and Caleb. Kate was in her own little world when she heard Mack's voice. "What's the matter, Sweet Pea? Can't you sleep?"

She quickly turned around and looked over at the king size bed. She had to have been hearing things because she could never accept the idea of Mack being in the same room with her, much less seeing him. But sure enough, there he was, sitting on the bed she'd just vacated. She stared at the life-size image of Mack for a few moments, and then thought about the wine she'd

47

consumed earlier with Emily, which wasn't all that much. She hadn't taken any meds, concluding that maybe she was just too tired and must be seeing things. That theory didn't work for Kate either because her mind seemed lucid enough at the moment. *Right. My mind is clear*, she thought, turning back to the window to look up at the moon again.

"Are you trying to ignore me, Kate?" Mack asked and wanted Kate to acknowledge him, but it wasn't happening. "Yes. I do believe that's what you're trying to do. You're ignoring me."

Kate continued to look up at the moon while her mind ran in a dozen different directions. That couldn't be Mack sitting on the bed. Mack was dead. She knew she wasn't crazy anymore because she'd been declared a sane person. Hadn't she easily handled the image in the mirror at Peter's house? Yes, she certainly had. And she could handle this situation too.

"Look, Mack, it's this way," Kate finally said, "I've had a few conversations with an image in the mirror and I got through that okay, although I never know when it might happen again. Now, all of a sudden, I think I see my dead husband sitting on the bed I just vacated. I'm very well aware of the fact that I was recently released from a mental institution, so I prefer to think this will pass and that I'm not talking to a dead man. I'd be a prime candidate for the loony bin again if anyone overheard me talking to you. They would be coming to get me with a straight jacket and with good reason."

Mack laughed that easy and unmistakable laugh of his, the one Kate knew so well. Then he said, "I know where you're coming from, Kate. It hasn't been easy for you."

"*EASY?*" Kate jerked her head back around and glared at him with immense anger. "Pardon me, Mack, but did I just hear you say *EASY*? Now that's really some way of putting what I've been through. Furthermore, if it's all the same to you, I refuse to believe that I'm standing here talking to my dead husband. That's because I refuse to think I might be going crazy again. If anyone heard me, they would have no choice but to assume that it's happening. But *EASY*? Come on, Mack. You have to know what easy was in all of this, don't you? Easy was dying to get you out of your misery. Easy was going to be with Caleb. Only I couldn't seem to do something that easy. All I could do was fall apart at the goddamn seams. So what the hell would you know about easy?"

Unrelenting bitterness swept through Kate again as the tears began to flow.

"That's hardly fair of you to say, Sweet Pea. Of course I was traumatized about Caleb's life ending like it did. But my God, Kate, I couldn't have gotten through that if it hadn't been for you. Honey, come on now. Think about it," Mack said, trying to reason with her.

"I have thought about it. I've thought about all of it, over and over again. Even after a year in the nut house, it's still all I can think about. You wanted to be with Caleb. So you drove right into an unsafe area of that coal mine, knowing full well the roof was working and could fall out at any time. You were just asking for it, Mack."

"Ah, Honey, come on. You surely aren't going to stand there and try to tell me you actually believe I had that accident on purpose? Come on, Kate, you know better than that," Mack argued.

"Yes! Yes, I think you drove into that unsafe area on purpose. And I thought you loved me more than that. I thought..." Kate stopped lashing out at him when she heard a knock on the door.

"Kate? Kate, it's me. Can I come in?" Emily asked.

Kate glanced back at the bed. If she thought she'd seen Mack, she wasn't seeing him now. She wiped her eyes as she crossed the room to open the door. "Of course you can come in, Em. Is something wrong?"

Emily had over-heard Kate's voice as she passed by the bedroom door. Looking a bit confused, she stepped inside the room and glanced around. "No, nothing really. I couldn't sleep, so I just took a chance you might be awake too and thought I heard you talking. Want to come downstairs and have a glass of milk with me?"

"Sure. I'll get my robe and be right down."

There was a glass of milk on the coffee table waiting for Kate when she came into the family room. Emily looked up at her sister and asked, "What's the matter, Kate? Too tired to sleep?"

"Too tired or too wired, I'm not sure which it is," Kate replied. Her nerves were on edge after that little chat with Mack. Whose nerves wouldn't be shot? Talking to a dead person was

49

something Kate vowed she would never reveal to anyone. Not even Emily.

"Me too. I guess I'm just so excited that you're really here. It's kind of like old times, isn't it?" Emily asked, remembering those months when she'd stayed with Kate and Mack.

"Sort of, I guess," Kate said and took a drink of the milk. Looking a bit troubled, she turned to Emily and said, "I want you to listen to me for a minute, Em, because there are a lot of things I need to get cleared up between us. Do you remember when Grandma used to tell us that God doesn't put more on a person than they can endure? Well, I think she was wrong about that, but then who's to be the judge of when enough is enough? But believe me, I've had enough. Are you with me on this? Anyway, just before I left the hospital I was given a piece of paper that says I'm mentally sound. So I take it to mean that I am. I realize that grief can push a person into a different state of mind, but believe me, Em, it's not even close to the same thing as going completely crazy. Trust me about this, because I've given it a lot of thought. Not being able to accept losing Mack and Caleb isn't the only reason I had to get away from Oakville. I couldn't stand the way everyone looked at me with all that pity in their eyes, wondering how I was able to even keep going, much less accept it. Little did they know I really couldn't, that I hadn't, or that I never would. I'm living with my loss because I don't have a choice. I'm too much of a coward to commit Hari Cari and I haven't figured out how to make myself just stop breathing." Kate had just unloaded all of her pent-up feelings to Emily.

"I know, Kate." Dumb-founded, that was about all Emily could say.

Kate shook her head. "No, Em, you don't know. And God, I hope you never do. I wouldn't wish the kind of torment I'm suffering on my worst enemy, even if I had one. I came up here to start over. I thought if I moved here and tried to pick up the pieces, then all I'd have to do would be to wait and see what happens. But I can't do that if everyone starts looking at me here like they did in Oakville." The thought of that happening was too much for Kate.

"No one knows you here in Toronto, Kate. Why would anyone look at you that way if they don't even know you?" Emily asked.

"That's exactly correct. No one knows me in Toronto except you and Gordon. I'm not worried about you talking, Em, but Gordon needs to keep quiet too. I want you both to promise that you'll never discuss my personal life or what happened to me with anyone. Not ever."

Emily noticed the anxious look in Kate's eyes. "We won't tell anyone, Kate."

"I want your word, Em. You have to promise me. So does Gordon."

"What? You want it signed in blood?"

"Damned straight I do if that's what it takes for you both to mean it."

Emily studied her sister for a moment. Was this really Kate? Cool, levelheaded, hardworking and loveable Kate. What on earth was going on in that pretty head of hers? "I'll tell Gordon to keep his mouth shut about your personal life. I'm sure that he will. But, Kate, you can't go through life running from what happened, or act like Mack and Caleb didn't exist and weren't a part of your life."

Kate looked down at the glass of milk in her hand and gently shook her head. "Oh, Em, I'm not running. I'm just asking for a little reprieve. Mack and Caleb weren't just a part of my life. They were my life. I have them with me in my heart. I'll always have them with me, no matter what happens. But it's a part of my life that I want to keep just for me and me alone. I don't have to share my memories with anyone else and don't intend to, especially not up here. I don't want any of my new acquaintants in Canada to find out what happened and feel sorry for me. They might start looking at me here like everyone did in Oakville. I know it's hard for you to understand, but please don't tell anyone about Mack and Caleb. Okay?"

"Yeah. Okay. You've got it."

"Good. Now I think I'll go back to my room and try to get some sleep. Don't wake me in the morning. Let that elusive, unconscious state happen for me as long as it will. That's if it does at all." Kate got up and set her glass down on the bar, told Emily goodnight and returned to the quiet emptiness of her bedroom... and the bed.

Susie Rigsby

A retired military special ops officer, Hank's eyes were trained to quickly observe danger. He'd spotted the Saint Bernard sitting close to the Jeep and asked, "Is that her dog?"

7 | CHAPTER SEVEN

Gordon Juenger had been addicted to fishing from the first moment his father handed him a fishing pole and explained the secret success of the sport, which was to keep his mouth shut. That was just before they climbed into a Jon boat and headed out for a day on the lake. Through the years, Gordon had discovered that the topic of fishing usually made for great conversation with most of his male dental patients. It rarely failed to take a man's mind off what was going on with his teeth. As a rule, Gordon just sang to his female patients. What the hell, it usually produced the same effect.

It wasn't exactly fishing that was on Hank Diamond's mind the first time he climbed into Gordon's dentist chair, suffering the mother of all toothaches. All the same, Gordon had talked incessantly about fishing while Hank's painful abscessed tooth was undergoing a root canal.

At the time, Hank would be the first to admit that he'd been more impressed with Gordon's ability as a dentist than the fishing tales, but they soon became inseparable fishing buddies and spent many lazy days together on the water. This worked out well for Gordon because Hank had been raised in the area and knew the best fishing spots. So Gordon usually made himself available when he got an opportunity to spend the day fishing with Hank. In fact, the fishing trip they were about to take this Saturday morning had been planned for weeks.

Even though Gordon had spent long periods of time in a fishing boat with Hank, he knew very little about the man's personal life. The one thing he had quickly discovered was that a friendship with Hank Diamond was a rare thing. Hank was definitely a man of few words and known to be a loner. While Gordon had put forth quite a bit of effort toward getting better acquainted with his fishing partner, it hadn't been easy for him to do.

It wasn't that Hank couldn't carry on an intelligent conversation about any subject that was mentioned, it was more that he never started a conversation about anything. Hank knew how to laugh at a good joke, but rarely told one. At first, Gordon thought his fishing buddy might be shy about meeting people, but that wasn't it either. The man was just different... in more ways than one.

Gordon was thrown for a loop after learning the Diamond name was widely recognized and quite influential in Canada. Hank's family owned several major discount stores from Ontario to British Columbia, super centers that gave Wal-Mart and the Walton bunch all the competition they wanted... or could stand.

However, Hank's participation in running the family business was non-existent. In fact, he was paid a hefty salary to just stay away, which Hank thought was the best job of all. He didn't bother with patronizing any of the Diamond Discount stores. And if asked, he couldn't remember the last time he'd been in contact with any of his family.

The monthly payroll check, coupled with his military pension, allowed Hank to live quite comfortably. He was a widower and not much of a socializing man, so he didn't spend much money.

Hank considered privacy to be one of his most highly prized possessions. He wasn't the least bit bashful when it came to letting anybody know he didn't want to be bothered. He might go for weeks without seeing or talking to another human being and that suited him just fine. But he always looked forward to spending a day on the lake with Gordon. More likely than not, it had a lot to do with the fact that Gordon was exceptionally serious about his fishing. Hank thought of Gordon as a quiet man and he liked that even more. He'd been looking forward to this fishing trip with the dentist.

As soon as he pulled up in Gordon's driveway, Hank spotted the fairly new Jeep Cherokee with Illinois plates. The Jeep had caught Hank's attention because he'd been shopping to trade for the same model, but hadn't quite made up his mind.

"Got company?" he asked as Gordon threw his fishing gear into the back of the truck.

In a hurry to get on the road, Gordon wasn't paying much attention. "What? Oh, yeah. Emily's sister is here visiting."

A retired military special ops officer, Hank's eyes were trained to quickly observe danger. He'd spotted the Saint Bernard sitting close to the Jeep and asked, "Is that her dog?"

Gordon looked over at Baron and grinned. "Yup, that's her dog all right. Big sucker too, isn't he? I don't think he'd bite unless he got pissed off about something. Then I wouldn't want to be around a dog like that one."

"No shit! Me either," Hank agreed. Then his eyes quickly shifted to the women coming out of the house. He had to chuckle when he overheard Emily sweet-talking Gordon on her way to the Jeep.

"Be a sweetie, Gordon, and cut your fishing trip a little short today. We should take Kate out for dinner tonight. I'm counting on you," Emily said, blowing Gordon a kiss.

Gordon looked at Hank and rolled his eyes. "I'll try to get back before dark. Right, Hank?"

Hank raised both hands into the air and snickered. Emily had total control over her husband and she knew it. So did Hank. "Hey, Buddy, you just say when and I'll bring you home."

"Right. Some friend you are," Gordon muttered as he was climbing into the truck. When Hank made no effort to start the engine, Gordon noticed his buddy was giving Emily's sister the once-over. "Come on, Hank, put your eyes back in their sockets and let's get going. You know damn good and well that I have to get back before dark."

"Emily's sister is a fine looking woman," Hank said.

The statement had caught Gordon by surprise. Other than a few melancholy remarks Hank had made about his wife, he didn't talk much about women. Before that moment, Gordon had never noticed Hank admiring any woman.

"Yeah, she was really a gorgeous babe before..." Gordon started, but stopped short of finishing the compliment because of his promise not to mention Kate's past.

He had Hank's attention. "Before what?"

"Before she... uh... lost a little too much weight," Gordon replied, hesitating too long before he answered Hank. "You know how silly some women can get about their weight. Always thinking they're fat and going on those stupid diets."

Hank's attention returned to Kate when she reached down to pet her dog. "Yeah, I know what you mean. It does look as if she might have gotten a little carried away with her dieting."

"No doubt. Now come on, Hank, let's get going. Daylight is wasting away," Gordon insisted, pleased when Hank started the engine, put the truck in reverse and started backing out of the driveway.

* * *

Emily's pretty sister had crossed Hank's mind several times during the day while he was fishing, but he didn't mention her again to Gordon. It seemed as though they'd barely gotten started when it was time to put away the fishing gear and leave the lake. The day had passed too quickly as far as Hank was concerned, even though he'd found it amusing to watch Gordon repeatedly glancing at his watch, keeping a close eye on the time.

Not the least bit happy about having to return home so early, Gordon griped, "Those damn women! You'd think they would be a little more considerate. It seems as if they are somehow compelled to ruin a man's day off, especially if they know he plans to go fishing."

Hank grinned. "Yeah. Damned women." Then he gave Gordon a knowing look. "But I'll just bet you won't be thinking that way later tonight when you're curled up in bed with Emily in your arms."

Gordon was astounded. He'd never heard Hank make such a comment about any woman, much less about Emily. The more Gordon thought about it, Hank had never discussed anything concerning the opposite sex with him. He'd just been given a prime opportunity to have a little fun and tease Hank. "You got that right, old man. You sure fooled me by making that remark, because I thought women were a thing of the past with you."

Hank's steel-gray eyes held a hint of sparkle. "I've been married, Gordon. I know how it feels to curl up in bed next to a beautiful woman."

Gordon was getting to be even more amused. "Well, I'll be damned! Maybe your dick's not as dead as I thought. So why don't you join us for dinner this evening and I'll introduce you to Emily's sister?" Gordon invited.

Hank raised an eyebrow at Gordon's remark before shaking his head to decline the invitation. "Thanks, but no thanks. I'll have a few beers while I'm cleaning this mess of fish we caught today, and then I'm going to relax and watch a little television. Besides, you don't need my help with those two women. You can handle Emily, and her sister isn't big enough to give you too much sass."

"Okay, Diamond, but you don't know what you're missing. Besides, it just might do you good to get out and enjoy a little female companionship. I would even buy your meal," Gordon offered, trying to bribe Hank.

Hank wasn't interested. "Nope. No offense meant, Pal, but your sister-in-law is too skinny for me. I like my women with a little more meat on their bones. But thanks again for the offer."

Gordon shrugged his shoulders. "Some damn buddy you are. But I guess it's probably just as well. Emily would be upset if she knew I was trying to fix her sister up with the likes of you. Then she'd get all pissed off and there I'd be in the damn doghouse because of your sorry ass. Forget I even asked."

"Don't worry, I will," Hank said, laughing as he climbed into his truck.

During the drive home, Hank gave Emily's skinny sister and Gordon's invitation to dinner a little more thought. Gordon was as tight as the bark on a tree, so what was he up to in offering to buy Hank a meal? Hank grinned. He'd always had a good eye for women, especially those that appeared to be of good stock, but he really wasn't interested.

He had to admit that Emily's sister was certainly an attractive woman, even if she was a tad too skinny. For sure, if she had been on a diet like Gordon said, then she'd probably carried it to extremes. Hank wondered if she might even be anorexic or bulimic. He'd read about women with those eating disorders. Now

57

that was a waste of good money. It was hard to imagine having a fine dinner with a woman that would get up afterward and head for the rest room, intent on emptying the contents of her stomach into a commode. He shuddered to think of a woman ramming her finger down her throat to induce vomiting. It amazed Hank, the extremes to which some women would go in their effort to make themselves look good.

Hank didn't need any of that crap. Not one bit of it. He didn't want it either. His life was just fine the way it was. Besides, he wasn't fit to hang around other women after Beth passed away. She'd endured so many sleepless nights with Hank, awakened to find Hank on his knees in the middle of the bed, swinging his fists and drenched in sweat from the terrible nightmares. Hank figured no other woman could or would tolerate sleeping with someone under those conditions. There had been no reprieve for Hank from those bad dreams, especially when Beth was no longer beside him. She'd learned how to calm him, had a knack for pulling Hank's head close to her bosom and holding him until Hank quieted down again.

Beth had been Hank's one and only love. He doubted there would ever be anyone that could take Beth's place in his heart. She was much too young to die and Hank was still bitter about losing his wife. The doctors told him that her death had been caused by a massive brain aneurysm. Without a doubt, they'd said Beth was probably dead before she hit the ground. Well, at least she was resting in peace now. For sure, peace was something she'd had very little of while she was alive... and living with him.

Four years later, Hank was finally getting used to living alone, but doubted that he would ever get used to being without Beth.

In an instant, Kate's hairbrush went sailing through the air and past Mack's head, hitting the bedroom door with a thud. He grinned. "Wow! I haven't seen that kind of temper from you in years. It's not healthy, you know."

8 | CHAPTER *EIGHT*

After treating Emily and Kate to dinner at *The Red Lobster*, Gordon suggested they rent a video and the sisters thought it was a great idea. Watching Jack Nicholson in "*As Good As It Gets*" and hearing Kate laugh again, he'd thought the evening had been a total success. He'd even forgotten about Hank's refusal of the dinner invitation until Emily mentioned Hank's name.

"Honest to God, I have laughed until my jaws hurt. Nicholson is such a riot and he played that eccentric part perfectly, don't you think? In fact, he reminded me a great deal of Gordon's fishing buddy, Hank Diamond, in that movie," Emily teased.

Resenting his wife's remark, Gordon immediately went to Hank's defense. "What the hell is that supposed to mean, Em? Hank doesn't have an obsessive-compulsive behavior problem and you damn well know it."

By the tone of Gordon's voice, Emily was forewarned that she had clearly touched a nerve. "Oh, my! Listen to him, Kate. He doesn't like me to make derogatory remarks about his hero."

"Damn it, Em! Hank is not my hero. He's my fishing buddy and a damned good friend and that was a real shitty remark you just made about him. If that's your opinion of Hank, then I'm glad now he refused my dinner invitation for this evening." Without thinking, Gordon had let that bit of information slip out into the open.

"*What* did you just say?" Emily's eyebrows arched up as her eyes grew big with surprise. "You've got to be kidding,

Gordon! Please don't tell me that you actually invited Hank Diamond to have dinner with us this evening."

"I most certainly did and I'm glad now that he refused," Gordon answered smugly.

"Thank God for small favors!" Emily was more than just a little annoyed by her husband's actions. "What on earth ever possessed you to do something like that in the first place?"

"I honestly don't know. It just seemed like a good idea at the time. Kind of make it a foursome, you know," Gordon replied in a matter-of-fact sort of way. Getting tactfully out of the mess he'd gotten himself into was going to be a bit touchy. Hank hadn't accepted the dinner invitation, yet Gordon could still end up in the doghouse because of his own big mouth.

With daring eyes, Emily shot her husband a look, then gave him fair warning. "Don't start it, Gordon."

"Start what? What did I do?" he asked, trying to look innocent.

Kate, realizing her brother-in-law had gotten himself in a hot spot, figured she could help him out a bit while setting him straight at the same time. "I think, Gordon, what my sister is trying to tell you is to mind your own business and don't be playing the matchmaker game. I love you dearly and I know you mean well, but I have to agree with Emily on this."

"I wasn't trying to fix you up, Kate. I swear. Hank really is a hell of a nice guy. I just thought he might enjoy the company of two witty women over a nice dinner." Gordon was still trying to make amends... with both women.

"For all we know, Hank Diamond may very well be a nice guy and I'm sure he makes you a great fishing buddy. But I happen to think he's a bit strange. He stays stuck up there in those hills, away from everything and everybody. He's a weirdo, or maybe a nicer way of putting it for you, Gordon, is he's an eccentric. So don't be inviting that man to dinner with us again," Emily said in a scolding manner.

Gordon's blood pressure was on the rise with resentment and he was still determined to defend Hank. "Damn it, Em! Hank is not a weirdo. There's nothing wrong with the man. If you have any reason at all to think he's strange, then I'd say it's because you don't understand him. Did you ever stop to consider that maybe Hank hasn't gotten over his wife's death?"

"Not really, but that could very well be true. I just prefer to believe that he's still a little brainwashed from being part of a Marine special ops unit. Wasn't it Force Recon or something like that? Anyway, it doesn't matter. Kate has just told you; do not attempt to fix her up with Hank Diamond."

"Or anyone else for that matter," Kate added, laughing at her brother-in-law.

"Okay, you two, I give up. I can never win an argument with Em, so I'm smart enough to know it's a losing battle when there are two Lingle women against me. But neither of you know Hank the way I do. And in my book, he's a real jewel."

"Oh hell, Gordon, why don't you just admit that Hank's whole life has been a replay of Rambo and that excites you? Just because he knows how to catch a few fish, survive in the wild, and slit a throat without remorse, that's all it takes to make a man a hero in your eyes. You probably wouldn't be Hank's bud if you hadn't bought that dilapidated old house up there in those God-forsaken hills next to his property," Emily said and laughed.

That remark caught Kate's attention. "Do you own a house up in the hills, Gordon?"

At the moment, Gordon wasn't too thrilled about discussing that particular piece of property. The place had always been a sore spot with Emily. "It's more like a barely standing structure than a house, Kate. I'd planned to fix it up some day but never found the time."

The thought of a house in the hills had grabbed Kate's interest. She wanted to have a look at Gordon's dilapidated and God-forsaken piece of property. "I'd love to see it. Would you mind taking me up there tomorrow?"

"Oh, God, Gordon!" Emily said disgustedly. "Tell her no."

"Now, Em, don't fret. I just want to look it over," Kate said, hoping to put Emily's mind at ease. But she was already thinking about the amount of time and abundance of energy required to fix up an old house, both which she had plenty to spare. But more importantly, it just might be the ideal place for getting her dog out of the city.

61

Later that evening as Kate sat at the dressing table and brushed her hair, she still had Gordon's hill property on her mind. For the first time in what seemed like ages, she was actually a little excited about viewing the property and looked forward to tomorrow. It's been a long time since Kate Corbin had looked forward to anything, she thought.

Mack was standing next to Kate even though his image wasn't reflecting in the mirror. He'd been watching her. "It's good to see you smiling again, Kate."

Hearing Mack's voice, Kate turned around to face him. "Well, Mack, are we going to have another conversation this evening?"

Mack snickered. "I guess so. You look rested tonight. Did you have an enjoyable evening?"

"Yes, I did. Gordon took us to dinner and later we watched a video. I enjoyed both very much. He's taking me up into the hills tomorrow to view a piece of property he owns."

"So I heard. You can't be serious about that place."

"Yes, Mack, I can," she abruptly answered.

"What's happened to you, Kate? You don't sound like the same person to me."

"That's because I'm not the same." She was looking directly at Mack, but tried to tell herself she wasn't really seeing him, let alone having another conversation with a spirit. It was just an illusion and it would pass.

"There's nothing wrong with the Kate that I know and love. It would be a mistake to make any changes."

"You mean knew and loved, don't you, Mack? Not know and love. We're past tense now. Remember? And believe me, I'm not the same. I have changed. You're with Caleb and I'm alone. I was told I'd have to get used to that idea," she said with sadness.

"You aren't alone, Kate. You still have your family and friends."

Kate forced a laugh. "I have Emily and Gordon. I don't have any friends in Canada. And just so you'll know, that's the way I like it. So I don't plan to be making any friends either."

"Just what are your plans, Kate? What exactly is it you're trying to do here?"

"Live! I'm trying to live, Mack. Just one day at a time. And one night at a time too, I might add."

"If you don't mind my saying so, it looks to me like you're running away from life. You should find a job, get back into the mainstream again, get active. Why don't you go to mass and try praying about it, Kate?" In an instant, Kate's hairbrush went sailing through the air past Mack's head, hitting the bedroom door with a thud. He grinned. "Wow! I haven't seen that kind of temper from you in years. It's not healthy, you know."

"Mack, why are you here? Why do you continue to make these little visits?" Kate was being sarcastic.

His eyes were full of love for Kate. With tenderness in his voice, he told her, "Because I love you, Kate. I can't leave you alone until I know you're going to be all right."

"Maybe you should have thought about that before you left me. God, I thought losing Caleb would do me in, but I still had you. I'm alone now and I'm not the same person any more. It seems as if the people I love the most are the ones I can't keep. I'll never put myself in a position to love someone else again, not the way I loved you. If I don't allow myself to care, then I can't be hurt. I won't lose anyone else like I lost you and Caleb."

"So then, your plan is to just go off into the hills and grow old, living all alone? Is that it?" Mack asked.

Emily was knocking at the door before Kate could answer. She'd heard the brush hit the door and was checking on her sister. "Kate, are you okay?"

"Yes, Em, I... ah... dropped a book."

"It sounded more like you dropped a bomb to me. Okay then, I'll see you in the morning."

Mack was gone when Kate turned around again, so she got up and pulled back the bed covers, climbed into bed and hoped for a peaceful night of rest. An hour later and wide-awake, Kate realized that sleep was still eluding her. She thought about the *Ativan* in her purse. The tiny white pill would probably help her fall asleep, but if she gave in and took it, she would probably want to take it again the next night, and then the next. That wasn't what Kate wanted to do.

Memories of Caleb and Mack danced around in her mind and tears began to trickle down Kate's face, silently being absorbed by the pillowcase. She wouldn't remember going from wide-awake into a semi-state of sleep, but sometime during the night Kate did manage to close her eyes and drift off into a black and deep abyss.

Impulsively, Kate reached over to touch Mack's face, only to find that it couldn't be done. Embarrassed, she drew back her hand. "That was rather silly of me, wasn't it?"

9 | CHAPTER *NINE*

Early the next morning, Kate found the map Gordon had drawn for her beside the coffee pot. There was a brief note attached with a paper clip. The map provided explicit driving directions to Gordon's hill property. The note was to apologize for not going with her. He had forgotten about the men's club breakfast meeting scheduled for that morning. He wouldn't be home until late evening.

Anxious to get on the road, Kate hurriedly ate a piece of toast and downed two cups of black coffee. After taking a quick shower, she slipped into a pair of jeans and pulled on a work shirt for the trip. With Baron sitting next to her in the Jeep's front passenger seat, they headed for the hills together.

For the first time since she'd been released from the mental institution, Kate actually had butterflies in her stomach. She really wasn't sure if the tiny adrenaline rush was caused by the thought of finding a place of her own, but this piece of property sounded like the ideal location for Kate and her dog.

It was good to know that she was always welcome to stay with Emily for as long as she wanted, but they both knew Kate's stay was temporary. Every time she saw the expression on Gordon's face when he watched Baron slinging goobers, Kate felt an urgent need to find a place of her own.

After memorizing Gordon's map, she drove the routes in the Caledon Hills that had been marked up. She tried to admire the topography along the way, but the roads dipped steeply and raised sharply, a warning for Kate to keep her mind focused on her location and driving. Observing the scenery would have to wait until later, maybe during the return trip.

When Kate finally spotted the road marker she'd been watching for, she turned off the main highway and traveled another mile to the narrow, rough lane marked on Gordon's map. Seeing that the lane was barely passable, she stopped to engage the Jeep's 4-wheel drive. The weeds had grown high and the lane was badly rutted, definitely in need of maintenance. But Kate was about to soon discover that the lane was in good shape compared to the condition of Gordon's A-frame dwelling.

With her first glimpse of the deteriorated structure, Kate brought the Jeep to a sudden stop. After shifting into park, she carefully viewed the run-down dwelling that was built into the side of a steep hill. Her first thought was that a person could easily die from exhaustion while attempting to make the necessary repairs to this place. Still, there was an ambiance about the property that was almost enchanting. And it seemingly called to Kate, inviting her inside.

She looked over at Baron, happily perched in the front seat beside her. "What do you think, Big Dog? Want to get out and do a little exploring?" She patted the dog's head before reaching past him to open the door. The dog quickly jumped out, ready to hike his leg and mark his territory.

Kate got out of the Jeep and closed both doors. Then, after taking in a deep breath of fresh air, she leaned against the Jeep and wondered if the dwelling's interior could look as rough as the exterior. She noticed Baron was busy sniffing out the place.

"Come on, Big Dog. Let's go see what it looks like inside." The dog followed along behind Kate when she started toward the porch.

The first mental note she made was about the deck and railing. Both would need to be replaced. She wasn't prepared for what she saw after stepping inside the house. Fighting the cobwebs, Kate tried to avoid kicking up the thick layer of dust that had settled on the floor, which was covered with old and cracked linoleum of an absolutely disgusting brown and turquoise pattern. The woodwork had been painted with a tan color of enamel, as if someone had tried to match the woodwork to the linoleum pattern. The same chipped and peeling tan paint covered the kitchen cabinets. The walls had been covered with wallpaper that was now faded and sagging.

She could visualize what the place would look like with new solid oak cabinets, new wall covering to go with stained and varnished woodwork, along with some new carpet and hardwood floors. Kate smiled at the idea of being totally turned on with this crazy idea of renovating the old house.

As Kate continued to explore the house, she found the layout of the floor plan to be quite unique. There was a flight of wooden steps leading up to the open loft bedroom. The railing looked out of place because it had been varnished instead of painted with the tan enamel like the rest of the woodwork.

She climbed the steps to inspect the open loft bedroom, which included another full bath that contained outdated and unsightly pink bathroom fixtures. As poorly decorated as this place had been, she was a bit surprised with the floor plan. The loft was fairly large and Kate could visualize the changes she had in mind to make. She was impressed with the stone fireplace that had been extended through the loft floor from the family room.

Using her imagination, plans for renovation of the entire house were already taking shape in Kate's mind. She would draw up a few rough-sketched floor plans of the changes she planned to make as soon as she got back to Toronto. The renovation would require a great amount of manual labor and a fat pocketbook. Luckily, she could easily manage both. When she was finished, the dwelling's physical appearance would look exactly the way Kate wanted.

The first floor would have a utility room, two bedrooms, bathroom, and a great room that included the kitchen and dining sections. The loft was big enough for a large master bedroom, to include a small private lounge area and the bath. An outside deck to the loft would have to be added so she could sit outside at night and gaze at the stars.

Kate's mind was made up. All she had to do now was locate an available carpenter who would stay with the job and work fast. Surely Gordon would know of a carpenter she could hire. If everything went as Kate planned, she could be living in the home within a couple of months. Providing, of course, the work started immediately and before bad weather set in.

She'd seen enough of the inside. There was landscaping to consider. Pushing the tall weeds down with her feet, Kate wondered about snakes as she moved around. Bug spray and repellant topped her mental list of items to be purchased. The yard definitely needed immediate attention and mowing was at the top of her list.

"Let's go, Big Dog. I've seen enough and I think this is the place for us. Too bad there's so much work to be done around here before we can move in," Kate said as she headed back to the Jeep.

*   *   *

That evening, as the Lingle sisters were having dinner together, Emily noticed that Kate had been unusually quiet. Gordon's hill property had consumed most of Kate's thoughts and she simply wasn't in a talking mood. Emily had watched Gordon drawing the map for Kate and read the note he'd written before leaving for work. She figured that Kate had already taken a tour of Gordon's unsightly real estate.

After dinner, Kate helped clear the table and load the dishwasher. When the kitchen was once again presentable, Emily poured two flutes of wine and handed one to Kate. "You haven't exactly talked my leg off this evening. What's on your mind?"

Kate had been in deep thought about remodeling Gordon's old house. "What? Oh, I'm sorry, Em, I didn't mean to ignore you. It's just that I drove up into the hills this morning and had a look at Gordon's property. I guess I've been thinking about it ever since."

"Oh no, Kate! Please don't tell me you like it up there."

Kate detected Emily's disapproval. "No, I didn't like it," Kate said, grinning after Emily let out a sigh of relief, then owned up to her true feelings. "I loved it."

"Oh, Katie, I was afraid that's what would happen. I've been begging Gordon to unload that piece of property for years. It would cost a fortune to fix it up. And it's so desolate up there." Emily argued.

"I knew that's what you'd say, Em, but I think the project of renovating that old house would be great therapy. I need to do something constructive, something I can be proud of when the job's completed. Besides, I don't think it's a good idea for Baron and me to stay around here much longer, not if you want to stay married to Gordon. I know he loves me but let's be honest with each other, your husband can barely tolerate my dog. He can't help the way he feels and I understand that."

"Forget about Gordon," Emily said, shaking her head. "Let's talk about that place. Why on earth would you even want to live up there in those hills? It's away from everybody and everything. I'm not real sure where civilization stops and that place begins. Have you noticed there aren't any neighbors living close to that property? And in case you haven't done any research about Canada, let me inform you that it is loaded with black bears, wolves, and other wild animals roaming those hills." Emily was trying her best to talk Kate out of the crazy plan to fix up the old house.

It wasn't going to happen. "It's right for me, Em. I can feel it. I felt it the minute I looked at the house. So don't waste your breath trying to talk me out of this move. I'm going to start sketching changes for the floor plans this evening. I want to talk to Gordon about buying his property the first thing in the morning. Be happy for me, Em. It's the first time I've actually looked forward to something since..." she couldn't finish.

Emily looked wistfully at Kate before taking another sip of wine. "Okay, Kate. I know where you're coming from and what you're saying. I just have to get used to the idea, that's all. Right now, I could just strangle Gordon for not selling that property to Hank Diamond when he had the chance. Now I'll have to worry about you being up there all alone." Kate's decision was enough to drive a person to drink and the wine was handy. Emily took another sip.

"I'll be just fine," Kate said, then finished off her glass of wine and stood up. "I'm going to my room. I want to work on the floor plans for a while before I go to bed. When Gordon gets home, will you tell him I want to discuss this matter with him in the morning?"

"Yeah. I'll tell him. See you in the morning."

Alone in her room, Kate grabbed a pencil and pad of blank paper off the Queen Anne desk. After plopping down on the loveseat, she kicked off her shoes and stretched her legs out on the ottoman to relax. With the pencil tip stuck in her mouth and thinking about several different ways to change the dwelling's floor plans, she wasn't surprised that Mack had decided to pay her another visit.

"Looks like you're in deep thought this evening, Kate," Mack said, sitting next to her on the loveseat.

Kate turned to look at him and suddenly realized that Mack's appearance was not one bit different than she'd remembered. His eyes still held that same twinkle they'd always had when she was close to him. He was still ruggedly handsome. Impulsively, Kate reached over to touch Mack's face, only to find that it couldn't be done. Embarrassed, she drew back her hand. "That was rather silly of me, wasn't it?"

Mack grinned. "No. It wasn't silly of you to do that. In fact, I've been expecting it to happen."

"Have you really?"

"Yes. We never could get close to each other without touching, could we?"

A sudden desperation was mounting in Kate's heart, mind and body and she had to turn away. She hated it. She hated this feeling of being so alone. This feeling she'd tried so hard to learn how to deal with, or to accept. "How do you expect me to ever get over losing you, Mack? It's never going to happen if you keep coming back to me like this."

"You will get over me, Kate. But there are a few things that will have to happen before I can stop coming to see you."

What did he mean? "Like what?"

"In time, Kate, you'll understand what I'm talking about. When that happens, and it will, then you won't need me anymore." He looked down at the notebook on her lap. "So you're drawing floor plans for the house in the hills. Is that really where you want to live?"

"Yes, Mack, it's really where I want to live. I love it up there. It's a good place for Baron and me."

"Well, Sweet Pea, I certainly hope so."

"Yeah, well, it feels right anyway."

"Time will tell, I guess. It looks like maybe you're headed in some kind of direction, Kate. I'm just not sure about it being the right one for you," Mack said, and then they both heard the

Second Chances

knock at the bedroom door.

"Kate, can I come in?" Emily asked through the door.

"Of course you can. The door isn't locked."

Emily entered the room and looked around before asking, "I thought maybe you'd like to have another glass of wine with me?"

Kate shot her a look. "Let's be truthful with each other, Em. You didn't come in here to ask if I wanted to have another glass of wine with you."

With a concerned look, Emily managed to smile. "No. Not really. I heard you talking as I walked past the door. It isn't the first time either, Kate. I'm worried about you. Are you talking to yourself?"

Kate looked down at the notebook. "Yeah, I guess I was at that. It's not a very good habit for me to get into, is it? Especially if I start answering myself. You might want to send me back to the funny farm if that happens."

Emily continued to look around the room. "Yeah, you're right. But I promise not to tell anyone. I'll leave you alone. I can see you're into some big time planning with your notebook. See you in the morning," Emily said, stopping short of an apology to Kate for what she'd been thinking.

Alone once again, Kate started working on her house plans.

* * *

Emily was in bed, but wide-awake and waiting for Gordon when he returned home from the men's club meeting. Completely disgusted, she was primed and ready to give her husband a good piece of her mind.

"I knew it would happen. I just knew it," she griped.

"What are you talking about, Em?"

"Kate drove up to that creepy property in the hills this morning and fell in love with the place. You should have sold it to Hank when he wanted to buy. Then we wouldn't be having this little problem, would we?"

71

Gordon sat down on the side of the bed and took off his shoes. "Christ, Em! How the hell was I supposed to know Kate would fall in love with the place? Besides, I think she's got great taste. I love it up there myself. What did she say?"

"She wants to talk to you in the morning about buying the property. She's in her bedroom drawing up the new floor plans. Tell her you don't want to sell it, Gordon." Emily was almost pleading with him.

"Is that what you really want me to do?"

"Yes. Kate has no business living up there all alone."

"Em, your sister is a grown woman with a mind of her own. I think telling Kate I don't want to sell would be a mistake. She'd know that it was your idea and you put me up to it."

"Why would she think that?"

He had changed into his pajamas and climbed into bed beside her. "Because, if your sister has her heart set on the place, she knows me well enough to know I'd let her have it. Kate's anything but a stupid woman, Em. You know that."

Emily sighed. "I suppose you're right. Then I guess there's really nothing we can do to stop her, is there?"

"I'm afraid not, Honey. I don't like the idea of selling Kate that property either. I'd feel like a heel if I took her money. I stole the place when I bought it and that old dwelling is in terrible shape. I think I'll just give the property to Kate. Then she can spend whatever she wants on the renovation. Personally, I think she would be smart to raze the old structure. She could build from the ground up a lot cheaper. But that's a decision Kate will have to make."

"Well, you'll hear all about Kate's plans in the morning. And so will I." More than ready to call it a day, Emily reached to turn off the bedside lamp. "Good night, Gordon."

Forever fascinated with Hank's ability to sense his presence, Dane was disappointed with his own failed attempt to sneak up on his older buddy. "Darn it, Hank! I keep tryin' to slip up on you but I never can. How do you always know when I'm behind you?"

10 | CHAPTER *TEN*

The days had started to cool down in the southern part of Canada, but Hank chose to split firewood closer to sundown, when he knew it would be cooler. The wood shed he kept well stocked for winter had been filled, but a large amount of logs were piled up to be split.

It might have been a sixth sense alerting Hank that someone was behind him, but more likely than not it was his years of training in a covert operations unit. When Hank turned around, he was looking down at his small young neighbor, Dane DaRoux.

Hank grinned. "What's happening, Pup?"

Forever fascinated with Hank's ability to sense his presence, but disappointed at his own failed attempt to sneak up on his older buddy, Dane replied, "Darn it, Hank! How do you always know when I'm behind you? I keep tryin' to slip up on you, but I never can."

Hank chuckled. "Guess you just aren't as quiet as you should be, Pup."

The boy watched Hank's muscled arms raise the axe, bringing it down hard to split a log perfectly down the middle. Then Dane said, "I've been over at Doc Gordon's place this mornin'."

"Is that right?" Hank asked without bothering to look at the boy while reaching for another log. "What grabbed your interest with that old place?"

73

"I saw a new SUV turn in there as I was riding by on my bicycle. So I decided to watch and see what was going on. A lady got out of it and went inside the house. She stayed in there for a bit too. And when she came back out, she walked all around the property like maybe she was lookin' the place over," Dane replied.

"Did you happen to get a good look at the lady?" Hank asked. It was right about then that Hank noticed the boy's right hand was jiggling around in his pants pocket.

"Well, I really couldn't tell too much about her, Hank. Not from that distance. But I think she was kinda pretty. I didn't get too close cause I didn't want her to know I was watchin'. But she drove that SUV right through all those tall weeds and it looked brand spankin' new to me. I believe she had the biggest dog with her that I ever saw," Dane finished, his voice filled with excitement. "And I'm talkin' *BIG*."

"I suspect that woman you saw is Doc's sister-in-law, Pup. Doc told me she's been visiting with him and his wife. I've seen that dog you're talking about and he is a whopper." Hank had to wonder why Gordon's sister-in-law would be looking around the old dilapidated house. He'd been persistent with his attempts to buy that property, but Gordon had adamantly refused to sell. It didn't matter to Hank that the property was an eye sore, as long as it remained empty. "I wonder what she was doing over there."

"I don't know cause I didn't talk to her. All I done was watch her." Dane's hand was struggling with whatever was in his pocket. Finally, the boy asked, "Hey Hank, would ya wanna buy a champion jumpin' frog?"

Hank tried not to laugh, had it figured the frog was in Dane's pocket. "Do you have a champion jumping frog, Pup?"

"Yep, I sure do. See. Here it is, right here." Dane pulled the frog out of his pants pocket and held it up for Hank to admire. "This one's a real champion, I swear it is."

"Is that right? How can you be so sure that frog's a real champion? Has it won any contests yet?" Hank inquired, giving it all he had to look serious.

"Well, no... not just yet, it ain't. But believe me, this sucker can really jump. I've been trainin' this frog myself. I'd bet he could out-jump any other frog in these hills. I'd be willin' to sell this champion frog to ya... dirt cheap too. That's if you talked

Second Chances

to me just right," Dane said, nodding his head as if Hank should be in agreement.

It wasn't easy, but Hank held on to a straight face. "Oh, you would? Well, tell me now, just how much money would a champion jumping frog like that cost a man like me?"

"Oh, I don't know. I figure a frog like this one would be worth at least two dollars. I'm sure when this frog jumps in the big leagues that it'll win you a lot of money." Dane kept the sales pitch going.

"Yeah, I'm sure it will too. But wouldn't you just hate to part with such a fine frog?" Hank finally had to grin in an effort to keep from laughing. He really didn't want Dane's frog, but the kid was his buddy.

"Well, sure I hate like the devil to part with my champion frog, but I've got another frog that I've already started trainin'. This one's ready to go into competition right now. I figure you can do more than I could about gettin' him into real competition, Hank, cause you've got a truck. I'd be willin' to sell this frog to you for a reduced price of just two dollars, but that's only because we're such damn good friends. I sure as hell wouldn't let anyone else have my champion frog for that price." No doubt, Hank thought, the kid was destined to be an expert salesman one day.

Hank didn't appreciate hearing a young boy like Dane use that kind of language, but being well acquainted with Dane's old man, Hank wasn't the least bit surprised. "I think you need to watch your language, Pup. I know your mother would be upset if she heard that kind of talk out of you. Tell you what I'll do. I'll buy your champion frog for five dollars if you'll promise to clean up your language. Is it a deal?"

"Five bucks! Wow! You got a deal," Dane agreed. Hank reached for his wallet, pulled out the money and handed it to Dane in exchange for the frog. "Thanks, Hank. You won't be sorry, I can promise you that."

After the swap, Dane jumped on his bicycle and rode off. Looking back at Hank as he pedaled down the driveway, he added, "Yep, that's one hel... I mean heck of a frog."

Suckered again, Hank thought and looked down at the frog he was holding. Then he chuckled, wondering if a beautiful, well-endowed woman might suddenly appear if he kissed that

75

sucker smack dab in the face. But Hank knew his luck didn't run that way and it probably wouldn't happen, so he set the croaker down on the ground, away from the woodpile. He'd already decided that a champion frog like that one surely wouldn't just start jumping away.

Picking up another log to split, Hank thought about Gordon's sister-in-law. Why would she be over there nosing around Gordon's old house? Maybe she was just out on a little exploring expedition while she was here visiting. No telling what went through a Yankee woman's mind these days? Holding that thought, he could just see Doc's pretty sister-in-law bouncing through that front door with Emily. She really was a good-looking woman. Being skinny hadn't taken anything away from her natural beauty. Then he wondered when the pretty lady might be making plans to return to the States.

* * *

Dane DaRoux was the sweetheart of the hills. The kid never met a stranger and had a personality that was loaded with charm. If he seemed a little shy at first, it didn't last long. As soon as someone offered Dane a smile, he was ready to be their friend. Most of the local folks found it hard to believe that a man like Charlie DaRoux could have sired such a great kid. Hank had often thought the same thing.

Hank knew that Dane's family life had never been easy. His mother, Ruth, had to marry Charlie when she was quite young. Charlie had raped Ruth one afternoon while she was working for him as a chore girl. Shortly after it happened, she had no choice but to tell Charlie that she was pregnant. Ruth was barely sixteen at the time and getting married wasn't exactly what Charlie had in mind. But he also knew if Ruth's father learned of her condition that the old man was capable of killing them both. Rather than risk the consequences, matrimony seemed to be the sensible route for Charlie to take, if not the safest.

Charlie held a strong resentment for his young wife and treated her badly from the very beginning. Ruth had never felt anything but contempt for Charlie, but was stuck in the marriage. As if having to live with a man she didn't love wasn't bad enough, she had to endure Charlie's physical abuse. With nowhere else to go or means to support her family, Ruth had to grow up fast and hard.

In her prime, Ruth was a tall and well-developed young woman with long wavy blonde hair and bright blue eyes, but bearing four children before the age of twenty-five had taken its physical toll on Dane's mother, and those features had long since faded with hard work and resentment. For Ruth, being married to Charlie was one hell of a life. Having sex with him was totally repulsive, which Ruth compared to having sex with a football player. She never knew when Charlie was going to tackle her or, for that matter, how hard.

His wife's welfare was the least of Charlie's concerns when he wanted sex. He couldn't have cared less if Ruth wasn't physically up to or felt like performing her conjugal duties. Even Ruth's menstrual periods didn't matter when Charlie was in the mating mood. Plainly, the man didn't care about anyone but himself.

After Ruth's first child was born, she knew getting away from Charlie would be difficult. But after the birth of three more children almost nine months apart, any hope she ever had of leaving was completely diminished. To make matters even worse, Charlie was furious with Ruth every time she told him she was going to have another baby.

Being a self-indulgent and self-centered person, Charlie had never been good to his family. It was only after his oldest son, Derek, had grown taller and was physically stronger than Charlie, that he showed the boy a bit of respect. That small amount of respect came about only because the kid had turned into a real workhorse for his father.

Ruth's daughter, Debbie, was the second child to be born into this miserable mess of a marriage. The poor girl was pretty enough, but she never knew from one day to the next what Charlie expected of her as to the daily chores. Luckily, she was capable of working like a man when Derek needed help, or else she stayed inside to help with the housework. Debbie was afraid to tell her mother about Charlie's incestuous ways, especially after Charlie threatened to beat her to death if she told anyone.

Deanne was Ruth's third child. Ruth had hoped this baby would be the last of her child bearing days, but it wasn't to be. Deanne was born six weeks earlier than expected and wasn't a healthy child. If Charlie paid any attention at all to this child, it was never in a pleasant way. To Charlie, the little girl was useless.

Dane came along after Deanne, but it seemed as if this little boy was extra special to Ruth. Besides, he was the baby of the family. Seemingly gifted with the knowledge of what it took to stay on Charlie's good side, it was a feat the little boy soon mastered and quite successfully at that. Dane was the only DaRoux child that could get Charlie to laugh once in a while.

If Charlie had just shown an ounce of affection toward any of his children, then maybe it would have made a difference with Ruth. But that hadn't happened. To do or say anything that might indicate he cared about anyone wasn't Charlie's way. Ruth had come to understand her husband's moods. Other than anger, she knew Charlie wasn't capable of any other type of emotion. His attitude toward his children, coupled with a miserable marriage, had caused Ruth a great amount of resentment and heartache.

Determined there would be no more babies, Ruth opted for sterilization after giving birth to Dane. Charlie thought his wife's sterilization was a great idea, regrettably wondering why Ruth hadn't smartened up before she'd produced four children.

The peace of mind that Ruth enjoyed in knowing she couldn't get pregnant again was good, but her life had been made miserable in another way, especially when Charlie came to bed in the evenings. It seemed as if he was always ready to have his way with Ruth, continually preaching that it was a wife's duty to surrender to her husband. After all, Charlie would boast, surrendering to a man was God's intention for all women. Ruth loathed hearing those words almost as much as she loathed Charlie.

Ruth often planned and schemed, wondering how she might go about killing Charlie and if she could get away with doing it, but in reality, she didn't have the nerve to follow through with his execution. She'd read one time about a woman down in Illinois that had presumably chopped up her husband's body and fed him to the hogs. She'd read that the man had been abusive to his family, like Charlie was to Ruth and the kids. Seems the authorities sifted for days through the mud in a hog pen, but were never able to locate any of the man's remains. Since there was no body to declare the man legally dead, then there wasn't any way to prove he had been killed. The woman was never charged in connection with her husband's disappearance.

All Ruth could do was dream about killing Charlie, because she didn't have enough nerve to get the job done. Thus, she continued to endure the mistreatment of her children, as well as her own physical abuse. More often than not, when Charlie came home after having a bad day, he would slap the kids around without cause or provocation. If Ruth tried to intervene, then she became the brunt of her husband's physical abuse. She'd suffered more black eyes, bloodied noses, busted lips, and fractured ribs than she could recall. On one occasion, she'd suffered a broken arm when Charlie twisted it too far behind her back.

Over the years, however, she'd learned to stay out of Charlie's way. She tried to avoid him by saying very little, not talking back and doing as she was told. This lessened the likelihood of causing Charlie to anger, while reducing the chance of having to endure another blow from his fists. She lectured the children often to do the same. They shouldn't speak at all when Charlie was around. If he asked them a direct question, only then were they to answer.

Because Dane was the youngest, he had more freedom and did less work than the other children. For some reason, Charlie got a kick out of the kid. He liked the way Dane could smooth-talk anyone out of a fast buck. A trait he truly admired in the boy.

Although Charlie was never able to keep a steady job, he made money by raising and selling a few hogs. Since he was a handyman of sorts, he would often do carpentry work on the side. It was well known that Charlie would do just about anything for a few dollars, even though he'd never made much of a living for his family.

Among his other faults, Charlie liked to drink and gamble. So the start of a new school year had always resulted in bad times for Ruth. Charlie hated having to work overtime for extra money to buy school clothes. About a month before school started, his short temper was always more noticeable to Ruth. It wasn't right to wish the young lives of her children away, but she wished they could grow up quicker.

* * *

Dane wasn't going home without first stopping by to see Needa Begay and her son, Raine. He had a hankerin' for a few of those sugar cookies that Needa usually kept baked and often shared with Dane when he stopped by. Besides, he was anxious to tell Needa about the lady he'd seen going into Doc Gordon's place earlier that morning. There would still be plenty of time to get home before supper.

Dane jumped off his bicycle and let it fall to the ground, ascending the porch steps with three jumps. Needa and Raine were sitting in the porch swing, watching as Dane jumped like a deer. When he was seated on the edge of the porch with his legs hanging loosely over the side, he looked up at Needa and grinned.

"What's Dane up to this evening?" Needa asked.

"I just came from Hank's place. I sold him my champion frog today," Dane boasted.

Needa looked over the hill toward Hank's property and laughed. "I'll bet that thrilled the heck out of Hank. What was he doing?"

"Splittin' wood, same as always. You wouldn't happen to have any sugar cookies, would ya, Miss Needa?"

"I'd imagine so. Wait here with Raine and I'll go fetch a handful for you," Needa told him as she got up out of the swing, leaving Dane to watch her son.

Dane moved to sit in the swing next to Raine. Needa's eighteen-year-old son had been diagnosed with fragile X syndrome, a disorder with characteristics similar to autism. The boy never said anything and rarely held eye contact with anyone.

Raine was Needa's love child. His father lived somewhere in California and had never known of Raine's existence. Needa dated the guy while she was attending college, still very much a wild and free spirit. She'd never really been in love, so when Needa discovered she was pregnant the idea of marriage was out of the question. Instead, she'd dropped out of college and returned to Canada with no intention of ever telling Raine's father about her condition. That was just Needa's way of doing things.

Second Chances

"Here you go, Dane," Needa said, handing the boy a ziplock baggie full of sugar cookies. "Sugar cookies for my little sweetheart."

Dane got up to give Needa her place next to Raine. He sat down on the porch, swinging his legs over the side again. Momentarily occupied with eating the cookies, he devoured three of the tasty treats before looking up at Needa and announcing with enthusiasm, "Doc Gordon's got company."

Needa laughed. "How in the world do you know that, Dane?"

"Cause Hank told me. It's Doc's sister-in-law. That's who Hank said the lady was anyway. She was over at Doc's old house this mornin'," Dane said before stuffing another cookie in his mouth.

"I wonder what she was doing over there at that old place," Needa quizzed the boy.

"Hank was wonderin' about that too. Boy, Miss Needa, you should've seen the big dog that was with her," Dane said, before licking the sugar off his fingers and lips. "She stayed for quite a while and looked around. She was drivin' a real nice Jeep. Can you believe anyone lettin' a big dog like that ride in a new Jeep?"

"What kind of a dog was it?"

"It looked like a Saint Bernard as best I could tell. I just know it was a big sucker," Dane answered and jumped off the porch. "I gotta go, Miss Needa. Thanks for the cookies. I'll stop by again real soon. Bye, Raine." Dane hesitated as if waiting for Raine to say something, but Raine wasn't paying any attention to the boy.

Needa watched Dane as he rode off on his bicycle. Like Hank, she was curious as to what the woman was doing at Doc's old house, thinking to keep a watchful eye on Doc's place. If anyone else showed up around there, she would see them.

Dane barely made it home in time for supper. When he sat down at the table, Charlie offered his young son a rare smile before he asked, "Where've you been, Boy? We was about to start supper without ya."

Not wanting his mother to scold him for eating cookies before supper, Dane chose his words carefully. "Nowhere in

81

particular, Pa. I've just been out ridin' my bike and I stopped by Miss Needa's for a quick visit."

Charlie frowned. "It beats the hell out of me, Dane, why you like bein' around that Beatnik and her mongoloid kid. Can't you find somethin' better to do?" he asked, picking up the bowl of mashed potatoes.

"Raine's not a mongoloid, Pa. That's not his problem. Besides, I like Miss Needa. She's always been real nice to me."

"She's a damn Beatnik, Dane. You jest mind your pa and don't be hangin' around over there with that woman and her idiot boy. No tellin' how simple that kid of hers really is," Charlie warned as Dane passed the potatoes on to Derek.

"There was a lady over at Doc Gordon's place this morning. She was drivin' a real nice Jeep," Dane was quick to say, wanting to change the subject. Every family member sitting at the table looked over to Dane. "Why's everybody lookin' at me like that? I was just ridin' by and happened to notice this SUV in front of Doc's old house. So I kind of... just watched. That's all," Dane lied.

"Dane, you can't just watch Doc Gordon's place from the road. Tell the truth, you idiot, you followed the Jeep after it turned into the lane, didn't you?" Derek asked, chewing a mouth full of food while he talked.

"Well, maybe I did just follow along. But that was just so I could get a better look at what was goin' on, cause she got out of the Jeep and went inside and stayed in there a long time. And when she finally came back out, she walked all around the place. She had this BIG dog with her too," Dane went on with his story.

Dane knew better than to reveal who told him the lady was related to Doc Gordon or that he'd been visiting with Hank Diamond. Charlie and Hank had been in an on-going feud for years that had brought about a strong dislike for each other. Their animosity had resulted from a dispute over property lines. Charlie was furious when Hank had the land surveyed. He kept pulling up the surveyor's stakes, saying Hank's old man had bought off the surveyors.

"Did you get all your chores done before you took off explorin' over at Doc Gordon's place, Dane?" Derek asked his kid brother.

Dane shot his brother a disgusted look. "I did what Pa told me to do."

Derek shrugged. "Good. That's what you're supposed to do, you little punk. Then I won't end up havin' to do your work too."

The family ate the rest of their meal in silence. Ruth and the girls didn't offer to say anything, but then again, they hadn't been spoken to either.

Susie Rigsby

With both hands on his hips, the carpenter walked further away from Kate and studied the project. "You could spend a small fortune renovating this old dwelling, but then maybe you've got more money than you do brains," he said, then looked back at Kate and smiled. "No offense meant."

11 | CHAPTER *ELEVEN*

"I can't sell you that old piece of property, Kate," Gordon told her during breakfast the next morning.

Kate's heart sank. "Why not? You aren't going to use it for anything, are you?"

Gordon winked at Emily but kept a straight face. "No, as a matter of fact, I'm not. But I'd feel real bad about asking you to pay me for a piece of property in that condition. It would weigh heavily on my conscience to be that underhanded. It might even cause me to lose sleep at night. Nope, I just wouldn't feel right about selling you that old place," he said before a big grin spread over his face. "But if you really want it that badly, then I'll give it to you."

Kate let out a sigh of relief before deciding to argue with him about giving away the real estate. "Oh, goodness, Gordon! I couldn't let you do that. At least let me pay you the amount you have invested."

"Oh, I don't think so. Em tells me that you have great plans for the place. My advice would be to bulldoze the structure down and start over, build a new home from the ground up. You'll save money in the long run if you do."

Kate laughed. "Nonsense. The wood is still sturdy and I didn't notice any termite damage. All it needs is a face-lift and a lot of inside remodeling. I've already sketched plans for the changes I'd like to make. Now all I need is a handy man with the right tools. Can you recommend a good carpenter who works fast and cheap?"

85

Gordon hated to enlighten Kate about Canadian carpenters. "Dream on, Sweetheart, because you won't find a carpenter that works cheap around here."

"Okay, so no cheap carpenters. Do you know of anyone that I could hire to help me tackle the job? There's a lot of work to be done."

Gordon thought for a minute. "Leo Staggner is the only carpenter I know, but I think he's about the best around. He just might be available this late in the season. I'll give him a call. You'll have to check on building permits too. When would you want to get started?"

"Yesterday would have been just perfect," she replied and grinned. "But the sooner the better. I'm going up there this morning after breakfast to do some mowing and weed eating on the yard. That's where I'll be if you can get in touch with him, he can meet me there. Once he looks the job over, I'm sure he'll know whether or not he's interested," Kate said and looked over at her sister. The expression on Emily's face indicated that Kate's sister was not at all pleased about this deal. "In the meantime, Em, would you mind checking into the building permits and see what I have to do?"

Emily had nothing to say, so she simply nodded her headed.

Preparing to spend the entire day in the hills, Kate packed a picnic lunch and iced down a cooler full of soft drinks and bottled water, after which she loaded a few of Gordon's yard tools and a lawnmower. She had never backed away from hard work and was all set to tackle the yard first. The weeds had to be removed and yard cleaned up before undertaking any of the major projects on the house.

*   *   *

It was a real treat for Leo Staggner to watch Kate whacking weeds. He sat in his truck for a long while, enjoying every minute of Kate's labor. After finally deciding to get out of his truck and go talk to the grass-cutting maniac, Leo walked up behind Kate and touched her on the shoulder.

"Oh, goodness! You startled me," Kate said and jumped back. She shut off the weed eater and wiped her forehead with the back of her hand, then smiled up at him. She noticed the pencil wedged over the big guy's right ear. That, coupled with the size of Leo's shoulders and dark tan on his face and arms, assured Kate the man might be her carpenter. He had character about him with a face that Kate thought looked honest.

Leo had looked her over as well. It was his nature to admire a beautiful woman and this one was well worthy of his admiration. "You must be Kate?"

"That's right," Kate said, extending her hand to him. "And you must be Leo Staggner."

Appreciating the firm grip of Kate's handshake, Leo nodded. "I am. Doc called me early this morning and said something about you being in need of a carpenter, said I'd find you up here working." Then Leo turned to look at the front of the dilapidated dwelling. "You got ideas about remodeling this old place, do you?" Walking further away from Kate and with both hands on his hips, the carpenter studied the project. "You could spend a small fortune renovating this old dwelling, but then maybe you've got more money than you do brains," he said, then looked back at Kate and smiled. "No offense meant."

No doubt about this guy being honest, Kate thought and laughed. "Maybe I do. And no offense taken."

Leo scratched his head, trying to size up his potential job. "You might want to consider razing this old house. I could build you a new home a lot faster than I could remodel this one. The lines aren't going to be true. It's just a whole lot of hard work, Kate, and you're still going to have an old house when the renovation is completed."

Shaking her head, Kate knew he was trying to change her mind. "Gordon tried to sell me on the same idea, but that isn't what I want to do. I love this place the way it is now. I think the old house has character, don't you? I feel certain there are still some good boards left in it. I've sketched a few rough drafts of what I'd like to have done if you'd like to take a look. I know it's a major renovation, but if you'll do the heavy part I can take care of the painting and staining."

Kate headed toward the Jeep for the drawings and Leo followed along behind her.

"The decision is yours to make, Kate. No job's too big or too small for me. I charge the same rate either way. You just need to know that it's going to take me a lot longer to remodel than it would to rebuild. I work by contract or by the hour, whichever you prefer. Doc says you're anxious to get started."

Kate handed him the drawings. "That's right. Here are the floor plans. I'll need a list of the materials you'll need to get started. I can go into Nobleton tomorrow and make arrangements for the materials to be delivered. If it's all the same to you, I'll deal directly with the supplier. That will allow me to keep on top of the material availability so delivery won't get us off schedule. It lessens your paper work too. You won't have to worry with getting lien waivers from the suppliers this way. It doesn't matter to me whether you write a contract or do the job by the hour. Either way will work for me. I'd like to start this job as soon as possible if that's okay with you."

He looked over Kate's rough sketches. "Not bad. This will make a world of difference in the old place. I'll do some measuring and take your plans home with me to make a material list this evening. I just hope you know what you're getting yourself into," Leo said, grinning.

"Yeah, so do I."

"Okay, then, you've got yourself a deal. Give me a call as soon as you have your building permits and I'll get started without delay," Leo said. Judging from the way Kate had been attacking the weeds, he suspected she might want to start without the building permits. But that wouldn't happen.

"I'll be in touch," Kate told him.

*   *   *

The sound of Kate's lawnmower was echoing across the hills. Since Doc's property was the only place close enough for the sound to reach Hank's place, he figured someone had to be over there working.

"Shit," he said out loud, thoroughly disgusted. He'd tried in vain on several occasions to buy the property from Gordon because the land adjoined Hank's and covered several acres. If he'd been successful with that acquisition, he'd fully intended to tear down the old house and clear the ground. It appeared as though that wasn't going to happen now.

Aggravated as he was, Hank decided to go over there and have a look around. He slipped into a pair of jogging shorts and running shoes, thinking to use the trip for an extra morning run and stop by Gordon's place on his return home. However, curiosity had gotten the better of Hank and he decided to stop by Gordon's property first.

Because the military demanded that their soldiers stay in excellent physical condition, Hank had become regimented to a routine of strenuous exercise. After retirement, he'd continued the daily ritual of running at least five miles or more every morning, and then enduring a thirty-minute workout. There was nothing about Hank's physique that would indicate he was reaching middle age, as if reaching middle age was supposed to mean something to a man like Hank. He hadn't even worked up a good sweat after jogging up the hill toward Doc's property.

As Hank neared the old house, he noticed the new Jeep parked in the driveway, giving him cause to wonder about the woman's big dog. His trained eyes scouted the area but didn't see any sign of the animal. Kate appeared to be totally oblivious to his presence when Hank sat down on the porch, so he just stayed there for quite a while and watched Kate mowing the grass.

She had a job to do and was too busy to notice anyone until she shut down the lawnmower. It was then that Kate took the time to look around, hoping to see a big improvement in the yard. She was startled again when she spotted Hank sitting on the steps and it showed.

"By the look on your face, I hope I didn't frighten you," Hank said and grinned. "I'm not really that ugly, am I?"

"You didn't frighten me." *And you certainly aren't ugly*, Kate thought as she glanced around for her dog. "It's just that I didn't realize there was anyone so close to me. I didn't notice you at all. How long have you been sitting there?" she asked, walking over to the cooler for a bottle of water.

"Not long. You mow with a real vengeance. Do you always take your yard work so seriously?" Hank asked.

She offered him the bottle of water, which he took. Reaching for another bottle of water, she told him, "I take everything I do seriously if I want to get it done."

He watched as Kate removed the bottle cap and took a drink, noticed the elegant lines of her long, slender neck, then wondered why it was her neck that had his attention. Given the opportunity to sink his teeth into this woman's body, he wasn't sure he'd want to begin with her neck. But then again, a guy's got to start somewhere and that area did look pretty inviting.

"Looks to me as if you're hell bent on making this place look presentable." Hank had actually meant the statement to be a compliment, but then he was just trying to make conversation.

"Is that right?" Kate gave him a look. Wiping the sweat off her forehead and with a noticeable hint of sarcasm, she added, "And I'll bet you arrived at that conclusion just by observing the way I work. You country boys think you have it all figured out, don't you?"

Hank wasn't prepared for the way Doc's sister-in-law was behaving or her flippant attitude. But instead of bothering with a quick come-back, he gave Kate that slow Diamond grin of his and replied, "The lawnmower got my attention. I don't live very far from here, so I thought I'd drop by and see what was going on, maybe offer to give you a hand. But I'll be on my way if I'm bothering you."

HE wasn't bothering Kate, but that cocky grin on his face hadn't set too well. Not to mention his muscled arms and legs, or the way his eyes had roamed over every inch of her body. It wasn't necessarily an uncomfortable feeling, but definitely one Kate hadn't experienced in a long time. Hoping to give the look back in a likewise fashion, Kate gazed down at his feet, then slowly moved her eyes upward over his legs until they reached his crotch.

With a smirk on her face equally as smug as Hank's, she told him, "It's rather doubtful that you could bother me, Mr. Diamond. And although it's been a pleasure chatting with you, I need to finish my job. Feel free to stay and watch me work for as long as you like and, by all means, help yourself to the cooler," she said and headed for the lawnmower.

Hank hardly knew what to think. Not of the woman, her reply, or her actions. "How did you know my name?"

Kate stopped and turned back around to answer him. "You men are all alike in believing that women never pay any attention to anything. Well, I hate to burst your bubble, but I remember you from the other day when you picked Gordon up to go fishing."

"But Gordon didn't introduce us. So that means you must have been talking about me."

Kate had moved to the lawnmower, preparing to start it again. "Maybe. But don't expect me to tell you what was said." Kate pulled on the cord several times but the mower failed to start. After waiting a few moments, she tried again, giving the cord several more pulls. The mower still wouldn't start. "Damn it," she said.

Hank got up and walked over to her. Displaying an even greater amount of arrogance and superiority, he said, "Please. Allow me to do that for you."

Kate despised looking so helpless over a stupid lawnmower. "The motor probably just got too hot and needs to cool off a little."

Hank gave her a devilish grin. "Yeah, I know what you mean. Some things start better when they're hot, but not lawnmowers." He reached down and pulled the cord, starting the mower with only one jerk and very little effort. He wanted to laugh, but instead he lifted the bottle of water as if to gesture a silent 'thank you' for it before he took off jogging down the lane.

Kate stood beside the idling lawnmower and watched until her handsome neighbor was out of sight. Hating the fact she couldn't get the lawnmower to start, she thought of how easily it had started for Hank. Well, with arms like that, why wouldn't it start when he yanked on the pull cord?

She'd never been physically attracted to another man after marrying Mack, but here she was, consciously aware of Hank Diamond's body. Why else would she have been so curt with him?

Upset with her randy thoughts about Hank, she went back to mowing with a vengeance, as the handsome hunk had so aptly described her work. It really didn't make much sense for

Kate to be putting out so much effort, because the yard was almost finished. So why was she still doing this? Then too, she kept wondering about Baron. Where was that dog while she'd been honored with a visitor? The dog rarely got that far away from her.

When Kate was finished with mowing the yard, she turned the mower off and glanced over toward the deck. She spotted Baron lying on the ground, within an arm's reach of the two new visitors that were sitting on the porch steps and watching Kate. Half amused and thinking this must be her day for visitors, Kate shook her head and walked over to the cooler.

"Hi. Have you been sitting here long?" she asked, but knew they couldn't have been there very long.

"No. Not long," the attractive, dark complexioned woman replied.

"I must apologize. I wasn't ignoring you. I just didn't see you sitting there."

Needa gave a soft, pleasant laugh. "There's no need to apologize. We came here the back way from over the hill. Seeing us would have been difficult for you. There's a path leading to my place from here," Needa said, nodding toward her property. Then she reached down to pet Baron. "Actually, we just sort of acquainted ourselves with your dog and followed him over here. He's very beautiful!"

"Thank you," Kate said and noticed the boy sitting next to the Indian woman. Obviously, his attention span wasn't normal and Kate tried not to stare, thinking he was a handsome lad to be afflicted in such a way. "The dog's name is Baron and I'm Kate Corbin. Gordon Juenger owns this property and I'm his sister-in-law. Do you know him?"

"Yes, he's our dentist."

Kate offered a soft drink to the boy, which Raine accepted. Then she took another soft drink and a bottle of water from the cooler, offering her other visitor a choice. "Would you like something cold to drink?"

"Thank you. I'll have the water. I'm Needa Begay and this is my son, Raine," Needa made the introduction while accepting the bottle of water from Kate.

Kate was quick to notice Needa's earrings and necklace, remembering her mother had worn the same type of jewelry many times. Needa's physical appearance was a dead give-away to her ethnicity but Kate asked anyway. "Indian? Right?"

"Yes," Needa answered with another warm smile. "I hope you don't mind our visiting when you're so busy. We didn't want to interrupt."

"No. Not at all. This seems to be a good day for visitors. I was just about to finish up here anyway. There's not much more I can do today," Kate said, removing the sweatband from her head.

"Are you planning to take up residence here, Kate?" Needa asked.

The impression Needa left with Kate wasn't so much that the Indian woman was trying to be nosy, just more curious than anything else. "Yeah, I am. I've talked my brother-in-law into parting with this piece of property. I've hired a contractor and he's supposed to start with the renovations right away. I hope to be moving into the house within six to eight weeks. Guess you think I must be crazy or else a glutton for punishment."

Needa looked directly into Kate's eyes and smiled warmly again. "Not at all. I can't think of a more suitable place for mending a broken heart."

The statement had caught Kate more than a little off guard. She gave Needa a puzzled look, wondering if Needa had talked to Emily or Gordon. "What makes you think I'm trying to mend a broken heart?"

"Oh, just a hunch, I guess. Aren't you?"

Kate felt uncomfortable. This woman was a stranger and getting a little too personal. Ignoring Needa's question, Kate started picking up the lawn equipment. "I really should be heading back to Toronto. I certainly have enjoyed meeting you, Needa. I hope you'll drop by and visit with me again real soon."

Needa knew that Kate had deliberately avoided her question. However, it wasn't necessary for Kate to answer. The tormented look on Kate's face had told Needa all she needed to know. She had seen the sadness in Kate's eyes, a sadness that had loomed for too many months... and still remained.

"Raine and I will come back to visit with you again. If you need anything, my place is just over the back ridge and down the path a bit. If you follow the path, it will take you right to my back door. I'd be happy to help you do whatever I can," Needa offered in friendship.

Kate couldn't help but like the Indian woman. She was lovely, with a rare type of charisma that worked like a magnet. Though Kate didn't want Needa prying into her past, she felt certain that Needa's friendship would be a treasure. In a melancholy way, seeing Needa had reminded Kate of her mother, although Needa was closer to Kate's age.

"Thank you. I'll remember your offer. That's very kind of you," Kate said.

When Needa laid her hand on Raine's shoulder, he stood to go with her. As they were walking away, the boy stopped for a moment to pet Baron's head before following along after his mother.

When her latest visitors were out of hearing distance, Kate looked over at Baron. "So, Big Dog, you've been out visiting around the neighborhood, have you? Where else would all these visitors be coming from if you weren't dragging them up? Except for Hank Diamond. And where were you when that arrogant ass made his appearance?"

She petted the dog before climbing up the steps to put the lawn equipment inside the dwelling. After locking the door, Kate wondered if it wasn't a bit foolish. If someone wanted to take the lawn equipment, getting inside the old house would not be difficult to do. She locked the door anyway.

For Kate to assume he was married, Leo figured it was probably because he hadn't tried to hit on her. She was a beautiful woman and that thought had crossed Leo's mind several times, but he made it a practice never to mix business with pleasure. He reached up to remove his cap and scratch the top of his head. "I don't have a girlfriend either, Kate."

12| CHAPTER *TWELVE*

Kate was totally convinced after only a week of working with Leo Staggner that he was one hell of a carpenter. There were a few occasions when he had needed Kate's assistance, for which she made it a point of always being available and ready to help.

Leo was just as impressed with Kate's work ethics. She wasn't as physically strong as he would have preferred, but she was certainly better than no help at all. She never backed away from a job, whether Leo was asking her to grab the end of a board, hold a level, or bring him a tool. Kate had quickly responded. She'd stayed ahead of him in staining the woodwork and doors, impressing Leo with her taste in décor as the work progressed.

At the end of the eighth week, Gordon's old house bore no resemblance to the structure it had once been. The new siding, doors and windows, along with the new deck and steps, had made a big difference. For some reason, Leo had taken extra pride in building the upper deck that connected to Kate's bedroom. The additional deck had totally changed the front of the dwelling, giving it more character.

A genuine friendship had developed between Leo and Kate as the renovation project neared completion. The afternoon that Kate was writing out a check for the final payment of Leo's contract, he took a moment to admire the woman. When Kate handed him the check, Leo felt compelled to give her a compliment. "You certainly have been a real handy person to have around, Kate. You sure aren't a lazy woman. I'll have to say that much for you."

Kate looked up at her carpenter and laughed. "Thanks, Leo. My parents would be real proud if they could hear you bragging on me that way. I was taught that if you wanted something done right, then you'd best do it yourself. It's a lesson well-learned, wouldn't you agree?"

"I sure would." Wondering about Kate's personal life and the fact she hadn't mentioned one word about her family the whole time they'd been working together, Leo asked, "You know, Kate, you haven't said much about your parents. Do they live around here?"

"No, they live in California. I never cared much for California myself, but they seem to like it. I plan to invite them here for a visit after I get the house furnished. Which reminds me, I'm going to have a small get-together here next weekend and you're invited. We'll grill steaks and have a few beers. It will just be my sister and Gordon and perhaps a couple of others. I'd be delighted if you'd bring your wife and join us," Kate said, inviting Leo.

Realizing he hadn't told Kate anything about his personal life either, Leo chuckled. "Thanks for the invite, Kate, but I don't have a wife."

"Oh goodness, I guess I just assumed you were married." Kate shrugged her shoulders. "Well then, bring your girlfriend."

For Kate to assume he was married, Leo figured it was probably because he hadn't tried to hit on her. She was a beautiful woman and that thought had crossed Leo's mind several times, but he made it a practice never to mix business with pleasure. He reached up to remove his cap and scratch the top of his head. "I don't have a girlfriend either, Kate."

Kate thought about what he'd just said. Leo wasn't a bad looking guy. He worked hard and probably made good money in the building business. So why wouldn't a guy like Leo have a woman? "You aren't gay, are you?"

Leo's face blushed to a bright red. "Would it make any difference to you if I was? I mean, would you invite me anyway?"

She'd had no right to ask Leo such a question and hoped he wasn't offended. "You've done an excellent job, Leo. I'm not the least bit concerned about your sexual preference. You're invited, and feel free to bring whomever you please. My feelings would be hurt if you didn't join us."

Leo laughed. "Maybe I'd better set the record straight before this goes too far. I'm not gay, Kate. I've been that marriage route before and it didn't work out, but it did last long enough to get me a daughter. When the divorce was final, my ex-wife took my little girl and moved back to New York. My girl will be eighteen next month. I didn't get to see much of her through the years, so we're not very close. I've kept my child support payments up, but that divorce cost me a pretty penny. Guess it made me a little wary, so no more serious relationships for me."

"The marriage soured you on women?"

"No, not at all. When I get in the mood for a woman I usually hit one of the local bars. Otherwise, I know how to cook, clean, and pay my own bills. I get by just fine. For me, the best part of living alone is having control of the remote and picking the channels I like to watch on TV." Grinning, Leo slipped Kate's check into his shirt pocket and stuck his cap back on his head. "I'd be honored to attend your housewarming, Kate. But if it's all the same to you, I'll be alone."

"That works for me too, Leo. I'll be in touch."

As Leo drove away, Kate realized it had been more than a little uncouth to ask if he was gay. She valued Leo's friendship and should have known to leave well enough alone. But Leo had explained his situation quite well and now she knew.

Alone again, Kate took a moment to look around. She was proud of what she had accomplished, maybe more so than anything else she'd ever done. A lot of sweat, blisters and splinters had resulted from all the hard work, but the end result was well worth it. She finally had a home of her own. Buying furniture was all that Kate had left to do. Hopefully, she could get delivery before the weekend, then she would be set to move in.

Kate walked outside to look around in the yard, thinking autumn would soon be over. Gordon had forewarned her about the winters in Canada and how rough it could get. Except for getting the firewood delivered, Kate figured she was as ready as she'd ever be. But for right now, the air was still warm and the fall colors were beautiful. She really loved this place, she thought, sitting down in the swing.

Mack was sitting beside her. "You've worked hard, Kate, and the home is quite nice. You've done a good job."

"Would you like for me to give you the grand tour, Mack?"

"Thanks, but I've already had it. Are you sure you're going to like living up here?"

"Why do you keep asking me that question? I love it up here. It's so quiet and peaceful. Baron can run free and I don't have to worry about him getting hit by a car. What do I have to do or say to convince you anyway?"

"We'll see. I'm just worried about you."

"I'm fine, Mack."

There was a frown on Mack's face, or maybe a look of concern. "You are fine, Kate. There's no doubt about that. You're one fine woman. But there's still a lot for you to do yet and I'm not talking about this piece of property," Mack said, intent on having a serious conversation with Kate, but his visit was interrupted.

"Hi, Kate, are you busy?" Needa greeted, standing with Raine below the deck and looking up at Kate.

"No, not at all. Come on up and grab a seat. I'll go inside and fix us a glass of iced tea," Kate invited before glancing over to where Mack had been sitting. He was gone again.

Kate's company climbed up the porch steps and sat down in the swing. Raine giggled when Baron came over to him. A few minutes later, Kate returned with a serving tray and three glasses of iced tea.

"Help yourself," she said and set the tray on a table between the swing and rocker chair.

"Thanks," Needa said and reached for a glass, handing it to Raine. "I've kinda been wondering, Kate, if you spend much time talking to yourself?"

"Oh my, did you hear me?" Kate asked, embarrassed. "I wasn't talking to myself. Not really."

"I didn't think so."

"Why would you say that?"

"Because I know."

"You know? I beg your pardon. What do you know?"

"You speak to a spirit. It's the spirit of a person that once loved you very much. He still does. That's why his spirit remains here," Needa said before taking a drink of tea.

Kate smiled, ever so slightly. "Do you think I'm crazy, Needa?"

"Oh, no. Not at all."

"Anyone else would if they heard me."

"I'm Indian, Kate. Not your average Indian either, but then you'll probably learn about that soon enough." Needa decided to change the subject. "When are you moving in?"

"I hope this weekend. In fact, I plan to have a little housewarming next Saturday afternoon. I'll just be having my sister and Gordon. Oh, and I invited the carpenter too. I'd love for you and Raine to join us," Kate invited.

"Are you sure, Kate?"

"That's a silly question. Of course, I'm sure."

"I mean about Raine? I don't go anywhere without him."

"Didn't you just hear me invite Raine too? What is the matter with you anyway?" Kate asked, and looked at Raine. "He's such a handsome boy. I've noticed that he does respond to a few things. Have you ever thought about having him tested?" It was the first time Kate had offered to discuss Raine's condition with Needa.

"Of course, I have," Needa replied, touched by Kate's concern. "I do everything I can for him. I won't go into telling you about Raine's condition right now, but someday soon I will. I put as much money as I can into a trust for my son. It's to be used for his care if something should happen to me. I wish I had someone I could depend on to take care of Raine, but unfortunately I don't. Anyway, that's enough about that subject. I came to invite you over for dinner. It's nothing fancy, just spaghetti and meatballs with garlic bread. I've chilled a bottle of my homemade wine too. The food is ready if you're hungry."

Kate was thrilled by her neighbor's invitation, hoping they could get better acquainted over a glass of wine. "It sounds delicious and I'm starved. We'll take the Jeep to your place instead of walking the back path. Go ahead and get Raine loaded in the back seat with Baron while I lock up the house."

Once they were comfortably situated inside Needa's home, Kate was more than ready for that glass of wine. Relaxing as she sipped the wine, Kate's eyes wandered around Needa's spotlessly clean living room. The wall of bookshelves loaded with books caught her attention first. Then she noticed the beautiful altar, noting that great pains had been taken to decorate the altar in fall colors.

A small shelf above the altar held a beautiful crystal ball, black obsidian and a rose quartz among a few other crystals and stones that Kate recognized. An emerald green velvet cloth covered the altar. A brass chalice and bell were sitting to the left. A white handled knife, bowl of sea salt and censer had been placed to the right. A vase of fresh flowers were in the center, just above Needa's Book of Shadows. Incense holders were filled and ready to light, as were the colored candles. This was Needa's sacred altar and brought memories back to Kate of her mother's altar, along with a childhood that now seemed so long ago.

"Are you surprised about my life-style?" Needa asked.

"No, not at all," Kate replied and smiled. "In fact, I'd imagined as much the first day we met and I noticed your jewelry."

Needa smiled. "Then you must be familiar with the old ways?"

"It's more like I grew up with those old ways. Would you believe my parents are Hippies? I never looked down on them because of it. I just chose not to live that way. Your altar is beautiful and so are your crystals," Kate said as she walked over to the bookcase. Shelf after shelf contained books written by great authors. One shelf contained nothing but books written by Meredith Feira. "Meredith Feira! My mother loves Meredith Feira. She would have a field day if she could see these books. I'd be willing to bet my mother has every book Feira has written. But I do have to admit it looks as if you might have a few more. You must be fond of Feira's work too." Kate removed a book from the shelf and began to thumb through the pages.

A look of satisfaction crossed Needa's face. "I suppose Feira's published works are okay, but I personally think the author has a great deal yet to learn."

Kate was still admiring the collection of books when she said, "My mother would definitely argue that point with you. She thinks Feira is the one and only so I try to watch for Feira's latest releases. Nothing pleases my mother more than to get one of those books for her birthday or a Christmas gift. And I mean *nothing*."

"Then you should know that Meredith is about to release a new book titled *"The Sacred Stages of Life"*. I'll see that you get a signed copy to give your mother."

Kate turned around with a look of surprise. "That's very thoughtful of you, Needa. If you watch for Feira's work that closely, then she must impress you quite a bit too."

Slightly amused by what she was about to say, Needa chuckled. "I don't have to watch for Feira's work to be released, Kate. I know the exact date it's going to happen. And I do have a few extra of her previously published books. If there's one in particular that your mother hasn't collected, then I'd be happy to share with her."

Now Kate was really puzzled. "I'm afraid I don't understand."

"Meredith Feira is my pseudonym. I could hardly put Needa Begay on my book covers and expect them to sell, now could I? I mean a name like Begay isn't very impressive."

Kate was dumbfounded.

"No way! You have got to be kidding..." then she saw the amused look on Needa's face. "You aren't joking with me. You're really serious."

Needa laughed. "Apparently, you've never read anything about Meredith Feira. All of her book covers state that Fiera lives in Canada with her son. And yes, I am Meredith Feira. However, I've had to insist on my privacy because of Raine."

Kate swallowed the last of her wine before handing the glass to Needa. "Would you mind replenishing this glass of wine for me? It's delicious and I could use another drink."

This certainly wasn't what Kate had expected of her new neighbor. The Indian woman was famous for her literary works as Meredith Feira, yet she lived quite modestly, portraying the life of a Hippie that was living off the land and barely getting by financially. Kate was having a real problem with Needa's frugality.

Needa returned from the kitchen and handed Kate the glass of wine, then went to the window to check on Raine. The boy was outside playing with Kate's dog. It seemed an appropriate time to discuss Raine's condition with Kate. "It wasn't my intention to shock you about Meredith Fiera. But it's because of Raine that I've had to keep my identity a secret. The tabloids have a way of being very unkind, you know. So far, I've managed to

101

protect my son from that kind of cruel publicity. He's such a beautiful boy. He wouldn't know they were being mean to him. And believe me, they hardly ever tell the truth about anything. My contract agreement with my publisher has a strict clause about my privacy and no publicity. I don't do book signings or promotions. Of course, by now I don't have to do them anyway. My work speaks for itself. The name alone seems to get the job done for me. I'm sure you must be wondering why I live so frugally."

"Yes. As a matter of fact it has crossed my mind."

"I live this way because I'm putting as much as I can into a trust for Raine. I could never die in peace if I thought there wasn't enough money set aside to take care of him. The trust doesn't have as much in it as I think it should just yet, so I'll have to write a few more books before it does. I must tell you that it's very rare I invite someone into my home. But I do value your friendship as I hope you will value mine. I have complete trust that you won't reveal my identity as Meredith Feira to anyone. Up here in these hills, I'm just that crazy old Indian woman, Needa Begay. I'd like to keep it that way," Needa said, seeking Kate's assurance to never reveal Feira's true identity.

"You have my word. Your secret is safe with me. I am a little curious though, am I the only one around here that knows about you?"

"No. Hank Diamond knows. But Hank would have his tongue cut out before he'd reveal that information to another living soul," Needa replied.

The mention of her handsome neighbor's name caused a flush of warmth in Kate. She hadn't seen Hank since the day he'd stopped by and she'd been so curt with him in the yard. She figured her attitude was enough to ensure he wouldn't attempt another visit with her again. "I see. Do you and Hank Diamond have a... well, I mean, are you two... ah... I'm not sure just what it is I'm trying to ask you, Needa."

Kate was flustered.

Needa was amused. "Oh, I think I know what it is you're trying to ask me. I can read it in your eyes at the mention of his name. I see you've already encountered my Diamond in the rough. He's the absolute epitome of male, isn't he?"

"Christ! I hope you aren't reading anything about that man in my eyes, because it surely can't be there. Anyway, are you and Hank Diamond just good friends, or is it something more than a friendship?"

Discussing her relationship with Hank was easy for Needa. "Hank is a very dear friend of mine. If you ever need help with anything, you can always count on Hank to be there for you. He's always been there for me. I would trust that man with everything I have, even my life. Now, we've talked enough. Our supper is ready. You fetch Raine and I'll set the table. It's time to eat," Needa said, cleverly managing to close the conversation about Hank.

After dinner, Kate helped to clear the table and do the dishes, then told Needa she had to get back to Toronto. It was getting late and Emily would be worried about her. The events of the day filled Kate's mind during the drive into Toronto. Events that had blended together so strangely. Leo had finished the renovation project and invitations to the housewarming had been extended. She'd discovered that Needa was the famed author, Meredith Feira, which had been the real shocker. More importantly, Needa's statement about Hank Diamond had Kate wondering about her neighbor. He didn't appear to be the type of man to let a woman get the best of him, especially in a duel of body language. But then again, it seemed strange that he hadn't bothered to pay her another visit. Maybe Mr. Diamond was a recluse like Emily had thought.

It bothered Kate that she had gotten so flushed and flustered in trying to determine Needa's relationship with their handsome neighbor. It wasn't any of her business, so why would she even care if Hank was having a relationship with anyone. So what, she mused, if the guy had a fantastic body? His personality wasn't worth a shit and he apparently didn't care who had that opinion of him. He was vain and arrogant and probably quite proud of both those traits.

She looked over at Baron.

"This is all your fault," she said, causing the dog's head to turn toward her. "You probably brought Mr. Diamond over to the house that day on purpose, and then ran off so I couldn't see you. You knew I'd be pissed off about that, I'm sure." Kate laughed and the dog barked as if to know she was talking to him.

She had forgotten to call Emily about not coming in for dinner. Nothing perturbed Emily more than to cook a meal and no one show up to eat. However, Emily was very economically minded and dinner would not be wasted. There would be just enough left for Kate and it would be kept warm in the oven. If Kate didn't want to eat, then Baron would get the leftovers. So no big deal, Kate thought.

Kate found Emily and Gordon in the family room when she returned. Emily was reading the *Toronto Sun* and Gordon was watching television. "Hey guys, what's happening?" Kate asked.

Emily lowered the newspaper, her eyes peeping over the top. "You're late. We ate without you. Your dinner is in the oven."

"I've already had dinner, Em. I apologize for not calling, but I do have some good news. We finished the house today. I plan on buying furniture tomorrow. I should be staying in my very own 'Home Sweet Home' if I can get delivery before the weekend. It would be great if you could take a day off work tomorrow to go furniture shopping with me," Kate invited, hoping the invitation would get Em's forgiveness for not calling.

"Furniture shopping is my favorite pastime and I do have a few comp days coming. I'll call the office early in the morning and see about taking a day. I'm sure my supervisor won't mind. It'll be fun getting to spend someone else's money for furniture. We don't even have to worry about getting home early to prepare Gordon's dinner. The Jolly Boys are having a night out," Emily said, and turned to look at Gordon with annoyance. "Aren't they, Darling?"

"Good. Then it's a date. Now, if you'll excuse me, I think I'll head for the shower. I'm beat, so I'd better say goodnight to the both of you now. I plan to hit the sack early," Kate said as she headed for her bedroom.

Kate's heart melted as she observed the five fruit jars filled with honeysuckle in the boy's wagon. She grinned. "Well now, I must admit you do have some exceptional looking honeysuckle, but my yard is surrounded with the stuff. Don't you think it would be kind of foolish for me to buy yours?"

13 | CHAPTER *THIRTEEN*

The plaque that said "Home Sweet Home" and hung over Kate's kitchen cabinet didn't blend with the rest of the room's décor. She didn't particularly like the plaque, but getting rid of it wasn't an option since Gordon had given it to her as a house-warming gift. Emily told her that Gordon had personally picked out the gift, so Kate had to leave it hanging in full view where he could see it.

She'd worked the entire week at hanging pictures, putting knick-knacks in place, arranging and re-arranging the furniture, until she was exhausted. The checklist she'd prepared had dwindled, leaving only a few minor details to complete before the housewarming. She was still debating about how to decorate a remaining bare wall when she noticed there was a young boy standing on the porch, looking inside through the screen door.

"Well, hello there," Kate greeted the handsome lad.

"Hi," Dane DaRoux shyly returned her greeting.

"Is there something I can do for you?"

The young visitor turned away and walked toward the porch steps, where he stood and waited for Kate to come outside. With an aroused curiosity, Kate walked out onto the porch and stood beside the boy.

"Would you like to buy some of my honeysuckle, Ma'am?" he asked, pointing down at the small wagon parked in front of the porch.

Kate's heart melted as she observed the five fruit jars filled with honeysuckle laying in the boy's wagon. She grinned.

105

"Well now, I must admit you've got some exceptional looking honeysuckle, but my yard is surrounded with the stuff. Don't you think it would be kind of foolish for me to buy yours?"

This one ain't gonna be easy, Dane thought while giving Kate his best look of disappointment. "Yeah, I guess you're right."

"This area is sparsely populated. I suppose the prospect for customers in need of honeysuckle wouldn't be too good, would it?"

"No, Ma'am."

"Yeah. That's what I thought. Well anyway, let me introduce myself. I'm Kate Corbin. And you are?"

"Dane. I'm Dane DaRoux."

"Dane. That certainly is a beautiful name. Do you live close by?"

"I live on the other side of Hank's place," he answered, pointing his finger toward Hank's land.

"I see. Well, Dane, I'm not in the market for your honeysuckle. But I am looking for a handy man to do a little work for me. If you're interested, I'd pay you to help me wash my Jeep tomorrow."

"Yes, Ma'am. I'm interested. And I'm a real good worker. What time... ?" Dane started to ask, but was stopped short when he spotted Baron coming around the corner of the house. "Holy Smoley! That sure is a big dog!"

Kate laughed. "Yeah, he is a big dog. He has a hearty appetite too," she said, watching as the dog lumbered over to sit down beside the boy. Dane dropped to his knees and began petting Baron. "You'll make a life-long friend out of that dog by rubbing his back. He loves it," she added.

"What's his name?"

"Well, his registered name is Duke Brandon Von Baron. I call him Baron for short. And sometimes I call him Bear or Big Dog. Truth is, he'll answer to just about anything if he thinks food is involved," she teased.

"I can help you wash your car tomorrow, Kate. But I have to do my chores at home first. Will it be okay with you if we do it late tomorrow afternoon?" Dane asked, but didn't look up as he continued to rub the dog's back.

Second Chances

"That works for me. Does ten dollars sound like a fair wage to you?"

"*WOW*! Ten dollars!" He hadn't made that much in a week, sometimes even a month. "Are you kiddin'?"

Kate tilted her head to one side and raised her eyebrows, giving the boy a puzzled look. "Oh my, I never kid when I'm talking big business. Don't you think it's a fair wage?"

"Yes, Ma'am, it's more than fair. And I'll be here," Dane told her, jumping off the deck. Then he turned to wave at the dog. "Bye, Bear."

Kate laughed when the dog barked at Dane. "I think he likes you, Dane. See you tomorrow."

As Kate headed back inside the house, she wondered about the honeysuckle. Was there any kind of good use for sweet-smelling honeysuckle? She didn't know of one, but if there was then she couldn't imagine what it might be. Perhaps she should find a book relating to ground cover and get better informed about the sweet-smelling plant.

Later that evening and just before dark, Kate went to the door and whistled for Baron. When the dog didn't appear, she stepped out onto the deck and looked around. She whistled again and called the dog. Finally, she stepped down off the porch and started toward the side of the A-frame. That's when she spotted the stranger standing near the corner of the house, watching her.

"Have you lost your dog, Lady?" Charlie DaRoux asked in a deep, unpleasant voice.

Startled, but even more uncomfortable by the man's appearance, Kate wanted him to think the dog was somewhere fairly close. "I... no, I'm sure he's close by. My dog never gets very far away from home."

"I can't say as I'd agree with you about that, cause somethin's been killin' my rabbits and I think it's your damn dog. If I'm right, then I'm givin' you fair warnin' right now, I'm gonna fill your damn dog full of lead if I ever catch it with one of my rabbits in its mouth."

Kate was infuriated by the stranger's threat. "I beg your pardon. My dog has *NOT* been killing your rabbits. Furthermore, Mister, I wouldn't be threatening to harm anyone's dog if I were you, especially since you happen to be standing on my property," she responded hotly. Relief flooded through Kate when Baron appeared from around the other corner of the house and moseyed up beside her. The dog began to growl when he saw the stranger, but obeyed Kate's command when she said, "Sit, Bear."

Glaring first at Kate, and then at the dog, Charlie DaRoux repeated his threat. "You've been rightly warned about that dog. If you want to keep Cujo alive, then you'd best keep the damned animal tied up." Without giving Kate a chance to say anything else, Charlie turned around and walked away.

Kate's encounter with the ill-bred man had left her with an uneasy feeling. She grabbed Baron's collar and led the dog into the house for the night, after which she locked the doors.

* * *

The stranger, as well as his threat, was still fresh on Kate's mind when she awakened the next morning. She climbed out of bed and showered, hoping to direct her thoughts to something more pleasant. Later, as Kate sat on her deck drinking coffee, she recalled those Sunday mornings when she would attend Mass with Mack and Caleb. Thinking it hadn't been so long ago, why did it seem like another lifetime to her now?

Putting her memories aside, Kate decided to drive into Toronto and have breakfast with Emily and Gordon. She was anxious to tell them about the housewarming she had planned. During the trip into the city, Kate remembered that she would have to return home in the early afternoon and wait for Dane.

After breakfast, as they were cleaning up the dishes, Kate's mind was once again consumed with the episode she'd had with the offensive stranger. Emily had noticed that Kate seemed to be a little out-of-sorts. With the house renovation completed and now that Kate was living alone again, Emily wondered if Mack and Caleb were weighing more heavily on Kate's mind. "Is something bothering you, Kate?"

"What? Oh no, not really," Kate replied. "It's just that I encountered a very crude stranger in my yard yesterday. Em, are you acquainted with any of the neighbors that live close to me?"

"Are you kidding? I never go up there. Gordon might know a few of them. But other than Hank Diamond and Needa

BeGay, I've never heard him mention meeting anyone else. I think Hank is probably your closest neighbor. He lives on the hill just over from your place."

"Yeah. Gordon's fishing buddy. I've met him."

"Oh, you have? Gordon didn't say anything about Hank mentioning he'd made your acquaintance. But Hank is pretty much of a loner, so you don't have to worry about him bothering you."

"I'm not worried about being bothered, Em. Not by Hank Diamond or anyone else for that matter. It's just that this guy looked like a real creep that could be pretty mean."

Emily laughed. "Oh! Well, I tried to tell you, didn't I? Now the excitement begins."

"It really wasn't all that exciting. To be honest, it sort of upset me. I went outside to call Baron and discovered this guy standing in the yard at the corner of my house. I have no idea where he came from. He nearly scared me out of my wits when I first spotted him. He was filthy and obnoxious and appeared to be looking for trouble."

"Really? How so?" Emily asked.

"Well, first he accused Baron of killing his rabbits. Then he had the audacity to tell me he would shoot Baron if he caught my dog on his land."

Emily thought for a moment. "That sounds like something Charlie DaRoux would say. I'm pretty sure he lives on the other side of Hank's property. If I remember correctly, Gordon said the old bastard was nuts," Emily warned.

The name DaRoux hit home with Kate and she thought about young Dane. "I'd be inclined to believe Gordon's right about that. I certainly intend to keep an eye out for Baron after last night."

"Gordon needs to know about this, Kate, especially after all the preaching I've done that you have no business living up there," Emily said.

Kate wanted to talk about something more pleasant, like telling Emily about the cute, young boy she'd met. "I did get to meet someone new yesterday. Quite a charmer too, I must say," Kate said, and then she chuckled.

109

Emily noticed the sparkle in Kate's eyes, delighted to see her sister's enthusiasm about meeting someone again. Maybe Canada was going to be good for Kate after all. "Oh? Was he tall, dark and handsome?"

"Well, not really. Although I would bet money this young man is going to be a real heartbreaker when he grows up. He's got the most beautiful light gray eyes. He doesn't look to be over nine or ten years of age. His name is Dane. Isn't that a handsome name?" Kate asked, pouring herself another cup of coffee.

"That is a beautiful name. How did you happen to meet this young charmer?"

"He's a salesman. And get this one, Em, he's a door-to-door salesman. He almost had me charmed into buying a jar full of honeysuckle, but I somehow kept my wits and managed to resist. I did cut a deal with him to help me wash the Jeep. He's coming over this afternoon to do the job."

"Good. I'm glad you're making a friend even if it is a kid. Now I won't have to worry about you being so lonely up there." Emily raised her coffee cup into the air. "A toast to Dane."

Their cups met and clinked together. "To Dane," Kate said.

"I'm only going to tell you this just once, DaRoux. So hear me good," Hank warned. "I've already made my mark on that territory next door to me. The woman is mine."

14 | CHAPTER *FOURTEEN*

Immediately after graduating from high school, Hank Diamond left Canada to join the United States Marines. He'd scored exceedingly high grades on a series of written and oral tests, but his physical agility was also another strong point. Hank's combined attributes made him an excellent candidate for covert operations. He was intelligent, physically strong, and possessed a natural instinct for survival. Military training had only advanced and sharpened each of those traits for Hank.

Hank's covert training had landed him in some of the most unthinkable assignments, not to mention the most unimaginable conditions. He'd been disciplined to obey all military orders, basically those of search and destroy. The Marines had turned Hank into a trained killer and he was damn good at what he did, especially when thrown into a kill-or-be-killed situation. When a decision had to be made as to whether you lived or died, there were no options to choose from. Slitting the enemy's throat meant nothing more than survival of the fittest to Hank.

He'd witnessed every form of inhumanity that was imaginable in foreign countries, which drove Hank that much harder. Snuffing out life as part of the covert assignment had become all too easy.

Staying enlisted seemed to be the proper thing for Hank to do, since he was already trained for the job. He'd become so dedicated and regimented during active duty that the thought of mental fatigue never entered Hank's mind. That came later, after he'd retired. That was when Hank's nightmares had started, awakening him in the middle of the night, soaking wet with sweat.

Beth had always been there for him, offering her sweetness and understanding. It was doubtful there would ever be another woman who could understand Hank's troubled mind. Not as Beth had learned to do.

After retirement, Hank's military training had remained a way of life. He ate healthy meals. He ran a five-mile stretch every morning, exercised two or three times a day, and walked every evening. He was in excellent physical condition. Even before his military training, Hank had been exceptionally neat and clean about himself, orderly about his belongings, and spotless with his property. What had once been an intense part of his training was now a matter of Hank's pride.

Only a handful of Hank's military buddies lived in Canada, but he enjoyed having the guys over for an occasional game of poker and a few beers. Other than fishing with Gordon, this was about the extent of Hank's social life. He surely did look forward to those fishing trips more than anything else.

Hank's buddies had allowed for a decent mourning period after Beth's passing, then they started playing matchmaker, trying to fix Hank up with different women. Hank thought it was a nice gesture, but wasn't interested. He knew one of his nightmares could scare the hell out of a woman in the middle of the night, or she might be awakened by Hank's fists punching her in the face. It wasn't worth the effort. Not to Hank. There'd be no way in hell a man could apologize for abusing a woman that way, especially if he'd spent the earlier part of the night making love to her. He couldn't and wouldn't, which was the main reason Hank preferred to sleep alone.

But for some reason, being alone wasn't working very well for Hank at the present time. More often than not, he'd found himself thinking about his new neighbor, even though he'd deliberately stayed away from her place. He didn't care much for any woman with a smart mouth and was trying his damnedest to ignore Kate. Still, he couldn't deny the feeling he got in the pit of his stomach when she was around him. He had to smile every time he thought about Kate giving his body the once over. There had never been any doubt in Hank's mind that Gordon's pretty sister-in-law was definitely a gorgeous woman.

It hadn't helped that Dane had stopped by after helping Kate wash her Jeep, flashing his ten-dollar bill around and telling

Hank how sweet she was, adding Kate was downright pretty too. And damn it, Dane was just a kid.

Hank's thoughts about Kate Corbin were out of control and it was really pissing him off. Those thoughts were abruptly brought to a close by the sudden ringing of his telephone.

"Diamond here," Hank answered.

"Hello, Hank. It's Doc."

"Hey, Doc, what's happening? Are we still on for our fishing trip this weekend?"

"That's one of the reasons I'm calling. I don't think I can make it this weekend, Hank," Gordon apologized.

"That's too bad, Doc, but no problem. What's the other reason?" Hank asked.

"I hate like hell to ask this of you, but I need a favor. It may not be anything for us to worry about, but Emily is a basket case about this." Gordon sounded distraught.

"Sounds like you've got a major problem, Doc. What can I do to help?"

"Emily's sister, Kate, recently renovated that old house I used to own next to your property. She's living in it now. Word gets around pretty fast up in those hills, so I figured you were aware of this."

"Yeah, I knew she was over there."

"Anyway, it seems that some guy scared the hell out of Kate last evening. It was almost dark when she discovered him standing in her yard beside the house. To make matters even worse, Kate said the guy threatened to kill her dog," Gordon said.

"No kidding. Bet that didn't set well with her."

"You're right, it didn't. But this sounds exactly like Charlie DaRoux to me, and you know what a rotten bastard Charlie can be. Emily is worried to death about her sister. Would you mind keeping an eye on Kate's place for me? Don't worry about the damn dog. I'm confident that dog can take care of itself." Gordon sounded desperate.

"I think you're right about that dog," Hank said and chuckled. But the thought of Charlie DaRoux getting anywhere close to Kate nearly drove Hank into a fit of rage. "Charlie is one crazy son of a bitch, Doc. What the hell do you think he's trying to do?"

"Your guess is as good as mine, Hank. That's why I'm calling you," Gordon replied.

"Tell Emily not to worry about her sister. I'll personally see to it that DaRoux stays away," Hank said, hoping to put Gordon's mind at ease. "Are you sure we aren't fishing this weekend?"

"No, Hank. Honestly, I can't. I have some chores to do for Emily this weekend. Thanks again for helping me out with this, Buddy. I owe you."

"Don't mention it. Talk to you later."

Hank could feel the rage building as soon as he hung up the phone. And it wasn't just Charlie DaRoux that was putting him in a bad state-of-mind. Those disturbing thoughts he'd been having about his new neighbor were no longer going to be just a once in a while event. Thanks to old Charlie, the woman was going to consume his mind, just as Charlie DaRoux had often managed to do in the past.

*   *   *

If Charlie DaRoux was looking to find an odd job to do, then he'd usually head for the local restaurant in the early morning. This Monday morning wasn't going to be any different, except the neighbor that Charlie literally hated would be sitting at a table when Charlie walked in.

Since Hank Diamond wasn't the type of man to be found hanging around in a restaurant, Charlie was quick to take notice of Hank's presence. At first, Hank pretended not to see Charlie, but so far he hadn't missed a single move the despicable man had made.

Just as Hank had expected, Charlie's normal behavior would soon come into play. He looked over at Hank with a vile smirk, his nasty remark a bit garbled. "Looks to me like you got yourself a new bitch neighbor livin' next door to ya, Diamond. Guess you've already been over there showin' her where your property lines run."

Hank turned around slowly to look squarely at a man he thoroughly detested. "I can't see as how that's any of your concern, DaRoux."

Charlie's eyes narrowed with hatred as he pushed the conversation forward. "I hear tell she's a right smart looker too. But then I'm sure you ain't missed lookin' her over. Maybe you ought to do yerself a favor and pay her a little visit. Who knows, Diamond, you jest might get lucky and get yerself some of that sweet meat." There was a few brief moments of silence, then Charlie began to laugh, after which the other men sitting at his table soon joined in.

Hank glared at the filthy excuse of a man with eyes as cold as steel. "You know, DaRoux, I don't much care for you talking about my new neighbor that way. As a matter of fact, that woman you're talking about happens to be mine. So I suggest you don't make any more comments about my woman that I wouldn't appreciate. And if you want to keep breathing, it's for damned sure you'd best keep your distance from her," Hank warned.

"Are you tryin' to threaten me, Diamond? Cuz if you are, it ain't workin' for ya. I don't scare that easy," Charlie boasted, and then he winked at the guy sitting beside him. You could have heard a pin drop when Hank stood up, threw a tip down on the table for the waitress, and then walked over to stand beside Charlie.

"I'm going to tell you this just once, DaRoux. So hear me good," Hank warned, "I've already made my mark on that territory next door to me. The woman is mine. If I caught anyone going near my woman, I'd rip their heart out with my bare hands and make sure they ate it before they died. But that especially applies to you, Charlie. I don't want you to misunderstand and take that merely as a threat, because it's a solemn promise. I hope I've made myself perfectly clear." Hank waited a few seconds to see what Charlie would have to say next. Then he told Charlie, "Your property joins mine just like hers does, DaRoux. I could get to your place and do you in a hell of a lot quicker than I could get to her place and get off. But when I think about it, killing you might even get me off faster than she could."

Every person in the room heard Hank's threat as they sat and watched the two men. Hank figured his threat had to sound convincing enough. But then again, it's best not to be

115

misunderstood when you're dealing with someone as ignorant as Charlie. He stood beside Charlie's chair just long enough to give Charlie another chance to say something else. He waited to ensure Charlie had lost his sense of humor before walking out the door.

Leo Staggner was a regular customer at the restaurant before going out on a job. He'd heard every word Hank had spoken while eating his breakfast. Leo was well acquainted with Charlie, having hired the man a few times to help with some of Leo's bigger jobs. Leo didn't care much for Charlie as a person, but as a carpenter the man wasn't half bad.

Leo wasn't personally acquainted with Hank Diamond, but judging from the way the guy was built, and the look on Hank's face while he was talking to Charlie, Leo figured Charlie would be smart not to mess with Mr. Diamond. But then again, Leo had never thought of Charlie as being real smart.

If Charlie was going to save face after his confrontation with Diamond, then he'd have to say something witty. He couldn't let his buddies think that Hank had upset him. "I doubt Diamond has even met his new neighbor, much less be in a position to claim her as his property. The bastard's either lyin' or just tryin' to be a bragger. I'd say the woman's fair game fer any man that's interested. I know I could service that lady a hell of a lot better than Diamond could," Charlie boasted.

Leo had heard enough and got up from his table to leave. On his way out, he stopped beside Charlie's chair and looked down at the scumbag. "I did all the remodeling on that woman's house, Charlie. Hank Diamond wasn't just bragging. I've seen him there several times myself," Leo said before walking away.

Leo knew that what he'd said to Charlie wasn't true. He hadn't seen Hank anywhere near Kate's place. But he had an uneasy feeling about Charlie where Kate was concerned. If putting a little extra fear of Hank Diamond in Charlie would help Kate, then Leo was more than glad to do it.

By the time Hank had returned home, he appeared to be calm, when in fact his anger had not diminished in the least. If anything, it may have grown stronger and hotter. It gave him fits just to think about Charlie even looking at Kate Corbin, much less to imagine what else the filthy lowlife might have in his rotten mind.

But it wasn't just his resentment of Charlie that was really eating at him… and Hank knew it. It was that damned woman. Kate Corbin had been steadily consuming his thoughts and Hank didn't like it. He didn't need it and for damn sure didn't want it. So, if that was true, then why the hell couldn't he forget about the blasted woman?

Susie Rigsby

Hank grabbed her arm, spinning Kate back around to face him. "Now you listen to me, Kate, and hear me good. Charlie DaRoux is dumb and dangerous. I've warned the man to stay away from what's mine and I damn well meant what I said."

15 | CHAPTER *FIFTEEN*

By the following Wednesday, Hank's confrontation with Charlie DaRoux over the new resident in Doc Gordon's house had filtered through the Thrifty Mart, as well as every other business place in this small community. Nearly every person living in the general area had heard every little detail about the restaurant incident, even though nothing much was actually known about Hank Diamond's new neighbor. Except, of course, that she was a real looker and she was Hank's woman. Most of Hank's neighbors were pleased that after losing Beth, he'd found someone to spend time with. A man like Hank wasn't meant to be alone. It just wasn't natural.

When Kate decided a few days later to take Baron for a walk over to Needa's house, she had no idea that she was the talk of the community, or that she now carried the distinct title of being Hank Diamond's woman. She'd intended for the visit to be a short one, and mostly to inform Needa that the cookout was set for Saturday afternoon.

Needa had just sat down for a cup of Green tea when she heard the doorbell. After opening the door, she greeted Kate with a big smile. "Well, hello, you lucky lady."

Kate raised an eyebrow and looked puzzled. "Lucky? What makes me lucky?"

"You aren't going to try and pretend you didn't know this whole community is abuzz about you? And I honestly thought we were close enough that you'd have told me about this yourself. I can't believe I had to hear about it at the Thrifty Mart."

"Hear about what at the Thrifty Mart? What on earth are you talking about?" Kate asked and laughed. "I just came over here to tell you the cookout is set for Saturday afternoon and you're throwing riddles at me."

"Oh my, then you really haven't heard the latest gossip, have you?"

"I guess I haven't, because I still don't know what you're talking about. So why am I a lucky lady?" Kate asked again while fixing a cup of tea.

"I have a gut feeling that maybe I shouldn't tell you about this? But if I don't, and you do hear about it, then you'd probably be mad at me."

Kate smiled and sat down at the table with her cup of tea. "I could never be mad at you, Needa. But if the whole community is talking about me, then perhaps you'd better enlighten me as to what they're saying. We are friends, you know," she said, lifting the cup to her mouth for a drink of tea.

"Yeah. Well, the local gossips are saying that Hank Diamond has claimed you as his woman," Needa told her rather bluntly.

Hot tea spewed out of Kate's mouth, covering the white tablecloth. "He what? Why would he say such a thing?" She jumped up and grabbed the paper towels to clean up the mess. "Christ, look what a mess I've made. Will that stain come out of your white linen tablecloth?" Kate tore another paper towel off the roll and blew her nose. "Needa, are you sure about that? I mean I barely know Hank Diamond. I've only talked to him once since I've been here. God, look at this mess."

Needa was amused. "Goodness, Kate, most women would give their eye teeth to be labeled Hank Diamond's woman. We probably couldn't count the females that have been chasing after that man."

Kate shot Needa a look. "Oh yeah? Well, go ahead and ask me if I really give a damn so I can tell you that I couldn't care less. The thing is, I'm not Hank Diamond's woman and I'm definitely not chasing after him. Furthermore, I don't want him giving anyone that opinion. I have no idea what could have possessed that man to make such a statement. Needa, are you sure?" Kate quizzed her again.

"Well, Maribelle Martin told me and she said she got it first hand from Wanda Trousdale. Apparently, Wanda's husband was in the restaurant when Charlie DaRoux and Hank started having words over you. Mr. Trousdale said that Hank threatened to rip anyone's heart out with his bare hands if he caught them going near you, and then make them eat it before they died. For some reason, this threat seemed to be specifically directed at Charlie, or so it's been told anyway. Supposedly, Hank told Charlie he'd already marked that territory and you were *his* woman. I think it all sounds kind of romantic, don't you?" Needa's eyes glowed as she kept up the teasing.

"That bizarre, sick sense of humor has got to be the writer in you coming out. Other than you, I don't know another person living around here, and your Mr. Diamond has just given me one fine reputation. Thanks to him, there's no telling what kind of woman they think I might be. But whatever I am, it's for sure I am *not* Hank Diamond's woman. Christ! I can't believe he did that, and in a public place. Are you absolutely sure about this?" Kate asked again, wanting to think it couldn't be true.

"Honey, if what they're saying didn't happen, then someone has started one hell of a good story about you and Hank. Now sit down and let me fix you another cup of tea."

Kate shook her head. "No, I'm going home. I spewed tea on my blouse. I'll have to get it sprayed with a spot remover before it sets in. If I don't see you before, I'll look for you and Raine on Saturday. I'm expecting you to be there, so don't let me down," Kate said, setting her cup in the sink.

"We'll be there. Can I bring anything?"

"Nope. Just yourself and Raine, that's all. And be prepared to have fun. In fact, come a little early and we'll visit. Bye, Raine," Kate said and walked over to kiss Raine on the forehead. Raine looked up at Kate and smiled. Needa was dumbfounded that Kate's affectionate gesture had caused a show of emotion in Raine's expression. And it tugged at Needa's heart.

On Kate's return trip home, she gave serious thought to what Needa had told her. Why would a man she barely knew want to just openly insinuate they were in a relationship? The very idea of it was totally absurd. She still couldn't imagine what had ever possessed Hank Diamond to do such a thing.

The more Kate thought about what he'd done, the more determined she became to give Hank Diamond a good scolding

121

for his actions. He had to have known his actions would create a great deal of gossip. It was time to pay the arrogant man a visit and give him a good piece of her mind. It was exactly what he deserved.

As she pulled into Hank's driveway and parked in front of his home, Kate couldn't help but notice the immaculately maintained property. For a man living alone, it was as neat a place as she'd ever seen. Every window of the house was sparkling clean. The shrubs were ideally located and evenly trimmed, the lawn perfectly manicured. Off to her left, she saw what appeared to be a large trout pond.

Taking a deep breath, Kate got out of her Jeep and walked to the front door. She noticed Hank's truck in the garage as she was ringing the doorbell, which meant he should be home. When no one came to the door, Kate rang the doorbell again. Impatient now to confront him, she held the button in, causing the chimes to ring continuously. There was still no response from the inside. Just as Kate was about to give up and leave, she spotted Hank coming around the corner of the house.

"Are you looking for me?" he asked.

Hank's clothes were covered with wood chips, a good indication he'd been splitting firewood. Clad in only an old sweatshirt with the sleeves and neck cut out, and a pair of sweat pants that had been cut off above the knees, Hank looked like the proverbial bum to Kate. *Unfortunately, a too well-built bum*, she thought, and for a few seconds Kate had almost forgotten that she was mad.

"Yes. I... I came to... uh, I... I wanted to talk to you... ah..." she was stammering.

"What's the matter, Miss Corbin? Can't you speak your mind?" Hank asked with a boyish grin. "Or does my presence really have that much of an effect on you?"

The last question had managed to set Kate off again, remembering full well why she was there in the first place. She was throwing daggers at Hank with her eyes and he made note of her anger. "We've discussed that before and nothing's changed, so don't flatter yourself, Diamond. It's your mouth that upsets me. You've got a lot of nerve, blowing off your bazoo in the restaurant

Second Chances

and claiming me to be your woman. Just what in Sam hell made you do something like that?"

Hank's face quickly turned to a bright shade of red. "Oh! I take it you've heard about that incident."

"Did you think I wouldn't, or were you just hoping?"

"At the time, Kate, I don't think it mattered. I figured if I sent Charlie DaRoux the right message, then he'd know I meant for him to stay away from you. The son of a bitch is about half crazy," Hank said, attempting to explain.

"Stay away from me? How did you know he'd been around me in the first place?" Kate had no sooner asked when she remembered telling Emily about Charlie's visit. No doubt, Emily had told Gordon and this had to be Gordon's idea of handling Kate's problem. "Did my brother-in-law put you up to confronting Charlie DaRoux?"

Hank's color was gradually returning to a normal shade, and he grinned sheepishly. "Well... he didn't put me up to doing it quite the way I did, but Doc was worried enough about you to call me. DaRoux and I have been at each other for a long time over several different matters, so one more wasn't going to make much difference. Maybe I did come on a little too strong, but I meant for him to get my message."

"I'd say he got it all right, along with the whole damned community. You probably didn't faze Charlie DaRoux. But there's no telling what the folks around here will think of me now, and all because of your big mouth. Christ, Diamond! I'll be too embarrassed to even go buy a loaf of bread. Besides, my problem with Charlie DaRoux is just that... my problem. I'm not afraid of that man and I can take care of myself. So from now on you need to mind your own damn business. Thank you anyway." She spat the words at him, and then turned away to leave.

Hank grabbed her arm, spinning Kate back around to face him. "Now you listen to me, Kate, and hear me good. Charlie DaRoux is dumb and dangerous. I've warned the man to stay away from what's mine and I damn well meant what I said."

"I beg your pardon! I don't believe I fall into the category of *what's yours*. Now let go of me, you insufferable creep."

"Then maybe I need to fix that right now," Hank told her as a big hand went to the back of Kate's head, pulling her close

123

and covering her mouth with his. His kiss was long and hard and filled with such a strong desire that even Hank was confused by its effect.

Kate was well aware of his desire the instant Hank let go of her. She wiped the back of her hand across her lips as if to rub the kiss away. "You've got a lot of nerve. Why did you do that?"

He grinned. "Maybe I don't want DaRoux to think I'm a liar. You aren't going to complain, are you? I found it to be rather enjoyable myself."

"Complain! Are you kidding? I think you're probably about as crazy as Charlie DaRoux. Get this Diamond, and get it straight, because I don't intend to tell you again. I don't appreciate what you said to Charlie DaRoux in front of all those people in the restaurant, even if you thought it was your way of helping me. And it's for sure I don't appreciate being physically manhandled by you. I'm not your woman, you conceited jerk, nor will I ever be. It's my understanding you have women falling all over themselves just to be with you. So take my advice and go snag one of them," Kate said, her eyes glancing directly down at the sizeable bulge in the front of his sweat pants. She smiled smugly. "It appears as if you might need to go visit one of them right away. However, I'm really not impressed and I'm certainly not interested. Furthermore, don't ever try to put your mouth on me like that again or..." Kate didn't get to finish what she was going to say before she was silenced by Hank's next move, which was lightning quick as his mouth covered hers again.

With his eyes fixed on Kate's after releasing her for the second time, he tried not to look amused by Kate's open show of temperament. She was mad as a hornet. If nothing else, he thought being angry made Kate look even more beautiful to him. "Now, what were you saying?"

Kate cautiously began to back away from him. "You barbaric, arrogant heap of ego! I don't need your help with DaRoux. And as for what just happened, it would be a mistake for you to think that all women are unable to resist the size of that protrusion in your pants. You couldn't turn me on if you were the last man on earth."

Hank laughed. "And I thought you really liked me."

Kate had nothing further to say to the man. She climbed into her Jeep, started the engine and drove away.

As Kate pulled out of the driveway, Hank had to dodge the rocks that flew from the Jeep's spinning tires. The excitement of that woman was just about more than any one man could handle, he thought as he picked up his axe and headed for the wood pile.

The taste of Kate's mouth lingered on his lips. God she was soft. Lucky thing he had his feelings under control while she'd been throwing such a fit. Then he looked down at the front of his cutoff sweat pants and grinned. And she sure knew how to get a man excited.

Hank returned to his wood chopping. Maybe the physical effort he put into swinging the axe would eliminate the swollen problem between his legs. Damn. He had to exert some energy.

Susie Rigsby

Kate picked up her hairbrush and walked out on the upper deck. She thought of Peter as she looked up at the starlit sky. Maybe if she looked hard enough, like Peter had done, she would see Mack up there in the heavens and among the stars.

16| CHAPTER *SIXTEEN*

Weather wise, Kate couldn't have asked for a more perfect day to have a cookout. Even though the guest list was small and comprised only of those now presently involved in her life, everyone seemed to be enjoying the occasion. Gordon was busy preparing to grill the steaks and Emily was mixing drinks. Preparations to eat were nearly complete.

Kate was in the kitchen preparing a tossed salad when she heard the doorbell ring. Everyone that was invited had arrived, so she figured Raine was on the front porch and hit the doorbell. But when the doorbell rang again, Kate left the salad and went to open the door.

"Have I picked a bad time to pay my new neighbor a visit?" Hank asked, holding a freshly cut bouquet of assorted flowers in his hand.

Kate hardly knew what to say. "I... I... well no, of course not. It's just that I'm a little surprised to see you after..."

"After I made such a fool of myself," Hank interrupted, finishing what he was sure she was about to say.

Kate smiled. "Is that what you did?"

"Well, wasn't it?" he asked and watched Kate's smile widen, which was exactly what Hank had hoped to see.

Kate noticed his relieved look. "I'm sure you meant well, Hank. And perhaps I was a little out of line myself. I do sometimes have a tendency to over-react when I'm a bit riled," she said, pushing the screen door open for him. "I'm having a small get-together this evening. Please, come in and join us."

127

Hank stepped inside and handed Kate the flowers. "Thank you, the bouquet is beautiful. I must get it in a vase of water. Everyone's out in the yard, so why don't you join them and say hello. And tell Emily to fix you a drink."

They were actually being civil to each other, Hank thought on his way to join the others. That had to be a start.

As Kate filled the vase with water, she thought about the flower garden she'd seen at Hank's place, certain he'd cut the assortment of flowers himself. To imagine a man like Hank arranging something delicate and lovely as a bouquet wasn't easy. As Kate inhaled the fragrance of the flowers, a mental picture of Hank in those cutoff sweatpants sent a warm feeling through her body. This was no time to entertain such randy thoughts, so she put more effort into arranging the flowers in the vase. Hopefully, mingling outside with the others would help to keep those thoughts at bay.

She spotted Hank standing beside Gordon when she set the salad bowl down on the picnic table. He appeared to be comfortable in the mixed company, even though Emily had once described Hank as a loner.

Except for Leo Staggner, Hank was enjoying Kate's other guests. He'd heard about the carpenter but hadn't made the man's acquaintance. He didn't quite understand why he felt a bit resentful of Leo's presence. It couldn't be jealousy because that was an emotion Hank had never dealt with before. It did, however, help to ease his mind considerably when Hank noticed the attention that Leo was showing Needa.

Kate deemed her first cookout to be a success as she mixed and mingled with her guests. Everyone appeared to be having a good time. Even Raine seemed content while playing with Baron. Kate felt as if she could see a bond forming between the boy and her dog, which pleased her immensely.

The party came to an end just before dusk. Hank waited around while the others thanked Kate for her hospitality before departing. If things went as he'd planned, maybe he'd have the opportunity to spend some time alone with the gracious host.

"I really do owe you an apology for the way I acted the other day, Kate." He was standing beside her at the door, the last remaining guest.

Second Chances

Kate looked up at him and smiled. "Yes. I was thinking about that just a while ago. But the flowers will suffice, Hank, so spare yourself having to apologize," she said, trying to make Hank's effort somewhat easier for him. She had no idea that her warm smile had Hank's heart doing flip-flops.

"Thanks, but I really was out of line."

"So you were," she further agreed. "But honestly, I think perhaps I was too."

"No, you weren't. I had no right to say the things I did to Charlie DaRoux, especially in a public place where everyone could hear me. I wasn't thinking, I was just trying to get my point across to Charlie." Then he chuckled. "I figure he got the message alright. You don't know what a low-down scoundrel Charlie can be, Kate, but I do and I don't want him over here bothering you."

"Hank, you've given me a beautiful bouquet and offered your apology and I've accepted both in good faith. I think we both had some impulsive moments and we were both at fault. As for Charlie DaRoux, I'm aware there's a possibility he could cause me trouble, but I'd like to think I'm capable of handling any problem I might have with Charlie. Needa says you're a very good neighbor and I could call on you if I need any help. As for everything else that's happened between you and me, why don't we just forget about it and put it behind us. I can if you can."

Forget about it? If Kate was referring to the way he'd kissed her, then she had to be kidding. Hell, forgetting was the last thing Hank wanted or intended to do. In fact, standing so close to her at the moment, the idea of her lips covered with his was playing havoc with Hank's mind. Not to mention the heavy effect it had on the rest of his body. He could still feel the excitement of her kiss in his loins. What man in his right mind wouldn't think of wanting to do it again? Yet, Hank knew he had to get control of his impulses.

"Yeah, you're right, Kate. I'm your friendly next-door handy man. Just give a holler if you need my help. By the way, thanks for inviting me in this afternoon. It was great. Good night," he said and stuck a goofy looking hat on his head.

Hank was much too close as he passed by Kate going through the doorway. The chemistry was like a bolt of static electricity hitting between them.

129

"Goodnight, Hank. Take care."

Her eyes followed after Hank as he walked down the porch steps, out to the driveway, and then down the lane. She watched until her handsome neighbor was completely out of sight, then walked out on the porch to sit in the swing. She was tired. A lot of work had gone into getting ready for the housewarming, but it was a success. It seemed strange that having a few people over for a cookout could be so exhausting. It hadn't been so long ago when she and Mack would entertain as many as ten or fifteen fellow company workers at least a couple of times a month. She'd never felt this exhausted back then.

But there was a big difference between then and now. Back in those days when the evening was over, Mack would pick her up and carry Kate into the bedroom. After making love, they would fall asleep wrapped tightly in each other's arms. No way would she have felt exhausted back then. With only the touch of his hands and mouth, Mack had the ability to remove everything from Kate's mind... even the thought of exhaustion.

Tears welled up in Kate's eyes and she looked down at the dog. "Oh God, Bear, I miss him so much. Is the memory of Mack's touch going to haunt me forever?"

The night air had turned chilly, sending Kate inside to change into something warmer and more comfortable. Emily and Needa had helped to clean up after the party, so there wasn't anything left to do. She undressed and slipped into a sweat suit. The rest of the evening would be for relaxing and maybe read a few more chapters in Needa's latest published book.

Much later, after getting showered and ready for bed, Kate picked up her hairbrush and walked out on the upper deck. She thought of Peter as she looked up at the starlit sky. Maybe if she looked hard enough, like Peter had done, she would see Mack up there in the heavens and among the stars.

Kate brushed leisurely at her hair while she continued gazing up at the stars. Mack sat on the deck railing, watching her. He felt Kate's heartache. "It's a beautiful night."

Kate took a deep breath. "Yeah, so I've noticed."

"Did you have a nice evening?"

"It was okay, Mack. But things could be better."

"The way I see it, Kate, things have been a hell of a lot worse."

"Don't I know it? Are you here to tuck me into bed tonight, Mack?" she asked with a hint of sarcasm.

Mack ignored Kate's question and asked, "Why the tears, Kate?"

"Oh, you can see my tears in the dark?"

"No, Honey, I can feel them. Things should be getting better for you now. The house is finished. You've made new friends. Maybe you should concentrate on doing some type of volunteer work, or maybe even finding employment of some kind. You need to try and move forward into a new life, Kate."

She turned away from Mack and walked over to the other side of the deck. "That's what I've been trying to do, Mack. Or so I thought anyway. But as long as you keep showing up to remind me how much I miss you, how much I... I needed you, well, I..." now Kate's tears were flowing freely. "What is it that you expect from me anyway? There's not a night, not one single solitary night that I don't remember how you... how we were together. Sometimes I think I'll go mad from just wanting to feel you again."

Mack walked over and placed his hand on Kate's shoulder, even though he knew she couldn't feel his touch. "I know, Kate. You always were a loving woman. No man could ask for a better wife, or a better lover."

"Then why won't you set me free, Mack? Free me from this continuous torment of wanting you, of remembering the way we were."

Kate's words came as a surprise to Mack. "Oh? Do you really think it's me that is holding you back?"

"What is it with you, Mack? What the hell is it that you want from me or expect me to do?" she cried.

"I want you to open up your heart again, Kate. I want you to let go of all that bitterness you're still holding because of what happened to Caleb and me. Caleb is fine, Honey. And just as soon as I'm sure you're going to be okay, then I'll be fine too," Mack tried to assure her.

Still looking up at the stars, Kate wiped at the tears on her face. "So, is that it?"

"Not quite."

She began to brush her hair again. "Oh? There's more?"

"Yeah, there's more. He's in love with you, Kate." Kate didn't bother to say anything as she turned to go back into the bedroom. Mack followed her inside. He wanted an answer. "Don't you have anything to say about that? Or don't you like the idea of someone being in love with you again?"

Kate didn't want to have this conversation with Mack, but knew she had to say something. "*He?* Who is this '*he*' you're referring to, Mack? Am I to assume you're talking about Hank Diamond?"

Mack grinned, knowing it wasn't easy for Kate to discuss another man with him. "It kind of set you back a little when he kissed you, didn't it?"

Kate's face flushed to a bright red. "You saw that? Christ, Mack! Are you with me every minute? Do you know everything that's going on with me? And furthermore, if I thought you were watching, then do you honestly think I would consider having sex with another man?"

Mack's eyes twinkled as he gave a little laugh. "Maybe I shouldn't have told you that."

"I'm glad you did." I wonder what Hank Diamond would've thought if he knew my husband was watching him kiss me." Kate had to laugh a little about that too.

"I'm serious, Kate. He's in love with you. Give the guy a break. He's a good man."

"*NO,*" she said emphatically.

"Why not? Don't you find him physically attractive and personable?"

"Of course, I do. He's got great legs, Mack. He's a real turn-on in cut-offs. Or haven't you noticed?" she asked, teasingly.

Mack frowned. "I haven't been looking at his legs, Kate. He's not my type. But apparently you have. So, I'll ask you again, why not?"

Mack's persistence was beginning to anger Kate. "Butt out, Mack! It's no concern of yours what I do or with whom I do it. And as long as I think you're peeking over my shoulder, I can assure you I won't be making love to anyone. Anyway, I'm not looking for a relationship. I'm not ready."

"Okay, Sweetheart, I won't push you on the subject."

"That's good, Mack. Thank you for that much anyway." Kate pulled back the covers and climbed into bed. Reaching to turn out the light, she said, "Good night, Mack."

But Mack wasn't there.

Susie Rigsby

"Okay, so Hank Diamond may be a tad war-worn and that makes him a little strange. I'm not what he needs, believe me," Kate said.

17 | CHAPTER *SEVENTEEN*

Sunday morning was Kate's favorite time to just kick back and relax, even try to stay in bed and sleep late... if she could. But she'd made other plans for this day and was up early for an invigorating four-mile run. The morning air was cool so she moved at a brisk space to keep warm.

Kate was only a mile into her run when she noticed the white, older model pickup truck slowing to move along beside her. She recognized Charlie DaRoux as soon as she turned her head to get a look at the driver. Kate chose to ignore him, maintaining her pace in hopes Charlie would take the hint and drive on away from her.

She wasn't that lucky. Instead, Charlie rolled down his window and with a sly grin he asked, "Can I give you a lift?"

Kate didn't bother to acknowledge him and continued to run, thinking the old kook couldn't be right in the head. He was actually offering her a ride after he had threatened to shoot her dog. Unfortunately, Kate had no way of knowing that Charlie hated rejection, which made him even more determined. He wasn't going to go away until Kate acknowledged him in some manner.

"No, thank you," she finally told him. "I jog for the exercise. I don't need a lift."

"Whatever. I was jest tryin' to be neighborly," Charlie said, laughing as he pulled away.

She'd never met anyone like that man before. He definitely wasn't dealing with a full deck. In fact, there wasn't anything normal about Charlie DaRoux or his actions. It gave Kate the creeps just thinking about him.

On her return run, Kate stopped by Needa's place for a cup of coffee. As always, Kate knocked before opening the back door. Needa was at the stove fixing pancakes, but looked up when Kate entered the kitchen.

"Oh boy, pancakes! Looks as if I may have timed my run just right to get breakfast this morning," Kate said, hoping for an invitation to eat as she reached in the cabinet for a coffee cup.

"I bet you could smell the bacon frying."

Kate laughed. "Something like that. And I have worked up a pretty good appetite. Jogging will do that for a person. I could probably eat a couple of those pancakes if you have plenty."

Kate sat her coffee cup on the table before walking over to Raine. Needa observed her son's expression when Kate bent down to kiss the top of his head. Could it be possible that Raine had feelings for Kate? *Surely not,* she thought.

After breakfast, when the dishes were done and the kitchen was clean, Needa poured two cups of coffee and joined Kate at the table. She reached for a cigarette, lit it, and then took a deep drag.

"Smoking is a terrible habit, Needa. Those cigarettes will probably be the cause of your demise someday," Kate warned.

Needa frowned. "Hey, will you lay off about my smoking? It's the only vice I have left, so indulge me a little with this one."

"I didn't mean to sound like I was lecturing you."

"That's good, because I don't intend to quit smoking."

Kate took a sip of her coffee. "I've been thinking a lot about Leo Staggner lately."

That caught Needa's attention. "Oh yeah? Do you like him?"

"I think he's one heck of a nice guy. I noticed that he hardly left your side at the cookout. I think he might have eyes for you," Kate replied in a nonchalant manner.

Needa smiled. "Do you now?"

"Yeah, I do. Perhaps you should invite Leo over for some of your famous tea. And while you're at it, you might want to lace the tea with just a small amount of love potion." Grinning, Kate winked at her friend.

"You've just been dying to bring that up, haven't you? I haven't thought to invite him for tea yet, but I expect to be seeing

Second Chances

him again. Leo appears to be such a warm and sincere person. He seems to think a lot of you, Kate."

Kate snickered. "I think maybe it was those fat paychecks I gave Leo every week that impressed him. I didn't begrudge a penny of his pay either. He has a great imagination for design and did an excellent job of renovating my house. I would recommend Leo to anyone. But I'd especially recommend him for you."

"That's if I intended to do any remodeling and was in need of a carpenter, which I'm not."

Kate chuckled. Needa had listened carefully to Kate's choice of words. "I know you don't need a carpenter. I'm not recommending him in that capacity to you, I'm recommending him as a male companion for you. Leo is a good man. And in case you haven't noticed, he's not a bad looking guy either. I could tell he has eyes for you," Kate continued to tease.

Amused, Needa shook her head. "I'm sure you're a great judge of character and Leo is everything you say. If it will make you happy, I'll invite him for tea in the near future. Now, since we're on the subject of companions, why don't you tell me about Hank Diamond?" When it came to poking fun, turn about was fair play as far as Needa was concerned. And it was her turn at Kate.

Kate's smile suddenly disappeared. She gave Needa a puzzled look. "You're asking the wrong person about Hank Diamond. I don't know anything about the man."

"You wouldn't fib to me about that, would you?"

"Well, I don't think so. Whatever gave you the idea that I would know anything about Hank Diamond?" Kate asked.

"Are you trying to tell me you don't know how his lips feel when he kisses a woman?"

Clearly flustered, Kate's face turned red. "Did Hank tell you about kissing me? I can't believe he would have the nerve to tell anyone about that."

"Now, Kate, don't go jumping to conclusions. I haven't talked to Hank, but I will be seeing him this week when he brings my firewood. Hank has never mentioned your name to me." Needa said, jumping to Hank's defense.

"Then how did you know he'd kissed me?"

"Lucky hunch, I suppose. I was only teasing, but you sure fell for it fast enough. I must have touched a nerve," Needa replied

137

with highly stimulated curiosity. "Well, are you going to tell me about it?"

After taking another sip of coffee, Kate replaced the cup on the saucer and ran her fingertips around its rim, looking to be in deep thought. "I was pretty upset when you told me what Hank had said to Charlie DaRoux in the restaurant."

"Yeah, I could tell."

"The more I thought about it, the more it upset me, so I decided to visit Hank and give him a piece of my mind. I was mad as hell and thought I'd done a decent job of telling him off. I still don't know what possessed him to grab me and kiss me like he did. He said something about not wanting Charlie DaRoux to think he was a liar. As if Hank could really give a damn what that man thought," she said and managed to laugh.

"Hank's a good man, Kate."

"It's funny you should say that to me. It's the second time I've heard that remark about Hank lately. If he's such a good man then why is he single? My sister thinks Hank is strange, like he might be shell-shocked from the military. Emily has this thing about characterizing everyone, including me."

Needa got up and went to the coffee pot, poured herself another cup, then carried the pot over to freshen up Kate's coffee. "Hank's had his share of life's problems, Kate, but I can assure you that he is not shell-shocked. Hank retired from the military. He was trained in covert operations with the Marine's Special Forces. He's never mentioned it to me, but I think those guys are trained to do some really mean shit."

"Marines? Are you saying he was in the U.S. Marines?"

"Yeah, he was quite young when he joined up. I never really understood too much about it and like I said, Hank doesn't talk about it to anyone. I don't think he ever fit into the picture with his family. He was a rabble-rouser as a young buck. I guess he had to get all that shit out of his system some way, so that's the route he took," Needa said.

"Okay, so he was a misfit and rebel-rouser. Why would that be a problem for him now?"

"Well, I don't know, but from what little I've read about covert operations, I think it can get to be pretty hairy for those special ops guys. Hank won't talk about it, but I think he was involved in some real unpleasant situations under the worst of conditions. Most guys do okay during active duty. It's when they return home that their heads get all screwed up. I have no idea what it would be like to take orders under those conditions. But I'd think killing on command as those guys have to do, especially in the way they're trained to do it, well, it's bound to have some type of lasting effect on a man. I'm just guessing, but I'd say Hank was so good at his job that the military wanted him to stay and train others in covert operations. His wife told me that sleep didn't come easy for Hank after he retired." Needa said.

"You knew her?" Kate asked.

"Oh my, yes. She was a beautiful woman and Hank's only salvation at the time. Beth knew what to expect and how to handle the situation. They had a good marriage. Then one day about four years ago, she just dropped dead from a brain aneurysm. Hank worshipped that woman. I don't think he's ever gotten over losing her and stays pretty much to himself. I was shocked to see him at the cookout yesterday. Did you invite him?" Needa was being nosey.

"Not until he showed up at my door with a beautiful bouquet. Then I asked him to join us. He came over to apologize for what happened between us. I think the flowers were a peace offering. I accepted them as that anyway," Kate said. Then, looking quite serious, she told Needa, "I'm not looking for any kind of relationship. Not with Hank or any other man. Hank and I are just neighbors. I'd like to think that if we both tried hard enough, we might even become good friends. I just want to make myself clear that I have no intention of ever falling in love with anyone, especially not Hank," Kate said with a look of determination.

"That's an awful strong statement for a young woman to make, don't you think?"

"No. Not really. I lost the love of my life and I was devastated when it happened. I don't intend to ever go through anything like that again. It's really fairly simple, Needa. If I can keep from falling in love, then there's no risk for that kind of pain and heartache. Besides, being alone isn't so bad," she concluded.

Needa didn't agree and shook her head. "Are you kidding? Being alone sucks, Kate. There's nothing in this world like the feel of a man's warm body next to your backside on a cold winter night. In case you didn't know, the snow gets damn deep up here in these hills."

"Not as deep as the bullshit you're putting out. And darn, I'm not wearing my boots either," Kate said, laughing as she looked down at her feet. "Okay, so Hank Diamond may be a tad war-worn and that makes him a little strange. I'm not what he needs, believe me."

"Hank's not strange, not the way your sister seems to think anyway. He just has this thing about keeping to himself. That's just until he gets to know you. If you're lucky enough for Hank to like you, then his presence can be a blessing. Personally, I think it's pretty damn nice just having Hank around to admire that gorgeous physique of his," Needa went on.

Kate's mouth turned up in a devilish grin. "I'm not blind, Needa. I've noticed."

"No, and you aren't dead yet either. Let the past go, Kate. Don't bury yourself in it, or run away from the future because of it. Life is too short as it is," Needa said, carefully choosing the words she spoke to Kate.

"You have no idea of what I've been through, Needa. Or for that matter, what it did to me."

Needa easily read the pain in Kate's dark eyes and reached over to pat Kate's hand. "Oh, but yes, I do have an idea. And you know I'm not very far away whenever you decide it's time to talk about it. Come on over and we'll hash it out. But only when you're ready."

Kate got up and walked to the door, turning back to Needa before she turned the doorknob. "Hank Diamond isn't going to be another one of my casualties, Needa. From the things you've told me, it sounds as if he's already had his share of life's problems. God forbid that he should have to suffer from any of mine. I wouldn't wish that on my worst enemy. And because I consider you to be a very dear friend, I for sure wouldn't want to burden you with hearing about my problems. I'll see you later."

When Kate started jogging back home, Baron was right beside her.

Mack continued to make his frequent visits, encouraging Kate to find a job, get into a daily routine and to start attending Mass again. He was patiently waiting for Kate to begin living her life to the fullest. Until then, his visits could not and would not cease.

18 | CHAPTER *EIGHTEEN*

The very thought of the up-coming holiday season was almost unbearable for Kate. Unlike her last Christmas that was spent in the mental hospital and totally oblivious to the world around her, Mack and Caleb's absence was already bearing on her mind. Without them, Kate preferred to just skip the holidays all together. She hadn't planned to put up a tree or do any other holiday decorating. Her heart just wasn't in it.

For the most part, Kate was content just being settled into a place of her own after finally getting it arranged exactly as she'd wanted. Most of her evenings were spent sitting in front of the fireplace, drinking wine and reading a good book. Baron remained her only companion. Although she visited often with Needa and Raine, she made every effort to avoid any kind of contact with Hank.

Every Sunday afternoon, she would drive down to Toronto and have dinner with Emily and Gordon. Overall, Kate wanted to think her life was getting back to normal. But as yet, she hadn't decided whether or not her way of life could be deemed as acceptable, much less normal. She wouldn't be willing to even give her existence a description. She was just there.

Mack continued to make his frequent visits, encouraging Kate to find a job, get into a daily routine, and to start attending Mass again. He was patiently waiting for Kate to begin living her life to the fullest. Until then, his visits could not and would not cease.

This evening, as Kate watched the huge snowflakes falling heavily to the ground, she was glad to be settled inside. It was a good night for staying close by the fire and reading a steamy novel that Emily had loaned her, *Lucky's Lady* by Tami Hoag. She was engrossed in a torrid love scene when the phone rang. Checking the caller ID, she recognized Emily's number.

"Good evening, Em," Kate greeted, laying the book down.

"Hey, what have you been doing to keep busy on such a snowy day?" Emily asked.

"Reading that steamy romance novel you loaned me, what else? And thanks a lot. This is hardly the kind of book a poor old widow woman like me should be reading."

Emily laughed. "I told you it was a good book."

"Yeah, well, do me a favor and don't loan me any more of your *good* books. My libido suffers enough as it is."

"Okay, no more of my books for you. I thought you might like to venture out for a day of Christmas shopping tomorrow? We can drag Gordon along and go out for dinner afterward," Emily said, hoping to sweeten the invitation.

Kate glanced out the window at the huge snowflakes that continued to steadily fall. "Jeez, Em, this weather isn't fit for man or beast. I'd rather not."

"I know what you mean. But if you haven't finished shopping, then this would be a good time to get it done. Besides, I bring you glad tidings this evening," Emily said and chuckled.

"I wonder why the way you said that just sent a cold chill up my spine."

"It should. I hope your house is in order and ready for company. Dad and Mom just called. They're flying up to Canada for Christmas. Now, go ahead and get excited."

Kate was amused. "I think Gordon is the person you should be telling to get excited, not me. After all, they are my parents too. How long are they staying?"

"They didn't say, but they've decided to stay with you. That was probably Dad's idea. Gordon is now convinced God's on his side, and that every dollar he's ever donated to the Church is actually paying off for him. He does plan to offer up a prayer for you, saying you'll need it." Emily could barely contain her humor.

"Tell your husband I really appreciate his concern." Kate took a deep breath, then asked, "Okay, whip it on me. How much time do I have before they arrive?"

Second Chances

"How much do you need?"

"Well, what do we have left, two weeks before Christmas? They surely wouldn't show up until about the twenty-third. Or would they?"

"Oh my, when did you suddenly become so naïve? I think they would. They'll be here the twentieth. Gordon agreed to pick them up at the airport. He said to tell you he would be delivering them immediately to Kate's comfortable little home in the hills."

Which meant Kate would be entertaining her parents for at least a week. "I suppose I'll have to load up on air fresheners. But then again, I doubt they could smuggle marijuana through customs. And that makes me wonder what our parents plan to do about their wild wood weed while they're here."

Emily snickered. "You should know better than to be concerned about Dad and his smoke. I'd never underestimate him about something that's so vital to his state of mind. Besides, if I know Dad, he has connections up here too. I suggest you go ahead and stock up with the air fresheners. Anyway, back to our shopping day tomorrow. Why don't you drive down early in the morning and plan on spending the day?"

Reluctantly, Kate agreed, realizing there wasn't much choice in the matter. And with her parents coming to visit, she would have to put up a Christmas tree. Laura would be upset if there wasn't a decorated tree to admire while she was getting high. "You're right, as usual. I'll be there unless the snow is so deep I can't get out. I'll call if I can't make it. If that happens, do me a favor and shop for me too. And don't forget to wrap the presents. After all, I am doing my part for Gordon."

When the conversation with Emily ended, Kate knew her plans had been squashed for a nice quiet holiday at home alone. She grabbed a pen and pad of paper to make a list of everything she would need to get done before Christmas.

Later that evening as Kate tried to read, she found herself reminiscing about the childhood she'd managed to survive with her parents. Foolishly, she tried to suppress memories of any past Christmas she'd shared with Mack and Caleb. It was just too painful to think about. In a melancholy mood, Kate had sipped entirely too much wine.

She was in a world of her own and barely heard a knocking at the door. Baron had been asleep on the floor, but the dog immediately raised his head and began to growl.

"Easy, Bear," Kate quietly said, petting the dog's head before getting up. She had a strange feeling, as if being warned not to open the door. The instant she spotted Charlie DaRoux standing on her porch, Kate realized she had made a mistake.

"Well, Mr. DaRoux, aren't you a little off your usual route this evening?" Kate asked.

Charlie looked over at the dog before allowing his eyes to roam over Kate's body, and then he replied. "Yeah, well, you see, my ole truck broke down out there at the end of yer lane. And I wus wunderin' if you'd be kind enough to give me a lift on home?"

"I see. Well, don't you think it might be a better idea if you called a towing company to come and get your truck? Then you could just ride on home with them. You're welcome to use my phone," Kate offered.

"It's Christmas, Miss Corbin, so I don't have the extra cash for a big towin' bill right now. You know how it is with a house full of rug rats. Besides, my oldest boy can help me get the truck goin' in the mornin' when it gets daylight," Charlie said.

"No, Mr. DaRoux, I don't know how it is with a house full of rug rats. But can't you just call your oldest boy to come over here and pick you up? I really don't want to get out in this weather."

Charlie gave her a disgusted look. "Look, Ms. Corbin, my phone's been out of order at the house. So I can't call anyone to come and pick me up. And I can't be payin' no big towin' bill right here before Christmas. All I'm askin' is for you to kindly give me a lift home. The way you're actin', you'd think I was some kind of criminal or somethin'. If you don't want to help me out, then I guess I'd best start walkin', hadn't I?"

Something told Kate to let him go on and start walking, but it was bitter cold and the snow wasn't letting up. And Kate could tell that Charlie had been drinking. She looked down at Baron, and then again at Charlie. "I'll get my coat and be with you in a minute, Mr. DaRoux."

The warm and fuzzy feeling she'd gotten earlier from the wine had quickly disappeared. Kate's heart was beating wildly when she shut the door and looked down at Baron again. "Get ready to ride, Big Dog. No way would I leave you behind."

After getting her coat from the closet, she nervously slipped it on as she started out. Baron was waiting for Kate at the door as if the dog had sensed her fear. Charlie was standing on the porch smoking a cigarette when Kate opened the door again.

"Let's go, Mr. DaRoux," Kate said, making sure Baron was between her and Charlie as she descended the porch steps. Charlie followed along behind, keeping his distance from the dog. The snow was coming down harder now and by the time they reached the Jeep, Baron's feet and coat were covered. Kate walked to the rear of the vehicle and opened the back hatch, then brushed the dog off before allowing Baron to jump up into the back area.

She'd been so engrossed with Baron that Kate hadn't paid close attention to Charlie's whereabouts, but Charlie had been watching her every move. He waited until Kate closed the back hatch, making certain the dog was confined securely inside the Jeep. Then Charlie shot from around the side of the Jeep and grabbed Kate's arm, while the other hand went to Kate's long mane, twisting it tightly around his fist. Baron saw what was happening and went wild, locked inside the Jeep where he couldn't get out to protect Kate.

"You snippety bitch," Charlie said while holding Kate's face close to his, glaring into her eyes. "You didn't even want to give me a goddamn ride, did you? That's cuz you think yer too good fer ole Charlie. Well, Miss High and Mighty, you ain't too good. You're nothin' but a slut, just like any other whorin' woman I ever knew. And I'm gonna show you what a real man can do fer a whore like you. Hank Diamond tried to blow his bazoo off about you, tryin' to make everybody think you wuz his woman. Well, I don't see that fucker's brand stamped anywhere on you, Missy. So I'm jest gonna show you what it's like to be with a real man." Keeping Kate's hair tightly wound around his fist, Charlie began pulling her back toward the house.

Kate was so scared she could hardly breathe, but tried to reason with Charlie. "You're making a terrible mistake, Mr. DaRoux. Turn me loose now and I'll take you home. We can both forget this incident ever happened."

"Turn you loose! Are you kiddin', Honey? Ole Charlie's gonna turn you ever which way but loose. And I can promise you ain't ever gonna forget what happened. I don't aim to scare you, Miss Fancy Pants, but yer gonna get to see what a real man looks like. Did you ever see a mule's dick? I'll bet not. Well, I ain't braggin' or nothin', but I've got what you might call a mule's dick, if you can jest imagine it. And I'm gonna shove every single inch of it right up your ass. Look! By God, if I'm not hard as a rock, ready for you right now." Charlie was out of breath, gasping for air as he continued to drag Kate toward the house.

Kate felt like her head was going to snap off her neck when they finally reached the porch steps. The pain was unbearable when she lost her balance and fell. Charlie cursed at her. "Get up, you rotten bitch. Open that fuckin' door and let's get inside where it's warm. I'm freezin' out here." Kate felt his hand slide into her coat pocket. "Where's that damn key to open this door? Hell, I'm freezin'. I don't want to lose this ragin' hardon cause I'm ready fer you right now," Charlie bragged.

He found the key in her pocket and managed to unlock the door with one hand, while he kept Kate's hair tightly fisted in the other. Once they were inside the house, Charlie reached inside his pocket and pulled out a switchblade knife. Kate was nearly paralyzed with fear when she heard the knife open.

He dragged her over toward the fireplace and pressed the knife blade against Kate's throat. "Take off that damned coat," he scowled at Kate. "Right now, damn you."

Kate unbuttoned her coat, praying she could die right then and there, rather than have to endure what Charlie had on his mind. So scared she could barely move, she let go of the coat and it dropped to the floor. Charlie's knife blade moved to the buttons on her sweater, slowly cutting them off, one by one. When the sweater was gaping open, he ordered, "Take it off, you slut. There ain't a thing holdin' it on. Let ole Charlie get a good look at those perky little tits of yers."

When the sweater was off, Kate felt the tip of the knife blade moving over the exposed part of her breasts. "Maybe I oughta jest make a few marks on those pretty hooters of yers, so you'll remember what a little excitin' pain feels like. Come to think of it, if Diamond ever gets lucky enough to take a look at those tits, then he's gonna get a load of the mark ole Charlie's made on ya. I'd luv for that dumb fuck to know I got in yer panties first. Are those nips good and hard for ole Charlie yet?"

Second Chances

He ran the knife blade up under the front of Kate's bra, cutting through the center of it to expose her breasts. The pain was excruciating when the sharp blade sliced into the top of her left breast. Kate thought she would pass out as the blood trickled down over her nipple.

"Hot damn that sure is a purdy sight. Jest watchin' that sweet red blood runnin' down over that purdy white tit drives me wild. Lordy sakes, you sure are a well-built woman. I'm gonna love every minute of this."

After praying to die from the humiliation a few minutes earlier, Kate was now praying to pass out from the pain in her breast. She was close to an unconscious state when she heard the Jeep's horn blaring loudly. The noise distracted Charlie and his assault on Kate came to a halt as he listened. Only a matter of seconds had lapsed when there was an explosion of glass and Baron was jumping through the window. Caught by surprise, Charlie was totally unprepared for the dog's ferocious attack.

Almost in a state of shock but realizing she had to do something to help Baron, Kate managed to climb the stairs to her bedroom. She reached into the nightstand drawer and grabbed a loaded 9mm Luger. Then she hurriedly made her way back downstairs to help her dog.

"Get that goddamned dog off me! For God's sake, call him off!" Charlie yelled, rapidly losing his battle with the dog.

"Baron! Baron, NO!" Kate yelled at the dog. Trained to obey, the dog let go of Charlie's arm and went over to sit beside Kate. Even though her entire body was shaking violently, Kate's voice remained calm and direct when she pointed the gun at Charlie's heart. "Get out of my house, you filthy low-life. If you aren't out of my sight by the time I count to three, this gun is going to blow a king-size hole through you," Kate told him, her words filled with hatred.

Charlie had managed to crawl over to the door, grabbed hold of the doorknob and pulled himself up off the floor to stand on his feet. Kate noticed the blood dripping off his arm onto the floor when Charlie turned around and said, "You'd best be careful with that loaded gun. It might accidentally go off."

Kate pointed the gun barrel higher at Charlie. "You're wrong about that, you scumbag. If this gun goes off it won't be by accident. And if you ever set foot on my property again, I swear

147

I'll kill you. Now get out before I change my mind and shoot you anyway."

After Charlie went through the door and it closed behind him, Kate went over and turned the dead bolt lock. She gave no thought to the broken window, or that anyone could simply climb through it to get inside. Kate wasn't able to think. She was shaking so hard she could barely stand, let alone try to think. Then she looked down at her bare breasts, exposed to the cold air blowing through the broken window. She picked up her coat that was laying on the floor and somehow managed to slip her arms into the sleeves, wrapping herself in the bulky garment. Then she sat down on the sofa, buried her face in her hands and cried like a baby. Baron came over and sat down by her feet.

The cold air continued to blow through the house and Kate realized it would be impossible for the furnace to keep up. She had no idea of what to do about trying to keep the cold out. It was all she could do just to try and regain control of her emotions. She had to think. Something had to be done about getting the window covered. She didn't have anything but a blanket to hang over it, and a blanket wasn't going to help.

The laceration on her breast burned like fire and was still bleeding. She felt faint and knew she couldn't allow for that to happen. She immediately placed her head down between her knees and took several deep breaths to keep from passing out, wondering if she could freeze to death before she got the window covered. Think, Kate. She had to think.

"Think. Think. Think," Kate repeated over and over. Emily was too far away to help her now and she would insist on calling the police. It would be senseless to call Needa, since there was nothing Needa could do about the window anyway, and bringing Raine out in this weather wasn't a good idea either. Then she thought of Leo. He would know what to do about fixing the window. Luckily, she remembered Leo's phone number. Kate picked up the phone and called the carpenter.

"Leo, it... it's... this is Kate Corbin. I... I've had some trouble at my place and I... I need your help right away."

19 | CHAPTER *NINETEEN*

Leo was engrossed in a boxing match on television when he heard the telephone ring. He'd been waiting all week to watch this fight and didn't want to be bothered. Answering machines were made to take messages as far as Leo was concerned.

"Leo, it... it's... this is Kate Corbin. I... I've had some trouble at my place and I... I need your help right away. The front window has been broken out and I can't fix it by myself and..."

Leo reached over and grabbed the phone. "Hello! Hello Kate, it's me, Leo. I'm here. What's wrong up there?"

Trying her best not to start crying again, Kate wanted to speak clearly so Leo could understand what she said. But once she heard Leo's voice, all she could manage to say was, "I just need your help, Leo."

"Well you just sit tight and I'll be there in about twenty-five minutes at the most. I'm on my way right now," he assured Kate.

"Wait, Leo! The window is completely broken out."

"Don't worry, Kate, I'll take care of the window when I get there. Now you just try to calm down and I'll be there shortly." Leo slammed down the receiver, grabbed a jacket and ran out the door to his storage shed. In record time, he had a 4 x 8 piece of plywood loaded in the bed of his truck. Everything else he needed to fix Kate's window was standard equipment inside the truck's tool box. In less than five minutes after her call, Leo was on the road to Kate's place.

Leo could see that major damage had been done to the window as soon as the truck lights hit the front of Kate's house. Getting up Kate's lane had been hindered by the deep snow, but

Leo considered it record timing when he reached Kate's front door.

"Kate, it's me, Leo. You'll have to unlock the door to let me in," he said, gently knocking on the door. He could have just as easily stepped through the broken window, but decided that wasn't such a good idea because of the jagged shards of glass still barely hanging in the window frame. That wasn't the only reason he chose to use the door. He knew about the loaded 9mm Luger that Kate kept in the house. In Kate's frame of mind, she might accidentally shoot him.

Kate unlocked the door and Leo stepped inside.

"Oh, Leo, thank God you're here," she said and started crying again. Kate was trembling so that Leo grabbed her up into his arms and held her close. He saw the broken glass covering the carpet, and then he looked over at Baron. The dog didn't seem to be too spooked, but Kate was a physical wreck.

"It's going to be okay, Kate. I'm here. I've got you now. Everything's going to be okay. Can you tell me what happened to the window?" Leo asked.

"I... Oh God, Leo, he almost..." she started but couldn't talk about Charlie DaRoux.

"There, there now, Kate. Don't cry, Sweetheart. It's going to be okay. Everything's going to be okay." Leo held her close for a long while, then said, "Kate, I need to put more wood on the fire and I've got to get that window covered. Let me call Needa to come over here. You need some attention."

"*NO*! I don't want anyone else to know what happened here tonight." She clung tightly to Leo's hand, her eyes full of apprehension. "It was so awful and... and I feel so filthy."

"Just what did happen here tonight, Kate?" Leo asked as he picked Kate up and carried her over to the sofa, gently putting her down.

Leo was there to help her. She knew that. Of course she would eventually have to tell him about Charlie DaRoux, but not right now. She was too upset and ashamed. Still, she had to tell him something. "Baron broke the window when he jumped through it. He was closed up in the Jeep and I don't know how he could have gotten out, but..." Tears welled up in her eyes again as

Kate looked up at Leo. "He... he had a knife, Leo. And he... he cut me with it."

"Cut you! My God, Kate! You've been cut with a knife! Where? Show me." Leo was furious.

Kate opened the coat just enough to expose the gaping wound on her left breast that was still bleeding. "I'm afraid to look, Leo. How bad is it?"

"Honestly, I think that cut could use a few stitches. It was that no-good Charlie DaRoux, wasn't it? That low-life did this to you. Did he... I mean... well, you know?" Leo asked, wanting to kill Charlie with his bare hands.

"No, but he would have if my dog hadn't stopped him. I can't imagine how Baron got out of the Jeep. I heard the horn blowing just before Baron came crashing through the window. I managed to get my gun while Charlie was trying to stop Baron's attack. I wanted to kill that man, Leo. I thought very seriously about shooting him," Kate sobbed.

"You should have killed the no good son of a bitch, Kate."

Kate wiped away the tears and told Leo, "I'm so cold. Would you mind getting me a couple of quilts from upstairs, and then make some coffee. I'll stay here by the fire while you fix the window. We've got to stop that cold air from blowing inside."

Leo did as she asked and went to get the quilts. After seeing that Kate was warmly wrapped in the quilts, he set out to fix a pot of coffee. Then he left Kate long enough to get the piece of plywood out of the truck bed. By then, the coffee was ready and he fixed a cup for Kate. She sat by the fire and watched Leo making the temporary repairs to the window. The plywood would keep the cold out until a replacement window could be ordered.

Leo's next job was to clean up the shards of glass scattered all over the carpet. He put on a pair of gloves to handle the larger pieces, then plugged in the sweeper to vacuum the carpet. Finally finished with cleaning up the broken glass, Leo poured himself a cup of coffee and sat down on the sofa beside Kate.

"Kate, I still think you should let me take you to the hospital and have that cut looked at. Take another look to see if it's still bleeding," he told her.

Kate opened the coat just enough to look at her bare breast. "It's an open wound, Leo, so it's going to seep a little. If I went to the hospital, they would want to know what happened. There's no way I could explain a cut like this one and I don't want any trouble. Besides, I don't want anyone else to know about this incident. It's so degrading. After tonight, I don't think I'll have to worry about Charlie coming back. I told him I'd kill him if he ever set a foot on my property again." Kate pulled the coat together and took a deep breath. "I can't thank you enough for coming up here to help me. I simply couldn't think of anyone else to call. I knew your phone number by heart and that helped. I couldn't call Needa. There was nothing she could do to help me, and I didn't want Raine out in this weather."

"Damn it, Kate, you call me any time if you need help. That's what friends are for. But Hank Diamond could have been over here in a heartbeat if you'd called him. Then your problems with Charlie would have been over once and for all." Leo said.

"You're probably right about that, Leo. That's another reason not to let this go beyond you and me. I don't think it would be wise for Hank Diamond to hear about what happened. He despises Charlie. He tried his best to warn me about Charlie and I wouldn't listen. I told Hank that I could take care of myself, and thought I could. But if Baron hadn't jumped through that window when he did, Charlie would have..." Kate looked away, as if her mind had drifted off and she'd lost her train of thought. She hesitated before telling Leo, "He... he was going to rape me. I knew the scumbag was drinking the minute I opened the door. I didn't use good judgment and should have been more careful. Anyway, it's over. I'll take a hot shower in a little while, clean up this cut and put a butterfly bandage over it. You won't leave me tonight, will you, Leo?" she asked, looking rather pitiful.

"No way! I wouldn't think of it. You're safe now, Kate."

They sat together in front of the fire and talked for quite a while. Leo knew that idle chat would help keep Kate's mind off what had happened. A little later, she decided to have a shower and bandage her breast. When Kate returned to the living room, she found Leo stretched out on the sofa, sound asleep. She went upstairs to bed, taking Baron with her.

Kate awakened to the aroma of freshly brewed coffee the next morning. After slipping on her robe and house slippers, she headed downstairs to join Leo. He was sitting on the sofa, drinking a cup of coffee.

"Good morning, Kate. Did you manage to get a little sleep?"

She smiled at him. "I think I passed out as soon as my head hit the pillow. I can't thank you enough for coming to my rescue. I owe you big time, Leo," she said, gratefully.

"Don't talk silly. You don't owe me anything. But I have been giving a lot of thought to what happened here last night. I'm wondering if maybe you aren't making a big mistake by not reporting this to the authorities. Charlie DaRoux doesn't have a lick of sense. You may think you've scared him off, Kate, but guys like Charlie don't usually scare that easily. I'd say pulling a gun on him is going to be stuck in Charlie's craw for a while," Leo warned her.

"I know. And I've thought about that too. I just don't want any more trouble. So far, no one else knows about this except you, me and Charlie, so let's just lay low and see what happens. I know you won't say anything about this to anyone. And Charlie would be a fool to talk about it." Kate was adamant about her decision to not reveal what had happened to anyone else.

Leo was worried. "Have it your way, Kate. But I still think you're making a mistake."

153

Susie Rigsby

"You're stepping out of line again, Diamond," Kate said and opened the door. "I'm withdrawing my offer to give you a ride home. I think maybe the walk might do you some good."

20 | CHAPTER *TWENTY*

Hank routinely ran the same route every morning at 5:00 A.M. and this morning wasn't any different. Since the trees were now bare of their leaves, Hank had a clear view of Kate's house from the road. The security nightlight was shining brightly on Kate's driveway, making it easy for him to spot Leo's truck.

The thought of Leo spending the night with Kate had ruined the start of Hank's day, even though he tried to tell himself that it really wasn't any of his damn business. He wanted to give Kate and Leo the benefit of the doubt, wanted to think that perhaps Leo was there on business. Right, Diamond, it's just business, he thought. And if he believed that scenario, then he'd be a likely candidate for buying ocean front property in Arizona, as the song went.

At five o'clock in the morning, the only business Leo Staggner was probably conducting with the gorgeous neighbor was monkey business. Only a fool would try to talk himself into believing anything else. Hank knew what he'd be doing if his truck was parked in front of Kate's house at that hour of the morning, and he was inside with her. He sure as hell wouldn't be discussing business. More likely than not, Leo wasn't there to discuss a job either. Besides, hadn't Gordon told him that Kate was undecided about where to build a garage, and didn't intend to start construction until early next spring?

Hank was still fretting about Leo's truck being parked in front of Kate's house when he returned home. By noon, he was so worked up worrying about Leo being with Kate that he simply couldn't take it any longer. He boldly decided to pay Kate a visit, intent on finding out what was going on between his neighbor and the carpenter.

Leo's truck was gone when Hank headed up Kate's lane. That was a plus, he thought. He didn't need to have a confrontation with a guy he'd met only once, about a woman he barely knew, and over something they both would be quick to tell Hank was none of his damned business in the first place. As Hank neared the front of Kate's house, he spotted the plywood covering one of the windows. He moved quietly up the porch steps, knocking gently on the front door when he reached it.

Kate hadn't heard anyone on the porch, but the dog did and lifted his head to watch the door. However, Baron didn't seem to be too concerned.

"Who's there?" Kate asked through the door.

"Hank Diamond," Hank replied through the door. "It's colder than blue blazes out here, Kate. Can I come in?"

Kate opened the door. "You're right, Hank, it is cold out there. Please, do come in," she said, and then turned away, heading toward the kitchen area. "Can I get you a cup of coffee?" she asked rather nervously, which didn't go unnoticed.

"No, but thanks anyway," Hank replied, looking around the living room, and then at the plywood nailed over the window. "What happened to the window?"

Kate hadn't given a thought as to how she would explain the shattered window, should anyone happen to ask before it was repaired, and hesitated with her answer. "It... ah, it got broken out."

Hank gave her a funny look, followed with a slight chuckle. "No kidding. I think I can see that, Kate. How did it get broken? That's what I'm asking you."

It took too long for Kate to answer, which Hank didn't appreciate at all. Then finally, she told him, "Baron jumped through it last night and shattered the window."

Hank then had a puzzled look, quickly followed by one of total disbelief. What did she think? That he was totally stupid? "Baron! Is that some kind of a joke? Baron would have to be "Super Dog" to jump through that kind of window." Hank didn't like what he was seeing, or Kate's reply, which he considered to be an insult to his intelligence. "Now that you've had your fun, Kate, why don't you try telling me what really happened here last night?"

Kate walked over to the fireplace. "If you don't mind, Hank, I'd rather not talk about it."

"Oh yeah? Well, I do mind," Hank shot back in an irritated voice that caused Baron to sit up and growl at him. The dog got Hank's attention, aware the canine was on edge and very protective of Kate.

"Hank, I really am sorry, but I was just getting ready to leave. I don't have much time to visit with you right now. In fact, I was just on my way out to pick up my sister in Toronto. We're going to Christmas shop today. Can I give you a ride back over to your place?"

Hank realized she was trying to get rid of him. After running his fingers through his hair, he gave Kate an uncompromising look before pressing the issue further. "Let me explain something to you, Kate, and it's pretty damned simple. I'm going to ask you again what happened to that window. And if you don't tell me, then I'll go find Leo Staggner and ask him."

Kate grinned. "Go ahead. Leo won't tell you anything."

"Oh? You think not? Well, I seriously doubt that Leo Staggner is a stupid man. And the way I see it, he'll either voluntarily tell me what I want to know, or else I'll have to beat the information out of him," Hank said in a calm manner, but his steel-gray eyes were ice cold. It was a good indication he meant what he said.

Kate was infuriated by Hank's threat to Leo. "Hear me good, Hank Diamond. You just keep away from Leo Staggner. I can't believe you would even make such a stupid threat," she said, anger emanating from her dark eyes.

"Look, Kate, I saw Staggner's truck parked in your driveway early this morning, so I figure he must have stayed here all night. Since Leo's a carpenter, I have to surmise he nailed that plywood over the window for you. Common sense tells me that Leo probably knows how the window got broken. And I doubt he'd come up with some cock and bull story about your dog doing the damage. Now, are you going to tell me, or do I need to go see Leo. One way or the other, I intend to find out what happened to

157

that goddamn window." Along with his temper, Hank was about to lose his patience, but he kept a calm voice because of the dog.

Kate walked away from him, over to the door. "You're stepping out of line again, Diamond," she said before opening the door. "I'm withdrawing my offer to give you a ride home. I think maybe the walk might do you some good."

Hank moved to where she stood by the door and grabbed Kate firmly by the shoulders. She grimaced as pain erupted in her breast, causing Baron to stand up and growl. Hank saw the pained expression on Kate's face and didn't want to think he'd hurt her. "Jesus Christ! Did I hurt you?"

"It's okay, Bear." Kate was quick to tell the dog. Then she told Hank, "No, you... you didn't. Really. I'm just a little sore, that's all."

Hank knew better. "Are you nuts? Kate, I can clearly see that I hurt you. What's wrong with you? I don't understand what's going on here," he said, then gently wrapped his arms around Kate. "Please, Kate. Please tell me what happened here last night."

It felt good just to be held and Hank's warmth was comforting. Kate couldn't bring herself to draw back from him this time. "I really do have to go."

"No, you don't. Call Emily and tell her you're going to be a little late. Don't do this to me, Kate. You have to tell me what happened," Hank pleaded.

She didn't want Hank to know about Charlie DaRoux, or what the low-life had attempted to do to her. It was too humiliating. But sooner or later, she knew Hank would find out about the whole sordid ordeal. If she could just reason with him, make him promise not to get involved, then perhaps telling him might be the better idea. And if Charlie gave her any more problems, she could call Hank.

"I'll fix a fresh pot of coffee," she said, turning away from Hank and heading for the kitchen.

Hank followed behind her, watching every move Kate made, and the way she favored her left shoulder. He walked up behind Kate to gently place his hands on her shoulders again. "You've been hurt. I saw the pain in your eyes when I grabbed you. God, Kate, don't you know that I would never do anything to hurt you. But you grimaced when I grabbed you, and I can see you're favoring that left shoulder."

Keeping her back to Hank, she asked, "Hank, if I tell you what happened here last night, will you promise never to repeat it to another living soul, and that you won't get involved?"

"No, Kate, I can't make you that promise."

"Why not?"

"Because I have a gut feeling that I'm not going to like what I hear."

"Then I'm not going to tell you."

"Yes, I think you will."

"And just what are you going to do if I don't? Will you want to beat it out of me too?"

Very gently, he turned Kate around to face him. "Kate, listen to me. You must tell me what happened."

"Not if you're going to go off half-cocked with that temper of yours. I don't intend to tell you a damn thing unless you give me your word not to get involved. So which way is it going to be, Diamond?"

She drove a hard bargain, to which Hank gave careful consideration. Then he took a deep breath and agreed. "Okay. You have my word. Now tell me what happened."

No sooner had Kate finished telling Hank about her ordeal with Charlie DaRoux, until she saw a look in his eyes that scared the hell out of Kate. Perhaps telling Hank had been a big mistake and she reminded him once more. "You gave me your word, Hank."

"Yeah, well I lied," he told Kate, his voice shaking with rage.

"No, I won't accept that. Besides, I don't think Charlie is going to give me any more trouble. And I just want to forget about what happened. Believe that I won't be so foolish if he should ever show up here again."

"He won't."

"Well, I hope not."

"I can assure you that he won't, if I have to castrate the bastard to keep him away." Hank's expression had begun to

159

soften just a little, replaced by concern. "Now, let me take a look at that laceration of yours."

Kate's face turned a bright shade of red. "I most certainly will not."

"Damn it, Kate! Don't be so defensive. I just want to see how bad you're hurt. I have a tube of healing ointment that's great for lacerations, but you might need to see a doctor. Now show me," he insisted.

It was going against Kate's better judgment, but she unbuttoned the top two buttons on her blouse and carefully pulled the material away from her breast. She wasn't wearing a bra.

Hank's fingers gently pulled the bandage away from the wound. "Dear God!" he said after looking at her breast. "I'll kill him."

"It isn't so bad, Hank. I'm sure it's going to be okay."

Hank's fingers traced over the top of her breast, just above the wound. "The cut looks awful, Kate, but that breast is lovely," he said, bending his head down to lightly move his lips over the top of her breast, just above the wound.

Every nerve ending in Kate's body tingled from the touch of Hank's mouth. At the moment, she was not feeling, or remembering, any trace of the pain she'd endured earlier. "Hank, I don't... I really think... please don't do that."

Her words weren't convincing enough and Hank whispered in her ear. "Don't push me away, Kate. I want to hold you, be with you."

Kate's body begged for more as Hank's mouth brought sensations to life in her that had been dormant for far too long. Still, she pulled away from him, tears welling up in her eyes. "I have to go, Hank. You gave me your word about Charlie and a man's word is his bond," she said, walking toward the coat closet. If she was to maintain any kind of control, she had to get away from him.

He followed Kate outside to the Jeep. "I'll call you later to see how you're doing."

"That's very thoughtful of you," she said, turning to him when they reached the Jeep. "I'll give you that lift home I offered earlier."

"No thanks, I'll walk. It isn't that far and the fresh air helps to clear my mind. Drive safely, Kate," he told her, shutting the Jeep's door after Kate was seated inside.

* * *

That damn dog was going to die and to Charlie's way of thinking, the sooner the better. His right arm had been ripped open and was still raw from his encounter with the huge Saint Bernard. Charlie knew it would make him feel a whole lot better if he could just take a gun and blow that damn dog's head clean off. But that would be too easy. He wanted the dog to suffer a slow and painful death. He hated to waste good anti-freeze on a mangy-ass dog, but using the sweet liquid to destroy Kate Corbin's dog could hardly be considered a waste.

Derek DaRoux walked into the shed just as Charlie had begun to rub a healing ointment on his arm. "God, Pa! What happened to your arm? It looks awful."

Charlie shot the boy a hateful look. "That woman's goddamned dog attacked me over at Doc's place last night," Charlie answered, rewrapping the bandage around his arm.

"Attacked you! Are you kidding?" Derek questioned.

"Dammit, boy, ain't that what I jest said? My old truck quit on me at the end of her lane. The damn dog came out of nowhere and attacked me when I got out to raise the hood. That dog's a killer and it oughta be destroyed."

It wasn't just his mangled arm that had Charlie so upset. It was the idea of a woman pointing a loaded gun at him. No woman could pull a trick like that on Charlie DaRoux and get away with it. But then again, when Charlie thought about the little cut he'd made on that pretty breast of hers; it still sent adrenaline pumping through his veins. Just to picture the blood trickling down over her nipple gave him an erection. Maybe he'd leave a better mark on the bitch the next time they met. For certain, Charlie intended to finish what he'd started. Of course, in order to do that he would have to dispose of the damn dog first.

Dane had been standing outside the shed, quietly listening through the door to his father's conversation with Derek. The young boy could tell by the tone of his father's voice that

Charlie fully intended to get even with Kate's dog. Dane decided right then that he'd have to keep an eye out for Baron.

*   *   *

Leo Staggner couldn't stop thinking about Charlie DaRoux. The poor excuse for a man was as mean and dangerous as he was crazy. Mix those traits together and it becomes a combination not to be ignored. In the past, Leo had over-heard Charlie bragging about his sexual escapades with women. Even though Leo didn't believe a word of anything Charlie had to say, he did not appreciate Charlie's stories. It was disgusting to hear a man talk that way about women.

But after seeing Charlie's handiwork with a switchblade on Kate's breast, Leo was convinced that Charlie was not a man to be messed around with. He should have insisted that Kate go to the authorities and get a restraining order against the demented lunatic. If Kate refused to file charges against Charlie, then he might think it would be safe to have another go at her. If that happened, Leo worried that Kate might not be so lucky the next time.

With Kate's problems still on his mind, Leo was getting ready to head out the door when he heard the phone ringing. He thought about letting the machine answer the call, but the winter months were usually slow and he needed the business, that's if it was someone calling about a job.

"Hello," Leo answered before the recording machine kicked on.

"Hello, Leo. It's Hank Diamond here. I've got in mind to do a little remodeling to my place and thought I'd give you a call. I was wondering if you had time to come over and take a look. Then we could talk about the job." They would talk alright, Hank thought, but not about remodeling.

Leo could hardly imagine that a man like Diamond wouldn't be capable of doing his own carpentry work. But he wasn't going to kick a gift horse in the mouth, not when he needed the job. "I suppose I could. When would it be convenient for you?"

"I'm not doing anything right now. That's if you have the time to spare?"

Second Chances

"Suits me just fine, Hank. I'll be right over."

Thirty minutes later, Leo's truck was pulling into Hank's driveway. He was surprised to see that Hank's home had been decorated outside for Christmas, but was more impressed with the layout of Hank's property, which was very nice.

Within seconds after Hank heard the door bell chimes, he was greeting Leo with a smile and firm handshake. "Hello, Leo. Come on in. I've just brewed a fresh pot of coffee. Can I pour you a cup?"

"I wouldn't turn it down. I take mine black," Leo said, still wondering why Hank had called him in the first place. After looking around inside Hank's home, it didn't take a mental giant to figure out there was no work to be done here. Not to mention the house was spotlessly clean. Hank obviously had a reason for calling him, so all he could do was listen to what Hank had to say.

Hank led his guest into the kitchen where Leo sat down on a stool at the snack bar. After setting a cup of coffee down in front of the carpenter, Hank asked, "Do you have much work lined up right now, Leo?"

"My line of work is generally pretty slow in the winter months. I'm idle right now. What did you have in mind?" Leo asked, knowing he'd put Hank on the spot to tell him about the job and what he wanted done.

Hank thought about Leo's question for a moment. There was no point in beating around the bush about the information he wanted out of the carpenter. It would be a waste of Leo's time, and for that matter, his too. "Look, Leo, I might as well be up front with you. I didn't call you to come out here and talk about a remodeling job. I'm satisfied with my home just the way it is. I called you for another reason."

Leo looked a bit confused. "Is that right?"

"Yes. I want to know what happened over at Kate's house last night."

It was all coming together for Leo now, as he recalled Hank's run-in with Charlie at the restaurant, and then he'd showed up unexpectedly at Kate's housewarming. He had an interest, so it came as no surprise that Hank would want to know what was going on with his beautiful neighbor.

163

"Want to try being a bit more specific about what it is you're referring to?" Leo came back at Hank.

"I'm referring to that broken window that you covered with plywood, Leo. That's what I want you to tell me about."

Leo nodded. "I see. Well then, why don't you just ask Kate about the window? Seems it would have been a whole lot easier than calling me to come here about a job you don't need."

"Kate's not talking. I asked about it this morning and got very little out of her."

"Did she tell you anything at all about the window?"

"Well, Leo, it's like this. She did offer up some kind of cock and bull story that I didn't much appreciate. I wouldn't want to think Kate would just out and out lie to me, but let's just say her story seemed a little far-fetched. So that's why I'm asking you," Hank told him.

Leo grinned. "I have to admit that Kate truly is one of a kind. Thing is, Hank, she made me give her my word that I wouldn't tell anyone about last night. And I made her a promise that I wouldn't. When I give someone my word, I usually tend to keep it. I'm kinda funny that way."

Hank smiled. "She sort of gave me the impression you wouldn't want to talk. She also told me what happened with Charlie DaRoux."

Leo looked puzzled again. "Then what's left to tell? Did she show you what Charlie did to her?"

"Yeah. I got to see Charlie's handiwork with a switchblade. It wasn't very pretty," Hank said before taking another sip of coffee.

Leo had it figured out that Hank was no dummy and knew the seriousness of Kate's situation. But breaking his promise to Kate didn't sit well with Leo, even though the idea of leveling with Hank might be best. "Look, Hank, we both know they don't come any crazier than Charlie DaRoux. But I don't think Kate has any idea about the extent of danger she's in with that son-of-a-bitch. I thought what happened at her place last night was bad enough, but I can see the potential for things to get a whole lot worse."

"That's my sentiment exactly, Leo."

"Kate was so shook up by the time I got to her place last night that what she said didn't make good sense to me either. But I'll be damned if by the next morning she didn't appear to be the least bit upset. And she was adamant about not telling anyone else what happened. She's convinced Charlie will leave her alone now."

"I doubt that, don't you?"

"You've got that right. But Kate's so damned hard headed, and she insisted on handling it her way. She knows that idiot isn't going to tell anyone what happened. And she trusts me to keep my mouth shut. I did mention your name to Kate last night, told her since you were the closest she might have called you to come over and help her."

That last remark got Hank's attention. "What did she say about that?"

"She said you'd tried to warn her about Charlie and thought it best not to get you involved. I have to admit, I am kind of curious as to how you got Kate to tell you what happened?"

Hank chuckled. "That was easy enough, Leo. I told Kate if she didn't tell me, then I'd have to beat the information out of you. I guess she believed me."

Leo laughed. He liked Hank's style. "It's nice to know she thinks enough of me to save my ass from a beating like that. But seriously, I have given a lot of thought to Kate's problem with Charlie. I don't think she'll change her mind. Kate is convinced she's safe because of that dog. And I don't mind telling you, some of her story about that dog confused the hell out of me."

"In what way?" Hank felt he was getting somewhere with Leo now.

Leo removed his baseball cap and scratched the top of his head. "Well, for one thing, she said the dog was caged up inside her Jeep. Did she tell you that too?"

"Yeah, she told me the same thing."

"Then she said that just as Charlie was about to do her some real harm, he was distracted by the Jeep's horn blowing. The next thing she knew, the dog was jumping through the window and attacking Charlie. You pretty much have it figured out what happened between Charlie and the dog. Kate did comment that it was still a mystery as to how the dog managed to

165

get out of the Jeep. I wondered about that myself. I assume somebody had to open the door for the dog. But how the dog got out of the Jeep didn't puzzle me as much as the dog did."

Hank gave him a funny look. "What about the dog?"

"I'm sure you know a little bit about thermo pane glass windows, don't you, Hank? Well, I installed some pretty damned expensive double-paned windows in that house for Kate. Let me assure you, it would take a hell of a blow for a dog to shatter one of those windows. Kate said it sounded like an explosion when that dog came through the window," Leo said, then stopped talking for a moment, as if to think about what he was going to say next. "I cleaned up the broken shards of glass that were scattered all over the carpet. After Kate settled down and went to get cleaned up, I looked that dog over real good. And I do mean real good. Now get this, there was not one single cut to be found on that dog. None. I don't know about you, but that just beats the hell out of me."

"That is strange, isn't it? Kate told me she saw the dog jump through the window and I didn't believe her. Apparently, that's the way it happened." Hank now believed Kate's story.

So did Leo. "I'm sure of it. And from what Kate said, that big dog must've worked old Charlie over pretty good. If I know that rotten bastard like I think I do, he'll want to even the score with Kate and her dog too. That was my main reason for insisting she tell the authorities about what happened, but Kate wouldn't have any part of it."

"Yeah, she won't do it. I'll just have to keep a closer eye on Kate. As for the dog, let's hope it can handle any further encounters it might have with Charlie."

"Let's hope. If I was a betting man, I'd place my money on the dog," Leo said and reached for his jacket. "I should get back to the house, Hank. I'll see you later. And thanks for the coffee."

After Leo had departed, Hank poured himself another cup of coffee and thought about Kate's carpenter. He liked the guy.

When Hank finally got around to opening the door, he was amused to see Kate was holding a bottle of wine. Snowflakes covered her hair and eyelashes. For a moment, all he could think about was how beautiful she looked.

21 | CHAPTER *TWENTY-ONE*

For some reason, a dark cloud continued to hang over Kate's head. Whether it was because of what had nearly happened with Charlie or just her mood in general, she didn't know. Had she actually been so afraid of dying that night? Or was that cloud because of the strong feelings she had for Hank. Whatever the reason, the cloud loomed, along with the dreaded anticipation of her parents' arrival.

She'd said nothing of the Charlie DaRoux incident to Gordon or Emily. Gordon would have insisted she press charges and poor Emily would have gone into a state of shock. There was no need for either to happen. Leo had quickly replaced the window, so other than the ugly looking knife wound on Kate's breast, there was no tell-tale evidence to remind her of the sordid ordeal.

Much to her surprise, Kate wasn't afraid of being alone. As long as Baron was nearby, she had the dog's protection and felt safe. She had, however, memorized Hank's phone number in case she ever needed his help.

Every night, her terrifying experience of Charlie's attack was relived over and over again in Kate's mind. The whole ordeal still remained a puzzle. But for Kate, the biggest mystery of all related to Baron. How did the dog manage to get out of the Jeep? It would have been impossible for the dog to open the vehicle's door. She kept remembering the sound of the horn blowing just before the dog came crashing through the window. She knew the horn might blow if the dog's body pressed against the steering

167

wheel, but she could still hear it blowing after Baron was inside the house.

There was only one answer that Kate could come up with and chose to accept, it was probably Dane. He knew the dog well enough to turn Baron loose. But what about the horn? That same person would have been responsible for honking the horn to get Charlie's attention. And that person had to know Charlie was inside the house, which confused Kate all the more. Could Dane have followed his father over to her place? None of it made sense to Kate.

With only three days left before her parents were due to arrive; Kate sought the calming effect that only her good friend, Needa, could provide. She walked over early one morning for a cup of Needa's herbal tea.

While Kate was brushing the snow off her boots, Needa opened the door and told Kate to quit being such a pain in the ass and get inside the house. As if Needa had been expecting company, there was an empty tea cup sitting in place on the table.

"I sort of hoped you'd drop by this morning," Needa said as she poured the tea.

"Were you expecting company?" Kate asked.

"No. No one other than you," Needa replied, setting a small honey dispenser down in front of Kate. "Sweeten your tea with the honey. It's good for you. Very healing."

"Very healing for what, Needa?" Kate asked.

Needa gave her a questioning look. "For a lot of things, Kate. If you'd like, I can print you out a list."

Kate poured the honey into the cup of hot tea and stirred it with a spoon. She realized after taking a drink just how good the tea did taste. "I'm sorry, Needa. My ignorance really does show at times, doesn't it?"

Sensing Kate's uneasiness, Needa avoided the question by taking the conversation elsewhere. "So, Katie, do you have all your shopping done? Are you ready for company?"

Kate was looking around the room at the beautiful handmade Christmas decorations Needa had on display. "I've done all the shopping that I intend to do. As for my parents, they will be here in three days so I may as well be ready. I hate to say this, but I'm really not in the mood for Christmas. Maybe it would help if I'd get a tree and decorate it tomorrow."

Needa knew something had happened to cause Kate's malcontent, just as she'd known that Kate's heart had been troubled since the first day they met. Over time, she'd hoped that Kate would finally want to talk about it. But Kate had failed to initiate that conversation and it was something Needa couldn't do. If Kate was troubled by a spirit, she was the one that had to deal with it. Only Kate could free that spirit.

"Kate, for many, the holidays can be the happiest time of the year, yet may be the saddest time for others. Regardless, life is only what anyone makes of it, or what they want it to be. No more and no less," Needa told her.

Kate thought about what Needa had said for a moment. The Indian woman's outlook on life was exactly as she had spoken. Not once had Kate ever heard Needa talk about anyone or anything in a negative way. It appeared as though Needa's life rotated completely around her son, and nothing else really mattered.

Unexpectedly, precious memories of Caleb filled Kate's mind, recalling her son's outgoing personality and bright smile, the twinkle in his eyes that had been so much like Mack's, so full of energy when he was alive. She thought about all those times when Caleb would tease her into a wrestling match, always careful not to get too rough with his mother. Those memories brought tears to Kate's eyes.

Kate's good-natured son had performed like a super-star in everything he attempted. Mack would glow with pride every time he bragged about Caleb's athletic ability. And Caleb had been blessed with such a brilliant mind, excelling academically as a straight-A student, which pleased Mack even more. She smiled to think about the fishing and hunting trips that Caleb and Mack had loved taking together.

Along with the memorable flashbacks, Kate realized how lucky she had been just to have known Caleb, how honored she should feel that she'd been chosen to give birth to such a fine young man.

All those thoughts of Caleb had given Kate a warm feeling. Then she turned to look at Raine and smiled. If Raine were her son, she would be as over-protective and caring as Needa was about the boy. Raine was beautiful, just as Caleb had been, only in a completely different way. As if aware of Kate's thoughts, Raine turned around and looked directly at her.

"Look at all those books you've written, Needa," Kate said, turning her attention to Needa's library, thinking she had Needa's way of life all figured out. "You don't just write about how you think life should be, do you? You actually live it that way. It's the way you are, isn't it?"

Now she's getting it, Needa thought and smiled. "I've been very fortunate, Kate. And I know there are some folks around here who think I'm weird, but those who really know me prefer to think I'm just different. I couldn't care less what they think. I'm nothing more than what I am, which I hope is a good person. I strive to be honest and fair and do the very best that I can. Do you know what Karma is, Kate?"

"I think so. Isn't Karma our deeds and actions in this life for which we'll be held accountable in the next?" Kate said.

"You've got the right idea. It's an interaction between the higher and lower planes, bringing a state of balance between the two that will gradually raise the soul. Karma binds the lower self to the higher through the union of will, and the moral choices we make in this life. The spiritual law of cause and effect in a soul is made to yield just and right results, so that perfect balance is maintained between the planes. The outcome is stored away in the soul's inner being. As long as we are alive, Karma is incurred. When we pass away, the fruits of the spirit, so to speak, are reaped by the ego on the higher plane," Needa explained.

Kate listened intently, but was beginning to feel a bit uncomfortable. She thought Needa was getting a little too deep and decided to lighten up the conversation. "Yeah, in other words, be good and you'll go to heaven. Be bad and you'll burn. It's kind of like that old saying of 'what goes around comes around' type of thing."

Needa smiled. "We are in agreement that your current deeds and actions will pre-destine your next life, Kate. However, I believe your previous lives have made this life in advance for you, and I'm not so sure we see eye to eye about that. I know the things you've suffered have not been good, but you must release past heartaches and cherish the memories," Needa said, trying to knock a hole in the wall Kate had built around her heart.

She was wasting her time. It couldn't be done.

"I don't intend to let my memories get away, Needa. I will never let that happen," Kate said and thought it was a good time to change the subject. "My parents will be arriving soon and there won't be a dull moment. I've promised not to divulge the identity of Meredith Fiera, but I would never forgive myself if my mother didn't get the opportunity to meet you. I have my own special blend of eggnog for the holidays. I'll expect you over to meet my parents and sample my famous holiday drink."

So much for getting into Kate's mind, Needa thought. It was obvious she wasn't going to learn anything about Kate's life today. That was regrettable because Needa could do nothing to help Kate with the torment and pain she constantly carried.

Needa had no way of knowing that in her efforts to penetrate Kate's wall, she'd gotten closer than anyone ever had before. Kate had moments when she wanted to unleash all those pent-up emotions and tell Needa everything. Then she would catch herself and raise the wall again, not to let anyone near. She lived with the fear that if she cared deeply about someone, then she would surely lose them. For Kate, it was the same as signing their death warrant.

As she got up to leave, Kate noticed that Raine was standing by the window and looking outside. She walked over to him. "Raine, I could really use a big hug to cheer me up and make my day. Want to give Kate a big hug?"

To her surprise, Raine turned slowly and wrapped his arms around Kate. The gentle hug lasted only for a second or two before Raine pulled away, turning to look out the window again. Of course, he said nothing.

"Dear God in Heaven!" Needa said in amazement, tears welling up in her eyes. "I have never seen my son respond to anyone that way."

Kate winked at her. "I think he likes me."

"No, Kate, I think he loves you," Needa said, reaching for a Kleenex to wipe her eyes.

Kate had gotten through to Raine as no other outsider had ever done before. There could be no better Christmas present

171

for Needa than the one she had just witnessed with her son and good friend.

Visiting with Needa usually left Kate with a warm feeling and a better outlook on life. While walking the back path home, she was actually thinking about getting ready for the holidays. And there was very little time to prepare for the arrival of her parents.

* * *

Kate looked around the great room, trying to decide where to place a Christmas tree. The room was entirely too spacious for a small tree. It just wouldn't look right. But a large tree would never fit in the rear of her Jeep. She needed a pickup truck. But what she could really use was someone with a strong arm who could manhandle a big tree and get it placed in a tree stand.

She was certain Leo wouldn't mind helping, but felt she shouldn't keep imposing on Leo. There was only one other alternative to her problem, Kate thought and picked up the phone to call Hank. After dialing his number, she counted three rings before she heard Hank's masculine voice.

"Diamond here," Hank answered.

"Corbin here," she said jokingly, amused at the way he chose to answer a phone. "And you're just the guy I'm looking for. I need your help."

She'd caught Hank by surprise. "Kate! Are you okay?"

She laughed. "Yes, Hank, I'm fine. But thanks for asking. Can't I call without you thinking I'm in dire need of assistance?"

"I don't know. You've never called me before so I can't answer that. What's on your mind, neighbor?"

"Well, I hate to admit it, but I am in dire need of your assistance."

Hank loved the idea of Kate needing his help. "Oh boy, I'll bet that was real tough for you to accept, wasn't it? So what can I do to help you?"

"Actually, it's your physical ability that I'm in urgent need of," she teased.

"Hmmm... is that so? It sounds utterly wonderful. Tell me more."

At least she had his undivided attention, or so Kate thought. "We'll need to use your pickup truck too."

"My pickup truck?" Hank said and chuckled. "Don't you think the weather is a little unfavorable for bedding down in the back of a pickup truck?"

"That's cute, Diamond. Real cute."

"I thought so. You aren't going to break my heart and tell me you had something else in mind for me and my truck?"

"Yeah, I am, like help me find a real Christmas tree, and then maybe getting it set up in a tree stand?" Kate's reply sounded more like a question. Wanting Kate to think he was mulling over her request, Hank let a few seconds pass before he said, "I can do that. How about if I pick you up around noon? Just to show you my heart's in the right place, I'll even buy your lunch."

"You're too sweet. But I have a better idea. I'll fix lunch while you put the tree in a tree -stand. It's the least I can do to repay you."

Hank was disappointed if that was Kate's idea of a bribe, but still game. "Well, Kate, if you really wanted to repay me, I can think of something besides lunch that might work better," he said and laughed. "However, lunch will do for a good start. I'll see you about noon."

*   *   *

What the hell have I gotten myself into? Hank thought as he stood in the middle of a tree farm, agonizing over Kate's choice of a Christmas tree. The damn tree was huge. If she wanted to test his physical ability, he would much rather prove himself in some other manly fashion, rather than manhandling a monstrous Christmas tree.

No matter, he thought, cutting a tree would allow enough time for getting to know Kate a little better, which had been Hank's plan all along. If he was going to woo her with his natural charm and wit, he would have to delay the process of putting the tree in a stand for as long as possible. After which, he would offer to help decorate the colossal spruce. Being a gracious host, Kate would have to offer him a drink, maybe even two. And naturally, she would want to join him to toast his valiant efforts of mastering the tree. Yeah, Hank had a major plan alright, of which the enormous tree was only a small part.

The tree branches were bound together with a heavy twine, which Hank didn't intend to cut until the tree was firmly secured in the stand. He was hoping like hell that once he cut the twine, the tree wouldn't be standing lopsided. There would be no fixing the problem if that happened. Kate's job called for a bit more of Hank's ingenuity than he'd first thought it would, and had definitely taken more time than he'd intended.

With a tantalizing aroma of beef roast wafting through the air, Hank couldn't keep his mind on the tree. He was anxious to sample a taste of Kate's cooking. Then, if everything went according to plan, he fully intended to sample a taste of Kate.

"How's it coming?" Kate asked, bringing Hank a fresh cup of coffee.

"It is. That aroma coming from your oven tells me you have something mouth-wateringly delicious fixed for lunch. I can hardly wait."

"It's nothing special, just open-faced beef with mashed potatoes and gravy. Is that okay with you?"

"Are you kidding? It's my favorite," he said, looking up at Kate from under the tree. "I'm curious. Did your mother teach you how to do that?"

"Do what?" she asked with a puzzled look. "Are you asking if my mother taught me how to cook?"

With a devilish look in his eyes, Hank grinned. "Well, it has been said that the best way for a woman to win a man's heart is through his stomach. I thought maybe your mother might have helped you learn about the ways of life."

"Think again, Diamond. If my mother wanted to capture a man's heart, cooking would be her last resort," she told him nonchalantly.

"Is that right? Then just how would your mother go about doing it?"

"She would use her body," Kate replied rather flippantly, then laughed as she set Hank's coffee down on an end table and returned to the kitchen.

If she thought Hank would give up that easily, especially after making such a remark, then she thought wrong. Hank was getting up off the floor to inspect his work, hoping the job was finished since the tree appeared to be standing straight. He picked up the cup of hot coffee and took a sip before he asked, "So, what made you decide on food?"

She avoided looking directly at him. "You have me figured all wrong, Diamond. I'm not after your heart. As far as I'm concerned, you can keep it. I'm fixing your lunch because you helped me with the Christmas tree. It's the least I could do."

Hank wasn't interested in the *least* she could do. He was thinking more along the lines of the *most* she could do. He set the coffee cup down and moved to stand behind Kate, slipping his arms around her waist as she was slicing the roast. It was a gamble, he knew, but lowered his head so his lips could roam softly over the side of Kate's neck.

"Food's a nice gesture, Kate," he all but whispered. "But you should know that I'm a man with a big appetite. Does dessert go with this meal?"

Kate wasn't prepared for dealing with the sensations that ran through her body. She closed her eyes, enjoying the feel of Hank's mouth against her skin. "Wha... what would you like for dessert?"

He turned Kate around to face him. "What I just tasted works fine for me," Hank said, then his lips were all over her again. "I want you, Kate."

"I know."

"The roast beef can wait. I prefer to have the dessert first," he said before his tongue delved into the warmth of Kate's mouth.

She responded, just as ready to touch and taste. Bringing her arms up around his neck, Kate let her body settle in close against Hank's. It felt good. Their need for each other had been suppressed long enough.

Then suddenly Mack was there, alive in Kate's thoughts and watching her. She moved out of Hank's arms and walked over to the kitchen sink, trying to regain control of her senses. "It sounds to me as if you'd like to have your cake and eat it too, Diamond."

She never ceased to surprise him, Hank thought, slightly shaking his head but determined not to give up so easily. He'd come too far to quit now. "Well, I can't say that I see anything wrong with that picture. I didn't realize you had a problem with it either, Kate. It sure didn't feel that way just a second ago, when I had you in my arms."

"Look, Hank, I'll have to admit that you really do radiate a lot of charm and sex appeal. And I'd bet you rarely find a woman that can resist you, or doesn't want to sleep with you. But if it's all the same to you, I'd prefer to not let sex get in the way of a good friendship," she came back at him.

This isn't happening, Hank thought. "Friendship! You've got to be kidding! Christ, Kate, if you're trying to sell me on the idea that friendship is what I just felt out of you, then you're barking up the wrong tree, Sweetheart. I know better."

"Don't be silly. You aren't a stupid man."

He moved to stand in front of Kate, reaching over to run a finger along her jaw line. "That's right, Lady, I'm not a stupid man. I know desire in a woman when I see it. And by the way, yours was showing through pretty nicely."

Kate jerked her face away from his touch. "I'm sure going to bed with you would be quite pleasurable, but that isn't going to happen between us, Hank. Besides, you wouldn't want me to get the impression that I'd be obligated to have sex with you every time I asked for your help. Would you?"

Hank couldn't believe what she'd just said to him. Kate's ridiculous remark had not only been an insult, Hank felt as though he'd just been kicked in the groin. After picking up the scissors that lay on the counter, he walked over to the Christmas tree and cut the twine, allowing the bound tree limbs to open. The tree was standing perfectly straight.

"You don't owe me anything, Kate," Hank said, laying the scissors down on the coffee table, and then picked up his jacket. "In fact, you don't even owe me a meal. I'm not a man that expects payment of any kind when I offer to help someone, especially if it's what I want to do. And even if I was, I'd never settle for just another piece of ass. It's pretty well known in these parts that when I make love to a woman, it's always by mutual agreement." He slipped on his jacket and headed toward the door.

"Hank, I..." Kate started to apologize, but the door was already shutting behind Hank. *Shit,* she thought. She had not intended for her words to come out sounding the way they had. In all probability, she'd not only injured his male ego, she'd hurt his feelings as well. It shouldn't have happened. All she was simply trying to do was let Hank know she wasn't interested in having sex with him.

Disappointed that Hank was gone, and disgusted over the way she'd treated him, Kate looked at the roast beef and then over at Baron. "Are you hungry, Bear? Looks like you're going to get Hank's share of this meal."

Kate spent the rest of the afternoon decorating the tree and wrapping Christmas presents. Knowing she'd lost control and let her emotions run amok with Hank, she felt terrible about what had happened. And to think, he'd worked so hard to put up the tree. Hank didn't deserve being treated so badly. In fact, it was totally uncalled for. With her mind made up that she owed the man an apology, Kate grabbed a chilled bottle of wine from the refrigerator and drove over to Hank's house.

Hank was sitting by the fireside reading a book when he heard the doorbell ringing. He grinned. After giving Kate enough time to realize what she'd done, and certain she would want to apologize, he had perfectly timed her arrival. Hank took his time about going to the door, intent on letting Kate stand outside in the cold for a few minutes. Two could play her little game and now it was his turn.

When Hank finally got around to opening the door, he was amused to see Kate was holding a bottle of wine. Snowflakes covered her hair and eyelashes. For a moment, all he could think about was how beautiful she looked. But damn her, the woman had bruised his male ego and that was something Hank couldn't tolerate.

"What's the matter, Kate? Did your Christmas tree fall over?" he asked, rather sharply.

"I deserved that one, Hank."

"I'm not real sure just what it is that you deserve. But whatever it is, apparently I'm not the man to give it to you," he said flatly.

"I'm really sorry for what I said to you this afternoon."

"You damned well should be."

"Can I come in?"

"Whatever for?"

"I brought a bottle of wine. I thought we could talk."

Hank reached out and took the bottle of wine from Kate's hand. "Thanks. I can use the wine, but I can do without the conversation. Good evening, Kate."

After shutting the door in Kate's face, he waited for a few moments, wondering whether she would leave or attempt to apologize again. Finally, Hank walked over to the window and saw Kate getting into the Jeep, watched as she drove away.

If getting even with Kate was supposed to make him feel good, it didn't. Only a dumb ass would shut the door in a beautiful woman's face. Well, at least now they were even. For whatever that was worth, Hank thought.

"Hank accepted the bottle of wine all right. He took it right out of my hand just before he slammed the door in my face. There was no time left to apologize," Kate said, looking quite forlorn.

22 | CHAPTER TWENTY-TWO

Kate readily admitted that she couldn't blame Hank for shutting the door in her face. She had hurt his feelings and deserved the way he'd reacted to her. She couldn't stop thinking about the situation she'd created between them. She didn't want or need to have this problem with her good-hearted neighbor, especially during the holidays.

One minute Kate had thoughts of going back over to Hank's place and adamantly insisting that he accept her apology, but the next minute she felt that Hank really didn't want to see her again. So she stayed away.

There were two days left before Kate's parents were due to arrive. She was well-prepared for their visit with time to spare. It was the situation with Hank that continued to haunt Kate, playing havoc with her mind. She simply had to talk to someone about what happened and Needa was more familiar with Hank's temperament than anyone else. Kate trekked over the snow-packed path to Needa's place, hoping to get a few words of wisdom from the wise one as to how the situation might be remedied.

When Kate and her dog entered Needa's house, Raine got up and hurried over to Baron, bending down to wrap his arms around the dog's neck. The dog never failed to excite the boy.

Needa was watching Raine as she commented. "My son and your dog have definitely bonded."

Kate was thinking the same thing. "Yeah. Maybe you should think about getting Raine a dog? He sure does love mine."

"Maybe, but I'll have to give it some more thought. He's never shown an interest in animals before now. In fact, Raine has never shown any kind of emotion. I'm still in shock over the way he hugged you the other day," Needa said.

"I thought it was sweet," Kate said and reached for a piece of Needa's Christmas candy.

"Yeah, me too. I have a cat but it isn't a pet."

"You have a cat?" Kate asked, quite surprised. "That's odd. I don't believe I've ever seen a cat around here."

"You probably won't either. It's from the *Felis Rufus* family. Are you familiar with the breed?"

Kate laughed. "I think not. Has it got any other name?"

Needa chuckled. "Yeah. It's a bobcat."

"I thought bobcats were wild."

"Yes, normally they are, but I raised this one from a kitten. She'll come to me, but so far I'm the only one that can get very close to her. I hope Baron doesn't meet up with my cat. Those cats can be pretty mean. I don't think the end result would be very pleasant." Just thinking about the dog and cat having a go at each other made Needa a little weak in the knees.

"Baron's not a stupid dog. I'm sure he won't bother with your cat if the cat doesn't mess with him," Kate said, sitting down at the table with a cup of coffee. "You wouldn't happen to have a bottle of Kahlúa, would you?"

Kate's request caused Needa to frown. "As a matter of fact, I do. But don't you think it's a little early in the day to start hitting the liqueur?"

Kate laughed. "I don't plan on drinking the whole bottle. I'd just like to have a shot of Kahlúa in my coffee."

Needa detected a different kind of upset in Kate this morning, which wasn't all that difficult to do. While pouring the liqueur into Kate's coffee, she asked, "Do you have your Christmas tree decorated?"

"Yeah, I do. You must bring Raine over to see it. That tree is absolutely beautiful."

"I'm sure it is. So then, you're ready for your parents visit. Is there anything else I can help you do?"

"No. But thanks for offering."

"Then may I ask what's troubling you?"

Kate was thinking that Needa was much too observant, but then again, Needa did have a sixth sense that never seemed to fail her. "Does it actually show that much? I was hoping it wouldn't."

Needa laughed softly. "Honey, those big browns do all your showing for you. The eyes are a dead give away. Is there anything I can do?"

Kate sighed. "I don't know, Needa. Can you fix it so I could take back some terrible words that shouldn't have been spoken? I didn't mean for what I said to sound the way it did. It just came out of my mouth the wrong way."

"I'm sorry, Kate, but that's something I can't fix for you. This must be something you said to Hank. Am I right?" Needa asked, but intuitively knew the answer.

"Yeah. I really didn't mean to hurt his feelings. I just... well, the words just came out wrong. Maybe I was saying what I was thinking instead of thinking about what I should have said. You know I would never deliberately hurt Hank's feelings. He'd worked so hard getting my tree in the stand for me. I'd even fixed him a good lunch for helping me, and well... things just sort of got out of hand."

"How did that happen?"

"He made a pass at me."

Needa rolled her eyes and grinned. "I should be so lucky. What did you do?"

"I told you. I hurt his feelings. That's what I did. I don't even want to repeat what I said to him. But after I said it, Hank just quietly picked up his jacket and left. Later that evening, I drove over to his place with a bottle of wine and tried to apologize," Kate went on to explain.

"The wine was a good gesture on your part. What happened after that?"

"Oh, Hank accepted the bottle of wine all right. He took it out right of my hand just before he slammed the door in my face. There was no time left to apologize," Kate said, looking quite forlorn. "Guess he's really good and pissed at me. Wouldn't you agree?"

Needa tried to muffle her laugh. "Hank does have a way about him, doesn't he?"

Kate didn't see humor in the situation. "I don't think it's very funny, Needa."

"Nor do I. And I definitely wouldn't want a guy like Hank pissed at me."

"Then why are you trying so hard not to laugh?"

"I can't help it, Kate. I can just picture Hank taking that bottle of wine out of your hand before he shut the door in your face. That man is a real class act, isn't he? Knowing Hank as I do, I'd say he was betting you would knock on the door again. He was just trying to make you suffer a little, that's all."

"Do you really think so? Should I try again?"

"Well, my fine friend, I'm not any *Dear Abby*. But I do know Hank and I'd say that was his plan. It just backfired on him a little. When he made the pass, did he kiss you?"

"Did he ever! I felt that kiss all the way down to my toes. You're right, he really is a class act," Kate agreed, remembering the tenderness of Hank's mouth.

Trying to understand Kate was sometimes difficult for Needa. It was obvious that Kate was physically turned on by the man, so why wouldn't she want to take the relationship any further. "Then what is your problem? The last I heard, kissing is still perfectly normal between a man and woman if they're attracted to each other. And Hank Diamond is definitely all man if he's anything. Most women jump at the chance to be with him."

Kate thought about the intimate moments she'd had with her manly neighbor. "You don't understand, Needa. If I give in to have sex with Hank, then there's a good chance I would want to do it again... and again. I can't afford to let that happen. Getting to know Hank physically might work, but only if we could keep the relationship on a sexual basis. I've told you before that I don't intend to fall in love again. Not now and not ever. I'm as aware as you are that a strong physical attraction can mess with a person's mind. There are times when you just can't keep deep emotion in one place and sexual desire in another... if you know what I mean. Those two feelings go together like butter and popcorn."

"That's right, gal. One compliments the other and makes it better," Needa said and laughed again.

"Why do you keep laughing at me?"

"Because, my silly friend, it's obvious that you're probably already in love with him."

Kate jumped up from the table, upset by Needa's insinuation. "Don't say that! Don't ever say that to me. I... I don't care anything at all about Hank... not that way."

"Kate! Calm down for Chrissake. It's not the end of the world, you know. Did you ever stop to think that maybe Hank might even feel the same way? Of course, that's if you'd let him."

Kate had no intention of calming down. She looked away in order to avoid Needa's questioning eyes. "I can't... I can't care for him like that. And I won't. I'll sell out and move back to the States before I'd let it happen."

This is serious, Needa thought. Whatever had a hold on Kate and was eating away at her heart had done a genuine job. "Kate, does this spirit you talk to have an influence on your relationship with Hank?" Needa asked, touching lightly on the subject and with reservation.

Kate looked over at Needa. "Is your Indian intuition kicking in again?"

"I've always known you speak with a spirit. I told you so before. If you want to talk about this, we can. If you don't, then we won't. But you could at least give me an answer to my question. Does this spirit have something to do with your feelings for Hank?" Needa dared to ask again.

Kate's eyes shifted to focus on the boy and her dog, lying together on the floor. Several moments passed before Kate finally said, "Yes."

"I don't know what's happened to cause you such a tremendous amount of heartache, Kate. But I do know you can't dwell on it for the rest of your natural life. If that's keeping you from a relationship with Hank, then you're making a big mistake by allowing it to happen," Needa told her.

Kate hadn't finished her coffee, but was finished with the conversation. Perhaps coming to see Needa hadn't been such a good idea after all. She stood up and reached for her coat. "I have to go, Needa."

"You didn't finish your coffee and Kahlúa."

"I know, but it's just as well. I shouldn't drink this early in the morning anyway," Kate said, bending to give Needa a quick hug. Then she walked over and bent down to kiss the top of Raine's head. When Kate headed for the door, Baron got up and lumbered along behind her.

* * *

To see Kate in this frame of mind was disturbing to Needa. Her friend was a miserable mess. The wall Kate had built around her heart was steep and thick and impenetrable. The way things were looking, maybe the mighty Hank Diamond wasn't going to get through that wall of Kate's either. Whatever was going on, Needa felt that Hank could shed more light on the subject. She picked up the phone and called him.

"Diamond here," Hank answered.

"Good morning, you handsome devil. Did I catch you naked and wet in the shower?"

Hank laughed. "You wish."

"Oh well, it was a nice thought while it lasted. I've got a full pot of fresh coffee if you're interested."

"In other words, Princess, I'm being invited over for you to pick my brain."

"That's why I like hanging around with you, Diamond, you're so damned smart. Make it fast too," Needa said and hung up the phone without bothering to say goodbye. She knew Hank would run the distance, which would make it plenty fast enough.

The cold Canadian wind was full of bite this morning. By the time Hank had reached Needa's place and knocked on the door, he was more than ready for a steaming cup of coffee. He tousled Raine's hair as he passed by the boy, then kissed Needa on the cheek before he sat down. Two empty cups were setting on the table, awaiting Hank's arrival.

"What's up, my pretty Indian Princess?" Hank asked.

"Tell me about Kate," Needa all but ordered as she poured coffee.

"Whoa, Needa! This old boy can't work the same kind of magic you do, Sweetheart," Hank said and chuckled. "Besides, I'd have to know something about that woman myself before I could tell you anything."

"She has a sharp way with words where you're concerned, doesn't she?"

"Honestly, I think that would be putting it rather mildly," he told her before taking a sip of coffee.

"Did she hurt your feelings or bruise your pride?"

"I'd say a little of both. Why do you ask? Did Kate tell you what happened?"

"She tried, but I'm afraid her effort was quite pathetic."

"Is that right? Well, after the damage was done, I guess she decided to come over to my place and offer an apology. I'm sure she was serious about wanting to apologize, but I didn't give her much of an opportunity to get the job done. I'll have to make amends for treating Kate the way I did. I don't want her to have any hang-ups about calling should she ever need me." Quite sure of himself and with a wicked grin, he winked at Needa before cockily saying, "And she will need me. I'm just letting Kate stew in her own juice for a while."

"Kate is a very troubled woman," Needa said and wanted Hank to get serious.

"You're telling me. Did you happen to notice she wears a wedding band?" He hadn't mentioned it before.

"Of course. So did you, I see."

"Yeah. But she's never said anything to me about being married. Funny thing, neither has Doc. Has she mentioned it to you?"

"No, but I haven't brought the subject up either."

"Doc told me she wasn't married, but getting anything else out of him about Kate has been like pulling teeth. Damn hard to do."

"I see. Well, I will tell you that Kate is burdened with a great deal of heartache. You should be careful with her, Hank. Handle her gently," Needa warned.

He gave Needa another devilish grin. "I'd planned on being very gentle. That's if she ever gives me the chance, and believe me... I've tried. As you know, Princess, I don't take rejection very well, so I won't try again. If any more passes are

185

made between Kate and me, she will have to make the first move. Should she come knocking on my door and in the mood for sex, you can count on her having to beg me for it."

Needa frowned. "I wouldn't hold my breath if I were you."

"Come on, Princess. She's a woman, isn't she?" Hank said and laughed. "In fact, the last time I looked, she appeared to be every inch a scrumptious woman. So if you want to wager a bet about this, be very careful. Sooner or later, Kate will come around to my way of thinking. And I can hardly wait until it happens. Now, as much as I hate to part with good company, I have chores waiting for me. I must get back."

Unfortunately, Hank's visit with Needa was as short in time as it was in information.

"I see you've brought me another bottle of wine. Do you want to come in and talk?" Hank invited, pushing the door open for Kate.

23 | CHAPTER *TWENTY-THREE*

No matter how hard Kate tried to keep her mind occupied with the upcoming holidays, or tried to concentrate on the book she was reading, there was no forgetting about the way she'd treated Hank. Her ungrateful actions were still seeping into Kate's every thought. To make matters even worse, she couldn't get past his masculinity, vividly remembering the day she'd looked down to see his manhood about to punch a hole in his sweatpants.

And his mouth. Oh God, when those lips of his moved lazily over the nape of her neck, it felt like a shock wave traveling through Kate's system. Every time she thought of those moments, a tingling sensation went straight to the core of her very being.

There was no point in trying to deny the way she felt. She had a bad case of the hots for Hank's body

But she'd heard too much and couldn't help but wonder how many notches Hank had carved on the headboard of his bed, adding to his score every time he put out another woman's fire. Well, she wasn't that sex-starved. Yeah, right, Kate thought, wondering what had brought her into that line of thinking.

As Kate casually sipped some wine during the next afternoon, she'd managed to empty a bottle of Chardonnay while reading the last of *Lucky's Lady*. With the bottle emptied and the book finished, Kate had fallen into an excited state of mating desire.

The wine had Kate's blood flowing warmly through her veins, convincing herself that she could do anything her mind was set on doing. Along with those thoughts came an enormous amount of confidence that was much needed to face Hank again. She felt compelled to make one more attempt to tell Hank she was sorry. Only this time, she would ensure that Hank would accept her apology... without fail.

Surrounded by scented candles, Kate sat in the bathtub filled with steaming hot water and bubble bath. During the leisurely process, she drank two more glasses of a freshly-opened bottle of wine. She'd shaved her legs until they were as smooth as silk. Thinking to add a few more finishing touches, she generously applied a fragrant body lotion. While the wine continued to send warmth through Kate's body, it was also adding to her resolve.

She had a plan. Hank may very well have been trained in dangerous military maneuvers, but she was fairly well trained in a few fancy maneuvers of her own. She grinned devilishly, prepared to bet she could easily wear down Hank's defenses. That's right, she thought, Mr. Diamond would have no other choice but to accept her apology... this time. Before embarking on her mission, the last thing Kate had to do was grab another chilled bottle of wine from the refrigerator. It would do wonders for the apology.

Hank was pouring cream into his coffee when he heard the doorbell. He glanced out the window and saw Kate's Jeep in the driveway. The doorbell started ringing again before he could get to the door.

"Okay, Okay! Hold your horses. I'm coming," Hank yelled, slightly amused by Kate's impatience.

When Hank opened the door, Kate stood before him with a smile on her face and holding another bottle of wine. She was wearing a full-length fur coat that hugged her ankles in a provocative swirl. He first noticed her hair, which was lifted off her neck with combs. Loose strands curled sensuously around her face and neck. Although Kate's over-all appearance was definitely different, there was an aura of loveliness and softness about her that reached out to Hank.

And back so soon, Hank thought. He looked at the bottle of wine Kate was holding, and wondered what she was up to this time, figured he was about to find out. "Hello, Kate. This is an unexpected surprise."

"Hello to you too, Hank," she said, giving him a slow and wicked grin. "Let's try this one more time, shall we? I came to apologize for what I said to you."

Hank's mouth took on a lopsided kind of grin. This was definitely going to be good. It had to be. Maybe this woman wasn't to the point of begging... yet, but she was damned close. Yeah, this really was going to be quite good.

"I see you've brought me another bottle of wine. Do you want to come in and talk?" Hank asked, fully opening the door for her to enter.

"Oh, I'm definitely coming in, Hank," Kate replied, walking past him. "But not to talk."

With a puzzled look, Hank stepped aside for Kate's entry. "Oh?"

"That's right. Under no circumstances will there be any talking. And by the way, I brought you a Christmas present," Kate said as she walked past Hank toward the kitchen, taking the chilled bottle of wine to the refrigerator.

He thought Kate's behavior was quite strange. She mentioned a Christmas present but he only saw the wine. "That's very thoughtful of you, Kate. I do enjoy a good bottle of wine."

"The wine isn't your Christmas present, you silly man. I fully intend to help you drink the wine tonight."

"Oh, I see. Well then, where's the present?" Hank asked.

She opened the refrigerator door, set the wine on a shelf, and then turned around to face Hank. Undoing the belt to her fur coat, Kate replied, "Right here."

Hank watched as Kate let the coat slowly slide off her shoulders and drop to the floor. Obviously still overdressed, she was now wearing only her snow boots.

Taking a deep breath, Hank looked as if he had just witnessed a space invasion. Kate found his expression to be quite humorous, along with the fact that he was utterly speechless. Thus far, her apology seemed to be going as planned and Kate was well pleased.

She slipped a snow boot off with the toe of her other boot and kicked it away from her body, and then rid herself of the other boot. Without saying a word or losing eye contact with Hank, she moved slowly toward him. Wearing only a smile, she put her arms around Hank's neck and looked up at him. She then nipped gently at Hank's lower lip, a little teasing before she got down to more serious business, which would be slow, invasive, and productive.

Very smoothly, Hank's tongue found its way into the warm wetness of Kate's mouth, exploring areas that tasted of pure sweetness.

As the kiss held, Kate unbuttoned his shirt and pushed the flannel fabric off Hank's shoulders, revealing a thick mass of soft, black body hair that covered his chest. Her lips raked over his neck, nipping and biting as she went further down. Then he felt Kate's warm breath on his chest as her lips settled sensuously over a nipple.

"God, Kate, I..." Hank started.

She quickly pulled away, looked directly at him, and moved her right index finger to the center of her lips. "Shhh! I said no talking, Diamond. And that's what I meant."

Her lips were on his mouth again to assure that Hank couldn't, and wouldn't, say anything else. In the heat of the moment, Kate's fingers worked diligently at shoving Hank's sweatpants down from his waist. She was pleasantly surprised to discover he wasn't wearing underwear.

She pulled back again, wanting to observe what she was determined to conquer. She wasn't disappointed. His long lean body was smooth and magnificent from hours of physical workouts... just as she'd imagined it would be.

Being well equipped with all that was necessary to do battle, Hank was more than ready to wage war. He picked Kate up and carried her over to the fireplace, gently putting her down on a soft bearskin rug. The fire's amber glow gave off just enough light for Hank to admire her gorgeous body. Built for a man's pleasure, Kate was even more beautiful than he'd imagined. And the Gods were with him, because at this very moment the woman was his for the taking.

The thought of Kate as a Christmas present put a smile on Hank's face. If she was indeed his new Christmas toy, then he was ready to see how well it worked. A mountain of sensations rushed over Hank while he inspected, caressed, and pleased Kate. Then he lifted her foot and his lips began to tenderly nibble away, slowly working their way to the point of destination. As his lips grazed over the inside of Kate's thighs, upward, ever upward, he heard her low, throaty moan. His muffled warning was barely audible through Hank's busy lips. "Shhhh. No talking, Corbin. Remember?"

And then Hank feasted on the most sensitive part of Kate's body.

The onslaught of sensations provided by her worthy opponent had sent Kate straight to the point of no return. She clutched the bearskin rug tightly, her body quivering as Hank brought her to a long over-due orgasm. He loved every second of his accomplishment, given what little ground he'd managed to cover so far.

Kate was spent. "Oh God, Hank, I..." then she felt Hank's finger touch her lips.

"Shhhh. No talking," he warned her again. Moving up the length of Kate's body, he gently spread her legs with a soft push of his knee. There would be no reprieve for this woman. If she was intent on playing war games with a covert specialist, then it was required that she be in excellent physical shape... for endurance. The onslaught of Hank's driving passion was not even close to being over. It had, in fact, only just begun.

Hank introduced his opponent to a torturous pleasure while he touched, teased, and nipped at Kate's skin, driving her into seventh heaven. And still it wasn't enough. He understood quite well what Kate wanted. She wanted all of him and she wanted it right now. With a forever prevailing male ego, Hank knew he'd easily won the first round of this battle.

"Beg me, Kate," he murmured in her ear. And then Hank waited, but heard nothing. "Beg me, Baby. It's not going to happen for you if you don't."

For Hank, it didn't matter whether it was gambling, guessing, or a game of love and war; it was still just a game. And the fact remained that he was only playing with Kate. He was betting she couldn't, and hoped like hell that she wouldn't, call his bluff. Knowing if she did, then he was going to be the real loser.

But Hank had played this game too many times before. Like an expert, he had perfectly gauged Kate's insatiable need for him. She was helplessly under Hank's control, a prisoner to his lovemaking. The one word that Hank had been waiting to hear was barely audible as it escaped Kate's lips.

"Please."

"I can't hear you, Baby." He'd heard all right, but his inflated ego needed to hear it again.

"Oh, God, please..." Kate moaned.

She gasped as Hank filled her with his rock hardness, burying himself inside Kate until he was completely surrounded in her warm wetness. His body moved slowly at first, pacing himself until Kate was ready again.

It was as if Kate had been given the reinforcement she needed to carry on. She'd met his rise to do battle, accepted his challenge, knowing full well that she was completely bound to this body duel that raged on between them. After all, wasn't it a battle that she had initiated? Determined, Kate was in for the duration even if it killed her, or killed him, and she didn't know which one might actually die first. She didn't really care as long as it didn't stop.

Hank's control was unbelievable. Skin on skin, beads of sweat rolled off their bodies as they meshed into each other, meeting thrust for thrust. He savagely pulled Kate over on top of him, their bodies constantly intact and moving as if engaged in a bitter battle. They pounded each other harder and harder, until at last they both reached that winning plateau of their own private little war... together. It was perfect. He'd watched as Kate's eyes turned opaque with pleasure and her movement slowed, giving in to the ecstasy. Exhausted, she slumped down on his chest, her hair spreading over his neck and shoulder.

"No, Baby, don't quit now," he said as he grabbed a fist full of her hair, pulling her head gently up for his mouth to cover hers again. A smoldering fire of passion still burned within him. Without losing body contact and very much still inside her, he rolled Kate over on her back with a driving need to conquer her once again.

Once more he raised Kate to new heights of passion, and when his body gave in to the physical need pounding in his loins, she gave in to her need at the same time. Arching to meet his final thrusts, she had drained every ounce of strength from Hank's body that could possibly be left for him to give.

When it was over, they were both wringing wet with perspiration. For a few brief moments, Hank was helpless to move his body away from hers. When he did find the strength to move again, he reached for a floor pillow, tucking it under his head to lie beside her. There would be no talking between them now as they lay next to each other. For words, they both knew, would have ruined the moment.

By now, the wine's warm effect had completely left Kate's system. A long hot shower was in order and definitely needed. Kate moved to get dressed, aware that a coat was the only clothing she'd worn to this memorable event, and the coat was lying on the floor in the kitchen.

"Where are you...?" Hank started, but stopped when Kate turned around, put her index finger to her lips and shook her head, which meant not to say anything.

A few minutes later, Kate returned to the family room. He watched as she stood perfectly balanced to pull on her boots. After what he'd just put her through, Hank was amazed to see that this woman could even stand up. When she reached the doorway to leave, Kate turned toward Hank and smiled, blowing him a kiss before she left.

But she never said goodbye. That's nice, he thought. She hadn't even bothered to say goodbye.

After taking a shower, Hank returned to the family room and sat down in front of the fireplace. Languorously thinking about Kate's performance, he drowsily remembered every sigh and nuance of his fearless opponent. She'd made love to him far beyond his wildest expectations, lasting longer than he thought was even humanly possible... for a woman.

How could she be so sweet and innocent looking, yet more provocative and sensuous than any woman he'd ever known. She was insatiable, he thought. The taste of Kate lingered on his lips and her sweet scent in his nostrils.

Hank grinned like a Cheshire cat, quite proud of himself. By making up his mind to wait her out, he had outsmarted Kate. He'd been determined to let Kate make the next move, no matter how long it took. And his plan had paid off quite well for him. After the evening they'd just shared, he was mighty glad she hadn't taken her sweet time about coming back to apologize. As for that Christmas present from Kate, well, it was about the best gift he had ever received.

Hank's grin broadened. *And she begged too.*

Hank turned to face Kate. "I don't care what kind of pet name you give me when we're in the heat of passion. Just don't call me some other guy's name. It deflates my ego, Baby. And just who the hell is this Mack anyway?"

24| CHAPTER *TWENTY-FOUR*

The beeping sound of Kate's alarm clock brought her out of a deep sleep the next morning. After that fantastic round of apology with Hank was over, she'd returned home, showered, and slept like a baby. It was the kind of deep sleep Kate hadn't been able to enjoy for what seemed a lifetime. With one eye still shut, she glanced at the clock and thought the time couldn't possibly be right. It was almost 8:00 A.M. She never slept this late, and hadn't for years.

Then the events of the previous evening spent with Hank came to mind. After exerting all that energy, no wonder she didn't want to get out of bed. She glanced down at Baron lying on the floor beside her bed, and the smile that was seemingly fixed on Kate's face all but disappeared. Mack immediately popped into her mind, bringing pangs of guilt.

Oh no, please don't let this happen to me right now. It was ridiculous. Mack was gone, no longer a part of her life. Hadn't she been trying to accept that fact; live with it as well? Kate kept telling herself that she had every right to spend an evening with Hank, so why the guilt trip now.

Slightly upset with her thoughts, Kate got out of bed to brew a pot of coffee. After being with Hank, she had finally gotten a good night's sleep and felt certain that things were right between them once again. Weren't those two excellent reasons for feeling good about the previous evening?

As the coffeemaker belched out the final gurgle, Kate returned to the kitchen and poured herself a cup. And wouldn't you know, she was grinning again. It was the thought of her return trip to Hank's place that Kate found to be so amusing, clad in only the long fur coat and snow boots. It was so unlike her to act that way. Even so, the evening had certainly been a wild one. Kate was reliving every minute of being in Hank's arms when she heard the doorbell.

The last person Kate expected to see was Hank when she opened the door. But there he stood in all his splendor with a silly grin on his face. He'd worried that Kate wouldn't accept his presence so soon after last night. After removing the dippy-looking hat he always wore, he greeted Kate. "Good morning."

Heat flushed through Kate's body at the very sight of him. "Hank!"

He looked around on the porch as if to ensure no one else was with him. "Yeah. It's just me."

"Yes. Well, I... I'm surprised to see you... ah... so early this morning." She was stammering, which Hank thought was cute and made him feel comfortable with her again.

"Your coffee sure smells inviting. May I come in?"

"Oh, so it's a hot cup of coffee you're looking for this morning." Kate said, stepping out of the doorway for Hank to enter.

"Nah, coffee isn't what I'm looking for at all," he answered as he stepped inside. Kate glanced up at him with a puzzled look, shutting the door behind him. "I'm here after my Christmas present. I guess you forgot to leave it with me last night."

Kate was confused. Knowing she'd left the wine, she wondered what Hank could be referring to. "I don't... ah... quite understand, I don't think."

Hank moved in closer to Kate, leaving only inches between their bodies. Raising his hand to her mouth, a fingertip traced over Kate's lips. "When you left last night, you took my Christmas present with you. So I thought I'd come over this morning and see if I couldn't talk you into giving it back. I really wasn't finished playing with it, you know."

Kate was flustered. "I took... oh my... I don't know... you want to..." she began, still trying to figure out what he meant. Then suddenly it dawned on Kate what he was talking about. After blushing to a bright red, Kate smiled. "Hank, how could I have possibly left it with you?"

His lips moved slowly over her jaw and down the side of her neck, driving Kate crazy with wanting him again. "Well now, it appears as if that does create a bit of a problem for us. Doesn't it?"

She wasn't thinking clearly. "A problem for... for us? I don't understand."

Hank's mouth covered hers again, lingered, then slowly pulled away to explain. "Okay, then let me put it this way. Last night you brought me a Christmas present. I watched you unwrap it before you gave it to me. Best present I ever received, I have to admit. But when you left, you took it with you. Now that just doesn't seem right to me. In fact, where I come from, that's called Indian-giving. I don't think you should have taken it away. But since it would be virtually impossible for you to leave without it, then it leaves me no choice but to come over here when I want..."

Kate grabbed the back of his head, pulled his mouth hungrily down to hers and murmured, "Shut up, Diamond. You talk too much."

He picked Kate up and headed toward the stairs to the loft, but stopped dead in his tracks when the dog stood up and growled. "Maybe you'd better call off the dog, Kate."

She looked over at Baron and commanded, "Stay, Baron."

The rest of the morning was a repeat performance between the two hungry lovers, which was played even more superbly than the night before, giving each other the same amount of sexual pleasure. They rolled in each other's arms, using each other unmercifully.

Kate's body soared to new heights of ecstasy. Lost in the moment, she held tightly to Hank as she climaxed and whispered, "Oh, Mack!"

Those two words had unknowingly slipped out of Kate's mouth. Hank slowed momentarily when he heard Kate call him 'Mack', but nothing could have stopped his driving need as he planted his seed deep within Kate's liquid warmth. Even though he'd continued making love to Kate, those two words were embedded in the back of Hank's mind.

Perfectly content with each other's performances after their exhausting physical romp was over, Kate rested her head on Hank's shoulder, her fingers playing with the hair on his chest. Hank pulled at strands of Kate's long, soft mane, thinking about the name she'd spoken in the midst of their lovemaking, his resentment beginning to take hold. By damn, if she hadn't actually called him by another man's name. If that wouldn't be a low blow to any man's ego, he didn't know what would. There was nothing else he could do but bring it out in the open, confront Kate about what she'd done.

"Kate."

"Hmmm... yes?"

"I'd really appreciate it if you didn't call me *Mack* when we're making love."

A chilling silence filled the air. Kate's body grew taut and stiffened next to his. She pulled away from Hank, throwing her legs over the side of the bed and sitting up. A few moments passed before she looked back at Hank. "What made you say that to me?"

Hank moved to sit up in the bed. "Look, Kate, I don't care what kind of pet name you give me when we're in the heat of passion. Just don't call me some other man's name. It deflates my ego, Babe. And just who the hell is this *Mack* anyway?"

Tears welled up in Kate's eyes as she reached for her wedding band, nervously twisting it around her finger. "I'm so sorry, Hank. I... I didn't realize that I'd called you..." she couldn't finish the sentence that would include Mack's name. Obviously upset, she reached down for her clothes on the floor.

Hank moved quickly and grabbed hold of Kate's arm, turning her around to face him. It was then he saw her tears. "Hey, what's this?" he asked, his finger wiping at the dampness on her face. "I didn't mean to upset you, Sweetheart. I'm the one who ought to be upset, not you," he tried to tease, but his effort was a lost cause. "Please don't cry, Kate. Honestly, I didn't... it's just that you..." he was at a loss for words, and the hurt in Kate's eyes made him feel like a first class heel. Then Hank finally had to ask. "Who is he?"

Kate shook her head. She didn't intend to tell him about Mack. She couldn't, because if she did, then she would have to tell him about Caleb too. "Please, Hank, I wish you would just go. Being with you like this was probably a mistake on my part and I'm sorry. I know that I encouraged what happened between us when I came over to your place last night and, I... I shouldn't have done that." She looked up at him as if her heart would break.

Second Chances

What's this? She was actually kicking him out. He hadn't done one goddamn thing to deserve it, but she was kicking *him* out. Hank felt the anger mounting but tried not to let it show, keeping a calm voice. "I hardly think what happened between us was a mistake, Kate. Nothing as good as the sex we had last night and this morning could be called a mistake. Did Mack give you that wedding band?" he asked, believing he had every right to know.

With tears brimming Kate's eyes, she looked down at her wedding ring. "Mack is not a subject that's open for discussion between us, Hank. I really do think you should go now and leave me alone."

He didn't understand and he probably never would, but he wasn't going to leave without an explanation. "Wait a minute, Kate. I'm not ready to..." he started to object, but was stopped when Kate pressed her finger against his lips.

"Please do as I ask, Hank. Just go now and leave me alone," Kate said and bit nervously at her lower lip.

"Okay, I'll go for now. But I'll be back later."

"No. I think it would be best if you didn't come back."

So, it was like that for her, was it? A couple of rolls in the sack and Kate was finished. She couldn't be serious, Hank thought, but maybe she was right. Perhaps he did need to go. He sure as hell wouldn't have a problem finding another woman. And it was for damn sure the next woman he made love to wouldn't mistake his identity. It wasn't a good idea to speak his piece right now, or say what he thought needed to be said to Kate. Not while he was so mad. He could end up regretting it later. Words spoken in anger usually came back to haunt a person.

Hank backed away from Kate and reached down for his clothes that were piled on the floor. He slipped into his sweat pants and pulled on the sweatshirt as he hurriedly descended the stairs. He never said another word to Kate before leaving.

When Kate heard the door slam shut and knew Hank was gone, she fell across the bed and cried her heart out. Of all the crazy things to have happen, why had she called him "Mack"? And to have done such a thing in the height of passion... well, it was just unbelievable. He wasn't Mack. He wasn't anything like Mack. And he never would be.

199

Kate raised her head when she felt the dog's tongue licking her hand. She looked down at Baron through tear-blurred eyes. "Oh my, Baron, what have I done?"

It was noon before Kate could pull herself together enough to think about the arrival of her parents the next day. If she was going to get through the holidays, especially with her family here, then she had to keep her wits about her. This meant she had to try and think about what she was doing. She had to forget about Hank.

Getting involved again physically, or emotionally, had never been Kate's intention. Why had she so foolishly allowed that to happen with Hank? It was a dumb and foolish mistake. Dumb. *Get over it, Corbin,* she told herself. And yes, she was sure she could do that, too.

* * *

Making her usual batch of Christmas candy required concentration. If nothing else, it would take Kate's mind off everything else that seemed to be going wrong. She was checking the boiling sugar water with a candy thermometer when Mack appeared.

"White Divinity. That was always my favorite," he said, leaning against the counter.

"I was just wondering about you, Mack."

"Were you really? I guess that sort of surprises me since, well... since you've been so pre-occupied with your neighbor lately," he said with a sheepish grin.

"Don't, Mack. Don't you dare go there."

"Oh, come on now, Kate. There's no harm in expressing your warmest holiday wishes to a handsome neighbor," Mack teased.

"Warmest wishes?" she asked, miffed at his tasteless attempt to joke. "Is that what we're calling it now, Mack?"

"Wouldn't you agree that's an expression for spreading a little Christmas affection, and along with a nice bottle of wine, no less?" He watched Kate pull the pan of boiling sugar water from the burner, then reach to turn off the stove. "That sugar water won't be fit to use for candy if you don't finish it."

"I am finished with it." Mack was pushing her to the limit, or so Kate thought. "Why don't you just spit it out, Mack? Say what it is you came to say and get it over with."

"Oh my, aren't we touchy. What's wrong, Sweetheart? Is your love life getting you down?"

Lord, but he knew how to try her patience. "I believe we've been through this before. My love life is none of your business. So what is it you want from me?"

"I want you to have a happy holiday."

"Yeah. Right. Haha, Mack. Very funny."

"I'm serious, Kate"

"I doubt it."

"I'm in no position not to be. Think about it."

Kate took a deep breath and poured herself a cup of black coffee. Then she reached for the bottle of Kahlúa that was sitting on the counter. After pouring a shot glass full of the liqueur into the coffee, she looked over at him again. "No, Mack. You aren't here to wish me a happy holiday. I know better, but thanks just the same."

It was time for Mack to get serious. "Don't turn away from him, Kate. He needs you more than you think."

Now Mack really had her attention. "Come on, Mack, give me a break. You don't expect me to believe this visit is about my ultra-masculine neighbor, do you?" She gave a little laugh.

"No, it's not entirely about him. But yes, he is a large part of why I'm here. This morning when you looked at Baron, you thought of me. Don't do that, Kate. Never think that you're being unfaithful to me, because you aren't. Take the wedding band off your finger and start over. You still have the rest of your life to live. Let it happen. Let it happen with him."

Tears filled Kate's eyes. "NO. You don't understand, Mack. I can't bear the thought of loving anyone but you. Besides, I can't afford to love anybody else and risk the pain of losing again, not like I lost you. Hank was doing just fine before I came along. I'm sure he'll continue to do just fine without me in his life. I know he'll probably stay healthier and live a lot longer. What

201

happened with my neighbor was purely physical, Mack. Nothing more and nothing less and I won't let it happen again. I can't."

"Why not, Kate? Is it because each time it happens you might find yourself falling a little deeper in love with him?"

"I am *NOT* in love with him, so stop saying that. And furthermore, I never will be. I can't do this, so please don't hound me about it. For God's sake, Mack, I'm doing the best I can. I'm only human. If I can't touch you or feel you as I did when you were with me, then please..." she hesitated as the tears spilled from her eyes. "Oh God, Mack, don't you know what your coming here like this does to me?"

"Yeah, I know. I just wish you'd listen to me. But now is not a good time to discuss this any further, so we won't. Anyway, I guess Sam and Laura are on their way here for Christmas?" Mack asked, changing the subject.

"Yeah. They're due here tomorrow. We'll be having margaritas and marijuana. I can hardly wait," Kate replied with a small degree of ambivalence.

"Okay, Kate. I think it's time for me to go. That's the one subject I don't think we should be discussing right now. Not on top of everything else."

"You know, Mack, for once I'm in total agreement with you." By the time she'd reached for her coffee cup and turned back around to say something else, Mack was gone.

Unexpectedly, Laura looked over at Needa and asked, "I've been wondering, Needa, do you smoke a peace pipe?"

25 | CHAPTER *TWENTY-FIVE*

"Oh my, Sam! Just look at this place. It's so quaint." Laura Lingle beamed as she viewed the lovely winter setting around Kate's home from the back seat of Gordon's SUV.

"Yeah. This place is just alright. Didn't you say something about selling Kate this property, Gordo?" Sam asked, poking his son-in-law's shoulder from the rear of the vehicle.

It irritated the hell out of Gordon every time Sam poked him on the shoulder to get Gordon's attention. Frowning, he shot Emily a look. She must have told Sam about the real estate transaction with Kate. He looked up into the rear view mirror at Sam. "No, Sam, I didn't sell Kate the property. I gave it to her."

"I see. Well, Gordo, I have to say that was right nice of you."

Gordon cringed. Not only did he hate being poked on the shoulder, he detested Sam calling him 'Gordo'. He knew Sam purposely did it just to piss off his son-in-law.

"Tell me, Emily, how's our Katy doing? Is she getting back to normal?" Laura asked.

Emily glanced at Gordon again and noticed the smug look on his face. Being back to normal for Laura was the same as asking if Kate was over being crazy, which grated on Emily's nerves. Emily's voice was full of resentment when she answered her mother. "You mean since she was released from the mental institution, Mother? Isn't that what you're referring to?"

"You don't have to take that tone with your mother, Emily. She just wants to know if Kate's getting back to normal again. We both do," Sam said, immediately coming to his wife's

203

defense... as usual. Emily had always been quick about jumping to conclusions, as Sam well knew his daughter could do.

Emily sighed. "I'm sorry, Dad. I didn't realize my voice had a *tone*. But to answer Mother's question, I don't think Kate will ever get over losing Mack and Caleb. If Mother is talking about 'normal' as in getting back to her old self, then I do think Kate's much better. Physically, she looks wonderful. Kate was terribly thin when she first arrived, but she's gained a few pounds since then. She loves living in Canada," Emily said, hoping the information would be enough to stop any further questions about Kate's health.

When Gordon's vehicle pulled up in front of Kate's house, Baron's barking had Kate heading for the front door. She watched as her family got out of the vehicle and walked toward the house, carrying their luggage. She grinned, knowing that by now Gordon was probably more than ready to be rid of his in-laws. As it was, and the truth be known, Gordon almost felt guilty about dumping Sam and Laura off on Kate. *Better she than me though*, Gordon thought as Kate stepped onto the porch.

"Katy, darling, it's so good to see you again. And don't you look just fantastic," Laura said, hugging her oldest daughter.

"Thank you, Mother. You're looking fit yourself," Kate said, leaving Laura's embrace to exchange hugs with Sam. "It's good to see you again, Dad. The new haircut becomes you." She complimented Sam's neatly groomed gray hair before kissing him on the cheek, wondering at what point in time Sam had decided to part with his long ponytail. Perhaps age was changing her parents after all, she thought. "Come in and we'll have something hot to drink. The Canadian air can be brutal this time of year."

Thirty minutes later, Emily watched her husband's fidgeting, a true sign that Gordon had reached his limit for being around her parents in one afternoon. It was time to go home.

Kate took a while to show her parents around the house, telling them what all had been done during the renovation. After dinner, they sat in front of the fireplace, reminiscing over times now past. The conversation with Sam was enjoyable, which had Kate believing her parents were no longer so self-centered, and perhaps they were living a different lifestyle... finally. At least they hadn't pulled out any marijuana joints, wanting to get high on the wacky weed. And that was a plus in their favor. The Lingles' holiday visit seemed to be starting out on a pleasant note, for which Kate was truly thankful.

* * *

Early the next morning, Needa decided it was time to visit Kate and meet her parents. She'd even baked a loaf of date-nut bread for the occasion. When Laura discovered that Needa was another Meredith Fiera fan, a large part of the morning was spent drinking coffee and discussing the author's work. Kate wondered what Laura would think if she knew she'd actually been conversing with the famous author in person. But that was Kate's and Needa's little secret, and Kate had no intention of telling it to anyone, not even her parents. She'd been anxious for Sam and Laura to meet Needa, simply because her parents were both highly educated, certain that Needa would appreciate their point of view about the books Fiera had written.

Kate thought too, that it would be amusing for Needa to hear her mother's philosophical interpretations of Fiera's writing. Better yet, she could hardly wait to see the look on Needa's face after getting a load of Sam's outlook on life. Oddly enough, Sam was on his best behavior and Laura was enchanted with Needa, mostly because of Needa's ethnicity.

Sam grabbed the last few logs from the wood box and placed them on the fire, then reached for his jacket. "Show me where to find the woodpile, Kate, and I'll fill the wood box up for you."

"Let me get my coat and I'll help you with that, Dad. There's a small cart beside the shed that I use for hauling wood."

Laura waited until she was certain they were alone before she turned to Needa and smiled. "Kate looks so good, don't you think? Bless her heart. And after all she's been through too. Sam and I were so worried that she'd never be the same. We haven't seen our Katy since she was released from the mental institution. In fact, the last time I saw Katy was at Mack's funeral, and the poor girl didn't even recognize me."

Needa gave Kate's mother a strange look. "I wasn't aware that Kate had been in such a place."

Laura looked equally surprised. "Oh, my! Do you mean to say she didn't tell you?"

For some strange reason, Needa didn't want to hear anything more from Laura about Kate, even though it appeared as if she didn't have a choice in the matter. "No. I'm afraid not. Kate has never offered to discuss anything about her life before coming to Canada."

"That's strange. I wonder why she wouldn't want to tell you. I mean, well, you both seem like such good friends."

"We are good friends, Laura. Perhaps that's the reason I don't pry into Kate's personal and private life. And she graciously returns the favor. I'm sure Kate would have told me if she'd wanted me to know," Needa said, hoping to discourage Laura from saying anything else.

It didn't work.

"Well, that's all in the past now and Emily says Kate is doing just fine. Poor baby. I honestly don't know how she got through any of it. Everything happened so fast and, oh gosh, it was all so dreadful. I probably would have lost my mind too. Can you imagine how awful it would be to lose your son and husband just three months apart? And both accidents happened so tragically. My Katy went from being the happiest woman in the world right straight into the depths of hell. Sam and I were so far away when it happened, but we flew back as soon as we heard. I told Sam that our Katy didn't even realize we were there with her. If Mack's parents hadn't been close enough to see about her, I don't know what we would have done. But anyway, I'm just so thankful she's on the mend. Why, just to look at her now, one would never guess that she'd suffered a complete nervous breakdown. Would they?"

"No. They wouldn't." Needa took a deep breath and more out of curiosity than being meddlesome, she asked, "How old was Kate's son when she lost him?"

"Oh, let me think now, Caleb was sixteen at the time and that's been over a year ago. So he'd be seventeen, going on eighteen before too long. He was such a handsome boy, so much like his father, Mack. I still can't believe Kate's never told you a thing about either one of them." The very idea had totally baffled Laura.

"No, she's never mentioned them at all." So, Kate's son would have been close to Raine's age, Needa thought. There had been good cause for the sad and empty expression in Kate's eyes when they'd first met. It was clear to Needa now that Mack had to be Kate's visiting spirit.

"Well, considering that Kate has never told you, perhaps it would be best if you don't say anything to her that I mentioned Mack or Caleb. I don't understand why she can't talk about them, but I have noticed since I've been here that she doesn't have any pictures of them sitting around. I guess Kate has her reasons. Maybe she just can't handle seeing their faces on a daily basis. Who knows?" Laura concluded.

"Don't worry. I won't say anything to Kate about what you've told me."

Their conversation ended abruptly when the door opened for Kate and Sam to bring in the firewood. After the wood box was stacked full again, they settled down for another cup of coffee.

Unexpectedly, Laura looked over at Needa and asked, "I've been wondering, Needa, do you smoke a peace pipe?"

With a look of utter disbelief and embarrassment, Kate's face flushed to a bright shade of red. Never in her wildest imagination did she think her mother would dare ask Needa such a question. Kate was speechless.

Needa was amused when Kate loudly began clearing her throat to get Laura's attention, especially since it didn't work. Being the woman she was, Needa handled the question quite well. "No, actually, I don't. But I do smoke *Players* cigarettes. Kate fusses with me about that when I'm here, because she doesn't like to smell the smoke. So out of respect for Kate, I refrain from smoking when I'm in her home. However, I do give it hell when she comes to visit me," Needa said and laughed softly.

Laura's actions were simply too much for Kate to handle. She had to speak up, make Laura aware of her disapproval before it got completely out of hand. "Christ, Mother! I can't believe what you just asked Needa."

Sam had long ago learned to recognize that *tone* of voice coming from his daughters. He immediately came to his wife's defense, exactly as Kate had anticipated he would. "Now, Katy,

207

I'm sure Laura didn't mean anything by asking Needa if she smoked a peace pipe."

Did nothing ever change where Sam and Laura were concerned, Kate thought. "Please, Dad! I know exactly what Mother meant. So does Needa. But if Mother doesn't realize what she just insinuated, it really doesn't matter. She should apologize to Needa, and if she won't, then I'll have to do it for her," Kate said, fuming mad at both of them.

Considering everything else that was going wrong in Kate's life, the last thing she needed before Christmas was a family disagreement. Needa knew as much and tried to smooth things over. "Kate, there's no need for an apology. I'm sure your mother was just curious about my ethnicity."

Kate shot her good friend a look. "I only wish your ethnicity had been my mother's only reason for asking the question, Needa. Unfortunately, I happen to know better."

Before the conversation could progress any further, and as if it had been perfectly timed to diffuse a bad situation, Kate's telephone began to ring. Her voice was strained when she picked up the receiver and said, "Hello."

"Kate? Is that you?" Leo asked on the other end of the line, wondering if he had the right number. "I've been trying to get in touch with Needa but she doesn't answer her phone. I thought she might be visiting you."

"You thought right, Leo. Would you like to speak with her?"

"Yeah, I would, if you don't mind. I've barbequed a batch of ribs. I wanted to make sure she'd be at home before I headed over that way."

After the conversation with Leo was finished, Needa hung up the phone and turned to Sam and Laura. She graciously told them how pleased she was to have made their acquaintance, then apologized for having to return home and wait for Leo's arrival.

"I'll take you back," Kate told her.

"That won't be necessary. Raine and I can walk the back path."

"No, I insist. Let me take you. I need a breath of fresh air."

When they were settled inside the Jeep, Kate turned to face Needa. "I really am sorry, Needa. I guess it was too much to hope that my parents wouldn't disappoint me this time."

Needa smiled at her. "You are much too hard on yourself, Kate. I wasn't offended by what your mother said to me."

"Well, that's good to know, but I was offended by it. She figured if you smoked a peace pipe, then it stands to reason you'd surely have a supply of what Indians usually smoke in a pipe. I wanted to dig a hole and crawl in it," Kate said, reaching for the ignition.

"It's Christmas, Kate. Don't let them upset you. You've known for many years what your parents are like. Is that not true?" Needa asked, hoping Kate would let it go.

"Yes, I've always known. And the way they are is okay with me, so long as they keep it just around me. But when they start acting as they do around my friends, then I'm allowed to take offense. And I do. Jeez, by the time this holiday season is over and my parents are gone, I'll probably be ready for the nut house again." Kate spoke the words without thinking.

And Needa chose to ignore Kate's remark. "I'm having a small holiday get-together next week over at my place. Nothing special. Just finger foods and a few drinks. I'll call you later with the time. Please bring your parents and come over. I'll give your mother an autographed copy of my new book. I'd like her to have it as a Christmas present."

"But Needa, my parents will know you're the real Meredith Fiera if I bring them over to your house. I thought you didn't want that to happen," Kate said.

"Don't worry, I will keep my books well hidden during the party." Needa reached over to pat Kate's hand. "The holidays will be over before you know it, Kate. And then your parents will be returning to California. Try to enjoy them while they're here."

For Kate, that would be easier said than done.

Driving home alone gave Kate a chance to think about what she was going to say to Laura and Sam about the peace pipe incident. She had grown up accepting their hippie ways, which included their pot-smoking habits. But now they were guests in her home and it was no longer acceptable.

Then she smiled and thought about Mack. When they were first married, he hadn't objected to her parents' pot smoking when they came to visit. But after Caleb was born, he'd made it perfectly clear to Sam that they weren't to smoke marijuana around Caleb. Because Sam and Laura highly respected Mack, they had honored his request. Didn't she deserve that same respect? Kate guessed not, because they obviously felt comfortable smoking pot around her again. And that irritated the hell out of Kate. Just because Mack was gone, her parents shouldn't assume they could just do as they pleased while visiting her home, or treat her friends any way they chose. Thank God, Needa hadn't taken offense at Laura's remark about the peace pipe. Even so, Kate would ensure nothing like that ever happened again.

It was tough having to deal with the holidays and her parents at the same time. But on top of everything else, Kate couldn't stop thinking about Hank. How could she forget the way he'd touched her and made her feel? It would be next to impossible.

"Being mad at your parents is a hell of a way to start the holiday, Kate," Mack said, breaking Kate's chain of thought as he rode along beside her in the Jeep.

Kate knew he would show up sooner or later. She took a deep breath. "I know, Mack. They are my parents and I love them. But they do try me to the limit at times."

"Yeah, I know they do. But they both mean well, Kate. It's just that they've lived in their own little world for so long that they tend to forget about everyone else's. Let it go, Honey. Don't spoil your holidays over something that really isn't that important. Needa wasn't upset by Laura's remark." Mack offered, basically telling her the same thing Needa had said.

"Yeah. You're probably right. The holidays will be over soon and they'll be flying back to California. No need for everyone to get upset, especially this close to Christmas. Besides, I'm not up to butting heads with Dad. He always sides with Mom anyway. And if he thought I didn't want them smoking their dope while they were here, then he'd be just as apt to turn around and tell Mom they're flying back to California tomorrow. It would upset my mother terribly if she didn't get to spend Christmas with Emily and me. I guess I'll just have to forget about it."

They drove along in silence until they reached Kate's private lane. That's when Mack told her to pull over. "Let's talk," he said.

After she'd turned into the lane, Kate pulled the Jeep up a little further off the road, stopped and shifted the gear into park. Teasingly, she asked, "Do you want to neck?"

"Nah. I'd think you would've forgotten all about necking with me after being with..." Mack started, but Kate didn't let him finish.

"Don't, Mack! Don't go there."

"Oh? You don't want to talk about it."

"I don't intend to talk about it. I've told you that before. I wish it hadn't happened. And I'll make sure that it doesn't happen again. I... I actually called him Mack while we were... uh... I mean when we... well you know."

"Yeah, I know. I'll have to admit that was a rather dumb mistake on your part. But the thing is, Kate, he would have understood if you'd only tried explaining it to the guy. The man has a lot more going for him than just his body. He's human and he has feelings just like you do. He's got a good mind too."

"You're right. I'm sure he does have feelings. Just as I'm sure he didn't take kindly to being called *Mack*. I can understand that too. Can't you? Hank deserves better than what I have to offer or that I can give him. He really is a nice guy. I hope to keep him as a friend, but I don't know if that's going to be possible now."

"Yeah. I guess it would make a big difference after that kind of intimacy. I doubt I could have remained just your friend after we'd made love. We'll talk about this later, Kate. But there is one more thing I want to tell you."

"Oh, yeah? What's that?"

"Your friend, Needa, she's a very special person. She'll be your friend for life and you can trust her with anything you want to tell her. She won't reveal any family secrets."

"Oh, I'm sure you're right about that, Mack. And I do have a great respect for Needa," Kate said and turned to look at Mack, but he was gone. Shrugging her shoulders, Kate shifted the Jeep into drive and drove on up the lane. At least she wasn't mad

211

any more. And that made coping with her problems a whole lot easier.

"Kate didn't refuse my manliness, but she sure as hell knows how to deflate a man's ego." Hank hated like hell to admit it, but there was no fooling the Indian.

26 | CHAPTER *TWENTY-SIX*

Damn that woman! Hank's axe came down hard splitting another log. Nothing, absolutely nothing, had helped to ease his state of mind. Damn! Damn! Damn! He brought the axe down again, putting everything he had into it, trying to work off some of his anger. Just because Kate was drop-dead gorgeous and had the body of a goddess, it didn't give her the right to play games with a man's emotions any time she took a notion. Well, by God, she wouldn't be playing games with him again. He wouldn't let that happen.

Nope. Hell could freeze over before he would make love to that woman again, even if she begged him. Then Hank grinned, remembering that she had begged him. The memory of Kate saying "Please" did help to ease his wounded pride... a little. But even so, he still wasn't going to get involved with Kate again. He would rather face a gorilla in hand-to-hand combat than tangle with the likes of Kate Corbin. At least you knew what to expect from an ape. With Kate, you didn't know diddly-squat about anything.

Hank was so wrapped up in his thoughts about Kate that he hadn't noticed Dane climbing up on the pile of logs. There was a first time for everything, he thought, after Dane got his attention.

"Hi, Hank," Dane said, watching another log being split down the middle.

"Hey, Pup, what's happening?" Hank asked and looked over at the boy. He noticed the worried look on Dane's young face. Hank was concerned. "Hey, Kid, why are you wearing such a long face? It's almost Christmas."

Dane swept away the snow on top of a log that was beside him, but didn't bother giving Hank an answer. When Dane was quiet that way, Hank figured his little buddy wasn't ready to talk. Hank was smart enough to let it go. He figured the boy was in deep thought, maybe plotting his next move to make another fast dollar off an easy touch. It was a hell of a deal when a little kid got the best of a grown man.

Finally, Dane looked over at Hank and asked, "Hank, do you think Kate's dog would attack a man for no reason?"

Hank put the axe head down on the ground and leaned on the handle. "No, Pup, I don't think Kate's dog would attack a man for no reason. But if a man got that dog riled up, I'm sure it could do some real damage. Why do you ask?"

Dane was troubled, not quite sure if he should even be talking with Hank about his problem. But he was concerned about Kate's dog and had said enough to get the conversation going. The boy just couldn't imagine a gentle dog like Baron attacking anyone. "My Pa claims her dog attacked him when he pulled up into Kate's lane and got out of his truck."

"What was he doing in Kate's lane?"

"Pa said his truck broke down."

"You don't say. I wonder what provoked the dog that made it want to attack your Pa," Hank said, pressing Dane to tell him more.

"I don't know. Pa just said when he got out of the truck to check under the hood, the dog came out of nowhere and attacked him for no reason at all. Pa's arm got chewed up pretty good, Hank. He's real mad about Kate's dog too," Dane said. He felt better about letting Hank know what was on his mind.

Hank thought about what Dane had said for a few moments. "I see. Did your Dad tell you about the dog, Pup?"

"Nah. I overheard Pa and Derek talking about it in the shed. I think Pa plans to get even with Kate's dog. If that's so, I wouldn't give a plugged nickel for that dog's life. Would you?"

Hank couldn't let the boy know that he was aware of what had happened between Charlie and Kate's dog. For the lowlife that he knew Charlie to be, the man was still Dane's old man. Hank had no intention of belittling Dane's father in the boy's presence. "I think Kate cares a great deal for her dog, Pup. If your dad is smart, he'll leave well enough alone where that dog's concerned. I've split all the logs I'm going to for one evening. Want to come inside and have a cup of hot chocolate with me?" Hank invited, hoping to divert the boy's conversation toward something a bit more cheerful.

Dane jumped down off the logs. "I guess so. Have you got any marshmallows?"

"As a matter of fact, I think I do."

After Dane's visit was over and Hank was alone again, he decided it was time to pay Needa a visit. It wasn't so much that he needed the company; he was just in a lousy mood. For some reason, he couldn't get past the way Kate had treated him, but even that hadn't stopped Hank's incessant need for the woman's body. When all else failed, the attractive Indian woman's presence always came through to make Hank feel better. Then too, he figured Dane would be stopping by Needa's to talk about Kate's dog. If that happened, Needa would need to know the whole story beforehand.

As expected, Leo's truck was parked in front of Needa's house. Hank didn't want Leo to get the wrong impression about his friendship with Needa, so he knocked on the door instead of just walking inside as he usually did.

"Hank! What on earth are you doing standing out there in the cold?" Needa scolded after she'd opened the door. "Come inside, you ninny."

Hank stepped inside and greeted Leo. "Hello, Leo." Leo stood up to shake hands. Then Hank threw his head back and sniffed the air. "My compliments to the chef for whatever it is that's cooking in the oven. It sure smells delicious."

"I just warmed up some left-over barbecue ribs and there's plenty left. Pull up a chair and I'll fix you a plate. We've finished eating, but we'll sit with you at the table while you have a bite," Needa invited.

Hank noticed that Raine was watching television in the living room. It had never been a problem for Hank to discuss anything with Needa in Raine's presence. The boy paid little attention to what was going on around him, probably wouldn't understand what was being said even if he overheard it. And at the moment, Raine appeared to be in a world of his own.

Hank took a bite of the barbecued rib, chewed for a minute, swallowed, and then took a sip of coffee. He wiped his mouth with a napkin before looking over at Needa to say, "Dane was over at my place this afternoon. He's a little concerned about Kate's dog."

Hank was quick to notice the funny look on Leo's face.

"Why is that, Hank?" Needa asked.

Hank shifted his attention to Leo. "Does she know anything?"

Leo knew where Hank was going with this conversation and just shook his head, instead of giving Hank a verbal reply.

"Know anything about what?" Needa asked, inquisitively.

Seeing that Needa's curiosity was piqued, Hank grinned and winked at Leo. "We aren't supposed to talk about it. Are we, Leo?"

"Aren't supposed to talk about what? And who told you not to talk about it?" Needa asked, clearly agitated.

Hank was having fun with her. "Oh my! Do you mean to say you haven't heard?"

Now that she'd been pushed to the limit, Needa rolled her eyes. "Okay, Diamond. Unless you'd enjoy being turned into a frog, I suggest you quit playing games. If there's something going on with Kate's dog that I should know about, then you'd best spit it out."

Hank wasn't all that convinced that Needa could actually turn him into a frog, but why take the chance. Besides, Needa could usually find out what was going on if she really wanted to know. "Well, the way I get it, Kate's dog almost chewed Charlie DaRoux's arm off over at her place a while back. Charlie's real pissed about the dog too. Or so Dane tells me."

Needa looked puzzled. "I don't understand. Kate's dog isn't vicious. Why would Baron want to attack Charlie DaRoux?"

"Charlie's been telling around that his truck stalled in front of Kate's place. Says he pulled into Kate's lane to get the truck off the road. When he got out and raised the hood, the dog came out of nowhere and attacked Charlie for no reason. That's Charlie's story anyway. And I'm sure he'll be sticking to it. You agree, Leo?"

"Yeah. Sounds just like a story that scumbag would concoct. I'd think Charlie's arm would be in pretty bad shape after being mauled by that dog. He'd have to make up a pretty good story about how it got that way. I've been wondering how Charlie would go about explaining what happened to him."

"You guys are just making this whole thing up. You're both so full of shit," Needa said and laughed. Then she noticed that Hank and Leo weren't laughing or making light of what they'd just told her. "You guys aren't kidding. Are you?"

Leo shook his head and Hank lowered his.

Needa poured herself a fresh cup of coffee and sat down at the table again, more concerned than ever. "Kate's dog isn't vicious. He wouldn't have attacked Charlie without good reason. Charlie must have provoked the dog. So why don't you two tell me what really happened?"

Hank picked up another barbequed rib from his plate. "Why don't you tell her what happened, Leo? I'll finish eating before my food gets cold."

After Leo had finished telling Needa about Kate's ordeal with Charlie and what the dog had done, she was speechless, not to mention clearly upset. "I don't understand. Why wouldn't Kate call me to help her after that happened?"

"Kate was so upset that her frame of mind was shot to hell. She did say later that she didn't call you because it was snowing and she didn't want Raine out in the bad weather. Besides, there wasn't anything you could have done for her. After I got there and fixed the window, Kate seemed to calm down. The next morning while we were having coffee, she made me swear not to tell anyone about what had happened," Leo said.

Needa looked over at Hank. "Then how did you find out about it?"

"Well, during my early morning run I happened to notice Leo's truck parked in front of Kate's house. At that hour of the morning, I couldn't help but wonder what was going on. So, a little later, I moseyed over that way and saw the plywood over the window. I'll have to admit that it took some real persuading to get Kate to tell me about what happened," Hank replied and looked humorously over at Leo. "But I managed."

217

Leo grinned. "Yeah. The big bastard told Kate that if she didn't tell him, then he was going to beat the information out of me. How do you like that one?"

Needa laughed. "It's nice to know she thinks that much of you, Leo." Then she turned back to Hank. "I'll bet she made you promise not to get involved in this. Didn't she?"

"That's right, Princess. She wanted my word."

"Kate doesn't know Charlie like we do. If he's been badly mauled by Kate's dog and Kate threatened to kill him, then I'd say it isn't over. Not by a long shot," Needa said. She was worried about Kate and her dog.

"That's the way I see it too. And I told Kate the very same thing," Leo said. Then he stood and picked up the jacket he'd draped over the back of a chair. After kissing Needa on the cheek, he told her, "I gotta go, Babe. I'm expecting a phone call about a job. I'll call you later." Turning to Hank, he asked, "Want a ride home, Hank?"

"No, I think I'll stick around for another cup of coffee. But thanks for the offer."

When the door shut behind Leo and they were alone, Hank looked over to see Raine standing in the doorway. He had no idea how long the boy had been standing there, or why Raine had such a strange look on his face.

Needa had noticed Raine's presence as well. "Do you want something, Raine?"

Raine didn't say anything, but walked over and sat down at the table across from Hank. It was a first for Hank. He couldn't recall the boy ever doing that before. Then he watched Raine pick up the saltshaker, unscrew the cap, turn the saltshaker upside down and pour a pile of salt on the table.

"Raine! What on earth are you doing?" When Needa grabbed for the saltshaker, Raine pulled it back out of her reach. Confused by Raine's actions, she wet a dishcloth and came back to wipe up the salt. But Raine pushed her hand away, and then he began to draw in the salt with his finger.

"Leave the boy alone, Needa. He isn't bothering me," Hank said.

"But Hank, I've never seen him act that way."

"Yeah. I know what you mean," Hank agreed, but was more concerned with their discussion about Kate than he was about Raine playing in the salt.

"Back to Kate, there's something you should know. But I must ask you a question before I tell you what it is. And you must be honest with me when you answer," Needa said.

"I would never lie to you, Princess."

"Are you in love with her?"

Hank was a little puzzled by Needa's question and wasn't prepared to answer. With all the different emotions he'd felt about Kate over the past few days, the idea had never entered his mind that it had anything to do with love. Hank was still thinking about Needa's question when Raine got his attention again. The boy had quit drawing in the salt with his finger and wasn't moving a muscle. *He's listening to us*, Hank thought. Then he looked back at Needa. "That's a tough one, Princess. I can't say."

"I'm sure. And I can understand why you must think that way. However, if you aren't in love with her, then I have no right revealing to you what I've recently learned about Kate. And I won't," she assured him.

Hank stood up from the table. "Then I guess you'll have to keep what you know about Kate to yourself, because I can't give you an answer to your question. Right now, I'm so pissed off at that woman that I think I could wring her beautiful neck right off her gorgeous shoulders."

Needa chuckled. "You really don't know how to take her. Do you, Diamond?"

"It's not funny, Needa."

"Then you must forgive me for laughing. What did she do, Hank? Refuse your manliness? Or did she bruise your ego again?" Needa teased.

"Kate didn't refuse my manliness, but she sure as hell knows how to deflate a man's ego." Hank hated like hell to admit it, but there was no fooling the Indian.

Needa laughed more heartily this time. "She didn't laugh at your size or anything like that, I hope."

Hank snickered. "No, I almost wish it was something that simple. I think what really bothers me, is that Kate didn't mean for this to happen. It just slipped out. She got very upset about it. I could tell."

Needa had stopped laughing. "I don't think Kate would intentionally hurt anyone's feelings, Hank. What did she say?"

"Damn it, Needa, she called me Mack while I was making love to her. I politely asked her not to do that again, and then I made the mistake of asking her who the hell Mack was. She told me that subject wasn't open for discussion. Then she asked me to leave and not come back." Hank could feel his anger mounting.

"What the hell, Hank! So there was an honest slip of the tongue. And you blew up over something so meaningless?" Needa asked.

"Meaningless! We were in the middle of making love, for Chrissake. And yeah, I took offense. Okay? Hell, I don't know of a man who wouldn't. I didn't get shitty with her or anything like that, but I thought I had a right to know who this Mack character was.

"Do you think she really meant what she said to you? I don't."

"How the hell would I know? The damn woman runs so fucking hot and cold all the time that I can't figure her out. In fact, I've just about given up on the idea of trying." Yep, Hank was mad alright... and it showed. He rarely used such language with anyone, much less Needa.

"Her parents are here, you know?"

"Yeah. Kate told me they were coming for the holidays. I don't think she was particularly excited about that either," he said and looked over at Raine again. The boy was still sitting perfectly still. Hank was certain now that Raine had been listening to every word they said. He got up and slipped on his jacket, then kissed Needa on the forehead. "I have to get back over to the house and check my fire."

"I'm having a little holiday get-together next week. Just a few close friends and neighbors. I'll expect you," she invited.

"Will Kate be attending?"

"I invited Kate and her family. I certainly hope they attend."

"I wouldn't count on it if you told her I'm on your guest list. Really, Princess, you know I'm not much on parties. So if it comes down to inviting me or Kate and her family, then I can make it easy for you."

"That's nonsense. I haven't set the exact date and time, but I'll give you a ring to let you know. And I'll expect you to attend."

"What if I wanted to bring a date?" he teased.

Needa laughed. "That's entirely up to you, Hank. Stag or drag, either way suits me just fine."

"Tell me something, Princess. This carpenter guy that hangs around you all the time, is he winning your heart from me?"

"Are you jealous?"

"Damned straight, I am. I don't want to lose you."

Needa giggled. "Don't worry, Lover. You won't. I'm not going anywhere. Don't you like him?"

"Like him?" Hank asked, hesitating a few seconds like he was in deep thought. "Yeah. As a matter of fact, I do. Do you?"

She grinned. "Yeah. As a matter of fact, I do too."

As Hank passed by Raine's chair, he reached over and tousled the boy's hair. When they were alone again, Needa looked over at Raine. He had gone back to drawing in the salt with his finger. When she glanced down at the salt, she saw that Raine had drawn a dog.

Susie Rigsby

"Don't look now, Gordon, but I think your fishing buddy has spotted us. Yeah, he's coming this way. Gracious me! Look at that gal's figure! Maybe Hank's not such a nerd after all," Emily kidded and winked at Kate.

27 | CHAPTER TWENTY-SEVEN

Treating his in-laws to a holiday dinner at the Red Lobster restaurant wasn't exactly Gordon's idea of a fun evening, but would simply have to endure. Just as his dinner party was about to be seated by the hostess, Emily tapped Gordon on the arm and in a low voice, she asked, "Look, Gordon! Isn't that your fishing buddy over there?"

Kate and Gordon turned their heads simultaneously in the direction Emily had indicated with a nod of her head.

"Yeah, that's him," Gordon said, admiring the attractive woman with Hank. Quite impressed with Hank's taste in women, it was a perfect time to get even with Emily for her past ridicule of Hank. "Jeez, get a load of that chick he's with! Looks to me as if old Hank is doing okay for himself these days. Wouldn't you agree, Em?"

Emily was busy taking in Hank's appearance, but shifted her eyes to the woman. "Yes, she is rather attractive. Hank's dressed for the occasion as well... wouldn't you say? I must admit the man does clean up quite nicely. Do you happen to know that woman he's with, Gordon?" she asked after they were seated.

"Nope. But I'm going to ask Hank if he'll recommend me for her next dental checkup," he joked, and then felt Emily kicking his leg under the table.

Kate picked up a menu, trying to ignore Hank altogether.

"What do you recommend for dinner, Gordo?" Sam asked, scanning the menu.

223

It's starting, Gordon thought, his father-in-law was already grating on his nerves. He detected a faint smile on Kate's lips and knew damn well she was amused when Sam called him Gordo. "It's all good, Sambo. Take your pick. I'm buying."

Emily raised her eyes over the menu, giving her husband a cautionary *don't start it* look. That's when she noticed Kate looking toward Hank's table.

Hank had failed to notice Gordon and his family being seated, but spotted Kate when he looked around the room for a waitress. Kate was looking directly at him and their eyes held momentarily. *God, she looks beautiful,* Hank thought before returning his attention to Brandi Crampton, his dinner guest for the evening and best friend's new wife.

Bruce Crampton and Hank had served in the military together. At least once a month, they made a point of getting together for a game of poker with some of the other guys. Bruce had all but begged Hank to take Brandi out to eat while Bruce attended an out-of-town seminar. In fact, Bruce had made the dinner reservations for Hank.

"It was really nice of you to join me for dinner this evening, Hank. I hate eating alone. And with Bruce being away for the training seminar, I've been absolutely lost in the evenings without him," Brandi said, thankful for Hank's company. But Hank's mind was a million miles away. He wasn't paying a bit of attention to what Brandi had said. "Hank? Are you okay? You look as if you'd just seen a ghost."

"What? Oh... yeah... I'm sorry. I just..." Hank started to apologize when he was struck with a brilliant idea, or so he thought. "Listen, Brandi, I'm going to ask you to do something that might seem downright ridiculous to you. But I'd owe you big time if you could go along with me on this. A buddy of mine is sitting directly across from us with his wife and in-laws. He will probably drool when he sees you. So how game would you be at putting on a little show and pretend to be my date?" Hank asked, grinning sheepishly.

She'd noticed the twinkle in Hank's eye and grinned. "That sounds like fun to me."

All right, Hank thought, let the games begin. "Okay, now here's the plan, so listen carefully. In a few minutes, I'm going to pick up your hand and tenderly kiss the back of it. When I do, I want you to look directly into my eyes and smile, as if you're very pleased. Then, Sweetie, we'll proceed to make him think that you're my latest squeeze instead of my best friend's wife. Got it?"

God, he's such a wicked devil, Brandi thought. She was smart enough to know Hank wasn't going to all this trouble just to impress some hairy leg. If this little show was to make some woman jealous, then Hank was being a total comic with his effort. "Why, Hank Diamond! You aren't fooling me. Where's she sitting? I need to know what she looks like so I can run should she decide to come at me with a plate full of food," Brandi teased. Yep, no doubt about that Hank, he was anything but a boring man and just so full of surprises.

Hank smiled. "She's sitting across the room, directly over to the right from us. She's wearing black slacks and emerald green sweater. Remember, we have to make this look real, so don't let me down. From this moment on, Brandi, you've got to act as though you're so mesmerized by me that you're glowing with it."

"Wait, Hank. Give me a few seconds to get ready for this. I wouldn't want to burst out laughing. I'll tell you when I'm ready."

"She's sitting where you can see her easily enough. Wink at me when you see her looking this way," Hank said, intent on making sure that Kate didn't miss any part of their performance.

Brandi glanced over toward Kate's table. "Then I guess I'm winking at you right now, because she's looking this way again."

As soon as those words passed through Brandi's lips, Hank picked up her hand and seductively moved his fingertips over the top, then lifted her hand to his lips. Brandi was taken aback by Hank's slow, sensuous movement and warm soft lips, to the point her body was suddenly shivering with excitement. Playing the scene perfectly, her eyes lingered on his while Hank kissed the back of her hand.

Brandi was totally breathless. "Goodness, Hank!"

He grinned. "We've only just begun, Brandi. Are you still game?"

"Am I? I'd be a fool not to be. I can't wait for you to tell me about this woman."

"I'll explain later. Right now, I have another great idea. I'd like you to go along with me on this one too. That is, if you don't mind."

"I don't."

"Good. Now, Sweetheart, when you're sure she's looking this way again, just reach across the table and tenderly caress my face with your other hand. You got to do it as if you could just eat me alive with passion. Think you can handle that one?"

Brandi snickered. "Oh, I think that will be easy enough."

Kate had gotten an eyeful of Hank kissing the back of the blonde's hand. Her stomach turned flip-flops at the very sight of it. She couldn't even concentrate on the damn menu, not with her mind racing about the blonde with Hank. And forget about trying to ignore them, for that would be next to impossible. She was definitely glad that Hank was sitting in a position where they weren't looking directly at each other. After all, it wasn't polite to stare. But try as she might, Kate couldn't keep from glancing toward Hank's table.

"What looks good on the menu to you, Kate?" Laura asked, waiting for Kate to answer. Thinking Kate didn't hear her, Laura waited a few moments, then said, "Kate?"

"What? Oh, I... I'm not sure. I haven't decided yet. I think maybe the fried jumbo shrimp. I'm really not very hungry," Kate replied, glancing toward Hank's table again.

Brandi was right on cue, like a real super star in a big-time soap opera. Raising her hand to Hank's face, she smiled warmly and gave him a loving look, then murmured softly, "I kinda like this game, Hank. How am I doing?"

It was difficult for Hank to hold a straight face. Like Brandi, he was trying his best not to laugh. But this was serious business. "You're doing great, Kiddo. I'll have you nominated for an 'actress-of-the-year' award. Has she been watching?"

Brandi's eyes darted quickly toward Kate's table, and then back to Hank. "Oh, I don't think she's missed any part of our act so far."

"Great! Then keep up the good work. Remember, you've got to make it look real. I'll do my part if you'll do yours."

"I love a challenge, Hank. What's next?"

Hank leaned over and whispered in Brandi's ear. "Is she looking?"

"I think it's called staring. Go for it," she coached him.

When Hank's lips glided smoothly from Brandi's ear, over her jaw and on to her mouth, he'd completely taken Brandi's breath away. His kiss was long and wet and smooth. Kate would have to recognize an unmistakable passion between Hank and his new lady.

Tingling sensations shot through Brandi's body. When Hank's mouth left hers, Brandi was totally mesmerized by her husband's best friend. "Goodness, Hank!"

A lopsided grin spread over Hank's face. "How am I doing?"

"I don't think I could stand much more if it gets any better," she told him and giggled. "We aren't going to tell Bruce about this, are we?"

"Absolutely. Bruce will get a kick out of it."

"Oh my, do you think?"

"Of course. Bruce is a great sport. Did she see us kissing?"

"I really can't say. I must've had my eyes closed," Brandi said, looking diffidently at him.

Hank chuckled. "Yeah. Well, I guess it was kind of difficult to remember we were acting. I can't tell you how much this means to me, Brandi. Are we about ready to leave, or do you think we should continue on with this little show?"

It had been great fun, but Brandi didn't think it would be wise to carry Hank's little charade any further. It wasn't that she minded being a part of Hank's theatrics. It was because of the feeling in the pit of Brandi's stomach when Hank's mouth had covered hers.

She was only human.

"I... um... think maybe we'd better go."

"Okay. Now when we get up to leave, we're going to walk over to their table and I'll introduce you. My buddy is the younger fellow with them. We fish together all the time. Do you think we can still pull this off?"

"Oh, yes, I think so. Don't worry, I won't let you down."

"Thanks. By the way, maybe you'd better slip that wedding band off your finger and put it in your purse," Hank said and chuckled. "We wouldn't want her to think I was dating a married woman, now would we?"

Kate watched as Hank signed the ticket for dinner and handed it to the waitress. She didn't miss a move when Hank got up from the table and offered the blonde his hand to help his date up. She rolled her eyes when the blonde looked lovingly up at Hank and their gaze held. Infuriated with herself for even bothering to watch Hank, she glanced over at Emily. She'd been unaware that Emily had been taking in Hank's actions as well, or that Emily had been observing her sister watching Hank's romantic scenes, play by sensuous play.

"Don't look now, Gordon, but I think your fishing buddy has spotted us. Yeah, he's coming this way. Gracious me! Look at that gal's figure! Maybe Hank's not such a nerd after all," Emily kidded and winked at Kate.

"Yeah, he really is," Kate said, rather sarcastically.

Kate's remark was unexpected. Gordon gave her a funny look and Emily grinned, while Sam and Laura looked surprised that Kate had even offered to say anything. It wasn't at all like Kate.

According to plan, Hank and Brandi made a casual stop at Gordon's table as they were leaving.

"Hello, Gordon. It's good to see you again. Are the holidays going well for you?" Hank asked, ignoring Kate.

Gordon stood up to shake hands with Hank. "Yes, they are. Thanks for asking," Gordon said, turning then to Sam and Laura. "Hank, I'd like you to meet Emily's parents, Sam and Laura Lingle, and her sister, Kate Corbin. Or perhaps you've already met Kate since she's your new neighbor?"

Hank was ignoring Kate and Emily and that pleased Gordon as he continued with his introduction. "Sam, Laura, meet Hank Diamond. I'm sure you've heard me speak of him. Hank's my fishing buddy. He's also Kate's nearest neighbor."

Sam stood up to shake hands with Hank. "It's nice to meet you, Hank."

"Likewise, Mr. Lingle. Gordon has told me a great deal about you," Hank said. Then he looked directly at Kate. "Miss

Corbin and I know each other," he said, as his hand moved to settle at the back of Brandi's waist. "Let me introduce a dear friend of mine, Brandi Crampton. Brandi, this is Dr. Gordon Juenger and his lovely wife, Emily; his in-laws, Sam and Laura Lingle; and Emily's sister, Kate Corbin."

"It's nice to meet you all," Brandi said genially.

Kate noticed that Hank's hand was still making body contact with Brandi. The blonde was standing entirely too close to Hank and it was getting to be more than Kate could stomach. Even so, she still managed a slight smile and a polite nod.

"It's nice to meet you too, Brandi. Are you new to this area?" Emily asked, being nosey enough to find out more about Hank's date.

"Sort of. I've accepted a position as one of the nursing instructors with the University. I haven't lived here very long," Brandi explained.

"I see," Emily said.

"I don't get out very much. Meeting Hank was like a blessing in disguise for me," Brandi went on to say as she looked adoringly up at Hank.

Kate and Hank glanced at each other, briefly holding eye contact. Too briefly. Kate was about ready to gag. So she got up from the table and said, "It's been a real pleasure meeting you, Brandi. Now if everyone will excuse me, I'm off to the ladies room."

Pleasantries had been exchanged and goodbyes were said between Hank, Brandi and Gordon's family. Hank and his dinner date had departed before Kate returned to the table, and the waitress was serving their food.

Remembering how Emily had bad-mouthed Hank, and that Kate had pretty much sided with her sister, Gordon waited until Kate was seated again before commenting, "Christ, Hank's date was drop-dead gorgeous. Don't you ladies agree?"

Kate shot him a look. "Yes, Gordon, she certainly was." Then Kate picked up a napkin, spread it over her lap, and said, "Let's eat. I'm starved."

Emily gave her sister a funny look. Hadn't she just said a little earlier that she wasn't very hungry? Gordon, on the other hand, had already picked up on Kate's attitude.

* * *

During the drive to Brandi's home, Hank thought about her performance in the restaurant. He was grateful she'd gone along with his little exhibition. He told her so. "You carried that performance off like a real trouper, Brandi. I was very proud of you in the restaurant this evening and really appreciated your help."

"Well, it was fun while it lasted. She's really very lovely, Hank," Brandi said, complimenting the woman that had Hank Diamond playing games.

He wouldn't disagree. "Yes, she really is."

"Why were we putting on that little show anyway? Don't tell me you aren't getting anywhere with her." Brandi wouldn't have believed him even if Hank had tried to convince her there was a problem. So he didn't.

"Oh, let's just say the relationship isn't going as well as I think it should. She's my new neighbor."

"Damn! Some neighbor! I'm just glad Bruce didn't get a load of her before he met me," Brandi kidded.

"Don't worry, Babe, he would have still picked you. Now, let me tell you about the second act. I've been invited to a small holiday get-together and I expect she'll be there with her parents. How would you like to be my date and attend the party with me?" Hank asked, thoughts of his next performance with Brandi already in the making.

"Oh my! I wouldn't miss it for the world," Brandi accepted, wondering how far Hank would go with his little charade.

Well, at least there was a plan in motion. Hank wasn't sure if it was the right kind of plan, but it was a plan just the same. Win, lose or draw, he would see that this one was carried out for Kate's benefit.

Hank wasn't paying any attention and didn't see that Leo was grinning from ear to ear when Leo asked, "Don't you just hate it when a woman gives you that 'put out or walk' ultimatum?"

28| CHAPTER *TWENTY-EIGHT*

After meeting up with Hank and his blond bomber in *The Red Lobster,* a little angry wasn't the best way to describe Kate. Upset really wasn't the correct word either. She was furious and couldn't justify feeling that way. Why should she care if he was courting some beautiful blonde? Didn't she tell Hank to leave and never come back?

Yes, she certainly did.

Furthermore, she thoroughly understood that any woman would enjoy the company of such an extremely handsome, virile and charming man. But she definitely didn't want him, so why this humongous feeling of resentment for Hank... and his new girlfriend?

Nope, a fact is a fact. Kate was completely and undeniably peeved. That was all there was to say about that. Seeing Hank with the beautiful and sexy blond chick named Brandi might not have been so bad, if the blonde hadn't been hanging all over him. Hell, even her name sounded sexy, Kate thought as she walked over and sat down in front of the fireplace.

Hadn't she made it just fine through the rest of the dinner after Hank and the lovely Brandi made their shining exit? Sure she had. So why drag the crappy restaurant scene home with her now?

The grandfather clock chimed, telling Kate it was eleven o'clock. Laura and Sam had retired to their bedroom early in the evening, but Kate was too wired for sleep. She looked down at Baron lying on the floor next to her feet and smiled. The dog loved her even if no one else did.

Restless, Kate walked over to the French doors and looked up at the full moon shining luminously on a heavy blanket of snow that covered the trees and ground. It was a perfect evening to take a walk. Besides, thanks to Diamond and company, it was probably just what she needed to cool off.

Kate took a deep breath when she stepped out into the fresh air, thinking the walk would do wonders to clear her mind. She reached down to pet the dog's head. "Come on, Bear. Let's go for a late night stroll."

And out they went into the brisk night air.

Kate wasn't more than a hundred feet from the house when she thought she saw what appeared to be a shadow dart across the lane ahead of her. But Baron continued to lumber along beside her, seemingly quite unconcerned. *I must be seeing things,* she thought. After walking another hundred feet, Kate saw a shadow dart in front of them again. Baron still wasn't alarmed.

This isn't happening to me, she thought. If someone was up there ahead of them, or even following behind, then Baron would know. The dark shadow had to be some kind of optical illusion, perhaps created from the moonlight shining through the trees. Maybe Mack's spirit was playing a joke on her.

Maybe it was Hank.

Boy, that one's good for a laugh, Kate thought. Sure Corbin, old Hank just up and left that gorgeous hunk of woman hanging on his arm so he could follow you around on a bitter cold night. *You wish.*

Well, if Baron wasn't alarmed, then whatever it was Kate thought she saw couldn't be very dangerous. So why worry about it? She walked to the end of the lane, turned onto the main road and was headed toward Hank's property.

Kate was heavily clothed and her face was covered with a ski mask. So when Hank's headlights hit a walker on the road, he probably wouldn't have recognized Kate if not for Baron so close beside her. He glanced at the clock on the dash of his truck. Christ! It was eleven thirty. What the hell was she doing out here at this time of night? Hank pulled his truck over to the side of the road, next to Kate.

"Get in," he ordered, after rolling down the truck window.

Well, if it wasn't the mighty weekend warrior in the flesh. "No thanks," Kate told him, the sound of her voice slightly muffled through the ski mask.

"Damn it, Kate, I said for you to get in. And I don't intend to tell you again." God she was a hardheaded woman.

"Go away, Diamond. I'm not under your command, so don't be shouting orders at me. I happen to be taking a nice, peaceful walk, which I was enjoying immensely until you came along. Now blow off, Romeo," she said.

No doubt about it, she had the ability to thoroughly piss Hank off. Kate heard the truck door slam and kept walking, but quickened her pace. Within seconds, Hank had grabbed her and was lifting Kate's body over his shoulder, hauling her toward the truck.

"I guess beauty and brains would just be too much to expect in a woman. Now I understand what that old adage means," he said, carrying Kate as if she were weightless.

Kate beat on his back with her fists. "Put me down, you asinine, pompous brute. I'll sic my dog on you if you don't put me down."

"Yeah, sure you will. Come on, Baron. Let's go get in the truck, Boy," Hank told the dog and Baron quietly obeyed, following behind them. "See, Kate, even your dog knows you don't have any business out here at this time of night. Have you gone stark raving mad?" he asked, so mad he was about ready to whip the tar out of her. If it hadn't been for the dog, he'd have turned Kate over his knee... but good. He opened the passenger side door of the truck, roughly plopped Kate down on the seat and slammed the door shut. Then Hank walked to the rear of the truck and dropped the tailgate, prompting Baron to jump in.

Once Kate was certain that Baron was secured in the truck bed, she pushed the automatic door lock, locking both truck doors at once. Then she scooted quickly over to the driver's seat and looked through the window at Hank, standing beside the truck.

"Very funny, Kate. Now unlock the damn door and let me in," Hank ordered, his patience completely exhausted.

"Nah, you can walk home from here," she said, giving Hank a go-to-hell look through the window before shifting the

233

truck into gear. Then she smiled sweetly and flipped him the bird. That was just before she pressed down on the accelerator and drove away.

Hank couldn't believe it. She'd left him standing out in the cold, dark night. And he wasn't even wearing a heavy coat. As if that wasn't bad enough, damn her, she was driving off in *his* truck. Nothing, absolutely nothing, about Kate Corbin was easy.

The chance of another vehicle coming by at this time of night was slim to none, Hank thought, pulling his sport coat collar up around his neck as best he could. But no sooner had the taillights of Hank's truck disappeared from sight, than the headlights of another vehicle were shining brightly on Hank. *The Gods were with him.*

It sure did look like Hank Diamond standing alongside the road, Leo thought as he switched the range of his headlights from dim to bright for a better look. Then he pulled the truck up beside Hank and stopped. Hank opened the passenger door and climbed up into the cab of Leo's truck.

"What in God's name are you doing out here dressed like that, and without your coat? Wasn't that your truck that I just passed back there?" Leo inquired.

"Yeah, Leo, that was my truck," Hank answered, blowing warm breath on his hands as he rubbed them together.

"Who's driving it?"

"Kate."

"Kate?"

"Yeah, Leo, that's what I said. Kate," Hank replied, frustration clearly evident in the sharp tone of his voice.

"Do you mean to say Kate just drove off with your truck and left you standing out here in the cold dead of night?"

Hank really didn't want to discuss it. "That's just about the way it happened, Leo. Now are you going to give me a lift home, or would you rather sit here and listen to a twenty minute dissertation about why Kate is driving my truck?" Hank asked, almost wishing Leo hadn't stopped.

Hank wasn't paying any attention, but Leo was grinning from ear to ear.

"Don't you just hate it when a woman gives you that 'put out or walk' ultimatum?" Leo asked and burst out laughing.

"Very funny, Leo. Now, do me a favor, will ya? Just shut the fuck up and take me home? I'll get my truck in the morning," Hank told him.

Kate had hers coming, Hank thought. She'd get it too. Sooner or later, Hank vowed, he'd get even with Kate Corbin for pulling this little stunt.

Susie Rigsby

Hank's eyes twinkled like a star-struck teenager. "I'll admit that I don't have Kate figured out yet, but I'll get there. Just give me a little time."

29 | CHAPTER *TWENTY-NINE*

A festive spirit had filled the air inside Needa's brightly decorated bungalow. She had actually looked forward to the small annual holiday gathering of friends and now it was happening. Even Raine seemed to be enjoying the holiday activity. It was all Needa could do just to keep her son away from the table full of finger foods, including Kate's special blend of eggnog. Leo was a real life-saver by arriving early and offering to keep Raine occupied.

By 6:00 that evening, Needa was totally prepared for the party. Looking gorgeous in a long, solid red dress that clung to her figure like *Saran Wrap* and showing just the right amount of cleavage, Needa greeted her guests at the door. A few friends from Toronto had been invited, along with Kate and her family. And Needa's buddy, Hank.

The party was in full swing when Hank arrived, making his grand appearance with Brandi by his side. Purposely, he'd planned on arriving late for Kate's sake. The handsome couple grabbed everyone's attention as soon as they entered the room... including Kate's.

The blonde bomber is hanging on to his arm, looking more beautiful than ever, Kate thought. She watched as Hank attentively removed Brandi's coat, allowing his hands to linger much too long on Brandi's shoulders while he whispered in her ear. Then he handed the coat to Needa.

Kate took a deep breath, realizing the kind of effort she'd need to put forth treating Hank with some manner of civility. It wasn't going to be easy. But Kate was determined that no matter what else happened, she was going to be so sweet to the both of them that it would probably make Hank want to vomit.

She hadn't spoken to Hank since the night she'd driven off in his pickup truck and left him standing in the road. She'd intentionally left the keys in the ignition, knowing he would come by early the next morning to get his truck. In so doing, she wouldn't have to see him again, which was just as well because she had no intention of apologizing for her actions. Hank had deserved it.

According to his plan, Hank had been inseparable from Brandi during most of the evening. It was only by chance that Kate happened to notice him standing alone by the table, looking over the selection of finger foods. While on the other side of the room, Needa's collection of crystals and stones had claimed Brandi's attention.

Kate waited until after Hank had filled his cup with eggnog before casually walking over to join him. She took the cup from his hand and smiled sweetly up at him, just before taking a sip of the eggnog. Hank felt a strong urge to wring Kate's gorgeous neck because of the smug look on her face. Then she had the audacity to say, "Thank you. It's good stuff."

"Think nothing of it," Hank said as he reached for another cup and the dipper.

"You look very nice tonight." *Still as handsome as ever*, Kate thought.

"Thanks. So do you." *You beautiful bitch.*

"Thank you."

"You're welcome."

"Your date looks quite stunning too," Kate complimented.

"I'll have to agree. Brandi is a beautiful woman."

"Have you known her long?" Damn it, that really wasn't what Kate had meant to ask. Oh well, what the hell.

"Long enough, if you know what I mean," Hank replied, smiling devilishly and hoping Kate would get the message.

"That's nice." It wasn't easy, trying to be nonchalant while doing a slow burn.

"Yeah. It's real nice being with someone that doesn't call me MACK." The cutting remark had slipped out of Hank's mouth unintentionally. It wasn't at all what he'd intended to say.

He watched as Kate eyes filled with resentment and pain, his words cutting into her like a knife. Then, without any forethought whatsoever, Kate threw the full cup of eggnog she was holding at Hank's face. "Fuck you, Diamond."

The sudden outburst had caught everyone's attention. In the midst of her fury, Kate wasn't aware of the other guests watching them, nor did she care. Without saying a word, Hank picked up a napkin to wipe the eggnog off his face.

Realizing what she'd done, Kate set the empty cup down on the table, then headed toward Needa's bedroom to get her coat. The walls were closing in on her. In order to breathe, she had to get out of the house and away from Hank.

Brandi hurried over to Hank, grabbing a napkin off the table to help wipe the eggnog off his sport jacket. "I think maybe you're pushing her a little too far, Hank," she warned.

Hank grinned. Kate's emotional display wasn't exactly what he'd expected, but his plan was obviously working wonders. "I think maybe you're right."

Kate was wearing her coat when she came back into the room and walked directly over to Needa. "I've caused a terrible scene and interrupted your party, Needa. And I'm so sorry. Coming here tonight was a big mistake," Kate apologized. Then Emily had joined them and Kate asked, "Will you make sure that Mom and Dad get back to my place after the party?"

Emily nodded.

There was nothing more for Kate to say or do, except to get out of there as fast as she could before falling totally apart. Tears were pouring down Kate's face as she climbed into the Jeep and started the engine. *I can't believe I did that,* she thought. Not in her wildest imagination was she the type to do something so stupid. And she never used such foul language. She felt so ashamed. No doubt, she would have to call Hank tomorrow and apologize. But what on earth was she going to tell Emily and her parents?

The answering machine was beeping when Kate stepped inside the house. The message was from Peter. Her in-laws were coming up for the New Year. *Great, that's just what I need,* Kate thought. At present, she wasn't fit for man or beast to be around. Peter and Maureen deserved better.

* * *

The remaining guests at Needa's party didn't have the nerve to comment on Kate's actions. Most were still in shock from seeing Kate throw the cup of eggnog at Hank. Gordon was speechless. He had no idea what might have provoked Kate, thinking Hank wasn't a man to make crude remarks or insult a woman. Emily was still trying to make up her mind as to whether or not Hank was a nerd. And Kate's parents couldn't believe what they had just witnessed. Totally baffled by their daughter's actions, they were ready to go off somewhere and smoke a joint.

All Needa could do was smile. She had the whole chain of events figured out. As far as she was concerned, there could be no denying that Kate was in love with the mighty Hank Diamond. It was Hank that Needa wasn't so sure about. There was no second-guessing that man.

After thanking Needa for her gracious hospitality, Kate's family loaded up and headed for Kate's place. Once they were inside the vehicle, Laura was poking Gordon's shoulder from the back seat. "Gordon, have you known your fishing buddy for very long? He surely must have said something that provoked Kate into taking such drastic measures."

"I've known him for a while, Laura. Hank's a very nice guy."

"Did you see that look she gave him? I don't recall ever seeing such a look on Kate's face. She was steaming hot," Sam said.

Then Emily chimed in. "You know him better than anyone else, Gordon. Do you have any idea what that was all about?"

"No. Em, I don't. Furthermore, it's none of our damn business," Gordon replied curtly, hoping to shut them up and drop the subject.

They seemed to take the hint and rode the rest of the way to Kate's house in silence. For Gordon, the silence was golden.

* * *

After his shocking scene with Kate, there was no way Hank would have departed before the party was over. Luckily, the eggnog was in a small cup and covered more of Hank's face than his jacket. However, he was relieved when the evening finally came to an end.

He wasn't sure whether Emily was treating him like a second-class citizen, or just trying to avoid him altogether. Either way, her cool treatment wasn't acceptable to Hank. He'd done nothing wrong. It was bad enough that he felt responsible for Kate's actions, but damned if he was going to admit it.

As for Needa, he knew she would be calling him bright and early the next morning, full of questions that Hank couldn't answer.

Through it all, Brandi had been a real sweetheart, teasing him good-naturedly. "I think it's time for you to write me out of the script, Hank."

He laughed. "What's the matter, Sweetheart? No guts?"

"Oh no, it's not that. I've enjoyed playing your game. I just think our theatrics have run their course. If you really care for that woman, then I don't think you should keep pressing your luck. So tell me, has throwing eggnog in your face added a little more fuel to your fire?" Brandi asked.

"She's got a lot of moxie. I'll give her that. But I think maybe I should just lay low and let Kate cool down a little before I whip anything else on her."

Brandi chuckled. "Yeah, Hank, that's probably a good idea. Bruce will be home tomorrow. I can't wait to tell him about the eggnog incident. He'll never let you live that one down."

"Yeah. I know what you mean. I can just hear him now. Oh well, I'm game for letting the guys have a good laugh on me once in a while," Hank said, pulling into Bruce's driveway and stopping the truck. "I owe you, Kiddo. Big time too."

"Nonsense, Hank, you don't owe me anything. It was my pleasure. I'm sure Bruce plans on getting together with you for New Year's Eve. We'll be in touch." Brandi reached over and kissed Hank on the cheek, then opened the truck door.

"Let me walk you to the door."

241

"Don't be silly," Brandi said, getting out of the truck. "We're only talking twenty-five feet. Good night, Hank."

Hank waited until Brandi was inside the house before backing out of the driveway, his every thought still about Kate. Maybe those scenes he'd been playing with Brandi hadn't been such a good idea after all. It certainly wasn't his style. And the stupid remark he'd made to Kate that resulted in his eggnog bath was totally uncalled for. Any other time, he would have been livid over a woman throwing a face-full of eggnog at him. But under the circumstances, it was exactly what he'd deserved.

Hank's remorse over what he'd said to Kate was great. He thought about calling her to apologize. But then again, he might want to give that idea some more thought before it happened.

* * *

Hank was amused when Needa called early the next morning to invite him over for coffee. She wasted no time in getting right to the point. "Who's the blonde, Hank?"

Hank snickered mischievously. "Gorgeous, wasn't she?"

"Very much so. Now who is she?" Needa persisted.

"She was my date, Princess," Hank answered, teasing Needa.

"Hank Diamond! I'm in no mood for any of your horseshit. So what was the deal? Who is she?" Needa insisted.

Hank figured the Indian couldn't stand much more suspense, so he'd better explain the whole game plan to her. "Actually, it wasn't a real date. Brandi is just a good friend of mine. In fact, she's Bruce Crampton's new wife. I told you he'd re-married a few months back. I'm sure I did."

"Bruce Crampton's wife! Why in the world would you bring her to my party? And where was Bruce?"

Hank grinned. "Bruce is away at a training seminar. He's due back home on Sunday. He asked me if I would mind taking Brandi out for dinner one evening while he was away and I told him that I would. Next thing I know, we're sitting in *The Red Lobster* having dinner and in walks Kate and her family. I talked Brandi into playing this little game in the restaurant for Kate's benefit. And then, I got the brainy idea to bring Brandi with me to your party, sort of give Kate a double dose of my good-looking date. I do owe you an apology, Princess. The game got a little out of hand last night at your party."

Needa looked bewildered. "Then Mrs. Crampton wasn't really your date, she was just more or less on loan to you?"

"Something like that. You know I don't go for dating married women, especially if it's my best friend's wife. I only invited Brandi to attend your party with me because I wanted to make Kate jealous," he admitted.

Needa stared at him in amazement. "That is so unlike you, Hank."

There was a gleam in Hank's eyes. "Oh? Do you really think so?"

"Yes, I do. And you didn't just make Kate jealous. Whatever it was that you said to her, Kate was furious at you for saying it."

"Yeah. Well, I have to agree, I'm guilty as charged. I did say something to Kate that was totally uncalled for. I deserved every ounce of eggnog she threw in my face. It sure was a move I didn't see coming. But what happened wasn't entirely my fault either. Kate does have a way of getting under a man's skin." He lifted the coffee cup to his lips, took a sip.

"This doesn't have anything to do with the truck incident, does it?" Needa teased.

"I knew Leo would shoot his big mouth off about that too, but I don't think so. I'm not real sure just what it is that's happening to me over that woman. I just know she's got my testosterone level totally fucked up, and I can't figure out why I stay so damn mad at her."

"Perhaps you're in love with her," Needa offered.

Hank still wasn't going that route with Needa and gave her a look of reservation. "I don't know that I would call it love, Princess. I will admit the woman knows how to rattle my cage, but love is something altogether different. I haven't known Kate very long. And I've been pissed off most of the time since I met her. That's not me."

Needa shook her head. "Nope, I read you like a book, Hank. You couldn't keep your eyes off Kate last night. Kate's anything but easy and that alone drives you wild. You're used to having women call and proposition you. They fall all over you and make being with them too easy. Kate's not like that and you haven't figured out what makes her tick. Admit it, you're in love with her," Needa insisted.

Hank's eyes twinkled like a star-struck teenager. "I'll admit that I don't have Kate figured out yet, but I'll get there. Just give me a little more time."

"Surely, you wouldn't try and fool the Indian and say you don't love her."

Hank grinned wickedly. "Not at all. But I'm not going to admit that I do either," he answered and reached over to pat Needa's hand. "You're not going to tell Kate our little secret about the sexy date I had with me last night, are you? I'm not ready for the truth to be known just yet."

Hank was a smart man. But as Needa knew, even a smart man could be as dumb as a box of rocks when he's in love with a woman. And Kate wasn't the average woman. It wouldn't do to play games with Kate, especially if her feelings were involved, which they obviously were or else she wouldn't have reacted as she had at the party.

"Kate's life has been quite complicated, Hank. I can't tell you about it unless you're willing to admit you're in love with her."

"Not today, Needa. I've got work to do, so I'd best hightail it out of here and get started." He got up and set his empty coffee cup in the sink. When he got to the door, he turned around and winked at Needa, blowing her a kiss before he left.

She grinned. God, he was such a devilish man.

* * *

Charlie DaRoux picked up the overturned pan that had contained the anti-freeze. This was the fifth time he'd set the pan out, only to find it had been turned over again. The contents had been purposely poured on the ground. Someone had to be watching him, and then pouring the anti-freeze out after he was gone. The damn dog was never going to die if it didn't have a chance to drink the anti-freeze, not to mention the time and trouble to keep replacing the liquid poison.

      Charlie hated that damn dog with a vengeance. He even had dreams of watching the dog die. But someone was definitely interfering with his plans for the dog's demise. And right now, as Charlie held the empty pan, he was mad as a hornet. If nothing else, he'd set a trap and hide, then watch to see who was responsible for the dirty deed. Whoever it was, Charlie had a little something in store for them too.

Susie Rigsby

"You just don't get it, do you, Diamond? There's nothing for us to work out. I'm not interested. We had some great sex, but that certainly doesn't mean we're joined at the hip. I'm sure you've had better and so have I. I'm not mad and I'm not hurt. I'm just not interested." That was about as blunt as Kate could get with him.

30 | CHAPTER *THIRTY*

Getting through the holidays had taken its toll on Kate, not to mention the dramatic events that had occurred with Hank. She was glad to finally get back into a normal daily routine. However, she did have to admit that some of her holidays had turned out to be very pleasant.

Having Peter and Maureen up for the New Year had been very enjoyable. Kate hadn't realized how much she missed Mack's parents until now. They were still very much a part of her life. Before leaving, Peter made Kate promise to fly down for a visit in the spring or early summer. Kate had agreed to make the trip.

Seeing her parents again hadn't been all that hard to take either. Other than the small misunderstanding she'd had with her mother concerning the peace pipe incident, everything else had gone fairly smooth. She'd decided not to tell Emily about that particular misunderstanding with her parents. Some things were just better left unsaid.

For the most part, Hank had kept his distance from Kate since Needa's party. And for some reason, Kate couldn't bring herself to call him and apologize for the eggnog incident. Maybe, she'd told herself, she wasn't all that sorry for her actions. Nearly two months had passed since her dramatic and idiotic display of foolishness. Time, as Kate well knew, had a way of making people forget unpleasant events, no matter how big or how small.

Kate had seriously considered looking for some type of employment, but of late, she hadn't physically felt up to working outside the home. She was losing weight again and seemed to be living with an upset stomach. Before she got too serious about finding a job, she would need to make an appointment for a physical. Even Emily had shown concern about her sister's weight loss.

She'd been sleeping better and figured it was because she was so tired all the time. If she felt up to it, she was still running every morning and again late in the evening. It seemed that Kate always felt better after getting out into the fresh air. After this morning's early run, Kate decided to stop by Needa's place on her way back home. She found Needa in bed with a raging case of the flu.

"Why didn't you call me?" Kate fussed at her.

"Oh, what for? There's nothing you can do for me. You know the flu has to run its course. If you're smart, you'll high-tail it out of here before you catch this crap from me. I do have a fever," Needa warned.

"Nope. First, I'm going to fix you a bowl of hot chicken noodle soup. And if I can get Raine to go with me, I'll take him over to my house and keep him there until you feel better," Kate offered.

"That's sweet of you, Kate, but I don't think he'll go with you and he's not being very rowdy. I just hope he doesn't get sick too. I don't know when I've ever felt so bad. Darn it anyway," Needa complained, suffering the mother of all headaches. Every muscle in her body ached and she hadn't been able to keep anything in her stomach.

Kate straightened up around the house, prepared the soup and left it covered on the stove, and then turned to Raine. "Hey, Raine, how would you like to go home and stay with me for a few days? Your mother is sick and needs to rest."

Raine was busy playing with Baron and didn't offer to respond.

Needa managed to muster a faint laugh. "He's ignoring you."

"That's not a first for me. Well at least I tried. I'll come back later this evening and check on you again," Kate said, grabbing her coat to leave. But before she could open the door, Kate noticed that Raine had gotten up from the floor and was following along behind her. Surprised and pleased, she looked back at Needa. "Hey, get a load of this, will you? Wait a minute, Raine, and we'll throw some of your clothes into a bag."

A few minutes later, Kate was holding Raine's hand as they walked the back path with Baron toward Kate's place. It had done much to lift Kate's spirits knowing that Raine would come and stay with her. She was certain that not having to worry over the boy was a big relief to Needa.

As it turned out, Raine stayed with Kate for two days and two nights. His behavior was great. Baron seemed to have a constant soothing effect on the autistic boy. He listened to music, watched television, and sat in front of the fireplace for hours at a time with the dog.

Kate made a point of tucking Raine into bed both nights, always kissing his forehead before pulling the covers up around him, always wanting to cry when she left the room. For some reason, being around Raine often had her thinking of Caleb and Kate couldn't understand why. Physically, they didn't look anything alike. They weren't anything alike either. But he just did.

By Saturday morning, Needa was feeling much better. Dane had stopped by earlier to visit and decided to accompany Needa across the back path to Kate's house. When they arrived, they found Raine lying on the floor in front of the television, perfectly content, his head resting on Kate's dog.

After entertaining Raine for two days, Needa was sure that Kate would have multiple unfinished chores and didn't intend to visit for very long. When she finally picked up Raine's coat and told him they were going home, Raine became unruly and didn't want to leave.

"Would you get a load of him? Maybe he'd like to take up room and board with you, Kate," Needa said and laughed. It wasn't until Baron got up to follow Dane outside that Raine allowed Needa to put on his coat and go with her.

Needa and Raine took the back path toward their place, while Dane headed down Kate's lane toward the main road. Baron followed along behind Dane and playfully nipped at the boy's pant legs, making Dane laugh.

They had reached the end of the lane and Dane was still laughing while he played with the dog. He didn't notice Charlie's pickup truck stopping on the main road, not until Charlie rolled

249

down the window and yelled at Dane.

"What the hell are you doing, Boy? Get your damned scrawny ass over here and get in the truck," Charlie ordered angrily.

The dog immediately turned toward the sound of Charlie's voice. Growling viciously, Baron ran toward the truck. When Charlie saw the dog coming at him, he quickly rolled up the window. The dog was barking ferociously at Charlie and lunged into the truck's door.

Scared out of his wits, Dane ran to the other side of Charlie's truck, opened the door and jumped inside. Within seconds, Charlie was shifting gears and pulling away from the dog.

"You stupid little bastard, are you crazy? That dog's a killer! I ought to tan your hide good for hangin around this place," Charlie screamed at his son, sweat popping out on his face from fear of the dog.

"I'm sorry, Pa. I'm not afraid of the dog. He was just playing with me. That's all. I didn't mean any harm. Honest."

During the brief ride home, Charlie thought about Dane and the dog playing together. No one knew of his plan to do away with the dog. So who could be turning over those pans of anti-freeze he'd been putting out for the mutt? It had to be someone that knew Charlie was trying to poison the dog. Maybe it was his own son. Maybe Dane was responsible for keeping that damn dog alive.

Charlie was so worked up about the dog and the spilled anti-freeze that he was in a fit of rage when they reached the house. The minute they walked through the door, he turned to Dane. "You've made friends with that damned dog, haven't you, boy?"

"I don't have any trouble with the dog, Pa. I never have," Dane told him.

Charlie eyes narrowed as he glared at Dane. It was a look he usually got just before all hell broke loose. Dane was familiar with that look. "By all rights, that dog should already be dead. I've set out several pans of anti-freeze for that fuckin' dog to drink. Someone keeps turnin' the pan over and pourin' out the anti-freeze. You wouldn't know anything about that, would you, boy?"

Dane shuddered and swallowed hard. "No, Pa. I don't. Honest. It wasn't me. I didn't do it, I swear I didn't."

Charlie glared at the boy. "You little bastard. You're lyin' to me, ain't ya? I can always tell when you're lyin'. Your eyes get real big and you have to swallow real hard," Charlie said as his hands reached to undo his belt buckle. "I'm gonna teach you not to interfere with destroying that dog once and for all."

No one was there to stop Charlie from giving his youngest son an unmerciful beating. Derek had driven Ruth and the girls into town to shop for groceries while he went to the barbershop. By the time they returned home, Charlie was well on his way to being in another drunken stupor.

Aware of Charlie's drunken state and trying to avoid him as best she could, Ruth went about her business of putting up the groceries. Some time had passed before Debbie came into the kitchen and whispered to Ruth that she should go see about Dane in the boy's bedroom.

Lying on his stomach, Dane was barely able to lift his head when Ruth stepped into the room. She walked over beside the bed and looked down at her small son. Dane's eyes were swollen shut and his face was badly bruised from Charlie's blows. When Ruth reached down to touch Dane's backside, he flinched.

"Don't! Don't touch me, Mom!" The side of Dane's head was badly bruised and dried blood covered his nose and upper lip from a nosebleed.

"It's okay, Dane. Just let me look, Baby," Ruth said as she gently lifted his shirt and gasped, "Oh my God! What has he done to you?"

Dark bruising surrounded the ugly, bulging, red and bleeding welts that covered Dane's small backside. He was simply too weak to move.

Insane with hatred for Charlie and deep concern for her son, Ruth went back into the kitchen. "You rotten son of a bitch, you could have killed my little boy. He needs medical attention. I'm taking him into town to the emergency room," she said, grabbing her coat from the closet.

"You bitch! You ain't takin' that damn kid nowhere. Leave him be. He'll survive. I had to teach the little bastard a lesson," Charlie said with slurred words.

Ruth ignored him, intent on taking her son for the much needed medical attention. When Charlie noticed Ruth was putting on her coat, he got up and grabbed her.

"That's where the kid gets that shit, from you. He sure as hell ain't nothing like me. I said the kid was stayin' right here," Charlie screamed at his wife. In yet another fit of rage, Charlie's fist sent Ruth reeling across the room.

Determined, Ruth got up off the floor and started past Charlie. This time, Charlie's blow was harder, sending Ruth's body spinning against the stone fireplace. There was a loud popping noise when Ruth's head hit the stone and she fell unconscious to the floor.

Charlie walked over to Ruth's limp body. "Get up, you bitch. I ain't done with you yet either," he said, kicking Ruth in the side of the head with the toe of his work boot. The force of Charlie's striking foot was the only movement from his wife's body. Ruth's daughters stood back and cried as they watched the brutal assault, too scared to say or do anything to help their mother.

After Derek had finished feeding the hogs, he headed for the house and found his mother's motionless body lying on the floor. When he couldn't get Ruth to respond, Derek looked up at his sisters and said, "She's hurt real bad. Call an ambulance," he ordered and glared at Charlie. "You could have killed her, Dad."

Charlie was too drunk to care. He went out and climbed into his truck. He wasn't going to stay around for any more of this sorry shit.

* * *

Not long after Needa and Raine had left Kate that morning, she decided to bake a batch of cookies for Dane and Raine. She had just removed the first batch from the oven when she heard the doorbell. Out of habit, she glanced out the front window but didn't see a vehicle sitting in the driveway. Then she went to the door and looked through the peephole to see Hank standing on her porch. She opened the door and looked up at her handsome neighbor, thinking his face was pale and drawn and he physically looked like shit, even wondered if he'd had a bout with the flu.

Hank reached up to remove the goofy-looking hat he usually wore. "Good morning, Kate."

"What do you want, Hank?" she asked rather bluntly.

Hank sensed her mood. "Look, Kate, I'd like to set some things straight and make it right between us again. We've both made some mistakes, but I'm ready to forgive and forget if you can," Hank said in an effort to mend their relationship.

Looking a bit blank, she was silent for a few moments, then said, "Get lost, Diamond."

She attempted to shut the door in Hank's face, but he quickly moved his arm to keep the door from closing. "Kate, just let me come inside and talk this over with you."

"You know, I think I've heard that line somewhere before. And it didn't work for me then either. Go away, Hank. I don't have any time for you today. I'm very busy."

"Oh? Doing what?"

"Reading a book."

"Come on, Kate, let me come in. Don't you think we can act like two mature adults and try treating each other with a little civility?"

Kate rolled her eyes at him. "If *we* both wanted to do that, *we* probably could. There's just one little problem with that plan. I don't want to. Besides, *we* have nothing to talk about, so good day." Kate attempted to shove the door shut again, but Hank was persistent in holding it open. "Look, Diamond, I can't afford to heat all of the Caledon Hills. I'm losing valuable heat because you're holding the door open. I have nothing further to say to you... other than goodbye. Why are you even here? Has the blond bomber already ditched you and moved on to something bigger and better?"

Now was not the time to display a sense of humor, even though Hank felt the urge. He managed to hold a straight face and attempted to explain. "She was nothing more than a good friend, Kate. In fact, she's my best friend's wife. He asked me to take her out for dinner one evening while he was away at a training seminar, and I obliged. It was the least I could do."

Hank was doubtful that she would believe him.

She didn't. "That's one hell of a story, Hank. No doubt you're sticking to it."

253

"I'm serious, Kate."

"Then what about all that lovey-dovey stuff between you two at the *Red Lobster*?"

"I was just having a little fun trying to ruffle your feathers. It was all perfectly innocent. I asked Brandi to go along with me and she agreed. At first, she thought it was kind of cute, but later said she thought I'd pushed you a little too far. Regardless, I wasn't really with her. I was merely keeping her company while Bruce was away."

"You have a sick mind, Hank. You really do."

"Look, I'm sorry, but I just wanted to make you jealous. I swear to you, Kate, I haven't been with another woman since we were together."

Kate managed a little laugh. "And that's supposed to mean something to me?"

"I thought it might."

"Well, you thought wrong again. And if you're practicing celibacy because of me, then don't be a fool. It doesn't become you."

"You aren't going to let me in, are you?" he asked.

"No, as a matter of fact, I'm not."

"Are you that mad at me?"

"No, not really."

"Are you hurt?"

"Why would I be hurt?"

"Kate, if you'd just let me inside, I know we could work this out."

"You just don't get it, do you, Diamond? There's nothing for us to work out. I'm not interested. We had some great sex, but that certainly doesn't mean we're joined at the hip. I'm sure you've had better and so have I. I'm not mad and I'm not hurt. I'm just not interested." That was about as blunt as Kate could get with him. "Now will you please move your arm so I can shut the door? And go away."

The pitiful look on Hank's face nearly broke Kate's heart. But he did as she asked and removed his arm so Kate could close the door. He looked out over the hill, and then Hank turned and walked away. There was nothing more to say.

Second Chances

* * *

Although it was later than usual for Kate's morning run, she needed the fresh air. She had missed running for two days because of Raine. So she was making up for lost time and hoping like hell the workout might erase all thoughts of Hank from her mind. With Baron at her side, she'd made it onto the main road and was moving at a steady pace when Charlie's truck topped the hill.

Charlie spotted the dog first, and then he saw Kate running along beside the beast. This was too good to be true, he thought, realizing that he could get them both with one hit. Kate was running on the opposite side of the road, toward the truck. Charlie speeded up to close the short distance between them, then swerved over to the other side of the road in his attempt to run Kate down and kill her dog at the same time.

Baron's heavy body suddenly lunged into Kate before she realized what was happening. Then they were both tumbling down the steep, snow-covered ground, hitting trees and rocks before finally landing at the bottom of the ravine.

Kate was barely conscious, unable to decide where she hurt the most. Baron was licking her face. "Stop it, Bear," she managed to say. Realizing she was unable to move, Kate knew her only hope of getting help was the dog. "I can't move. You've got to go get help, Baron."

Kate's head was spinning with excruciating pain. Doubting she could be seen from the road, she realized that she could freeze to death before anyone found her. Baron obeyed only certain commands, so what could she say to make him understand? "Hank. Bear, fetch Hank," she mumbled. But the dog wasn't going to leave Kate.

Wondering if she would soon die at the bottom of the gorge, Kate finally closed her eyes. If only she could make Baron understand. If only the dog knew enough to go for help. Seconds, minutes, Kate had no idea of how much time had passed before she opened her eyes again, aware that the dog wasn't still beside her.

255

Running at phenomenal speed, Kate's dog jumped onto Hank's front porch with a loud thud. Standing on hind legs and barking loudly, Baron pawed at Hank's front door demanding attention... and got it.

After opening the inside door, Hank jumped back at the sight of Kate's big dog. Baron dropped to all fours, turning to run down off the porch, stopping, and then running back up on the porch again. All the while, the dog was barking continuously at Hank.

Something's wrong, Hank thought, or else the dog wouldn't be acting that way. He slipped on his boots, grabbed his coat, and went outside to join the dog. "Okay, Baron, I'm with you. Where are we going?"

It was all Hank could do to keep up with the dog. In fact, at times he couldn't. When Baron got too far ahead, the dog would stop, turn around and start barking at Hank again. Baron stopped running at the location where Kate had fallen, but continued to bark while looking down over the side of the gorge. When Hank caught up with the dog, Baron started his descent down the gorge to Kate. Hank had already spotted Kate and began his descent behind the dog.

When they reached Kate, the dog laid down beside her. Hank knelt down, gently lifting her head. "Kate? Honey, can you hear me?"

Kate barely opened her eyes. She had to be dreaming. No, maybe she was dying. Maybe the last face she was ever going to see would be Hank's. God, she hurt all over.

"Yes," she replied, her voice barely audible.

It was the last thing Kate remembered.

Having seen so much misery and physical mutilation in the service, Hank didn't appreciate Kate's negativity. She's lucky to be alive, he thought. "I'd try being a little more grateful if I were you. You'll be pretty sore for a few days, but you'll mend."

31 | CHAPTER *THIRTY-ONE*

Like every other emergency room in a large city hospital, some were waiting to be treated while their family members quietly sat around talking, reading magazines, staring out the window, or else trying to take a nap in an uncomfortable chair. They all had one thing in common; they weren't there because they wanted to be. If they weren't waiting to be treated, then they were waiting to obtain medical information about the condition of their loved ones.

Ruth DaRoux's children were huddled together in a corner, looking worried and out of place while waiting to be told about their mother and Dane. Emily and Gordon were sitting across from Needa, Raine and Hank, emotions tense as they waited for a report on the extent of Kate's injuries.

Conversation was almost non-existent as there wasn't a whole lot left to say. Hank had talked to Derek and knew that Charlie was responsible for what had happened to Ruth and Dane, but had no idea that Charlie had caused Kate's accident. It was a mystery to Hank how she'd managed to fall and end up at the bottom of the gorge. But at the moment, he was more concerned about the extent of Kate's injuries.

Everyone looked up when one of the physicians came through the swinging ER doors, stopped and looked around the room, searching for family members of the patient he'd just treated.

"Are there any family members here with Kate Corbin?" the physician asked before looking impatiently at his wrist watch.

Gordon and Emily both stood up simultaneously with Hank.

"We're here with Kate Corbin, Doctor. How is she?" Gordon asked.

"Well, she's pretty banged up. She'll have some dandy bruises and be sore as the dickens for a few days. And I sutured a couple of her lacerations. But overall, I'd say she is one lucky lady. Are you the patient's husband?"

"No. I'm her brother-in-law," Gordon said.

"I see. Well then, perhaps you can relay the good news to her husband for me."

Gordon gave the doctor a puzzled look. "What good news?"

The physician grinned. "The baby is just fine. I was told she took quite a long fall over some pretty rough terrain. It beats me how a fetus could survive such a trauma, but this one did."

"*BABY!*" Gordon bellowed in disbelief. "I hardly think so. There must be some mistake, Doctor."

The physician raised his eyebrows. "I beg your pardon, Sir. There's been no mistake made here. Now if you'll excuse me, I have other patients waiting," he said.

"Can we see her, Doctor?" Emily asked.

"She's resting quietly right now. I would prefer that she not be disturbed for a while. I'll have one of the nurses let you know when she's awake. I'm going to have her admitted for observation, just to be on the safe side. I'll check on her again a little later."

After the physician had walked away, Gordon turned to Emily, Needa and Hank. Emily looked as if she might faint. Needa appeared to be in a state of shock. And poor Hank looked as if every drop of blood had just been drained from his body. He was as white as the painted wall he leaned against.

"This has to be your fault," Emily angrily spat the accusation at Hank.

Gordon was quick to diffuse the situation. "Now Em, don't be speaking out of turn."

Hank ignored Kate's sister. Dumbfounded, he looked over at Needa. "I think we need to have that talk now, Princess."

Then the swinging doors to the ER opened again. A different physician walked into the waiting room area to claim everyone's attention. He glanced around momentarily before asking, "DaRoux family?"

Derek and his sisters stood up. Derek replied, "Here we are, Sir."

The physician eyed the children carefully. "Where's your father, young man?"

"I don't... he's not here right now, Sir," Derek answered.

"I see. Can you get in touch with him?" Just what was he supposed to tell this kid, the physician wondered.

"Maybe I can a little later, but not right now. Will my mother and little brother be okay?"

"Your brother has been brutally beaten, son. Fortunately, he's young and his physical injuries will mend in time. Emotional scars are another matter. Is your father responsible for doing this to the boy?" the physician asked.

"I'd say so, Sir."

This was that particular part of a medical profession that any physician found difficult to handle. No amount of training ever totally prepared them for such horrendous and intentional abuse, or dealing with it. "I see. And your mother? Was your father responsible for her injuries as well?"

Derek looked over at his sisters, then down at the floor. "Yes, Sir."

The physician shook his head in pity and concern. "Son, your father is in some very serious trouble. The authorities have been notified. I'm sure they'll want to speak with you about what happened."

"I understand, Sir. How's Mom doing?"

The physician detested these situations. He scanned the adults standing close to the DaRoux children. Wasn't there an adult present for these kids? *Apparently not.* So how do you go about telling three kids that their mother is dead? Or that it's a blessing she didn't make it, because had she survived, she would never be their mother again? That she would be a vegetable. "I'm sorry, son. We did everything we could, but your mother didn't make it."

Ruth's daughters began to cry, but Derek fought back the tears. "I see."

259

The scene was more than any strong-willed person could stand, Hank thought, well aware the DaRoux children felt alone in their grief. "Hey, kids, give me just a few minutes to talk with Needa, and then I'll take you home with me. I'll see what I can do to help you. Do you have any aunts or uncles?"

Derek nodded his head. "Just Mom's sister, Aunt Marie and Uncle John."

"I'll get in touch with them when we get to my place. I won't be gone long," Hank said, taking hold of Needa's arm. He gave Gordon a pleading look. "Would you mind watching Raine for a few minutes, Gordon?"

"No problem, Hank. Take your time. We aren't going anywhere until after we've seen Kate," Gordon told him.

With a firm hold on Needa's arm, Hank ushered her down the hallway toward the coffee shop. "Come on, Princess. I'll treat you to a hot cup of coffee. It's time for us to have a long heart-to-heart talk."

Once they were seated and sipping their coffee, Hank looked over at Needa and said, "Jeez, Princess, this has been one hell of a day."

"It certainly has," Needa agreed.

"So, after that bomb the good doctor just dropped on us about Kate, maybe it's time for you to tell me what you know about her past."

"Do you love her?" Needa asked.

"Damn it, Needa. I seriously doubt that Kate's had sex with anyone other than me. So stop pussyfooting around and tell me what I need to know," Hank insisted, his patience wearing thin.

Needa shook her head. "I don't intend to tell you jack shit about Kate until you answer my question." The situation was serious, but it was all Needa could do to keep from grinning before she asked, "Haven't you ever heard of condoms, Diamond?"

"Don't get cute with me, Princess," Hank said and shot her a look. "And yeah, I do love Kate. So start talking."

Needa wasn't convinced. Saying he loved Kate in such a matter-of-fact manner didn't set well with Needa. It was as if Hank was just trying to appease her so Needa would talk. She frowned at Hank. "Oh, you do, do you? So, just how much do you love her, Hank? Tell me how you really feel right now? Does the fact that she's carrying your child make a big difference? Is Kate's pregnancy a result of your love for her? Or do you feel it's a big mistake, like maybe it's the result of your carelessness during some wild sex?"

"Damn it! I love the woman! I'll repeat it as many times as it takes to convince you. I love her, Needa. But for God's sake, what is it that you've been trying to tell me?" Hank did manage to sound a bit more convincing.

"Fate has not been kind to Kate. She was looking to start a new life when she came to Canada. She had just been released from a mental institution after suffering a nervous breakdown. She's still very fragile," Needa said, thinking it was time to tell him.

Hank thought he might be sick. "A nervous breakdown? Why? What happened?"

"She was married to Mack Corbin, a man she loved with every fiber of her being. They had a son, Caleb. He was their only child. Caleb was only sixteen years old when he was killed in an automobile accident. Three months later, Kate's husband was killed in a mining accident. That's when her mind snapped and Kate fell apart at the seams. And that's why I warned you to handle her gently. Looks to me like you've been handling her the only way you knew how," Needa said, adding insult to injury.

"So that's where the name "Mack" came from while we were making love," Hank said, thinking out loud.

"Of course."

"And I thought I'd get even with Kate by flaunting Brandi in her face with our little performance. She didn't deserve any of that crap. What I did was totally uncalled for, Princess." Hank felt terrible, wondered if he might even qualify for sleazebag of the century.

"Oh, don't be so hard on yourself, Lover. You didn't know. And unless I'm badly mistaken, you really do love Kate. If you didn't, you wouldn't have concerned yourself with trying to make her jealous. I honestly believe Kate feels the same way about you, Hank, but she's afraid. Kate's got it in her mind that loving you would be the same as signing your death warrant, and then something bad might happen to you. If Kate doesn't allow herself

261

to love, then she's not in a position to lose either. I've told you this before, my friend, that you must be very careful with Kate. She's been nursing a broken heart for quite some time. Now she's nursing a badly bruised body. And it looks as if before too long she'll be nursing a new baby. *DAD.*" Needa emphasized that last word with a wicked grin.

Hank managed a weak lop-sided grin. "Kinda looks as if I got a little caught up in my own game. Wouldn't you agree?"

"Sure looks that way to me. Now let's get back to the waiting room. I must take Raine home. I'll see Kate tomorrow, but you should try to see her as soon as possible. Then you'll have to take those poor DaRoux kids back to your house and get them fed. Those poor darlings." Needa's heart was aching for the children.

"Yeah, let's go. I do need to see Kate."

* * *

When Kate finally opened her eyes, she felt as if she'd been run over by a freight train. Why did she ache so badly? Where was she? What happened? Then she thought about Baron. Yes, she remembered now, she was jogging and Baron had lunged at her. She'd lost her balance and fell down into the gorge. Turning her head on the pillow to look around, she saw Hank sitting in a chair beside her bed, reading a magazine.

Hank sensed Kate's movement and looked over at her. "Hi."

"Baron?"

"He's fine, Kate. That dog saved your life."

"The way I feel right now, I'm not so sure Baron's done me any great favor," Kate said.

Hank didn't appreciate Kate's negativity. *She's lucky to be alive*, he thought. "I'd try being a little more grateful if I were you. You'll be pretty sore for a few days, but you'll mend."

Kate closed her eyes and suddenly remembered every second of her fall down the steep gorge. It was like a bad dream. She could have frozen to death and joined Mack and Caleb. But instead, her last thoughts had been of trying to send Baron for help. Then she opened her eyes and looked at Hank again, saw the concerned look on his face. "Yeah, I guess you're right. It's just that right now every inch of my body is aching."

Hank's eyes were locked on hers. She had to know about her condition. She's a woman, so how could she not know? Was she upset about it, maybe even trying to kill herself? Then he remembered Needa's words of warning. *Go easy, Hank.* "Do you remember anything about the accident? What caused you to fall?"

"Not much. I remember Baron's weight hitting me, which must have caused me to lose my balance and made me fall," Kate replied.

Hank laid the magazine down and moved to sit on the hospital bed next to Kate. Gently, he reached for Kate's hand and raised it to his lips. "You scared the hell out of me, Kate. I thought I'd lost you. And I love you too much to lose you."

Kate was speechless for a moment, then managed to chuckle. "Wow, Diamond! I may owe you for saving my life, but let's not get carried away about your doing it," she joked, wanting to remove her hand from his, but didn't have enough strength to put forth the effort.

"I told you, Kate, your dog is responsible for saving your life. Not me. I knew something was wrong because of the way Baron was acting, so I followed the dog and he led me straight to you. Baron is your hero. Not me." He wanted Kate to understand what he was saying.

"Are you saying that Baron found you and brought you to me?"

"Yeah. The dog damned nearly broke down my front door trying to get my attention. I followed him on foot to where you went over the side of the road. Don't you remember anything else about the accident?" Hank asked. He knew that dog worshipped Kate, so what caused Baron to throw his weight into Kate and make her fall?

Kate's head was throbbing. And trying to remember what happened before she fell only made it worse. But she wanted to remember. They were running on the side of the road and Baron lunged at her. But why? Was there a truck? Yeah, there was, and Kate remembered the truck was suddenly coming at them. The throbbing ache in her head was getting worse and it hurt just to think. "I'm not sure, Hank. Maybe I can remember more tomorrow. Right now, it hurts even to think."

"Then don't. Try to rest," Hank said, then kissed her forehead, after which Kate looked up at him. "Kate, before I go, I do have something else to tell you."

"Oh? More good news today?" she asked, rubbing her fingers back and forth across her forehead.

"No, this isn't good news. And maybe I shouldn't be telling you about it right now, because it's pretty upsetting. I don't know all the particulars about what happened, but Dane's in the hospital too," Hank told her.

Kate's mind was spinning. She remembered that Dane was at the house with Needa earlier and he was fine. "What's wrong with Dane?"

"Charlie tried to beat the kid to death. Dane's in pretty bad shape," Hank said.

Kate turned her head away. "Oh, dear God! *NO!*"

"Yeah, and that's not all of it. For some reason, Charlie worked Dane's mother over real good too. She's dead." Hank was finished with the bad news.

"Oh, my! Is there anything else I need to know?"

"I think that's enough for one day. We'll talk later. Try to get some rest. Gordon and Emily are in the waiting room. Do you want to see them?" Hank asked.

"Just for a few minutes. Would you mind getting them for me?"

"Sure, I'll tell them on my way out," he said, leaning over to kiss Kate's forehead again. "By the way, I'm taking the rest of the DaRoux kids home with me. The authorities have issued an APB (all points bulletin) on Charlie, but I don't want to take a chance of him getting near the rest of his kids again if he isn't found. I'll see you in the morning."

"Don't worry about me, Hank. You've done enough for me already and I'll be fine. But thanks anyway," Kate said.

Hank smiled. "No, Kate, I haven't done enough. But I'll make it up to you. And I will be back tomorrow whether you like it or not."

"I'm not a man for much conversation, Kate. And it's for damn sure I never say things I don't mean," Hank said.

32 | CHAPTER *THIRTY-TWO*

It was late and Charlie was still drunk. He was headed toward home when he drove by Kate's place and spotted that damn dog again. "Goddamn it! I thought sure I'd fixed your ass."

There was a brand new bottle of anti-freeze and a pan in his truck. Now that Dane wasn't around to dispose of the liquid poison again, putting more anti-freeze out for the dog was no trouble. Determined to see that Kate's dog got a good drink of the sweet stuff, Charlie climbed up a nearby tree and waited for the dog to appear. He was close enough to Kate's place that the dog should be able to pick up his scent. When that damn dog came looking for old Charlie, it would find that nice little treat waiting for the dumb animal.

Over an hour had passed and there had been no sign of the dog. It was getting colder and Charlie began to shiver. Time was running out and he'd have to head for home if the dog didn't show up pretty soon. Charlie's vision was beginning to get a bit blurry when he finally noticed a movement down in the bushes. A few minutes later, Charlie watched as someone emerged from behind the trees. He could determine that it was a male figure, watching as the boy walked over to the pan of anti-freeze and kicked it over.

As if to be aware of Charlie's presence, the young man then walked over and stood beside the tree that Charlie had climbed and was sitting in. When the boy looked up, Charlie managed to get a good look at his face. Raine was grinning up at Charlie, waiting for Baron's enemy to make a move.

It's the beatnik's kid, Charlie thought and almost fell out of the tree. "You stinkin' Mongoloid! I never dreamed it was you.

265

I'll fix your scrawny ass," Charlie yelled, sliding down out of the tree. Raine took off running as soon as Charlie's feet hit the ground.

Right behind Raine and in hot pursuit, Charlie kept trying to grab hold of the boy's coat. Raine was pacing himself as he ran, staying just close enough to keep Charlie in the chase. They ran through the woods for a good distance and Charlie was beginning to wear down, yet determined to catch the kid.

As if it had been carefully planned, Raine slowed his pace and allowed Charlie to get within inches of grabbing Raine's jacket. Confident the boy was just within his reach, Charlie was putting every ounce of energy he had left into the chase. Then, like a deer, Raine suddenly leaped into the air and landed several feet ahead of Charlie.

Raine's plan had worked. Dedicated in his pursuit of catching Raine, the old man didn't have a clue that he'd been set up to meet his demise. Raine listened to Charlie bellowing loudly as he dropped into a deep well full of freezing water.

After sinking into the water, Charlie struggled against the wet enclosure to reach the water's surface again. He finally managed to grab onto a tree branch that had grown through the deep well's brick wall. The water's freezing temperature sent deep chills through his exhausted body.

Charlie was stone-cold sober now. "Hey! Hey, kid! Help me! I need a rope. Throw me down a rope," he yelled, looking up at the small round opening above him. He could see Raine looking down at him. "Help me," Charlie yelled again.

Raine continued to look down into the well for a few minutes. Just as Charlie was beginning to think the boy might be going to help him, Raine turned and walked away. Charlie DaRoux's fate had now been sealed.

* * *

"Does your father make a habit of staying away from home very often?" The detective was asking Derek the next morning at Hank's house. The DaRoux home had been under surveillance the entire afternoon and night, but Charlie had not returned.

"No, sir," Derek answered, certain his old man would run like hell if he knew the authorities were looking for him. Derek seriously doubted he would ever see his father again.

"Well, we'll continue to keep a lookout assigned to the house. I understand you and your sisters will be residing with your mother's sister for a while. I know where to find you if we should need to talk again," the detective said.

"Yes, Sir."

What a raw deal for a boy his age, Hank thought, giving Derek a sympathetic look as the detective walked away. Then Hank said, "Tell me about your Aunt Marie, Derek."

"There's nothing much to tell, I guess. She's my mom's baby sister."

"Do you like her?"

"Oh, yeah! There's nothing about Aunt Marie that a person wouldn't like. It's just that she's raising four kids of her own. So I kinda doubt she's going to appreciate four more. I don't know that she'll even want to take us in," he told Hank.

Hank ran his fingers through his hair. *What a mess.* And he was anxious to get back to the hospital and check on Kate. Right now, she was the most important person in Hank's life.

Before Hank left the hospital with the DaRoux kids, he'd made Gordon and Emily swear not to mention Kate's condition to her. They'd both agreed it was the right thing to do and would be best for Kate.

"You know, Derek, I've had my differences with your old man, but I've always respected your mother," Hank said. "I'll see to it that your little brother gets taken care of when he's released from the hospital. I plan to keep Dane here with me. But for now, I've got to take care of some important matters of my own. You just have to hang in there and be strong for your sisters."

"Sure, Hank. We appreciate everything you're doing for us."

On his return trip to the hospital, Hank had decided it would be best to check on Dane first. Then he would spend the rest of the day visiting back and forth between Kate and his little buddy. He didn't intend to leave the hospital again until all was right between the three of them.

Dane's eyes were closed when Hank stepped into the room and sat down quietly in a chair beside the hospital bed.

"Hi, Hank," Dane said and opened his eyes.

"Hey, Pup! How'd you know I was here? Your eyes were closed," Hank kidded.

"Guess I'm learnin' like you did."

Dane's physical appearance was so pitiful that it broke Hank's heart. He'd seen his share of broken and bloody bodies in his lifetime, but this was different. This was a kid that Hank liked and cared about. "Guess so."

"Have they found my Pa yet, Hank?"

"No, I don't think they have."

"Kate's sister, Miss Emily, came to see me this morning. I know about my mom."

"I'm sorry, kid. I really am."

"Do you know what really troubles me, Hank?"

"No, Pup. What troubles you?"

"I can't even remember what my Mom said to me the last time I saw her," Dane told him.

Hank felt a lump forming in his throat. "Tell me something, Pup. What provoked your old man that he whipped you like he did?" To Hank's way of thinking, Charlie had to be the devil himself to severely abuse such a small child. If Hank ever found the son of a bitch, he fully intended to tear the rotten bastard apart with his bare hands.

"He whipped me because of Kate's dog. Pa was mad at me about Baron," Dane said.

"I don't think I understand," Hank told him.

"I'd gone over to Kate's place with Needa to get Raine. Needa had the flu, so Kate had been keepin' Raine at her house for a few days. Just until Needa felt better. When we left Kate's place, Needa and Raine took the back path as usual. I wasn't goin' back to Needa's. I was goin' home, so I took Kate's lane. Baron wanted to play and followed after me, nippin' and pullin' at my pant legs. By the time we'd reached the end of the lane, Pa had seen me and stopped his truck. Pa started yellin' at me and Baron took out running toward the truck. Gosh, Hank, I ain't never seen a dog get that vicious before! I thought Baron was gonna break right through the glass on Pa's truck when he lunged at it. When we got home, Pa started accusin' me of pourin' out the anti-freeze he'd been puttin' out for Baron to drink. I tried to tell him I didn't do it, but Pa said I was lyin' about it. No one else was there when we got home. Honest to God, Hank, I didn't think Pa would ever stop hittin' me. I can't rightly say that I remember when he did. I didn't deserve that whippin' either, did I?" the boy finished, exhausted.

"No, Pup. You surely didn't," Hank agreed.

"Miss Emily told me Kate's in here too. She said Kate took a pretty bad fall. I haven't seen her yet, but I will," Dane promised.

"I think maybe you'd better wait and let Kate come to you, Pup. Right now, kid, you are one ugly looking dude. It's going to take a few days to get that mug of yours back into shape. How are you feeling?"

"Better than I did yesterday," Dane said and tried to muster a grin.

"Listen, kid, I'm going upstairs to see about Kate, but I'll be back before too long. Let me know if there's anything you need or want and I'll get it for you," Hank told the boy.

"Thanks, Hank," Dane said. Just as Hank started to leave the room, Dane stopped him. "Hey, Hank?"

"Yeah?" Hank answered, turning back around to face the boy.

"Do you think there's a chance they'll let me go to Mom's funeral?"

Hank looked away, trying like hell to keep his composure. "I don't know, Pup. The doctors will have to decide if you're physically strong enough. We'll see. Okay?"

"Yeah. I guess you're right. Well, be sure and tell Kate I asked about her."

"You bet I will. Now try to get some rest and I'll be back shortly," Hank said, closing the door behind him. Then he quickly wiped the water out of his eyes. He was a grown man. What would Kate think if she knew he was blubbering over some kid? He hadn't cried since Beth's funeral. It was good that Dane was on one floor and Kate was on another, giving Hank enough time to regain his composure.

When Hank stepped out of the elevator, he came face to face with Emily. This wasn't exactly the way a day should start, Hank thought and greeted Emily. "Good morning, Emily"

Emily didn't like Hank and resented his presence. "Look, Mr. Diamond, why don't you do us all a favor and stay away from Kate. Haven't you already done enough?"

"She hasn't said anything about... well, I mean, she doesn't know that we..." Hank was stammering.

"If Kate knows we're aware of her condition, she hasn't said anything to me. I've kept my promise to you. I haven't confronted her about it either," Emily said. Why she bothered to tell him anything, Emily wasn't sure, but then said, "She does know about Dane and all of that mess. She's worried sick about that little boy."

"Sounds like Kate. Look, Emily, I know you're really pissed off at me right now and I can't say that I blame you. But give it a rest, will you? I care a great deal about Kate and we're going to get through this." He wanted to be friends with Kate's sister, if that was possible.

Emily looked at him for a moment, shook her head, then turned and walked away.

Hank was carrying a dozen red roses for Kate. After leaving Dane, he'd stopped by the florist shop on the first floor to make the purchase. Before entering Kate's room, he took a deep breath and inhaled the bouquet's scent, hoping the flowers would work magic and weaken Kate's attitude toward him.

"Good morning," Hank said, greeting Kate with a smile and the roses. She looked much better this morning. Pale, but better. Who the hell was he trying to kid? Kate was beautiful. She had always been beautiful in his eyes, and now, even more so.

"Oh, Hank, the roses are absolutely beautiful! But you shouldn't have."

"Yes, I should have. How are you feeling?"

"Like every part of my body has been hit with a baseball bat, but at least the throbbing headache has stopped. Thank goodness," Kate replied, then asked, "Have you seen Dane?"

"Yeah, I just left him. He's holding up pretty good. He's young."

"I must get down there right away and visit him."

Hank shook his head. "I'd wait a day or two if I were you."

"Emily said the same thing. Is it really that bad?"

"Yeah, Honey, it really is. I think Dane may have to stay in the hospital for a while. I haven't said anything to him about this yet, but I'm going to see about getting temporary custody of Dane. I thought Emily might use her position with Family Services to help me do that."

Tears welled up in Kate's eyes. "Why, Hank Diamond! I do swear. There must be a warm heart beating in that broad chest of yours after all."

"More than you know, Baby."

"That's very admirable of you, but I've already informed Emily that I want Dane to stay with me. I'm sure he'd be just fine with you, but Dane needs to be with me so I can take care of him. Besides, you know how fond he is of Baron."

"Yeah, I know," Hank said and bent down to kiss her. He wasn't going to argue with Kate about Dane.

"What was that for?"

"Because I felt like it. And because I love you, Kate," he added.

She chuckled. "There you go with that *love* crap again. Love is just a four-letter word to you, Diamond. I really am grateful to you for saving my life, but don't consider yourself bound to me forever because of it."

Kate casually picked at the bouquet as if she didn't have a care in the world. Maybe she didn't know about the baby yet. Realizing just how touchy the situation could get, he remembered Needa's warning to "go easy".

"I thought we'd been through this yesterday, Kate. Perhaps you don't remember. You can't credit me with saving your life. Baron deserves that honor," he told her again.

"Oh, I know. But if you hadn't used good judgment and followed Baron, then I'd still be there, wouldn't I?" Kate was adamant that he'd played a big part in saving her.

"No, I don't think so. I think your dog would have found someone else to go with him if he couldn't find me. He probably would have gone after Needa. Maybe I was just the luck of the draw." He took the bouquet from Kate and laid it on the table.

Then he sat down on the bed, close to her. "I'm not a man for much conversation, Kate. And it's for damn sure I never say things I don't mean. But I thought I'd lost you when I saw you lying at the bottom of that gorge. It made me realize how much you mean to me."

Kate thought about what he'd said for a moment before she told him, "I don't love you, Hank."

A sharp pain centered itself in Hank's gut, but he wasn't going to give in. He reached to pick up Kate's hand. "I hope to change your mind about that, Kate."

Kate pulled her hand away from him. "I rather doubt you can."

"Are you going to shoot me down before I even have a chance to prove my worth?"

This was difficult for Kate. "Look, Hank. We've had some really great sex, but that's all it was. Since you aren't the type of man to go without great sex for very long, I'm sure it won't take you very long to find another partner. As for me, well, I don't appreciate you coming in here to give me this cock-and-bull story about loving me. It's almost like you're digging around in a box of Cracker Jacks for the toy prize. In the first place, and if you want the honest truth, I don't believe a word you're saying. God only knows why you persist in saying it anyway. And so you'll know, *love* is just a four letter word to me too," Kate finished and took a deep breath.

Hank looked deep into her eyes. *She's not being honest with me.* "Don't try to tell me how I feel, Kate. And don't push me away. I need you." He watched the rise of Kate's breasts as she took another deep breath, thought about the scar Charlie had left with his knife.

"Oh God, Diamond, that was good. That's a really great line. You should use it more often." Then she laughed, as if she were making fun of him. "*You* need *me*? Ha. I hardly think so."

"You're wrong, I really do."

She snickered again, rather nastily. "Oh, really? Since when did the mighty Hank Diamond ever need anyone? And what on earth gave you the idea that you need me of all people?"

"I... I just do, that's all. I think we're good for each other. I want to be with you. I... I want to marry you, Kate." He almost choked. Hank's words came out sounding like he had a mouth full of peanut butter, or his tongue was stuck to an ice cube. Stammering wasn't Hank's style.

He's nervous. In fact, he was too nervous. It wasn't at all like Hank. There was only one way for Kate to find out why he was so uptight. "You know I'm pregnant, don't you?"

Hank nodded his head, then looked down at the floor.

"Do they?"

Still focused on the floor, Hank nodded again.

"Oh, God!"

He looked up at Kate. "Listen to me, Kate. I want..." She interrupted Hank by putting a finger against his lips.

"No, Hank, you listen to me. I don't need your damn sympathy. I don't need your love either. And I sure as hell don't need your name. What kind of a fool do you take me for anyway? If you didn't know about my condition, would you even be here now? Would you be bringing me roses, trying like hell to convince me how much you love me? I rather doubt it. I'm a big girl, Diamond. I can take my licking and keep on ticking. I've done it before and I can do it again. Now do me a favor and just get the hell away from me," she said, almost all in one breath.

"Just like that?"

"Yeah, just like that."

"I'm not supposed to have any say in this whatsoever?"

"Why should you?"

"I don't know what happened to turn you this way, Kate. But somewhere inside you there's a woman with a lot of love to give. I know it."

"Oh yeah? Well, maybe so, but it's not for you. Now beat it, Diamond," she said, sarcastically, convincing Hank that it was time for him to go. When Kate was sure that Hank was gone, the tears began to trickle down her cheeks.

Hank didn't go back to see Kate again that day. He didn't want to upset her. He visited off and on with Dane before going home later that afternoon. After making arrangements for the DaRoux kids to stay with their Aunt Marie, he called Needa. "I need a shoulder to cry on, Princess."

273

* * *

Two days after Kate's conversation with Hank, she was being discharged from the hospital. Even though Emily had advised against it, Kate was determined to see Dane. She'd been through a lot and wanted to believe she was prepared for the worst. She wasn't. Kate almost fainted when she saw the injuries Charlie had inflicted upon the little boy.

"Hey, Dane, how are you feeling?" Kate managed to ask, a huge lump stuck in her throat.

"I'm doin' better now, Kate," Dane told her.

"That's good. You'll probably be getting out of here in a few more days. I've made arrangements for you to stay with me, Dane. Would you like that?" she asked.

She noticed a bit of a troubled look on Dane's face. "Yeah, Kate, that would be nice. But Hank said he's expectin' me to stay with him. And I don't want to hurt Hank's feelins."

Kate smiled. "Oh? Did Hank say he'd already arranged for you to stay with him?"

"Well... not exactly. He just said he was seein' about it. He mentioned that you wanted me to stay at your place too," Dane said.

"Did he now? Well, that Hank is a really great guy with a good heart. But don't you think I'd be better than Hank at taking care of a young boy like you. I know I'm a better cook than Hank. Besides, you would have Baron to keep you company at my place. Hank doesn't have a dog." Kate admitted to herself that maybe she was being a little under-handed with Hank, but where Dane was concerned all was fair in love and war.

The thought of getting to be with Kate's dog sparked a bit of excitement in Dane. "Yeah, that would be great. I can't wait to see Baron," Dane said. Then another worried look crossed the boy's badly bruised face. "Kate, they haven't found my Pa yet, have they?"

"No, I don't think so."

"If Pa found out that I was stayin' with you, he'd be real mad. I think that's why Hank wanted me to stay at his place," Dane reasoned with her.

"I know, Dane, but we'll have Baron there to protect us. Besides, I'm not afraid of your father. We'll be just fine, I promise," Kate said as she walked over and kissed Dane on the forehead. "You just hurry up and get better so I can get you out of here. I'll be back tomorrow," she promised.

If the authorities didn't locate Charlie, or if he ever set foot on her property again, Kate vowed to rid this world of the old man. Shooting the son of a bitch was the least she could do for Dane. It was the only payback Charlie deserved for the death of Dane's mother.

Susie Rigsby

Hank was amused by Kate's inquisitiveness and chuckled. "I never could understand why any woman would want to keep a diary. Maybe women are afraid if they don't write down all those major events in their life that they'll forget what happened in their old age.

33 | CHAPTER *THIRTY-THREE*

A hunter found Charlie DaRoux's body in the deep well a month later. He'd tripped and almost fell into the open well. That's when he spotted Charlie's frozen body hanging on the side of the well's brick wall. Charlie had managed to snag his coat over a sharp edge of stone to keep from sinking to the bottom. It had kept him from drowning, but nothing could have saved Charlie from the cold temperatures and dying of exposure. Fittingly, Charlie had frozen to death.

Hank had cleared it with the authorities about breaking the news of Charlie's demise to Dane. He pulled into Kate's driveway and parked his truck. Before he could reach the front door, Kate stepped out on the porch to greet him. The look on Hank's face alerted Kate that his visit had to be about Dane.

She was cordial, but a bit reserved. "Hello, Hank."

"Kate," Hank said. "How are you?"

"I'm doing fine, but thanks for asking," she told him. "Are you here to see Dane?"

"Yeah. Charlie was found this morning."

"And?"

"We don't have to worry about him hurting anyone again, Kate. He's dead."

"I see. Then you'd better come in," Kate said, turning to go back into the house. "I just made a fresh pot of coffee. Can I get you a cup?"

"Yeah, that would be nice," he accepted, following behind Kate.

Hank spotted Dane lying on the floor with Kate's dog. He walked over to the sofa and sat down. "Hey, Pup, looks like you're doing pretty good this morning?"

"I am, Hank. I'm doin' a lot better. Kate's been takin' real good care of me. Baron's been helpin' her too," Dane beamed.

"I would imagine so. Dane, I've come to tell you something and..." Hank cleared his throat and nervously fingered his hat. "Well, I hardly know how to put this, kid, except to just come right out and tell you."

Hank had never called Dane anything other than "Pup". So something wasn't right. And the boy had never seen a time when Hank couldn't speak his mind. From the sound of Hank's voice and lost expression on his face, Dane figured that Hank had news about his Pa. "It's about my Pa, ain't it, Hank?"

Hank cleared his throat again. "Yeah, Pup. It is."

"Have they found him?"

"Yeah. They did."

"Is my Pa gonna go to jail now?"

"No, Pup, your Dad won't be going to jail. They found him in an old well not too far from here. A hunter found him early yesterday. It looks as if he accidentally fell into the well and he... uh... he died from exposure, Dane. Your Pa froze to death."

Dane understood and nodded his head. "What's gonna happen to me now? Will I have to go live with Aunt Marie too, like Derek and my sisters?"

"I don't think so. I wouldn't worry about that right now if I were you. I have an idea or two about where'll you be staying, but we'll discuss it later. We need to take care of getting your dad buried first, and I've been looking into his funeral arrangements."

"Okay, Hank, whatever you say." With that, Dane rolled over on the floor and rested his head on Baron's body. As Hank got up to go into the kitchen, Dane looked up at him. "Want to play a game of checkers with me?"

"Maybe. Do you think you can beat me?"

Dane smiled. "Do you think I can't?"

Hank wasn't surprised at Dane's lack of emotion over his father's death, figured the kid was probably glad his old man wasn't coming to get him. With that thought in mind, he headed for the kitchen to get the cup of coffee Kate had offered. He knew she'd listened to his conversation with Dane. She'd set his coffee on the countertop beside the cream and sugar containers. He poured a dab of cream into his cup, stirred, took a sip, and then waited for Kate to say something.

"I'm glad it's over," she finally told him.

"Yeah. Me too."

"I know what you're thinking, Hank, but I want to keep Dane here with me. I can raise him. I can do it as good as anybody else," she said stubbornly.

"I don't doubt that for one minute, Kate. But a young boy like Dane needs a man around to help raise him, teach him all the things a boy needs to know about being a man. Dane's never really had much of a father. He's a great kid and I'd cherish the opportunity to raise him too. I came over here to tell Dane about Charlie, but I wanted to talk to you as well."

"Is that right?"

"Yes. And I have a bit of information you should know. Before Charlie was found, I went over to his place and had a look around."

"You were looking for Charlie?" she questioned.

"What do you think?" he asked, grinning. "But I figured since I was there and all alone, I might just as well nose around the place a bit."

"And?"

Hank was amused by Kate's inquisitiveness and chuckled. "I never could understand why any woman would want to keep a diary. Maybe women think if they don't write it all down they'll forget what happened in their old age. But it's difficult for me to imagine a woman like Ruth DaRoux keeping a diary." Hank noticed the strange look on Kate's face. "Now mind you, I certainly wouldn't want anyone to think I'd be low down enough to read someone else's diary, but I doubt Ruth will be caring too much about that now. Dane's mother was an amazing woman and, much to my surprise, she'd written some pretty interesting stuff in her diary."

Kate's interest was piqued. "Really?"

"Yeah. Why don't we take our coffee and go up to the loft where we can talk in private," Hank said, tipping his head toward

Dane. The boy hardly noticed when they left the room, still lying with Baron in front of the fireplace.

Kate was anxious to hear more of Hank's story once they were settled together on the loveseat. "Now tell me about Ruth's diary."

Hank smiled. *Just like a woman.* "Well, it seems that Ruth had one true love in her life when she was a younger woman. This was before Charlie came along and ruined everything for her. The young man's heart was broken over Ruth having to marry Charlie like she did. And I guess the poor guy never stopped loving her. According to Ruth's diary, she felt the same about him. Apparently this young man came back for a visit about the same time that old Charlie had gone up in the Yukon for a spell. It's hard to believe, but according to Ruth's diary, she arranged to spend some time with the guy while Charlie was away."

Kate's eyes lit up with excitement. "You aren't going to tell me that Dane's not..."

A big grin flashed across Hank's face. "That's right. Ruth knew that Dane wasn't Charlie's son, but what could she do about it? She wrote in her diary that she'd never told the love of her life about conceiving his child. What's so strange though, is that she didn't even write down the guy's full name. She only referred to him as *James*."

"That's amazing, Hank. So what did you do with Ruth's diary?"

"Now, Kate, what would you think I'd do with something like that?"

She hesitated, as if in deep thought. "The diary is never going to be found, is it?"

Hank smiled again. "I don't know how you feel about it, but I don't think it would be right to tell Dane about his mother."

"Oh, I agree. He's been through too much already. Sometimes, as they say, it's best to just let sleeping dogs lie, you know," she philosophized.

"Yeah. Sometimes, it is best to just let..." Hank caught himself before he said the wrong thing. He reached for Kate's hand, wanting to touch her in some small way. "Kate, I have something more to say to you. I'd appreciate it if you'd hear me out and think about it for a while. Fair enough?" he asked, handling Kate with kid gloves as Needa had told him to do.

Kate grinned. "I'll listen to what you have to say, Hank. But be careful."

"Good. From the first moment I first laid eyes on you, I knew you were going to be somebody special. In the beginning, I'd be lying if I told you what I felt wasn't purely physical, just like you said. But somewhere along the way that all changed," Hank said, and then hesitated for a bit, wanting to get it right.

"I'm still listening, Hank."

"I know. Well, I just wanted to say that I've seen a lot in my life, Kate. I survived being a covert operations specialist, even survived against all odds in a rotten jungle. God knows I've seen more than my share of death and misery, pain and suffering, and tortured souls. You name it and I've been there, done that. And when I lost Beth, I thought my whole world was going to fall apart. She'd always been there for me and I loved that woman more than life itself. But when you came along, well, there was just something about you that told me it was time to get on with my life. I've been giving this a lot of thought, Kate, and I've loved you from the very beginning," he said. No words passed between them, so he asked, "Should I go on?"

"You mean there's more?"

"Yes, there's more."

"Then by all means, Hank, don't quit while you've got the floor."

"Thanks. Well, I've been thinking that if we could work things out so we could be together, then we could both have Dane. I know how pigheaded you can be, and you probably do believe that you can raise Dane and our baby without my help. But believe me, Honey, that's not the way it's supposed to be. A kid needs both parents. And well, what I guess I'm trying to say is... ah, I mean..."

"You'd better spit it out, Diamond, before you choke to death," she teased.

"Marry me, Kate," Hank blurted out the words. "I'll make you happy. I swear to God, I will."

Kate chuckled and clapped her hands. "That was some speech, Diamond. And such a beautiful performance too. Tell me,

281

what do you do for an encore?" she asked, amused by Hank's display of uncertainty.

He grabbed Kate up into his arms. "If it's all the same to you, I'd rather show you about my encore." The next thing she knew, Hank's mouth had covered hers. Nothing about Hank had changed; his kiss was still slow, deliberate and breathtaking. "Let me hold you, Kate. I want to make love to you so bad right now that I ache all over from just thinking about it. Please, Honey, don't send me away again."

She wasn't going to send Hank away. "Stay for dinner, Hank. I think Dane would like that," she invited.

"What about you?"

"Yeah. Me too."

"What's on the menu for dinner?"

"What! I just invited you to dinner and you're worried about the menu?"

"No, just the dessert," Hank answered, grinning sheepishly.

"Well, we're having hot roast beef with mashed potatoes and gravy. If I remember correctly, it's the same meal you walked out on once before," she reminded him.

"I won't make that same mistake again," Hank said and kissed her on the forehead. "Will you think about what I've told you? And consider what I asked, Kate?"

"Yeah, Hank, I'll do both."

"Good," he said and kissed her again. "Now, I'm going back downstairs to be with Dane. He challenged me to a game of checkers, you know."

"Yeah, so I heard."

Kate remained in the loft, alone with her thoughts as she sat in front of the fireplace. She gazed into the flickering flames and something told her that Mack was nearby. Then she realized he was sitting beside her in the loveseat.

"Well! I must say, Kate, that guy's speech really touched me too."

"Come on, Mack. Give me a break, will you?"

Mack laughed rather lightly before getting very serious. "This is going to be my last visit with you, Kate. I've brought a buddy with me this time. Take a look."

Kate looked over to see Caleb standing beside the fireplace. Her son was smiling at his mother. Tears welled up in Kate's eyes. "Oh, Mack, can he talk to me?"

"No, I'm sorry, but he can't. I just thought you should see how happy Caleb is. Look at his face, Kate. His eyes are glowing. Caleb is doing just fine," Mack told her.

"But why can't he say something to me? I don't understand. You talk to me."

"Yes, I know. But Caleb has already crossed completely over to the other side. He's kind of on loan to me for this visit. As for me, well, let's just say that I sort of cut a little deal before I had to join Caleb once and for all. After losing us both and almost at the same time, I knew what it would do to you. I couldn't leave you in that kind of shape. Caleb didn't get a chance to say goodbye and neither did I. Then you were in such a mess in the hospital. It's so difficult for mortals to understand when death removes their loved ones. Grief is such a sad and lonely affair, Kate. That's why I just couldn't leave you for good until I was assured you'd be okay. It took awhile, but I was given the chance to make it right for you and I took it. That's why you can hear me talk, but not Caleb. Like I said, this is going to be my last visit. You've been given a second chance for a new life now. That young boy needs you. That man needs you too. He loves you, Kate. And if you'd just admit it, you love him too. So don't mess this up. By the way, about this new life you're carrying, do me a favor and name that little boy after me."

"Don't make jokes, Mack."

"I'm not joking, Kate. Oh, and there is one other little matter I should clear up with you before we part. If I don't come clean with you about this now, you'll wonder about it for the rest of your life," Mack said and grinned.

"What's that?"

"Remember that night you were attacked by that creep, Charlie DaRoux, and Baron jumped through the window to save you."

"Of course, I remember. What about that night?"

"Well, you do remember the horn started honking first. Right?"

283

"That's right," she answered and thought about the sequence of events that transpired on that night. "You surely wouldn't try and convince me that it was you honking the horn, would you?"

Mack was laughing. "Of course not, but let's just say I had it arranged."

"Oh? You want to share that little secret with me now, while you're telling all?"

"Sure, I do. It was Raine."

"Raine! Get real, Mack. The boy is autistic."

Mack grinned again. "So he is. And Baron's just a dog too. You know, Kate, we folks residing over on the other side do have our ways. Between Raine and Baron, I'm really kind of proud of the way things turned out that night. If I were you though, I don't believe I'd tell anyone that Raine helped you. They'd never believe you anyway."

Kate couldn't take her eyes off Caleb. Her son was still smiling at his mother when Mack got up and walked over to stand beside Caleb. The husband and son who had been a major part of Kate's life were with her now, but not for much longer. "We're going now, Kate. Have a good life with your new family. And be happy," Mack said as he looked over at Caleb. "Wave goodbye to your mother, Caleb."

Caleb was waving and still smiling as they faded out of sight, forever removed from any further contact with Kate, but never from her heart or memory.

Kate wiped away her tears before heading downstairs to be with the new men in her life. She'd invited Hank to stay for supper and it wasn't right to keep a hungry man waiting. She found Hank and Dane at the table playing a game of Chinese checkers.

"Are you two guys hungry yet?"

"Yeah, but I don't want to eat until I finish kicking Hank's ass..." Dane caught himself, remembering his deal of long ago with Hank about using bad language. "I... I mean... I'm kicking his butt with this game, Kate," Dane bragged.

"That's good, Dane, keep it up. There are times when even the mighty Hank Diamond has to be shown a thing or two. He's pretty hard headed, you know."

Hank looked up at her. "Listen to who's talking. It takes one to know one, my lady."

"That's right, it does. Oh, and by the way, Mr. Diamond, the answer is 'yes.'"

"Yes to wha...?" Then it dawned on Hank what she meant. He jumped up and grabbed Kate by both arms. "Do you mean it? You'll marry me? Did you hear that, Dane? She's going to marry me."

Susie Rigsby

Kate's heart skipped a beat, nearly stopped for a second. She turned around in Hank's arms and looked directly into his eyes. And there it was. Unmistakably, she saw the same twinkle that Mack always had in his eyes, especially when Kate was close to him like this. "What did you just call me?"

EPILOGUE

"Hurry, Kate. We're going to be late," Hank scolded his wife.

"I'm hurrying, my love. Have we got everything? Did you put a new box of wipes in the diaper bag for me?"

"Yes, honey, I did. What else needs to be done? We're supposed to be at the Judge's office by one o'clock to sign those adoption papers. Let's try not to be late for this event.

Hank was holding his nine-month-old son in his arms and the baby was all over the place. "Let's get this kid into the car seat and get going. Jeez, he won't stay still for a minute," Hank said and laughed.

"How do I look, Hank?" Dane asked, modeling his new suit that Kate had purchased for the special occasion.

"Like a million bucks, Pup. Now let's go and get this over with." Hank was as nervous as the day he'd waited for his son to be born.

Needa, Raine and Leo were waiting at the courthouse. Looking like Cox's Army as they walked inside together, Needa quickly offered to hold the baby before Hank, Kate and Dane entered the Judge's chambers.

The adoption papers lay on a table in front of the judge. He looked first at Hank, then to Kate. "Have you both looked over the papers? I'm sure you've found everything to be in order. If you'll just sign on the line above your names, then this matter will be concluded," the Judge told the adoptive parents.

After the papers were signed, the Judge looked at Dane and winked. "Well, young man, it's official now. These two adults have just legally become your new mom and dad."

287

Dane beamed at the thought of being Hank's son. "Does that mean my name is Dane Diamond now?"

The Judge grinned at the young boy. "That's exactly what it means. From here on out you will be known as Dane Diamond. It sort of has a nice sound to it. Don't you think?"

"I think it does too, Sir," Dane agreed.

The Judge looked over at the baby in Needa's arms. "Is that your baby brother?"

"Yes, Sir. It is," Dane replied.

"And what's his name?"

Dane glanced at the squirming baby. "Him? Oh, that's just Mack. But he's too young to be concerned about his name. His last name is Diamond though, just like mine," Dane beamed.

The Judge stood up and extended his hand to Hank. As they shook hands, Hank thanked him for everything. The Judge walked back into his private office and Hank turned to Kate. "Let's get home and start celebrating."

The adoption party was waiting to begin at the Diamond residence. Gordon and Emily were already there, helping to get the food ready. Peter and Maureen had driven up to spend a few days. Bruce and Brandi Crampton had just arrived. Needa, Raine and Leo returned with Hank and Kate and their two young sons.

"You know, I hate to admit this, but marriage looks good on that man of yours," Brandi told Kate later as they were sipping a glass of wine.

"Yeah. I still have to laugh when I think about that little performance he put you through. I guess the joke's on me though, because Hank's cleverness in making me jealous did work. I was literally green-eyed when I saw him with you."

Kate looked around the yard at her family. Maureen was lovingly holding little Mack. Peter, smoking his pipe, looked more than content to be playing Chinese checkers with Dane.

Hank walked up behind Kate, slipped his arms around her waist and whispered in her ear, "Hey, Sweet Pea, I've got a great idea."

Kate's heart skipped a beat, nearly stopped for a second. She turned around in Hank's arms to look directly into his eyes. And there it was. Unmistakably, she saw the same twinkle that

Mack always had in his eyes, especially when Kate was close to him like this. "What did you just call me?"

Hank smiled, exactly as Mack would have done. "What? I called you Sweet Pea. Why?"

Kate smiled. "Oh, nothing. It's just that I haven't heard that expression in a while. What's your great idea?" she asked, snuggling up against him.

"Why don't we retire early tonight? I'll bet if we tried real hard, we might even make a baby sister for our two boys," Hank whispered while kissing her neck.

Life had started over for Kate. With a second family, she had been given a second chance for happiness. Kate didn't intend to waste one minute of it. Not in this lifetime.

Susie Rigsby